RHETT C BRUNO
TITAN'S SON

TITAN'S SON

©2019 RHETT C. BRUNO

Published by Aethon Books LLC.

Cover Art by: Jasper Schreurs

Cover Design, Print and eBook formatting and cover design by Steve Beaulieu.

CHILDREN OF TITAN

**Pick up the whole
series.**

PROLOGUE

PETER SILDARIO, CAPTAIN OF THE *SUNFIRE*, FELL FORWARD onto Rin's naked chest. The middle-aged Ringer woman lay on her back near the edge of his bed, one arm pinned beneath his body and the other gripping the blunt end of a shiv carved out of a rusty metal bolt. She'd stuck it into the captain's throat, and not even his fat fingers could keep the blood from pouring all over her.

At first, his body twitched while she held it there, then he went still. She tried to slither free, but the layer of sweat and blood smeared across her pasty skin didn't help. His Earther body was too heavy considering how deep the *Sunfire* flew within the atmosphere of Saturn.

Her ribs grew sore under his weight, making it difficult to breathe, and after a minute, she imagined she might suffocate. She'd never wanted to be a maintenance worker on a gas-harvester in the first place and had only done so for the good of her people... Now she was going to die on one. She wasn't as afraid as she thought she'd be; she only wished she could pass on far away from the captain's foul stench.

Three pairs of gloved hands slipped between his body and

hers just before the weight caused her to pass out. They pried him up just barely enough for her to slip out from beneath his sagging belly.

She tumbled to the floor, gasping for air. The captain was rolled back onto his chest, half-hanging off the bed with his face dipped in a deepening pool of his own blood.

"We heard screams," a Ringer com operator named Hayes said as he ran in, his tone panicked. He too was born on the icy surface of Titan and had a permanently crooked nose that had been broken by security too many times. "What the hell did you do, Rin?"

"Trass, he's dead," said Joran, who, like Rin, was a *Sunfire* maintenance worker.

Rin ignored them. She lunged at the captain and punched him in the side. The fat on his stomach jiggled, but the weighty corpse barely budged. "How does that feel, Captain!" she screamed as she struck him again. "You like that! You want it harder?"

Gareth, the third Ringer who'd helped dislodge her, grabbed her by the shoulders and tore her away from the corpse. Working with the engines made Gareth the strongest of them despite him also being a Ringer, so he picked her up and sat her on the red-stained bed.

"Are you all right?" he signed with his long, thin-fingered hands. His tongue had been sliced off at the back of his throat by the Earther captain lying dead before them, so he couldn't speak. They called it a work accident.

Rin glanced down. Her boiler suit was torn along the back, so far down that it wrapped around her thighs. Rows of finger-shaped marks along her slender hips stuck out against her white flesh as if drawn on with a pink highlighter. She was almost entirely exposed to the germ-infested air, a rare sight for a Ringer outside of the Lowers. Her three saviors were clothed from head to toe in boiler suits and wore sanitary masks and gloves as was customary.

"I'm fine," she panted, throwing her arms back through her still intact sleeves. Gareth helped her. The fit was loose from having been stretched time and time again by the voracious captain. Hayes took a step to help as well, then regarded the bloody captain and stopped.

"You've really done it now," Hayes said. "They'll space us all for this."

"He deserved far worse," Rin growled.

"Others will have heard the screams," Joran said. "We've got to get you out of here."

"Yeah, where are we going to go?" Hayes asked. He was sweating even more than Rin, his gaze glued to the body. "I hear Pluto is lovely this time of year."

Gareth shot him an angry glare as he finished helping her back into what was left of her outfit.

"Just shut up, Hayes, and let me—" Rin was interrupted by the three-man *Sunfire* security team suddenly appearing in the room's entrance. All of them were Earthers, painting short, broad figures compared with her tall, slender one. They wore dated suits of Pervenio Corp-fashioned armor, but their shock-batons were top-of-the-line, tips crackling a vibrant blue.

"You skelly bitch!" one of them yelled. They rushed into the room, weapons raised.

Gareth didn't hesitate. He ripped the shiv out of the captain's neck and charged. He was naturally weaker than the Earthers, but he'd grown up a brawler in a fighting pit deep in Titan's Darien Lowers. Joran promptly followed, and though he wasn't a fighter, he knew how to hold his own as a distraction. Hayes wasn't as lucky. He froze somewhere between fleeing and fighting and got prodded in the side by a shock-baton. His convulsing body toppled forward, vomit spewing from his mouth.

The mess slowed the guard coming at Rin and gave her enough time to think. She'd been invited to the captain's quarters a few times before she'd had enough and killed him, and she knew he kept a loaded pulse-pistol in a stand by the head of his bed in case the crew got rowdy.

She sprawled across the mattress and fumbled through the drawer until her reedy fingers found the rubberized handle. She whipped around and saw a shock-baton speeding toward her head. She caught the Earther's burly arm before it shocked her. At the same time, he grabbed her pistol-hand and shoved it upward. Born on Earth, under Earth-like g conditions, he was multiple times stronger than her. Both of her arms were ready to give out when she decided to pull the trigger.

The shot hit a power conduit running along the exposed wall behind them. Electricity coruscated through the air toward the baton's lit end. She squirmed away from him just in time to escape the current as the guard screamed. His back wrenched, and he shook violently. While he was incapacitated, Rin reached around him and put a second bullet into the head of the guard kicking Hayes's curled-up body. Gareth and Joran didn't need her help. The former was plunging his shiv into their guard's chest over and over as the latter held him down.

With the wailing, electricity-filled Earther stuck in front of her, Rin was trapped between him and the wall. She tried to slide her thin body around him without making contact, but as she did, there was a crackle, followed by a deafening bang. The power conduit overloaded and went off like a stick of dynamite centimeters away from the right side of her face, launching her across the room.

Rin rolled over, her vision foggy, her ears ringing. There was no pain. Shadows raced toward her, screaming her name. Hayes reached for her face, appearing horrified as he hesitated to touch her.

She ran the tips of her fingers across her own cheek. Still, she felt nothing, but when she pulled them away, charred flesh was stuck beneath her nails. She clawed at her face again, this time peeling away skin as if she were a wax sculpture held to a torch.

Gareth pulled her to her feet while Hayes yelled for her to focus. She pushed them aside and grabbed a baton off the floor. One of the Earthers crawled toward the fallen gun. Rin's vision remained cloudy, but she didn't need to see straight to hit one of their fat bodies.

She spit out a glob of blood, skin, and liquefied sinew, then cracked him across the head with the baton over and over until his legs stopped twitching.

ONE

I FOCUSED ON THE OFF-DUTY XO OF THE *PICCOLO*, A rickety, Saturn-based gas harvester on its last legs. Earther John Barnes was enjoying his time off by fleecing the Darien Lowers for cheap drinks while he gambled away his paycheck.

He sat between two members of the ship's security crew at a card table in the Sunken Credit. I knew him well after spending the last two years working maintenance on that very same ship. He had a tendency to pick fights with his Ringer subordinates just for the sake of it, and his bulging muscles meant he always won. He gave even Earthers a bad name. Not an easy task.

He was my mark.

A pretty server placed a tray of drinks down for them. Their fourth round. She winced as John grabbed her arm before she could hurry away. I slid my stool a tad closer so I could hear what he said to her over the din of the Sunken Credit, mostly the desperate voices of old, worn-down Ringers at slot machines and tables who'd been trying and failing to catch a break every day since they were unfortunate enough to have been born in the Darien Lowers. Noisy clusters of thick pipes ran along the rocky ceiling as well, feeding the water purification plant on the other side of its rocky walls.

"Aye, you mind telling your Ringer bosses to turn up the heat?" John barked.

"Of course," the server replied. "I'll—"

He cut her off, instead wrapping his arm all the way around her waist and pulling her close to the table. A full transparent bodysuit and sanitary mask kept her safe from direct contact, but she wore nothing underneath—just her skinny, malnourished figure.

"And I thought I said to bring it neat?" he blustered. "I said that, right, boys?"

His two smirking mates nodded. "That's how I heard it," one remarked. "If we wanted ice rocks, we'd go outside."

"That's right. Now how about you take your skinny Ringer ass back there and fetch us another." He handed her the tray but first took his drink and chugged half. He slammed it down, his Earther strength causing her to scramble to keep the tray level as she hurried away.

She slipped right between me and an old Ringer who'd long since passed out with his face on the bar. I struggled not to glance over at her. The transparent plastic outfit the bosses made every server wear to help garner more tips for the house sure wasn't doing her any favors when it came to lecherous Earthers like John.

"I don't know why we still let those mud stompers in here," the bartender remarked.

"They tip well," the server replied. I caught a glimpse of the parts of her face not covered by a sanitary mask, expecting to see signs of tears after she'd endured a barrage of insults over the course of the night. Instead, she appeared relatively unfazed. A real pro.

"Well, if you want a break, just let me know."

She shook her head. "Just refill them. Neat."

The bartender poured more liquor for the Earthers, then reached into each glass and scooped out the ice with his gloved fingers. "That ought to do it. And I'll be sure to turn down the temperature too. Freeze their fat backs to the inside of their coats."

"Thanks, Chev." The server's mask lifted from a smile, then she picked up the tray and sauntered back toward the tableful of goons.

"You having another?" the bartender asked me. I was too busy peering at John's table to hear him at first. "Drayton?"

I looked up at him, then down. Ice inside rattled against the sides of the empty glass in my hand. I nodded and flashed him my ID to transfer some of the last few credits I had to my name. The transparent card bore no information but for a data chip linked to the Pervenio database. Words and images were too easy to falsify.

The charge went through, then purple synthahol lifted the perfect spheres of frozen water as the bartender filled my glass. People didn't bother selling the good stuff in the Darien Lowers since barely any Ringer could afford it, but water, Titan had plenty of. It was one of the few things we did have and freezing it was easy. If there was a definition of cold, it said *Titan* next to it, and my people had lived there for three centuries since Darien Trass's first settlers fled Earth to escape a meteorite large enough to wipe all life from the planet. Zero degrees Celsius was like a warm summer's day on our former homeworld for me.

I lifted the glass to my mouth and pretended to take a sip. The only reason it even needed ice was to dilute the dreadful taste of the lab-brewed concoction. Lucky for me, I had no plans of drinking a second. One was all I needed to strengthen my nerve, and now I had to keep my head straight.

After John and his crew received their drinks, he smacked

the table to compel their Ringer dealer to distribute digital cards across the display built into the tabletop. No physical cards meant the dealer didn't have to touch anything his patrons did, though that didn't keep him from checking his gloves and sleeves every time he had to swipe the screen just to make sure none of his pasty skin was showing. Contact with an Earther could get a Ringer stuck in quarantine. Staying out of there was the only thing more important than a good tip.

While John and his crew played, I watched him drink with one hand and with the other whip out his hand-terminal and struggle to read whatever was open on the screen. He barely paid attention to the game, as if he had too many credits to spare... which may well have been true. The device—a Pervenio-issued V_3X model, just released in the past month—was worth more than I'd earn in one whole shift on the *Piccolo*. The screen was double the size my Venta Co terminal had been before I sold it to be able to pay for the previous month's rent without starving. It was exponentially faster and able to connect to Solnet broadcasts originating from anywhere in Sol. The entire device was thin as a sheet of glass, its silvery back-casing shimmering brighter than anything else under the Sunken Credit's failing lights.

I was going to steal it. After leaving the *Piccolo* to be closer to my mom after she caught something and got stuck in quarantine, I was desperate for credits. My plan was to use the expensive new terminal to try to get back into the good graces of one of the fences I used to run for. They were all still bitter about me leaving the shadows behind to try to make an honest living.

After two years on a gas harvester, I was out of practice, so John made for an easy warm-up. I knew from experience that he liked to get so drunk he wouldn't remember how he got the bruises from the night before. The fact that he deserved to get swiped was just a bonus. I had standards, at least. I never liked stealing from people I didn't know anything about. Earther or not, there was no saying what they'd been through. Mom taught me that, even though she hated what I used to do and was preparing to do again.

Thirty minutes passed quickly. My staring didn't appear suspicious, because everyone else in the gambling den had an eye on the Earthers from the moment they'd entered. Ringers came and went, most with heads hanging in defeat and a few wearing looks that said they'd broken even and would be back tomorrow to try getting rich again. John and his friends were on another round of drinks. If they had a shred of decency—which I knew they didn't—it was long gone. John was swaying. He went to hug the server and fell off his stool onto his knees, cackling hysterically.

"Oh, c'mon, girl," he slurred. "I don't bite." He grabbed her leg. She kicked at him to pry free, but he didn't budge. Waves of fear finally flooded her face. John drew himself to his feet, then tugged her tight against his puffy thermal coat. His mates chuckled the entire time.

"I swear I'm cleaner than any of the Ringer filth you've screwed before," he said. He ran his fat fingers up her back and through the ends of her hair. Seeing direct contact like that between a Ringer and an Earther made my skin crawl. She yelped and slipped down out of his grasp, causing him to again stumble to his knees.

That was when the bouncers had finally had enough. Just what I'd been counting on. I stood and used them as cover to get closer. I wasn't worried about John or the others recognizing me with my sanitary mask on. That was the one benefit of having to wear one everywhere: It made me difficult to differentiate from any other Ringer at first glance. What I was worried about, though, was the baton hanging openly from John's broad hips. Weapons weren't allowed to be worn anywhere in Darien without special permits, but no gambling den manager in the Lowers was going to stop him, considering what he was spending.

"All right, fun's over," a bouncer said. "Let's go, all of you." The slender man towered over the Earthers by at least half a meter, but three centuries of breeding in Titan's low g had rendered him significantly weaker than them. John could probably throw him clear across the room if he wanted, and when the bouncer leaned down to help him up, he pretty much did just that.

"Get the fuck off me!" he grunted. He shoved the bouncer with one of his meaty arms, and the Ringer flew back into a nearby table so hard that the fastenings at the base went loose. John's companions jumped to their feet. They wobbled, but their stocky legs kept them upright. The other Sunken Credit bouncers surrounded them, wiry fingers curled into fists. Every patron stopped what they were doing.

"Do it, skelly," John said. He stood as tall as he could. "I'm begging you."

The Sunken Credit went silent. Everyone stopped what they were doing and gravitated toward the debacle. *Skelly* wasn't a term anyone with a brain would use in the Lowers. It originated because many of the Ringers stuck in quarantine looked like skeletons, with their pale skin, their emaciated bodies, and the black bags under their sunken eyes.

I hurried over to a structural column near the disturbance and leaned against it, chin in my palm, sanitary mask pulled as far up over my nose as possible. I had to fight the urge to join everybody else in approaching them. With my mom in quarantine, *skelly* hit closer to home than ever before. But knowing that I was about to hit his wallet was reprisal enough.

John gripped the handle of his baton and glared at the bouncers. "C'mon!"

He lost his footing for a moment but caught himself on the back of his chair. "Give me a reason!"

The crowd around the Earthers' table continued to swell. John didn't back down, but the two others with him got shifty-eyed. Strong as they were, they were vastly outnumbered. The only reason fists hadn't started flying after what he'd said was that the Sunken Credit would have lost some of its best customers. That, and it was never smart to hit an Earther out in the open in Darien, Lowers or not. You never knew who they were connected to with their extensive clan-families. Any Earther could be related to a member of Pervenio security, a Director, or worse, a Collector. If there was one thing any Ringer knew, it was not to do anything bad enough to have one of them hired to hunt you down.

"Leave them, John," one of his team said, dozens of glowers seeming to sober him up in a hurry. "Let them enjoy their shit-filled cave."

John scanned the crowd one last time then broke out into laughter. He patted one of the bouncers on the shoulder. "You Ringers can never take a joke." He laughed. "Let's go, boys, before we run them out of credits and have nothing to come back to."

He shoved through the bouncers, his crew following so close behind they were almost stepping on his heels. The gathered crowd parted to let them pass, but their glares didn't shift.

"I fuckin' love this place!" John shouted. He pointed to the craggy ceiling. "So much more fun than up there."

His path toward the exit was going to take him right past me. The hand-terminal was in the left pocket of his jacket. I'd watched him place it there before he went for the server.

My fingers wriggled in anticipation as I started toward him, head down so he wouldn't recognize me. Not that any of us looked different to trash like him. My palms got clammy, and my heart raced. I should've had that second drink. It'd been so long since I'd lived in the shadows. It felt natural, though, anxious as I was. Going back to something familiar always seems easier than leaving it behind.

I braced my body for the impending impact. I knew from similar undertakings that walking into a muscle-bound Earther was like slamming into a stone wall. I fixed my gaze on the floor until I saw his feet, then held my breath.

My long fingers slithered into his pocket as we collided, and I snatched his hand-terminal. The fact that he was drunk and wasn't stepping with purpose was the only thing that kept me from falling, but the force still made me stagger backward. I transferred the device into my pocket behind my back as I did.

"Watch where you're going, Ringer!" John barked.

"Sorry," I mumbled. I turned my head and squeezed between him and one of the other drunken members of the *Piccolo* security team. I made it only a few steps away before John must've realized something was missing and patted his coat.

"What the..." he said. "Hey, my terminal!"

I didn't wait to start sprinting. I blew past the Ringer bouncers, who made a half-assed effort to grab me and gave chase for a few seconds just to seem like they cared before giving up. I was counting on that too.

"Get back here!" John shouted, surprising me with how near his voice sounded.

A glance down at the elongated shadows cast across the floor told me that he and the other Earthers were in hot pursuit. I'd expected them to be slower in their drunken state, but weighted boiler suits under their coats held them tight to the surface. That allowed them to move quicker under Titan's low-g conditions, whereas my stringy frame protracted every one of my long, hopping strides. I leaped over a dealer's table, John's baton just missing me before it came crashing down and snapped off the edge.

My chest heaved. There was a service hatch at the back of the Sunken Credit. I'd made sure to slice the lock earlier that day as I planned my escape route. Maybe I was out of practice, but I wasn't stupid enough not to be extra cautious.

"I'll break your skinny neck!" John roared, sobered by rage. His crew couldn't even keep up with him.

I yanked open the hatch and rushed through, and as I tried to seal it behind me, his baton poked through the gap to pry it open. The move didn't buy me much time, but it was enough for me to distance myself as I took off again. The service hatch led directly into the upper level of a water purification plant, where I was welcomed by a forest of massive vats, pumps, and pipes being used to siphon water out of Titan's subterranean ocean. Steam poured out of exhaust vents, obscuring the floor like I was in some sort of mythological grotto.

John's heavy feet slapped against the grated metal of the catwalk we emerged onto, echoing down to the plant's imperceptible bottom. Ringer maintenance workers and engineers shouted in confusion. John yelled something, but I couldn't hear what. The racket of the purification equipment was exponentially louder than it had been next door.

I took a twisting path along the catwalks strung between each vat to try to slow John down. It didn't work. My weight forced me to take wide turns, whereas his allowed him to whip around corners. He grew so close that I could hear him wheezing.

"Got you now!" he said. One of his hands extended to grab me, but it caught only air as I leaped up the side of one of the lofty water vats. My rangy fingers gripped the sloping edge of the lid, and I heaved myself up. There was no way he could copy that move at his mass.

"I'll fucking kill you, Ringer!" John continued to shout obscenities while a group of clamoring workers wearing ear protection arrived to see what was happening. I was glad for the neutral term, which meant he hadn't recognized me. Like he'd remember much of this anyway.

I stood and scurried across the top of the vat through a wall of steam. A service ladder ran up the wall, only a short jump away. Everyone was too busy staring up at where I had been earlier to notice me clamber up and pull myself through the access hatch at the top.

Warm, humid air stemming from the Uppers blasted my face, and in an instant, my brow was dripping with sweat. I rolled onto my back to gather my breath.

I was in the service tunnels running beneath the Darien hydro-farms. A second access above led directly into them, but the lock controls were well beyond my ability to slice. The tiny porthole in the center provided my only light and allowed me a glimpse of the world above.

Row after row of green leaves extended for kilometers in two lateral directions—all different shapes and sizes, growing fruits and vegetables I'd never tasted in their natural forms. The farms surrounded the two-kilometer-long rectangular enclosure of Darien and were considered part of the Uppers, despite being sunken into Titan's frozen crust. They were constantly patrolled, so that the mostly Ringer workforce tending the plants had no chance at stealing anything.

About twenty meters above its floor, beyond a series of suspended planters and water-channels, was the farm's transparent ceiling. Thick, polished trusses braced a layer of glass against the ceaselessly stormy skies of Titan. All I could see beyond it were wisps of white sand and flashes of lightning.

I sighed before continuing my crawl through tunnels so cramped only a Ringer could fit. It'd been years since I'd used that escape route, but I found my way back toward cold air through the labyrinth of increasingly dark passages with relative ease. After a short slide down a vertical shaft, I was able to exit through a busted exhaust vent into the heart of the B3 Lowers' central node.

Not a soul cared enough to notice me emerge. A sea of Ringers were all too preoccupied with their own affairs, swarming the market stands for ration bars or "fresh" produce covered almost entirely in brown spots. The enormous lift-shaft running up the center of the spacious cavern was currently letting off. It pierced every level of the Lowers, and Pervenio security officers in full regalia were posted along the decon-chambers wrapping it. John and his team already stood at one of them, probably giving a report. The officers wouldn't care. The shiny pulse-rifles strapped to their backs meant they had more important things to worry about than some Earther dumb enough to get too drunk where he shouldn't.

I headed down a tunnel branching off the node. Familiar smells of salt and soldered metal greeted my nose—the scents of the many factories and water-plants sprinkled throughout the Lowers. It was impossible to go far without running into one of them.

I leaned against the wall in a shadowy nook near an opening to a series of residential hollows and took out John's terminal. It was a beauty. Seeing it in my hands got me to crack a smile, my first in Trass knows how long. I opened a slot in the back using a pin I always kept in my pocket while on a job and removed the fingernail-sized battery so that the device couldn't be tracked.

"New hand-terminal?" someone asked me.

My gaze snapped upward. Approaching from the direction of the central lift, I saw what had been the only pleasant thing to look at while serving my two-year stint on the *Piccolo*: Cora

Walker. She was the chief navigator on the ship since before I started. A lofty title for someone born in the Lowers.

I momentarily lost the ability to formulate words. Even being within a few meters of her usually made me freeze. Her skin was fair as snow-powder and the cascading blond hair tumbling over her slender shoulders was so light that it appeared silver when struck by the right light. Together, they made her rich blue eyes stick out on her face like two brilliant gems.

"Cora, I..." I stuttered. I'd kept my past life a secret on the *Piccolo,* and as much as I hated lying to her, I planned on keeping it that way. I couldn't handle her disappointment right now. "Yeah. Just got it."

"Looks nice," she replied, her voice so gentle that you had to really be paying attention to hear it.

"Yeah. No wonder the thing was sold used, though." I shook it playfully to show her the blank screen. "It's busted."

"Want me to take a look?"

I hesitated, then realized that I didn't want her to think I didn't know how to replace a battery. Being a navigator within Saturn's tumultuous atmosphere meant she was a whiz with tech.

"No, that's okay. I'm just going to bring it back to the scrap shop and get my credits back."

"Oh... okay." She glanced down at her own hand-terminal. "Well, I better get moving, then. I'm supposed to be meeting with Culver soon to discuss the next shift. See you in two days?"

My heart sank as I remembered that was when the next *Piccolo* shift was scheduled to start. A shift I wasn't going to be taking part in. I hadn't told anybody that except for the ship's captain, obviously, and my mom, who couldn't leak the news, considering where she was. I hadn't told a soul about her yet either. It would've made the whole situation feel more, well, real. I had this image in my head of Mom strolling back into our home, completely cured before anyone realized she was gone.

"Yeah," I lied again. I didn't have the heart to let Cora know I wasn't coming back. Seeing her around the *Piccolo* was the only thing that made scrubbing filth out of canisters while dealing with John and the rest of the crew's bullshit tolerable. She was the only thing I'd miss.

The corners of her lips twitched a bit as if she was considering smiling, then she nodded. "Good," she said. "Well, I'll see you around then, Kale."

She went to walk away, but I tapped her shoulder to stop her. She turned her head, face lighting up like she expected to hear something thrilling.

"You have the time?" I asked, gesturing to John's ineffective hand-terminal. Earth-time, that was. Titan's days were extremely long, and even the first Ringers sent by Trass continued using the far more manageable Earth-time since they were within enclosed settlements anyway.

"Oh, sure," she said, biting her lip. "Four thirty-five."

"Shit!" I blurted. "I, uh, I've got to run. Bye!"

She watched quizzically as I sprinted past her. Visiting hours at the Darien Quarantine Zone weren't going to last much longer, and I had to find someone who would take care of John's hand-terminal before I went to see my mom, then make it to the Uppers for the legitimate job I'd taken after resigning from my post on the *Piccolo*—cleaning the floors of Old World Noodles. I needed to do something to pay rent until a fence came through.

Sometimes I wondered what it'd be like to have been born into some wealthy Earther clan-family. There'd be a lot less to do.

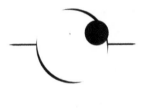

TWO

THE DARIEN LOWERS WERE CLUTTERED WITH FACTORIES, gambling dens, and clubs that put those in the Uppers to shame. Like pretty much everything else on Titan, they were nearly all funded by Pervenio Corp, even if their managers liked to pretend they weren't, so the only relatively well-off Ringers I ever knew were fences working the black market. They tucked themselves into the shadows of legitimate enterprises, and even though I was only eighteen, I'd met more than my fair share. Some were safer to work with than others.

One by one, I hurried between the shops of all my old connections with John's hand-terminal as my ticket in. They wouldn't even open their doors to see what I had to offer, let alone say hello. A step onto an Earther-run gas harvester, and it was like I'd betrayed my people or was guaranteed to be a rat.

Growing frustrated, and with the end of visiting hours at the Q-Zone rapidly approaching, I decided I'd skip to the last fence I ever wanted to see again, but the one I knew was my best shot. Dexter Howser was the grubbiest, greediest man I knew, which meant he'd never say no to easy credits. He liked to use children who hadn't developed any connections and bring them into his fold, so I'd met him when I was very young. His headquarters was a parts and repair store fronting for a chop shop in Level B6, the lowest occupied section of the Darien Lowers, almost fifty meters below the surface of Titan. The hollow where my mother and I lived was four levels up, but down in B6, the smell of salt was so pungent it made my nostrils sting.

I pulled my sanitary mask tight over my nose. The beggars lining the walls of the level's central node were so skinny their chins were like knives. A few here and there were even coughing. It was likely from breathing in the fumes from a dozen factories escaping through the worn-down air recyclers, but I wasn't about to risk getting sick.

Dexter's place was down a long tunnel, right beside a factory transforming chunks of metal imported from throughout the Ring into circular hatches. The clamor of welding torches and machine belts was so raucous that I couldn't hear my footsteps. It was just how any fence would like it. Nobody could listen in, even if they tried.

I knocked on the hatch of the unnamed chop shop, and after a few seconds, a voice spoke through an intercom.

"What's your business?" a man said.

"I've got a delivery for Mr. Howser," I replied. "It's delicate."

A camera was nestled into the ice-rock above the hatch. I watched the lens tilt, aim at me, and zoom in. I was out of the life for only two years and, even though I'd grown a bit taller, my gaunt face hadn't changed. Not a hint of stubble, let alone a beard. They'd know exactly who I was.

"Mr. Howser will see you immediately." There was a *click* and a *hiss* as the hatch popped open.

The space inside was little more than a waiting room with a rusty counter. Scraps of metal lay against the walls, and a haze of dust floated in the air, so thick that everything appeared speckled.

Howser's muscle consisted of four grungy Ringers, one on either side of the counter and two by the entry-hatch. Their narrow faces were coated in grime, matching their rotting teeth, which appeared even more yellow in contrast to their pasty skin. The area beneath their noses was chapped from snorting foundry salts—a synth-drug made from residue in water purification plants.

They had the kind of look in their eyes that said they weren't just willing to use the decade-old pulse-rifles strapped to their backs but would enjoy it.

"Kale Drayton!" Howser said, sitting behind an unexpectedly new-looking console set on the counter. "Mr. Gas Harvester. Never thought I'd see you all the way down here again."

His appearance was similar to his henchmen's, only dirtier. Wild hair fell to his shoulders, and his messy beard went even farther. He grinned as he saw me, and I could smell his putrid breath from across the room. I counted only three natural teeth in his mouth; the rest were fillers made of chrome.

"Neither did I," I admitted.

I started forward cautiously, my eyes darting between his armed henchmen. Their weapons may've been ancient, but if they were able to fire, they'd still be enough to riddle me with fist-sized holes. It'd been a long time since I'd dealt with people of their sort. Earthers like John could be cruel, but they weren't desperate... or hungry.

"Hurry now. Let me get a look at you." Howser snorted a bit of white powder sprinkled on the counter before he rolled out from behind it on an automated wheelchair. Both of his mangled legs were covered by loose pants that dragged across the floor. Rumor had it they'd been crushed by machinery a long time ago. The finest doctors in Sol probably could've put his lower half together again, but a man like him wouldn't pay an Earther for help, even if he could afford it.

He rolled a circle around me, scanning me from head to toe. I couldn't help but stare at the handle of the razor-sharp knife I remembered being hidden in the arm of his chair. My muscles tensed.

"I worried you might've wound up with more color up there," he said. He stopped in front of me and stared up into my eyes. He grinned, his teeth like a row of train tracks. "What brings you back to your favorite old fence?"

I glanced over my shoulder at the nearest henchman. He breathed down my neck, nostrils flaring. "Mr. Howser," I began. "I think you know why I'm here. I'd love to catch up, but can we please skip to business?"

He grimaced. "You're not still bitter about your last job, are you, Kale?"

I was hoping he wouldn't bring it up. Other than his stench, the job was the reason he was last on my list. It was the reason I'd wound up taking the job on the *Piccolo*. For the parts of my life I remember, my mom worked as a servant for a wealthy Earther merchant named Tanner Saunders. Because of that, Dexter knew that I had a better shot at robbing him than any of the other kids under his thumb. He promised me a fifty-fifty share of whatever I could get from Tanner's place in the Uppers. Naturally, the Earther's security was tighter than anything I'd ever dealt with, and I got pinched.

I never thought my mom would look at me the same way afterward. My father was shot doing something similar when I was barely four, and my whole life she'd preached about me staying on the right side of the law. But instead of allowing me to go to a cell like I deserved, she convinced Tanner to have me pay off my debts by working on the *Piccolo,* a gas harvester captained by his clan-brother, Weston Saunders.

Since the alternative was spending years in one of Pervenio Station's infamous cells, I accepted the deal. If all the Ringers who'd returned from them with half their minds left weren't lying, the cells were airlocks with a view of space, keeping prisoners under the constant threat of being ejected until they lost their minds. If the Q-Zone was the worst place a Ringer could wind up, that was a close second.

Work on the *Piccolo* was tedious compared with the shadows of the Darien Lowers, but it allowed me to slip out from beneath the thumbs of seedy fences. The crew was tiresome, though Cora made up for them, and Captain Saunders was actually pretty fair for an Earther. After a year I got even on my debt too, and was placed on salary, where I started to earn some legitimate credits.

Everything in my life turned around until two years later. My mom and I managed to exchange the occasional message over Solnet while I was on the *Piccolo* harvesting Saturn's precious atmosphere. During my latest four-month shift, however, she went totally silent. That was until the last day when I received the message that flipped my world over and placed me right back where I'd emerged from.

KALE,
    I'VE BEEN SICK. THEY HAD TO TAKE ME IN...

That was all I needed to read. I would honestly have been ready to hijack the *Piccolo* and drive it straight to Titan if the shift hadn't been ending anyway. I resigned the moment I got back to Darien so I could stay near my mom. I knew she would tell me to keep working hard and not to worry, but I couldn't leave her alone to wither away. I was all that she had left in the world, and she was the same for me. The *Piccolo* could be decommissioned and gutted for all I cared if it meant being there for her.

"Kale," Dexter repeated, drawing me back to the present.

"No," I said, shaking the memories out of my head. "I knew the risks of what I was doing. I just don't have a lot of time."

"Got an appointment with that Earther captain of yours? I bet he loved you." He made a lewd gesture with his hand in the direction of one of his henchmen. They all laughed.

"I—" I stopped myself. I'd stolen my first ration bar when I was seven, and if all those years working the shadows of the Lowers had taught me anything, it was never to let a fence know how desperate you really were.

I decided to move things along myself. I took out John's hand-terminal and slapped it on the counter. Dexter's eyes went wide. "Pervenio V3X model hand-terminal," I said. "Brand-new."

He wheeled over, snagged it, and spun it in his hands. He looked like he was about to start drooling; it glistened as brightly as his false teeth. "How in the name of Trass did you get your hands on this?" he asked.

"I still know a few people," I said.

"Anybody else know about this?" He tapped the screen a couple of times and then checked the missing battery port.

"Only you."

"Now, now, Kale. I thought we were beyond lying. I've heard talk you were back, asking around, trying to wriggle back into our life. I may not be able to walk, but I have ears everywhere."

The two henchmen by the counter edged closer. I took a deep breath. "Nobody else would open their hatch for me but you," I said.

"The people you knew, you're lucky nobody had you removed after you decided to go up," he said.

I was well aware of that. For a while, people from my old life and kids from schooling gave me crap. They'd write EARTHER LOVER on the hatch of my mom's hollow when I wasn't there, or threaten to gut me if they ever caught me conversing with certain people. Eventually, it died down, and I knew if anyone really thought I needed to be removed, it'd happen with my back turned. A shot to the head seemed preferable to breaking the deal my mom had secured with Tanner Saunders and winding up a Pervenio prisoner.

"Look, Dex, if you aren't interested—" I said before he cut me off with a wave of his hand.

"Let's not say that," he said. "I'm just hurt you didn't come to me first. You know who always offered you the best jobs."

"Best jobs to get caught, you mean?"

His glare hardened. "It's all part of the trade, Kale. You know that."

"I know." I sighed. "So do you want it or not?"

He wove his fingers through his mess of facial hair as he ogled the shiny device. His eyes betrayed him. I knew he wanted it. Other fences were willing to pick and choose, but Dexter Howser couldn't keep his paws away from anything worth more than a handful of credits.

"Terms?" he asked.

"We split the revenue fifty-fifty," I said, the words coming out more softly than I'd hoped. Negotiation was a muscle I hadn't flexed in a long time.

"Fifty-fifty?" Dexter eyed his men and then started to chuckle.

"Yup. I did this freelance. No tips, no help. Consider it a gift."

"A gift for old Dexter?" His features suddenly darkened and

he stared daggers my way. "How about I just get rid of you and take the whole thing?"

The two henchmen I could see armed their rifles, grinning ravenously. There was no saying what the ones behind me were doing, and I didn't have the nerve to check. I tried my best to ignore them.

"Dex, c'mon," I said.

He continued staring for what seemed like half a minute, his face not shifting. Then he broke out into hysterical laughter, spittle spewing all over his beard. His men lowered their rifles and joined him.

"You should've seen your face!" Dexter chortled. "Oh, Kale. You always were fun."

I laughed nervously with them but said nothing.

"I'll tell you what," Dexter said after gathering his breath. "I'll do sixty-forty, and unless you've set up a shop and have a troop of back-channel dealers to get top credits for this thing, you'll take it."

"I know what it's worth," I replied. "Fifty is generous."

"It's very generous. And you're welcome to see if anybody else is interested, but I think you'd have to go far away from Darien to find them. You leave us behind, we leave you behind."

He was right, and he knew I knew it. If I wanted my mom to remain comfortable in the Q-Zone, I needed to take the offer. Her entire credit savings had dried up since she'd never earned much more from Tanner Saunders than what it took to pay rent and buy food.

"Why did you agree to meet with me, then?" I asked, not wanting to appear overly eager to accept.

"Curiosity, mostly," he said. "I've heard two years on a gas harvester could give a Ringer wrinkles, and I had to see if that was true. Looks like you made it out smooth as ever. Like a baby."

"Two more and I might not be so lucky."

He smirked. "Look, I know you're no Earther lover. You took the blame back then and kept your mouth shut when you got caught. Any of us would've accepted the same deal to stay out of one of their cells." He shifted his chair and then drove it closer to me. "My real question is, are you back home for good?"

"I'm back," I declared. "I'm ready to move on, tired of sitting around in high g getting ordered around and making shit credits."

"Then don't be an idiot and deny my offer."

I maintained the ruse that I was still considering as best I could. "If I do agree, how long until the credits come in?" I said.

"Something this new?" He picked up the terminal again to examine it, licking his lips as he did. "Probably a week. Maybe longer."

"A week? C'mon, Dex, you can't be serious."

"If I could sell it to some uppity Earther, no problem, but I've got to mask the product key, get it off the Pervenio network, and Trass knows what else just to make it Solnet-capable without it registering as stolen. You want instant gratification, strap your collar back on and return to the *Piccolo*."

I accidentally groaned loud enough for him to hear. My job at the noodle shop might be able to hold me over, but my credit account was starting to be stretched as thin as my mom's. Getting her placed in the preferable quarters of the Q-Zone wasn't cheap, and I was paying the full rent on our hollow now too.

"I'll tell you what," he said. "Say yes now, and I'll have something else for you by tonight. Others said no because they looked at you and only saw a traitor. I see a worthwhile invest-ment for both of us."

I could tell by the glimmer in his eyes that I wasn't a good enough actor and he'd already gained a clear picture of my desperation. Rather than hurt my cause any more, I swallowed my pride and extended my hand.

"Fine, Dex," I said. "You've got a deal."

"Outstanding!" he exclaimed. He grasped my hand and shook, his palms as rough as sandpaper. "Let's start fresh, and maybe soon, we'll find a way to make a little bit more than shit together."

"Fine by me. I'll be back tonight. Just try not to get me caught again."

"I'll do my best."

Dexter's lips lifted into a predatory smile, his chrome teeth shimmering like the icy rocks of Saturn's belt against the black of his mouth. I faked a smile in return, and as I went to let go of his hand, he squeezed harder and pulled me closer. His breath made me want to vomit. "Oh, and Kale, a word of advice," he whispered. "For Trass's sake, lighten the hell up, or I'll drop you so fast you'll never step foot in Darien again."

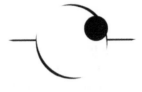

THREE

As I rode the inter-block tram to the visiting area of the Darien Quarantine Zone, I couldn't imagine a more depressing place in all of Sol. Every seat in the car was occupied by a Ringer like me off to visit a sick loved one. It was easy to tell who was making the trip for the first time—their eyes were wet with tears. Mine weren't. I'd been to the Q-Zone every day for the last month since returning to Darien and I was out of tears. My mom had already been stuck inside for six months.

The tram emerged from the Lowers and ascended to Titan's surface. Outside, a midday storm whipped up the ruddy sand covering Titan, obscuring most of my homeworld. It made it hard to avoid focusing on the bright red Pervenio Corp logos—a helix wrapping around a tree branch— reflected in every window. Each of them had a mark above them with the date the Q-Zone had been built, 2285 A.D., just a year after the Great Reunion between Ringers and Earthers.

After Darien Trass sent the earliest Ringers to Titan, the Earthers who survived the Meteorite rebuilt their world, all while seeking new ones so that Armageddon could never happen again. They spread from Earth to Mars, to the asteroid belt, and then beyond. Fifty years ago, they reached Saturn, where my people had already been focused on establishing a new, peaceful civilization for humanity based around Titan for over two hundred years. It was supposed to be an incredible moment of unity after centuries apart, but with the Earthers came all the sicknesses our weakened immune systems had forgotten about. No measure of precautions could stop it: Thousands upon thousands of my people died off, peace died, and the Earthers had to step into our cities and establish order with quarantines and separated living areas before the rest joined them.

The one I was headed to was the oldest, to go along with Darien's being Titan's earliest settlement. That meant that countless Ringers had succumbed to illnesses within its unsanctified halls.

It didn't seem right that my mother could wind up as one of them. She'd always been rigorous about cleaning her body, about wearing her gloves and sanitary mask no matter where she was. She'd taught me to be the same way, to keep them on even while I slept aboard the *Piccolo,* despite its living quarters being segregated. That was probably the only thing I was ever smart enough to listen to her about when I was younger.

In the end, none of it mattered. She caught something, same as everyone else thrown into one of the many Q-Zones dotting Titan's frozen surface had. Didn't matter what the disease was either.

Sure, they'd separate people with different ailments, but most of the diseases had no names, or did once but were lost in the annals of Pre-Meteorite Earth. All I knew for sure was that getting the right medicine through Pervenio Corp cost a fortune in credits. I'd already put aside all the money I'd ever earned, and it barely scratched the surface.

I wasn't going to give up, though. I owed my mom everything. From first giving me life, to later helping me straighten it out.

It grew dark as the tram slipped into the Q-Zone's entrance, carved into a lonely plateau rising from a plain of bleached sand. After it came to a screeching halt, Earther security officers garbed in the red and black of Pervenio Corp marched up and down the aisle, letting each row out one at a time. When my turn came, I fell in behind a somber line consisting almost entirely of masked Ringers, shuffling along as if they didn't actually want to get where they were going.

Security guided us into a long, bright lobby with sterile white walls that tended to give me headaches over time. It seemed like every other Ringer on Darien had the idea to arrive in the Q-Zone at the same time because it was taking even longer than normal. On most days, I tried to visit when opening hours commenced rather than toward the late afternoon. My date with John in the Lowers had destroyed that possibility.

Enhanced security measures never helped things move along either. Every visitor was patted down twice. Life in Darien was more tense than it had been when I'd left for my last gas-harvesting shift. There was news of a bombing back on Earth carried out by an unknown faction of offworlders while I was away, as well as multiple riots that had taken place throughout Titan's colony blocks during M-day a few months back.

My feet tapped nervously as the line slowly trudged along. Warm, Earther-comfortable air had me sweating. By the time I reached the reception window outside of the decon-chamber, I was one of the last few Ringers who would be permitted through until the next morning.

"Name and ID," the elderly Earther woman sitting at the desk on the other side said. She was so short I could barely see her frog-like face over her computer screen. It was obvious she didn't recognize me despite how often I'd been visiting. Hundreds of masked Ringers passed by her every day.

"Kale Drayton," I said as I handed her my card. She glanced up at me from her computer a few times while she looked it over. Satisfied, she gave it back.

"Visiting?" she asked.

"Katrina Drayton."

"One moment." She typed so speedily that her stubby fingers became a blur. It made my stomach turn to imagine how many times she'd probably searched for a name in her files. It was a job that nobody should have to do, Earther or not.

When she was done, she extended her palm and requested my hand-terminal.

Pervenio security didn't permit handheld devices in Q-Zones. They didn't approve of pictures of the suffering leaking onto Solnet without context or consent. Of course, that didn't matter to me. I'd already sold mine so I could help pay for my mom to stay on one of the higher levels of the Q-Zone, one where she'd get a soft mattress.

"Got none," I said.

"Proceed." She waved me on and then turned back toward the line. "Next!"

I took a step forward. Two Pervenio security officers immediately signaled me to spread my arms and legs. They left no part of me unsearched.

"Clear," one of them grumbled.

I was beckoned into a boxy decon-chamber. It was amazing anybody ever got sick given how many of them were sprinkled throughout Darien. They were at the Q-Zones, between the Uppers and Lowers, outside of every tram to another colony block, along every dock and hangar— everywhere. All it took was a single germ, though. Or so I'd been told by myriad ads throughout the Lowers preaching safety and cleanliness.

"Clothes," an automated voice announced.

I removed all my clothing, even my undergarments. After depositing them through a chute, I stood in the center of the room completely naked. The decontamination process initiated. As usual, I waited nervously.

A whistling sound met my ears as balmy air rushed through air recyclers into the chamber. Then a tight web of pinkish beams that made up the electrostatic cleaning matrix spread across the room. They gave me a tingle as they passed across me, once through the front and then again in the other direction.

"Clean," the automated voice announced after a minute, easing my concerns.

My clothes, now warm from being washed, appeared on a shelf by the exit. I put them back on and hurried out of the decon-chamber, and they were instantly cooled. Like most exclusively Ringer-occupied places on Titan, the air in the Q-Zone was chilly enough that I'd see my breath if I wasn't wearing a sanitary mask. That was the only comfortable thing about the place.

"Visiting room C-7," an officer indicated from behind a glass screen just inside the Q-Zone. He wore a full helmet and a visor so dark he seemed faceless. No Earther was permitted to enter the Q-Zone without clearance and an insulated suit. It was one agreement between our peoples nobody had the nerve to ever break.

A middle-aged Ringer woman exited as I approached the entry of room C-7. She stared blankly forward, tearless. All I wanted to do was place my hand on her shoulder and tell her everything was going to be all right, but I wasn't in the mood to lie. I shuffled silently past her and into the contained visiting room.

The walls were white and shiny, but through a glass divider in the center, I could see the dreary adjoining visiting area within the quarantine proper. It was bright enough for me to be able to tell that the metal-clad walls were in disrepair.

I sat in the single chair set in front of the glass. Shortly after, my mom hobbled over to a seat across from me. The centimeter-thick transparent divider separating us might as well have been a kilometer.

Like all full-blooded Ringers, she was tall and lean, with white-as-paper skin and knobby joints that appeared more delicate than they really were. The first sign indicating something was wrong with her was that her brown hair was uncharacteristically frizzy. Frayed strands stuck to her soaring, sweaty forehead and clung to the tip of her flat nose. She'd always kept her hair clean and straight. The second sign was her bloodshot eyes and the dark creases wrapping around them, which only made them appear redder. She looked worse than she had just a day earlier. Like a salt sniffer hankering for a fix.

"Hi, Mom," I whispered through the two-way intercom system built into the glass.

"Kale... You didn't have to come again," she responded, appearing as heartbroken as I imagined I must've. Her voice was muffled by a sanitary mask far more extensive than mine, but I could still tell it was uncharacteristically raspy.

My mask lifted as I forced a smile. "I wasn't about to let you be alone."

"You don't need to fake anything with me. I know where I am."

I took her advice. "So how are you feel—" I was cut off when a racking cough seized her.

She turned away and bent over so I wouldn't be able to hear it clearly through the intercom. It didn't work. The struggle of her lungs was evident, and before long, she was dry-heaving. There was nothing left inside of her to regurgitate.

No matter how many times I'd heard the sound since I'd

started visiting her, it still made me cringe. By the time she was finally able to withdraw her skinny arm from her mouth, she was laboring to breathe.

"I'm fine," she grated, as if nothing had happened. I decided not to draw attention to it. "How are you, Kale? Shifts are starting up again soon, right?"

"Yeah. In a few days," I said. I paused and took a measured breath. There was no reason to keep hiding the truth from her, since I was going to keep visiting anyway. "Look, Mom, I'm actually staying behind this shift. I've already told Captain Saunders. I don't want to be trapped in Saturn for four months while you're in here."

"Stop that," she said. "Good work is hard to find these days."

"It's only temporary, I swear. I found a job sweeping up a noodle restaurant in the Uppers, and I plan on finding something else for nights. Maybe the engine factory by home. With both, I should at least make the same as I did on the *Piccolo*."

"Kale." She said it the way she used to when I came home late, and she'd known I'd been out getting into trouble. "The proudest day of my life was sending you off to board the *Piccolo* so you could see something in the universe beyond the enclosure of Darien. Don't throw that away for me."

"Mom, really, I'll be fine. After we figure this out, I'm sure Captain Saunders will take me back—he gave me a shot in the first place. For now, we just have to think about getting you out healthy. Have you talked to Tanner about helping?"

"I told you not to worry yourself about that."

"You served him for two decades! By Trass, his clan-brother owns the damn *Piccolo,* so he's got to have something lying around. It's worth trying."

"Always the optimist." She exhaled, so congested that she sounded much like one of the faulty air recyclers in the depths of the Lowers. "Fine, I'll message him, but for now, I want you to focus on you. You need credits too, you know."

"Of course. How else am I going to convince a woman as good as you to give me a chance?"

"Still after Cora, are you?"

I blushed and shot a playful glower her way.

She chuckled for as long as she could manage, then began coughing again. Once that abated, she said, "Please, Kale, just think about it." She regarded her bony hands and shrugged. "It can't get any worse."

"After all these years, you must know you can't stop me. As long as I'm still breathing, there's no way I'm letting you be reduced to ashes."

I meant that literally. The Ringer dead were almost always cremated, ever since the days of Darien Trass's first settlers, when the dead were burned for energy... recycled into the wealth and majesty of Titan. After the Great Reunion, when sickness became prevalent, cremation was required by mandate.

"Better than anybody," she admitted. She raised her hand to place it against the glass divider, wincing during the entire effort, as if even that small task was a struggle.

"As long as you promise to keep fighting, I'll be here trying to get you out." I pressed my long, latex-clad fingers on the glass across from hers. We held them there for as long as possible—a minute, maybe two—until her weak arm started shaking. It was hardly long enough for me, but that was the closest we could get.

"Would you mind..." she began before hesitating. Her lips drooped into a frown, and she stared straight into my eyes. I could tell immediately that my least favorite part of every day was arriving early. "Letting me get some rest?" she finished.

"Already?" I glanced up at the digital timer on the wall. It'd been only seven minutes. Security allowed each visitor to get a maximum of fifteen. "It's still early."

"I know, I'm sorry. I just haven't been getting much sleep lately, and you came so late."

It was difficult for me to regard her and not picture the vibrant woman who'd somehow managed to deal with all the shit I'd put her through, who'd cared for me since before I could walk. But she did seem exhausted.

"It's fine," I said. "I've got to start getting ready to sweep the floors at Old World Noodles soon anyway. I can't wait."

My mother wasn't amused. "I really hope you reconsider the *Piccolo*," she scolded. "I don't want you to have to—"

"I know," I stopped her. Sick or not, I could tell where she was going. "Wind up like my father. I promise I'm staying on the right side of the law still." It stung my throat to force the lie out, but for her sake, I had to. She was frail enough without having to fear for my safety.

"Okay..." she said.

"I'll be back first thing tomorrow," I said. "Same time as usual if the lines aren't bad."

Her lips began to tremble, but she steadied them enough to speak. "You really don't have to keep coming back every day."

"I know that." I forced another grin. "But I look forward to it from the moment I wake up. I really don't mind it here. It's nice and cold. I just wish the glass was gone."

She muttered something under her breath. I expected my response to at least make her expression brighten a little, but all it managed to do was get her to angle her despondent gaze away from me.

"I love you, Mom," I said.

"I love you too," she replied before being beset by another bout of coughs. This time, she didn't bother to let it pass. She just got up and shambled away into the Q-Zone without looking back.

I lingered for a minute while another Ringer with the same affliction limped in to take her place. This one was in far worse condition. His pale flesh was stippled with rashes, and he was skinny, even for a Ringer. His medical gown barely fit, allowing me to see ribs so visible they appeared like the keys of a xylophone. The poor man couldn't have had more than a week left.

I rushed from the room. It took a lot out of me, visiting. I lumbered back through the decon-chamber, again waiting anxiously the entire time I was inside for me to come up clean. I did.

After I exited, the elderly receptionist cleared me, and only on her screen did I realize the time. My shift at Old World Noodles was starting in thirty minutes. I really needed to get a new hand-terminal so I could tell the time on my own. There was too much to do.

FOUR

"Where've you been, Drayton?" the manager of Old World Noodles asked me before I could even get through its entrance. The squat Earther wore a cross glare on his broad face and stood with his thick, hairy arms crossed. I could tell he was propped up on his toes to pretend he was taller than he was. Even then, I still had a good half-meter or more on him along with every other working Ringer scattered throughout the Uppers,

"Security was tight at decon," I replied. "I couldn't get through. It won't happen again." It was the best excuse I could come up with, if only because it was true. Sure, I should've left earlier, but there was no predicting that the Ringer ahead of me would be caught trying to smuggle something in and hold everyone up.

"Sure," he replied, his voice dripping with skepticism.

"Mr. Belview, I—"

"Save it. You're finished. There're thousands of others like you in the Lowers who would kill for a job here. I've got no time for another lazy-ass Ringer. First to flee Earth, first to ditch a little bit of hard labor. Typical."

He slammed the door in my face, leaving me with a bevy of additional excuses stuck on the tip of my tongue. Through the glass, I could see some of the patrons at the tables snicker.

My heart sank. Barely five minutes late and I was out of a cover job. I slowly backed away, deflated and wondering where to go next, when I bumped into something as solid as a boulder.

"Watch it, Ringer!"

I caught my balance and whipped my body around. My gaze dropped to see a security officer in full red-and-black Pervenio regalia. Unlike me, our collision didn't affect him in the slightest, both due to his stocky build and a weighted boiler suit calibrated to help him acclimate to the low, one-seventh Earth-g conditions on Titan. The tinted visor of his sleek helmet aimed directly at my face, and he gripped the handle of his sheathed shock-baton a little too comfortably for my taste.

I decided to move on quickly.

I was in the ground level of the central atrium at the heart of Darien's Upper Ward, so if I caused even a hint of trouble, there'd be more Earthers on me in a second than I could count.

Before I took the job on the *Piccolo,* the Uppers wasn't a place I often found myself, and even afterward, I rarely did more than pass through on my way to the docks. Ringers like me couldn't afford most of what was sold there anyway, so there was rarely a reason to linger.

Besides the serious risk of sickness, I found it too bright, with countless ads lining the pure white walls. And definitely too loud. The airy spaces allowed you to hear voices and advertisements echoing from every direction. They all wound up muddled together into a frantic commotion far less melodious than the hum of Lowers machinery.

It was also hot. Just standing around made sweat leak from every pore. The Uppers were constantly heated to around fifteen degrees Celsius to remain comfortable for its mostly

Earther populace. Way too warm for my blood. On the *Piccolo,* everywhere but the Ringer dorms was kept to the liking of Earthers, so I'd grown somewhat used to dealing with it, but it was always nice when I got to return home to a bed where I actually needed covers.

What I found most discomforting about the Uppers, though, was how spotless everything was. Not that I particularly enjoyed staring at the rusty, grated ceilings and ice-rock-carved walls characteristic of the Lowers, but everything seemed too perfect. I couldn't even find a wrinkle in the uniforms of patrolling security officers—whose prevalence also didn't help put me at ease. No matter which direction I looked, there were at least two in sight for every Ringer hard at work performing janitorial jobs similar to the one I'd just lost.

It'd been like that since I could remember, but things had been growing worse ever since the Titan-wide riots that occurred while I was away. Pervenio kept it off Solnet, but I'd heard that three security officers wound up beaten to death in the Ziona Colony Block on the other side of Titan during the latest M-day. Things always got heated between our races around that day—when Earthers reveled as if they'd conquered the universe just because Earth wasn't dead—yet in other years, people rarely died of anything but their own carelessness.

The holiday never really bothered me much. Earth was barely more than a series of old tales and pictures as far as I was concerned. I knew I'd never step foot there. Earthers had their unifying holiday just like we Ringers had Trass Day, named after the man who built the ship that carried our ancestors to the Ring before the Meteorite nearly extinguished all life on Earth. It was celebrated November 10, when they are said to have first touched down on Titan in the year 2036.

Trass's towering statue, which rose through the center of the atrium, was the only visible thing in the Upper Ward that remained untouched from before the Earthers arrived and the Ringer Plague left them in charge of renovation. It depicted Darien Trass on his final day on Earth, standing beside a little girl as they pointed toward the sky. The base was surrounded by real plants with frilly pink flowers that were still slick from being watered. A plaque embedded on it read: HE GAVE HIS LIFE TO GIVE US THIS RING.

The ship he built to escape the Meteorite had limited space, and only the most qualified people were permitted to board. It's said that the girl beside him was his daughter and that he sacrificed his position on his ship so that she could go, even though she didn't meet the requirements. He chose to sacrifice himself rather than any of the other three thousand passengers, none of whom had done much to make the exodus possible. I don't know many people who would've done the same. He could've been King of Titan if he'd wanted. Instead, his line merely became one of the many families that helped establish the Ring in the centuries that followed. The last of them were said to have died during the plague following the Great Reunion.

I took a seat on the bench beside the memorial so that I could gather my thoughts. It was my favorite spot in the Uppers for that, not that it had much competition. Trass gave his life to save what he thought would be the last remnants of humanity. Surely he wouldn't have sulked after missing out on a job at Old World freaking Noodles.

I tried to imagine myself being happy working in the Uppers for the rest of my life like my mother had. It wasn't all bad. Many of the generous walkways were lined with planters like the one around the memorial, displaying all manner of colorful flora that had supposedly thrived outside on Pre-Meteorite Earth. It was a bit pretentious, but I'd always been fond of plants. We didn't have them in the Lowers. Translucencies cut into the dense enclosure of the Darien Colony Block permitted the whitish glow of Titan's sky to shine through as well. Down in the Lowers, we never got to see any real sunlight.

I looked around the atrium. There were plenty of other jobs I could apply for. Employers were always looking for Ringers who had experience working amicably with Earthers to do the jobs that Earthers didn't want to do. I had that. And I was happy to accept the low wages. They were still higher than what I could make in the Lowers or at the hydro-farms performing similarly menial tasks, since most Ringers refused to take work in a place mobbed with Earthers.

My confidence renewed, I went to stand. A Ring-wide Pervenio transmission suddenly popped up on every ad and view-screen in the atrium. The image of Director Sodervall—the voice of Pervenio Corp throughout the Ring—appeared all around me.

I approached the largest view-screen in sight. A crowd formed around it. Earthers, Ringers, everyone stopped what they were doing. It wasn't often he publicly addressed the entirety of the Ring, so when the Voice of the Ring spoke, everybody listened. He typically spoke of unrest or a new policy, but today, he appeared extra cheerful, although that wasn't saying much. His craggy lips seemed to be permanently stretched into a thin, straight line.

"People of the Ring!" Director Sodervall began. "Why should we remain divided? Why should we bicker and brawl? Recent troubles on Earth have inspired our great benefactor, Mr. Luxarn Pervenio, to petition the United Sol Federation to reconsider its position on the Departure. Under his proposal, all offworlders, including those from Titan, will be permitted to enter their names in the Departure Lottery, provided they are healthy and have received all available immunizations. The USF Assembly's vote will be held next week, on November 10.

Soon the fight to ensure our survival will rest in *all* of our hands!"

A palpable ripple of discontent passed across the entirety of the Upper Ward. The Earthers sitting at a nearby bar grumbled under their breath. I heard one mutter, "Mr. Pervenio is losing his mind," and another, "Great—next they'll name one of the Ringers king, and we'll wind up bowing to him. You'll see."

Talking heads appeared on the screens to discuss the announcement. Every Ringer in my vicinity stopped what they were doing and ignored their bosses' shouts for them to return to work. It was hard to get a read on any of their expressions with their masks on, but many of the eyes I saw bled with contempt. Just like mine were.

The Departure was the main reason the majority of my people hated M-day, but it wasn't because they were upset they couldn't participate in the Lottery to win a place on an Ark-ship bound for the stars. It was because they believed that there was no reason to spend billions of credits on sending a ship beyond any realistic means of contact—that the Departure was a mockery of what Darien Trass had accomplished under the stress of a meteorite bearing down on Earth.

I'd never concerned myself with that before. If Earth-born citizens wanted to brave space, I was happy there'd be fewer of them. And yet, the Director's line about requiring "all available immunizations" caused the hairs on the back of my neck to stand on end and my teeth to grind. I knew firsthand how that essentially discounted 99 percent of Ringers, who if they'd been able to afford them, would obviously have sprung their loved ones from quarantine. It was like spitting in our faces. And holding the vote on the 10th, Trass Day, was just rubbing it in.

"Better off sending them all to Earth," I heard one of the Pervenio security officers beside me whisper to his partner. "Maybe some real gravity will teach them to be human again."

His partner snickered. "It'd solve our problem, that's for sure."

My fists clenched. I turned to face them, but before I could do anything impulsive, a bottle sailed across the atrium from somewhere behind me and smashed into the view-screen above. The impact was so loud that it sounded like a gunshot. Terrified screams rang out as I was showered in sparks.

"Keep your damn Lottery!" a voice hollered.

"Trass chose us!" shouted another.

"The Children of Titan already have a home!"

The ring of flowering plants wrapping the base of the Trass Memorial suddenly went up in flames. Then, while I stood frozen, the situation escalated beyond anything I'd ever experienced in the Uppers. A group of Ringer workers grabbed the security officer beside me and beat him with his own baton. They stole the pulse-rifle off his back and fired it at the officers attempting to subdue them.

The earsplitting sound of shouts and gunfire made my head spin. I was in the center of it all. I didn't know what to do besides cover my ears until someone grabbed my arm. There was no telling how I would've reacted if the touch hadn't been so tender.

"Kale, you've got to get out of here!" a woman yelled into my ear.

I turned my head and saw Cora. Her eyes were so close to mine and open so wide I could see all the myriad shades of blue encircling her pupils. I'd seen images of Neptune on view-screens, and even they couldn't compare.

"Kale!" she repeated. I snapped out of my daze and ran with her. Security officers raced by us toward the fray, and I lowered my head so they wouldn't notice my mask-covered face. It seemed pointless, considering how tall and lanky I was, but it worked.

We went as fast as we could. Blood-curdling screams and the sound of skulls cracking echoed across the Uppers as an endless stream of Pervenio security officers reestablished control. By the time we reached the lift down to the Lowers, I was so drenched in sweat it looked like I'd just been swimming. Groups of officers were positioned at every corner inside, wielding pulse-rifles now rather than batons. I leaned against the wall to catch my breath as we began to descend. Cora stood next to me. The heat hadn't left her nearly as exhausted.

She leaned in so that nobody would hear her. "What were you doing up there?" she asked crossly, as if I'd done something wrong.

I thought about asking her the same thing, but I knew the answer. There was a reason the heat didn't bother her, and it was the same reason she wasn't wearing a sanitary mask or gloves: She was a hybrid in the truest sense of the word. Her mother was a Ringer dating back to the first settlers like mine, but she'd been impregnated with Cora by some vagrant Earther who'd forced himself on her. Ringer mothers unfortunate enough to have to endure that abuse typically died of illness before they could give birth, so Cora was a rarity. As such, she was embraced by my people and had a strong enough immune system to be willing to spend time in the Uppers.

Being mixed-race also meant she had a unique look to her, which only made her more stunning. Her neck was long and shapely, the way pretty Ringer girls' were, but she was shorter than most and slightly curvier. She was also abnormally reticent for one of us. A majority of the Ringer girls I knew growing up were excessively outgoing, at least amongst their own kind.

I'd heard that before the Great Reunion, sex on Titan was as ordinary as conversation. Being crammed into tight, freezing living quarters when the Ring was first settled had had that effect on our ancestors. No longer. Monogamous relationships between Ringers was the way now. Sticking with someone you knew was safe went a long way toward avoiding quarantine. Honestly, the whole topic made me anxious. It was easy for Earthers, who with their vast clan-families didn't have to worry about finding somebody, since it was usually arranged. Sometimes, I worried I was the only Ringer my age I knew who hadn't already shacked up permanently with another person.

"Just passing through," was what I managed to say after an extended period of silence. Seeing her outside of the *Piccolo* once was a rarity; twice in one day had me tongue-tied.

"Same," she said. "Trass, I didn't expect that. What's Pervenio thinking?"

"Probably that they're helping," I said.

"Yeah."

We stood in silence for the rest of the ride. Her being timid and me being nervous just from sharing her air made for a painfully awkward combo. The lift stopped at Level B3, and I followed her off, even though I had nothing to do there.

Outside of the central lift, we were greeted by a ring of decon-chambers. I thanked Trass everyone had to pass through them alone. I think I would've fainted if I'd gotten into one with Cora and had to watch her strip down.

I stepped out of mine—clean, thankfully—and then an alarm suddenly wailed behind me.

"Contagion detected," an automated voice repeated over and over.

One of the chambers blinked red and Ringers throughout the node gathered to watch. Officers in hazmat suits ran through transparent halls stringing the decon-chambers together, and a short while later, I heard screams as a woman was dragged into an auxiliary lift. I didn't get a clear look at who she was.

I searched the crowd in a panic but didn't see Cora anywhere. Strong immune system or not, she looked enough like a Ringer, and that was a one-way ticket to quarantine, even if she'd probably survive it.

I shoved my way back through the accumulating crowd. I couldn't deal with the idea of having to make two visits to the Q-Zone every day.

"Cora, there you are!" someone exclaimed.

Air fled my lungs in relief. I spun my head around and saw that she was safely exiting one of the other decon-chambers. A Ringer man jogged toward her, grinning.

I knew him well. Desmond Parks was another member of the *Piccolo*'s maintenance crew. He was the fastest maintenance worker on the ship, probably good enough to be a real mechanic one day if he didn't like butting heads with the Earther crew members so much. It's safe to say we weren't friends. In fact, after leaving behind the shadows of the Lowers, I tried my best to avoid those. I considered Cora the closest I had to one, though our exchange on the lift was probably one of the longest continuous ones we'd ever had. Of course, she rarely spoke much to anybody. Sitting across from her in the Piccolo mess hall for meals every day was more than enough for me.

"Oh, hey, Kale," Desmond addressed me nonchalantly once we all convened. "Didn't know you two were together."

"We're not!" I replied, much more loudly than I intended. My cheeks went hot when Cora shot me a perplexed glare.

Desmond rolled his eyes. "Whatever you say. C'mon, Cora. Lester and Yavik are waiting for us so that we can all load up before heading down to the Foundry. You coming, Kale?"

I wanted to. I couldn't remember a day that I'd ever gotten to spend time with Cora outside of the *Piccolo*. Then I regarded her and remembered that I was no longer a member of that crew. In fact, I was currently unemployed... in a legal sense. I had no credits to waste on drinks. Only that salt-sniffer Dexter could help me with that.

Cora waited for an answer. The first thing that sputtered out of my mouth was: "I can't right now."

"Oh, right, I forgot," Desmond said. "I heard our beloved captain is busy searching for your replacement now that you've stepped down."

Cora stopped. She turned toward me, visibly shocked. "You're leaving?" she asked softly.

"He didn't tell you?" Desmond said. "Typical Kale. Got sick of kissing old Culver's ass, I bet."

I froze as well. Leave it to Desmond to ruin my plans to drop out as quietly as possible. But I hadn't expected her to seem so disappointed.

"It's complicated," I said.

"Well, hopefully, your replacement isn't as much of an Earther lover," Desmond said, calling me that for a different reason than people from my old life used to. Just because I didn't try to provoke fights during our shifts and focused on work so I could return to the coolness of my bed didn't mean I wanted to kiss the captain.

I ignored Desmond and held Cora's gaze. She was a girl of few words, but her expression was enough to make my chest tighten. "It's only temporary," I insisted.

She opened her mouth to say something, but Desmond grabbed her arm and towed her along. "Let's go, Cora," he said. "Leave him to his more important business."

She stared back over her shoulder for a few seconds as they set off across the node toward one of the branching tunnels before she bit her lip and turned away, leaving me standing alone like a fool and worried that this was the last time I'd ever see her. I knew it was for the best I didn't go, crew or not. It wasn't worth the risk of a few drinks loosening up my tongue enough to where I might mention something about John, Dexter, or my mom. It wasn't worth

Desmond ridiculing me in front of her for not having a drink either.

"Bye," I whispered as they disappeared into a tunnel.

It was time to focus on doing whatever I could to help my mom. Her condition was rapidly worsening. I exhaled, pushed Cora out of my head, and got back onto the lift. Dexter was waiting for me with work that might actually put a dent in the number of credits I needed to earn.

FIVE

IT TURNED OUT THAT I WAS GOING TO WIND UP AT THE
Foundry that night, though not with anybody from the *Piccolo*.
When I met with Dexter in his chop shop, he informed me he'd
just received a tip from someone about the registered parts of
Solnet. As usual, he said, it was going to be "as simple as finding
a starving Ringer." I doubted that, but I was glad the job didn't
include me going to the Uppers. After the riot in the atrium,
there was bound to be so much security up there I'd have to
cram through doors sideways.

My target was once again a hand-terminal, only this one
didn't belong to an Earther. I didn't like stealing from Ringers,
but Dexter's contact wanted the information stored on it so
badly he was offering ten thousand credits... close to double
what John's was worth. Enough to pay half a year's worth of
rent. The woman was supposedly an undercover Earther-
sympathizing informant, trading information in exchange for
special treatment.

The Foundry's musty air filled my nostrils as I stepped in. It
was a place Ringers went to forget—the largest, most renowned
club in Darien. Once the site of a production factory on Level

B5, it consisted of a series of gaping caverns. Male and female dancers in skintight plastic bodysuits like those in the Sunken Credit lined machine belts that cranked along through the swelling crowds of Ringers. Vibrant, pulsating lights refracted through clouds of mist that spilled out through exhaust vents once meant for safety. Bars were built into stacks of machinery, colorful bottles feeding through reallocated pumps to work the taps.

There was nothing else like it. In the Uppers, bars were quieter and filled with ads telling you what to drink and where to get it. In the Foundry, the rock-strewn walls were barren, and all that mattered were the hundreds of feet slapping across the floor as Ringers moved their bodies to pulsing beats. Earthers loved to tout their ancient stringed instruments and their slow-paced music, but I'd found those didn't help anybody lose themselves. Trass's settlers had no room for instruments on the Ark. My ears teemed with the synthesized rhythms of Titan.

I shuffled through a mob of masked men and women. Some of them swayed from drinking too much. Others danced like their lives depended on it, pupils rolled up into the back of their heads, probably from sniffing foundry salts. Sweat spraying in every direction made the floor slick. Shower stalls by the exit were available to be used whenever anybody wanted. Rudimentary decon-chambers stood at the entrance. There was everything necessary to help the Ringer patrons feel safe so they could unwind.

I'd enjoyed nights at the Foundry plenty of times, but I hadn't been in the mood since the news about my mom. It didn't feel right to dance or indulge, and drinking was the only way I could get myself to feel comfortable amongst the undulant crowd. I stuck to the walls and kept a lookout for Cora or Desmond. Wherever they were, I didn't want them to spot me.

My mark was across the club. The far side of the Foundry

was lined by raised suites with broad, tinted translucencies. They'd once been observation rooms for the factory but were presently used as private suites for some of the Foundry's wealthier guests. According to Dexter's contact, the terminal I was after was in the one on the far right.

Easy enough. Usually, I had to scope out locations, but the suite would be a single hollow, maybe with an adjoining bathroom. The only issue was getting inside.

An intimidating guard was posted at the base of the stairs leading up to the suite. He or she wore shiny white carbon-plated armor and a helmet with a visor so tinted that it was impossible to tell what was behind it. The pulse-rifle on his or her back was much newer than the ones Dexter's goons touted. That was going to be a problem, but the guard would have to piss eventually. I'd have to time the shift changes and figure out when to slip in.

I skulked over to an abandoned piece of machinery being reclaimed as a table, overlooking a group of dancers. It was the perfect spot from which to pretend I wasn't watching the suite. I was about to take a seat on one of the stools, when out of the corner of my eye, I noticed silvery hair.

I rushed around the side and ducked beside what had been a storage bin. Cora, Desmond, and a few more Ringer members of the *Piccolo*'s crew shoved across the dance floor toward my position, fresh drinks in their hands.

They seated themselves at the table, so close to me I could see their legs swaying through gaps in the machine's base. I couldn't hear anything over the blasting music, but Desmond and his friends were chatting it up like always. Cora remained silent. She seemed as somber as when I'd left her. I hoped it wasn't thanks to me.

Spilled drinks made my latex-clad hands stick to the rock as I stayed crouched. The floor had its own unique stench. More than a few people had clearly chosen to vomit in the bin beside me, with many hitting the side instead. I distanced my head as far as I could and focused on the suite. Three guards in identical white armor were outside now. Two marched down the stairs, and between them sauntered the woman I assumed the suite belonged to. Dexter hadn't given me a name or description, but I didn't need them. A glittering velvet dress hugged her lithe figure, cut high up on her thighs. It was an outfit of such extravagance that there was no wonder she needed the guards. True Ringer or not, she stuck out in the Lowers like my people did above.

She reached the bottom of the stairs in a frantic state and turned her head. Long, silken brown hair swept over her shoulders, and for a moment, it seemed like her eyes locked on me. I felt a chill. She was beautiful, but not in the way I was used to. There was ferocity to her features, like she knew she could have anyone she wanted pawing at her feet.

I was spellbound. Then she turned, hollered something at her guards, and they all hurried away. It didn't take long before the sparkle of her dress vanished within the mob of lanky Ringers. Questions like who she was and why in the name of Trass she was staying in the Lowers filled my mind. They were hushed when I realized that, in her rush, the lift door to her suite hadn't closed all the way. Jammed or broken, a rift along the bottom revealed the flicker of view-screens changing feeds beyond.

"It'll be easy," Dex had said to me about the job. I wondered if he had anything to do with getting her to rush out. There was no time to care.

"Sorry, guys," I whispered under my breath. I knocked into the machinery hard enough for one of the empty glasses on the portion being used as a table to fall off and shatter. Cora yelped. Desmond cursed. The move distracted my former crewmates for the few seconds I needed to sprint out toward the suite.

A pack of cavorting drunkards helped provide cover on my approach. Scantily clad dancers handled the rest. I casually leaned on the suite's stairs once I made it over, pretending I'd drunk a little too much and was having trouble standing. With my peripherals, I studied the door. My eyes hadn't been playing a trick on me. A bottle lay on its side in the opening, causing the fail-safes to keep it from closing all the way. The door was open, just enough, I figured, for my skinny body to fit through.

I scanned my surroundings. The woman in the violet dress was nowhere to be found. Neither were her guards. I took one slow step onto the stairs, then moved a bit faster as if I belonged. She probably had the device on her, but I could scope the place out. Or better yet, find somewhere inside to hide and wait for my chance. Vents were tight, but I'd squeezed into worse.

I kneeled and checked under the opening for guards. Seeing none, I took one last glance over my shoulder to make sure nobody was watching. The coast was clear, a sea of carousing as far as the eye could see. Except for Cora. I spotted her staring longingly into the bottom of her empty glass while Desmond nudged her in the side to try to gain her attention.

I turned back to the door. It was time to focus. I lay down and pulled myself through the narrow opening. My head made it in easy, but getting the rest of me through proved more diffi-cult than I'd expected. My ribs pressed against the unforgiving metal floor and felt seconds from cracking when I emerged, gasping for air. My foot accidentally tapped the bottle off the stairs, causing the door to slam down. Fortunately, a nearby control pad allowed it to be unlocked from the inside.

I got to my feet, groaning as a sharp pain pulled at my sides. It passed quickly but seeing what was within the room made my jaw drop. At first glance, it was an unassuming hollow—ice-rock walls and a dropped grated ceiling affixed with dim lights like any other. Across from me, however, was a curved array of view-screens the likes of which I'd never seen before. There had to be at least one hundred of them. They were deactivated, but I could think of only one purpose for such a workstation: surveillance.

My pulse hastened. Dex was far from trustworthy, but I wondered if even he knew who or what he'd sent me after. I approached the screens guardedly, despite being alone, and once I was close enough, I saw it. Sitting harmlessly on the counter by the station's seat was a hand-terminal. Not just any hand-terminal either. It belonged to me... or at least it had until I'd sold it off cheap so my mom could stay comfortable. I recognized the Venta Co branding, the bent portion of the casing on the upper right-hand side, as well as a series of scratches along the lower part of the screen.

"What the hell?" I asked.

I grasped the device and rechecked my surroundings. There was nobody else in the room. I held it up, and when I swiped the screen to see if it was on, a message popped up all on its own.

WE CAN HELP EACH OTHER, KALE DRAYTON. I NEED YOU TO SMUGGLE SOMETHING ONTO THE *PICCOLO*. DO THIS FOR ME, AND YOUR MOTHER WILL BE RELEASED FROM QUARANTINE AND CURED OF WHAT AILS HER. LEAVE NOW. VISIT THE FOUNDRY AGAIN BEFORE DEPARTING FOR YOUR NEXT SHIFT, AND THIS ARRANGEMENT WILL BE NULLIFIED. YOU HAVE TWENTY-FOUR HOURS TO REPLY WITH A DECISION.

FROM ICE TO ASHES,

R

The farther I read, the harder my heart thumped. By the end, my throat was dry, and my forehead dripped with sweat despite the icy temperature.

The contact address was unknown, and R might as well have been a word in Old Russian, because I had no idea who it could be. But I'd spent enough time in the shadows to know when someone was asking me to do something unsavory. That was when people were vague. Nobody ever worried about telling you the truth of what they wanted if the truth was clean.

I decided that all the stress on me was causing me to see things. There were thousands of hand-terminals like mine. It wasn't a stretch to imagine that another had similar blemishes. I took a deep breath and closed my eyelids tight so that I could reset my vision before giving it another read.

As my eyelids reopened, the entire array of screens blinked on simultaneously. Every single one displayed the same feed: a view of my mom's room in the Q-Zone. The sight caused me to stagger backward.

"Mom?" I whispered. Whether or not I was mic'd, she wouldn't have been able to hear me. She was half-asleep on a torn mattress—not exactly what they'd promised when I'd paid for a better room. One of her scrawny arms draped over the edge into a trash bin filled with bile, while the other was attached to an IV. A sequence of rashes dappled her face, which unless they'd just formed, had been covered by makeup when I visited her. There was no sound, but I could see her groaning. Every few seconds, her eyes opened slightly, as if she were checking to make sure she was still amongst the living.

I tossed the hand-terminal onto the counter and ran to the workstation's control console to try my luck at learning where the feed was coming from. A series of alien-looking algorithmic encryptions locked me out. I could slice through most rudimentary safeguards given the time, but this was well beyond my capability. My frustration built, and when I slammed down on the keys, the array went black again.

"Mom!" I shouted. I tapped one of the screens. It was still warm. Then I whipped my body around and scoured the empty room for anything that might help me figure out who I was dealing with. I didn't know anybody, not even a fence, who went by R. There was nothing. No stray clothing or closets. Not even a lavatory. Just metal, rock, and at least a hundred blank screens.

It suddenly hit me: This had to be Dexter's doing. Either a cruel prank... or worse: He feared his secrets being in my brain and wanted to get rid of me. Security could be on its way to detain me any second. Exchanging unsanctioned communications was considered highly illegal on Titan. It was enough to get you locked up on Pervenio Station for years.

I prepared to run, then froze. The hand-terminal had belonged to me. If it was still registered in my name and discovered with that message on it, I'd be screwed no matter what. I snatched it, shoved it into my pocket, and took off for the exit. It opened easily.

I launched myself over the railing of the stairs without thinking and plunged into the crowd. Cora or Desmond or anybody could have seen me. I didn't care. I needed to get out of the Foundry and to Dexter. If he really was setting me up, I'd get on my knees and promise that I wasn't being used by Pervenio as a snitch.

Level B6 was so quiet, the dark, yawning tunnels had the feel of an ancient crypt. The hullabaloo of its many factories was absent. Every hatch I passed was sealed tight. Exhaust vents and air recyclers moaned as if they were infested with ghosts.

I tried to act calm, but the device and the message in my pocket made that nearly impossible. The best I could do was to just keep from stumbling over any exposed pipes. I turned in to the tunnel leading to Dexter's chop shop, and the silence somehow grew even more unbearable. I could hear my own heartbeat.

Unlike the rest of the area, light poured through Dexter's wide-open hatch. I thought about what I was going to say to him while I approached. A whole slew of pleading and flattery—whatever it took to get him to keep to his word so that my mother wouldn't be left to die alone. It would hurt my pride, but I'd recover.

I stopped outside to gather focus. Once I felt as confident as I knew I'd ever get, I turned the corner.

"Dexter, you—" The words got stuck in my throat as I stepped through.

Dexter's shop bustled with Pervenio security officers. I counted at least four of them... alive. One clearly dead officer was slumped against the adjacent wall, blood oozing out of a gash in his forehead, and across from him was Dexter, sagging in his wheelchair. His throat was slit, and the knife that he kept hidden in his armrest glinted on the floor by his outstretched hand, the tip stained red.

"You, Ringer, this area is off limits!" a member of the security team shouted at me.

My gaze was ripped away from Dexter's gruesome throat. Four new-gen pulse-rifles aimed at me. My hands shot into the air. I stuttered, but no words came out.

All four of Dexter's henchmen were dead as well. Three lay behind the counter—messes of bloody, tangled limbs. The fourth was arranged similarly to the dead officer, but with the entire top of his head blown off. His limp body leaned against the room's open hatch, and on it, I saw something that hadn't been there earlier: An orange circle was painted on the metal face, so fresh that the point where the brushstroke had stopped still dripped.

"What are you doing here?" the officer questioned.

I bolted out of the room before any of them could grab me. "Get back here!"

I ran as fast as I could, tearing around corners so I'd be impossible to track. I didn't look back to see if they were following, and I didn't risk taking the central lift. A series of air ducts returned me to the same escape route underneath the farms that I'd used the day before.

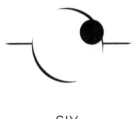

SIX

I FLUNG OPEN THE HATCH INTO MY HOLLOW ON LEVEL B2 of the Darien Lowers and rushed in, checking at least three times that it was locked tight behind me. Once I was sure, I fell against it and ripped off my sanitary mask. Steam from my mouth hung on the frigid air as I released a breath that had seemingly been trapped in my lungs since I fled Dexter's shop.

That unleashed a deluge of them, and I started to hyperventilate.

I'd seen death in the Lowers before—every Ringer had—but nothing like that. Whatever had happened, it was enough to drive Dexter to cut his own neck rather than be brought in; enough for his henchmen, depraved salt-sniffers, to give their lives as well.

I slid my hand into my pocket and withdrew my compromised hand-terminal. My fingers trembled too intensely to hold it steady. Dexter wouldn't have let himself die just to get rid of me. He certainly wouldn't to pull off a prank.

"Hello?" a voice hollered from outside my hatch. "Anyone home?" Then there came a few knocks, the metal causing them to echo along the rock and ice walls of my hollow.

I was so startled that I threw the hand-terminal across the room onto my bed. Then I jumped up, nearly hitting my head on the low, craggy ceiling. I thought about staying silent, but not answering whoever it was would only make me seem guiltier.

I slowly turned to face the hatch. It was difficult to see what I looked like in the murky reflection on its oxidized metal surface, but I wiped my sweating brow and drew a few lungsful for good measure. I told myself that if Pervenio security had decided to come after me, they would've busted through themselves. When I was ready, I pushed the heavy hatch open just enough to peek outside.

"Oh, Kale, it's just you," an older Ringer named Benji Reigar said. His pale face was creased with wrinkles so shallow that they appeared sketched on by a pencil. Generations in low g had made my people appear younger than our Earther counterparts of the same age. "I saw someone run in here, but I couldn't tell who it was."

I breathed a sigh of relief and opened the hatch a little farther. Benji was just another Ringer from the Lowers like me. He'd been living alone in the hollow next to my mom's since before I could remember.

"Sorry," I said. "I thought I forgot something."

"Must've been important. You look like you've seen a ghost." Benji leaned to the side to get a better look into my hollow. I moved with him to obstruct his view. He was a kind man, but he too often pretended like he was in charge of monitoring our little branch of the Lowers.

"I'm fine," I replied. I patted my empty pocket. "Just my hand-terminal."

He put on a wry grin and said, "Waiting to hear from someone, eh?"

"You could say that."

"By Trass, to be young again," he reminisced. "When are

you gonna find someone serious for yourself, kid? A Ringer boy your age ought to have a girl to keep his head on straight."

"I'm working on it."

He laughed.

"Well, thanks for keeping an eye on things," I said, not wanting to let him elongate the conversation like he tended to. "I better be getting to bed. Got work early." I went to close the hatch, but he blocked it with his elbow.

"So it is true?" he asked. "You're really going to stay on Titan full-time? People may give you a hard time down here about working on that harvester, but any of them would kill for a job like that, you know."

News traveled fast. Benji always seemed to find a way to learn everything about everybody who lived nearby. Luckily, I hadn't yet let anyone in on the real reason behind my choice, or he would've figured that out too and hounded me about my mother. The old man probably could've made thousands as an information broker if he put his mind to it.

"That's the plan," I said. "I landed a cleaning job in the Uppers for now while I search for something better. Those long harvest shifts were killing me."

"Staying out of trouble at least," he said. "Good. Your mother must be real proud of you." He peered over my shoulder into the empty hollow again. "Where's she been, by the way? I haven't seen her in a while."

I swallowed the lump in my throat. "Busy."

"That boss of hers giving her trouble again? I'll tell you, if those rich Earthers didn't have us to clean their sheets, they'd suffocate in their own filth."

I chuckled and placed my hand on the handle of the hatch assertively enough to warn him to let go. "Speaking of, I really better get going," I said.

"Well, I won't hold you," Benji replied, finally taking the hint. "Give your mother my best."

"I will."

I sealed the hatch and exhaled. My nerves were finally starting to calm. From what I'd seen behind Benji, Level B2 was busy, but not with Pervenio officers. They were easy to spot despite their stature. Nobody else in the Lowers could afford armor that shined like polished glass, or pulse-rifles with state-of-the-art digital ammo displays.

I headed to my bed. My legs felt weak, and I needed to sit before they crumpled. The hand-terminal lay next to me, having landed on my thin pillow. The screen was activated and the message from R shined as if mocking me.

I turned away from it and stared into my hollow—the six-meter-long cylindrical cave with ribbed walls exposed to the ice-rock crust of Titan and crooked light fixtures that were so hazy it made my skin appear gray. Two low beds were sunken along the flanks, with some area for storage, a limited kitchen, and a cramped bathroom. Once, the room had been filled with appliances and view-screens I'd earned both from stealing and working on the *Piccolo,* but they'd all been sold off for my mom's treatment.

The hollow wasn't much, but it was home. For as long as I could remember, I'd return from whatever kind of trouble I was off getting into, and my mom's face would be there to greet me, always smiling. She'd prepare whatever food she could manage to scrum up. Sometimes it would be a yeasty soup, which I'm told was seasoned to taste like the chickens that once roamed Pre-Meteorite Earth freely. I couldn't say for sure if that was true. Other times, it was a pair of condensed ration bars mass-produced somewhere by some corporation. On rare occasions, if the wealthy Earther she served was feeling particularly gener-ous, she'd even bring home some produce grown fresh in

Darien's Upper Gardens—something I wasn't able to steal. You had a better chance of getting murdered than finding a good, unprocessed meal in the markets of the Lowers, so those rare nights were my favorites. She'd always let me have the larger portion.

Not anymore. Presently, the bed across from me had been vacant for months. She'd apparently never even made it back from work the day she got taken in. She'd gone to the Lower Ward Medical Center to see about a minor cough, and that was that. It was also the only reason I was able to keep her condition secret from nosy Ringers like Benji: She hadn't set off a decon-chamber alarm and been dragged away screaming for all the Lowers to see.

I sighed and glanced back at the hand-terminal, finally with a clearer head. If the message wasn't Dexter playing games, did that mean it was real? I truly had no idea who R could be, but he or she was serious. The device had been planted for me, and only me, to find. Whoever had left it there knew my name and knew where I worked. Or at least where I *had* worked. The fact that I'd recently resigned from the *Piccolo* didn't seem to matter.

For a moment, I considered how displeased Captain Saunders was when I'd asked for a leave of absence and wondered if maybe he was the one behind the message, in an effort to get back at me. Until I realized how ridiculous that was. There was exactly one "R" in his name, and I doubted he'd go back to the second-to-last letter. Besides, I didn't do anything on the *Piccolo* significant enough to warrant a well-off captain risking his freedom by breaking Pervenio regulations. Yes, not reporting an act of unsanctioned communications was against the law, but being the one who sent the message was likely punishable with life behind bars.

. . .

DO THIS FOR ME, AND YOUR MOTHER WILL BE
RELEASED FROM QUARANTINE AND CURED OF
WHAT AILS HER.

It was an appealing offer, and a dangerous one. For my mother's
sake, I wasn't ready to say no—I couldn't ignore the view R had
shown me of her when she wasn't all prettied up for a visit— but
I wasn't foolish enough to leap blindly at the chance. I was good
at sneaking objects around Darien, occasionally smuggling them
between the Uppers and Lowers, but between worlds? And
why the *Piccolo*?

I couldn't think of a single reason why someone would be
interested in the ship. She was one of the oldest operating gas
harvesters in the Ring. So old, in fact, that a great deal of her
systems remained manual. Over the two years I'd worked there,
I'd never seen someone truly important walk its halls or even
mention it in passing.

I lay down and held the device in front of my face, reading
the message repeatedly, hoping I'd missed something. I had less
than twenty-four hours to make a decision, and I planned on
spending every one of them considering my options. My mom's
life depended on it.

I couldn't sleep. A few times I attempted to, but the message
rattled around in my skull. I tried to distract myself by switching
a newsfeed onto the hand-terminal, but that only made it worse.
An old Helix Engineering ad for bone-density boosters ran, and
its jingle got stuck in my head. *If you don't want your skeleton
a'droppin'*... R's message even started to take on the tune.

I sat up. My upper eyelids felt like they had tiny weights
strapped to them. My head ached from exhaustion. The hand-
terminal, which still operated normally despite all my contacts
being wiped, read 6:00 a.m. In all the hours of failed sleep, I

hadn't come up with a single helpful answer. The only ones I did find were that I was jobless, my mom was still in the Q-Zone, and the only fence who seemed willing to deal with me was dead, meaning the credits from robbing John would never come through. I could only hope that Pervenio had gone after Dex for reasons other than the message from R.

I decided I had to see my mom again. Not on a screen. I had to look her in the eyes to see if I really had any choice. If I hurried, I could beat the early rush for visiting hours at the Q-Zone. I got undressed and headed to my confined shower. Everything that had happened had caused me to slack off on my usual regimen. I scrubbed the stink of the Foundry off my body with water as warm as I could handle; it was the one thing there weren't many restrictions on. Titan and the Ring had plenty.

Once I was dressed and wearing a new pair of gloves and a clean sanitary mask, I tucked the hand-terminal into my pillow and covered that with a blanket. I couldn't risk anyone reading what R had sent me by bringing it along through decon-chambers and scanners. I rustled my blanket enough to make its placement appear accidental and then hurried out of my hollow.

The Lowers were quiet. Not uncharacteristically, like when I went to see Dex, but it was so early in the morning that the only people getting ready were those trying to make it to the Q-Zone. I fell in line behind a group of gloomy Ringers lumbering toward the tram station on Level B2.

I boarded the Q-Zone line, same as I did every day, and the vehicle rose up through twenty meters of rock toward the bright surface. The entire ride to the lonely plateau housing the Q-Zone, I stared through a window in hopes that I might see the silhouette of Saturn through Titan's cloudy sky. I never did. Dazzling strings of lightning flickered in the distance, and a storm gathered to obscure my view.

The line at the quarantine lobby was shorter than the day before, though security was even tighter. It made sense, considering what had happened after Director Sodervall made his address, but it also meant it took just as long as ever for me to reach the reception window. When I finally got there, the same crotchety receptionist croaked, "Name and ID."

I already had it out and ready to hand over. She studied it the same way she always did, as if it were her first time seeing it.

"Visiting?" she asked after she returned it to me.

"Katrina Drayton," I said.

She typed into her computer. "Hand-term—" She stopped herself. "One moment." She leaned in closer and stroked the keys more aggressively. My fingers tapped on the counter by the time she finally looked up again. The expression on her creased face was the same as usual, but I knew something was wrong.

"My apologies, Mr. Drayton," she said. "Update just came in. According to the nurses, she's not seeing any visitors today."

"Is she all right?" I questioned.

"No changes in conditions. Note just says she wasn't able to get much sleep last night and is under sedation."

The image R showed me of her sprawled out on her bed filled my mind. "Can you tell her it's me?" I asked.

"I'm afraid you'll have to come back tomorrow." The woman looked past me toward the rest of the line, as if I wasn't even there. "Next!"

I didn't budge. After the shittiest day I'd had since I discovered my mom's condition, I needed to see her. I needed to know what to do.

"No," I grumbled, a harsh edge creeping into my tone.

"Sir. Please step aside," she said.

Something snapped in me. I lunged at her window, my hands wrapping around the sill so tight that my pasty knuckles somehow went even whiter. "Tell her I need to see her!" I shouted.

A security officer seized me by the shoulders. He may have been shorter than I was, but his Earther brawn allowed him to easily tear me away from the window. I managed to squirm out of his thick arms, however, and leaped back at the window.

"Tell her!" I roared, pounding on the glass.

Suddenly, I felt like I was struck in my side by a bolt of lightning. I collapsed, drooling as my body convulsed from ten thousand volts of electricity surging through it. I'd been beaten plenty in my life, but this was the first time any officer had ever gotten me directly with the lit end of a shock-baton. My bones chattered, my organs felt like they were going to burst, and I think that at some point, I vomited. It didn't last long, but once I regained control of my body, I was as sore as if I'd just put in a full day cleaning the *Piccolo* at high g. The officer heaved me against the wall and sat me up.

"Next time you'll be locked up, Ringer!" he growled, waving his charged shock-baton. "Now get out of here!"

He kicked me in the leg and then returned to his post outside of the decon-chamber. There was no mistaking the pride in his expression as he and another officer exchanged a smirk.

The Q-Zone lobby was beginning to become a source of too much pain in my life. None of the Ringers waiting in line were foolish enough to try to help me up. I had to take my time and use the wall to haul myself back onto my feet because my fingers and toes still twitched from the shock.

As I struggled to steady my shaking legs, the same jaded woman I'd seen leaving visiting room C-7 the day before stepped up to the counter. She was beside an older man who looked like he could be her father. She had a quiet exchange with the receptionist, but then her face screwed and tears formed in her eyes.

"No!" she yelled. "No, he can't be!"

She stumbled backward, no longer silent and somber, but hysterical. She repeated "No!" as her father ran his fingers through her hair and attempted to comfort her. It was obvious he didn't know what to say.

"Yesterday he was fine and now..." She broke down. Her father hugged her and tried to hush her. It didn't work.

I felt bad for staring, but the entire line of Ringers joined me. Similar thoughts probably coursed through all their minds. My mother was wrong about what she said. It could get worse. At least *she* was still alive. Maybe it was the recent jolt to my system that made me realize it, but I couldn't just wait around wondering what I should do next.

I turned away from the crying woman and her father, wiped my mouth, and dragged my battered body back toward the inter-block tram. Before I could decide for sure if I wanted to do what R was asking, I'd need to reclaim my old position on the *Piccolo*. I wasn't going to risk searching Captain Saunders on Solnet with my compromised hand-terminal, and without his contact number, I'd have to try to locate him in the Uppers before I sweated to death. There were only fourteen hours left on R's offer.

Fortunately, I knew the captain's favorite place. I just hoped he wasn't too busy preparing for the imminent departure of the *Piccolo's* next shift to be there.

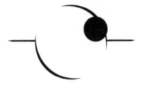

SEVEN

A ROUND OF HARVESTER SHIFTS WAS JUST LETTING OUT
when I arrived back in Darien. Unsurprisingly, more security
officers were present in the Uppers than ever before. Every
Ringer in sight had one in their shadow. Passing through the
checkpoints took so long, I thought I was going to explode.
Another hour wasted.

On most mornings, Captain Saunders frequented his
favorite coffee shop. The majority of Earthers did. To them, it
was considered a high-end beverage, though I couldn't figure out
why. I found it repulsive. The captain had bought me a cup
when I first signed on with the *Piccolo,* and it almost made me
throw up.

Despite having been there before, it took me longer to find
the place than I'd expected. The vibrant ads and white walls
throughout the Uppers were disorienting, and landmarks were
of no use since the lofty ceiling was masked by a uniform layer
of suspended gardens for the wealthiest of Earthers to enjoy. I
remembered for sure that the shop was in part of the Uppers the
path to the docks never took me on. It'd been nestled between

two of the towering residential towers, which rose fifty meters to support the gardens as well as Darien's enclosure.

I couldn't ask for directions since the many Earthers shopping and eating kept their distance from me, as if *I* were the one who could infect *them*. I didn't mind. My recent trip to the Q-Zone had me on edge, and I made sure my mask and gloves were on as tight as possible.

I grew frustrated with searching, when I noticed a familiar planter filled with broad, frilly leaves and purple flowers. It was located at the base of the tower the captain's brother lived in, directly across from the biggest viewport in the sector. From the correct angle, it almost seemed like the plants were growing on the surface of Titan. Of course, as I neared, I could see the moon's barren landscape stretching for kilometers toward a few distant factories alongside methane lakes, spewing black smoke.

The coffee shop was in a glassy pavilion across from it. A line extended from the faux-wood counter in its center and out the front door past where an officer was posted. I didn't see Captain Saunders anywhere inside, so I took a seat by the viewport and stared out at Titan while I waited. I needed to try to keep calm.

The view may have been nothing except for barren plains and distant, rock-strewn plateaus, but I found the moon's severity beautiful in its own way. It was the only natural world I'd ever known. Saturn had no surface—nothing to ground me while I was there—so it was hard to count it. I imagined when my people once soared the sky in winged suits before the Great Reunion, free to move about without fear of sickness or persecution.

Presently, a storm brewed in the distance. Lightning bolts danced across my view as if they were part of a choreographed light show. I must have watched it for thirty minutes. It was the only thing keeping me sane as I continually checked the ever-replenishing line at the coffee shop for Captain Saunders.

My stomach started to growl, and my neck got sore from supporting my head. At some point, two security officers arrived to loom nearby, trying to pretend they weren't watching me. It appeared the captain wasn't going to be found so easily. My next move was to knock on his clan-brother's door—my mom's ex-employer, whose home I'd once robbed—to see if he could help. I just had to hope that the captain hadn't already headed up to the *Piccolo*'s hangar on Pervenio Station, with the shift starting in a day.

I stood, but as I did, I noticed someone familiar approaching the line in the pale reflection of the viewport. I spun excitedly and spotted Captain Saunders. He had the typical pinkish skin and stocky build of humans from Earth, though his arms appeared relatively weak compared with most. A prim beard hugged his jawline, mottled on the right side by a series of faded burn scars that were common amongst harvester workers. He didn't move with the delayed hop-skip that walking under Titan's low g caused. I'd seen an ad earlier outside of the docks for a new line of form-fitting weighted suits, and the captain wore one under his synth-leather jacket.

"Captain!" I hollered and jogged toward him. The wary security officers mobilized to follow me.

Captain Saunders turned to me. His baffled expression didn't change when he realized who I was. He clearly wasn't used to seeing the Ringer members of his crew back on Titan.

"Drayton, what are you doing here?" he questioned. Every single Earther in line focused on us, which I'm sure only fueled the irritation in his tone.

I offered him a salute and took a moment to gather my breath. Sitting still for so long caused me to forget how much the heat was getting to me.

"I need to talk to you, Captain," I panted.

"Well, spit it out then, boy," he said. "I don't have time to waste."

"Sir, I made a mistake. I know what I told you last time we spoke, but I'd like my old job back."

The captain sneered. "Is that what you expect? You tell me you want to explore other options, and then I take you right back as soon as you have a change of heart. That's no way to run a business, boy."

"I know, but Desmond said you were still searching for my replacement."

"That bastard Desmond," the captain grumbled. He scratched his scruffy chin. "He is right. This break hasn't been much of one, thanks to you."

"I'm sorry, sir. But if you ju—"

He cut me off. "I wish it were only just you. People don't want to work on an old-model harvester anymore, even if she works fine. Bonuses for the extra gas those automated hunks can't gather aren't worth it anymore apparently. Earthers won't even respond to my postings, and last week, two other Ringer maintenance workers got taken into quarantine. Probably enjoyed themselves a little too much on break, as usual."

My features darkened, and he must have noticed because he cringed and momentarily dropped his gaze toward the floor. I doubted his clan-brother had told him the truth about my mom —he and the captain weren't close or anything—but the Q-Zones were a sore subject for any of my kind, and not to be brought up lightly.

"Right, sorry," he muttered. "Well, you're in luck. If we go up there undermanned, we'll risk becoming the next *Sunfire*. I need all the hands I can get back on board."

"Are you sure?" I cursed myself for giving him the opportunity to change his mind. I was expecting to have to beg him.

Getting a spot on any harvester had been difficult when I first started, since Earthers got their choice of newer ships and of every position above maintenance.

"I don't really have much of a choice," he said. "Shift leaves in a day, and like I said, the crew is light. You'll be in the same position, mostly maintenance, and Culver will continue seeing to it that everyone who works hard gets the occasional chance to earn some mechanical training on real repairs. Offer is as solid as ever, though I will be docking you a small fee for the trouble you've caused me. We'll call it five percent. Deal?"

He was a businessman before anything else, and I knew I shouldn't expect a promotion after almost leaving; I wasn't *that* important. I thought about telling him the truth about my mom to see if he'd change his mind, but the pay was no longer relevant. Captain Saunders was fair, and while I wouldn't consider us friends, he'd given me my first chance in the real world. That was more than most Ringers from the Lowers ever got.

"That's fine," I said. "Sign me back up."

"Good," he said. "Let it be a lesson that you can't just go quitting on a whim, boy. Work is scarce. You're not going to find much better on the Ring unless you know something about botany or can get picked up for a security detail."

"I know. It was a mistake."

"Don't let it happen again." He patted me on the arm with his uncovered hand before I could dodge him. "Report to the *Piccolo* by tomorrow. I've got to try and find another Ringer or two to replace those I've lost, and then we'll be off."

"Works for me," I said, attempting to distance myself from him in a way that wasn't noticeable.

"It'll be another four-month-long shift inside the gas giant, so pack a few shirts. Prove to me that you're willing to stay on for the long haul, and maybe in a year, I'll have you in line to be a mechanic. Maybe the head mechanic one day. We're all growing sick of old Culver anyway."

"Head mechanic?" I asked, shocked. Culver, the *Piccolo*'s elderly head mechanic, had creases on his face so deep that it looked like he'd been working on the ship since the day it was built. The crew used to joke that he'd die curled up in one of the harvesting tanks before he retired.

"Sure. You've always worked hard, and nobody seems to complain about you. I know you haven't had too many opportunities, but everything you ever repaired always ran smoother after. How many Ringers do you know that can say they're head mechanic of a gas harvester?"

"None," I admitted. "It's... it's good to be back, sir."

"It's not like you missed a shift, but it's good to have you back on board, Drayton. Good workers aren't easy to find these days." He glanced over at the coffee shop. We were nearing the counter. "You having any?"

"No, sir. Can't stand the stuff."

He shook his head. "I'll never understand you people."

I smirked. "Well, I'm going to head back to my hollow and start preparing," I said. "Thank you, sir. I won't let you down again."

"I hope not." He held out his exposed hand for me to shake. I gestured to my mask. I wore gloves, but after seeing my mother, I couldn't bring myself to risk touching an Earther willingly, no matter how safe the Pervenio newscasts claimed it was.

He shrugged. "Right, better you not go getting sick on me too. I'll see you tomorrow. Don't be late." He didn't wait for a response before turning to the coffee shop's counter and deciding on his order.

It was done.

I released a deep breath. I knew I was making the best choice for my mother's sake, though that didn't mean I didn't wish there was some other way. Maybe, as a mechanic, I'd be able to earn enough credits to help her honestly, but I'd have to wait years.

I left behind a spate of distrustful Earther glares and walked hastily back to the central lift down to the Lowers. A little too fast, apparently, because I didn't get far before another stout security officer shadowed me. I slowed down as much as my eagerness would allow. I didn't want to raise suspicion, considering what I was thinking about doing.

By the time I reached the central lift and took the plunge, I was so drenched in sweat that it was difficult to peel my clothes off for the decon-chamber. When I was finally through into Level B2, I sped up to a jog, and soon after a run. I could hardly contain myself.

A few beggars solicited me outside of a food stand selling the parts of plants nobody in the Uppers wanted. Groups of men snorted foundry salts in the shadows, their ragged sanitary masks and shirts making them appear guilty even if they weren't. They stared right through me as I passed.

My hollow was located along a long tunnel branching off the west side of the central node. Benji stood cleaning the outside of his hollow's hatch with a rag that was probably only making it dirtier. I raced by him without bothering to say hello. My thumb extended to work the print-based locking mechanism, and that was when I noticed the view-screen posted adjacent to my hatch.

The month's rent to Pervenio Corp had come up short. Apparently, paying for both our home and my mom's upgraded stay had now depleted my account as well as hers. We had a week to come up with the credits, or the hollow would be leased out to another poor Ringer scraping along for a living. Without John's terminal or the noodle shop, I wasn't going to be able to raise them. Even if she got out, my mother would be homeless.

"Everything all right, Kale?" Benji asked.

"Not now, Benji," I said, seething. "Fuck!" I punched the screen as hard as I could. It was Pervenio-made, so the thing didn't even crack, but it sure as Trass hurt my knuckles.

"Kale!" Benji approached me, his face flush with concern.

"Would you just stay out of it!" I shouted, shoving my finger into his chest.

I flung open my hatch, stormed inside, and locked it. Then I hurried over to my bed and tore the hand-terminal out of my pillow. My chest heaved as I typed a response.

IF YOU CAN REALLY HELP MY MOTHER, I'LL HELP YOU. WHO ARE YOU AND WHAT DO YOU NEED?

-KALE

I struck "Send" before I could second-guess myself. I wasn't sure if I felt a sense of relief or nausea afterward, but my response to R streamed invisibly out into the ethers of Solnet, bouncing off laser-com relays throughout Sol toward wherever R was.

I sat quietly for a while, barely able to tear my eyes off the bright screen. I tried switching on the Darien Newsfeed to distract myself, but again, that didn't help. A story about Pervenio Corp's decision to ask the USF Assembly to include offworlders in the Departure Lottery played. The reporters said Titan's locals were thrilled and depicted the riot in the Upper Ward's atrium from an angle that made it seem like it was a celebration. On one of the clips, I could see myself standing in the corner of the screen, looking bewildered.

"Liars," I grumbled.

I switched it off and decided I preferred staring at a blank screen. I'd started to doze, when suddenly, my hand-terminal vibrated. I fumbled to hold it upright and steady the screen so that I could read the incoming message.

MY IDENTITY IS IRRELEVANT. HAVE FAITH THAT MY END OF THE BARGAIN WILL BE FULFILLED AS LONG AS YOU SUCCEED. I NEED YOU TO LINK THIS HAND-TERMINAL TO THE MAIN NAVIGATION CONSOLE OF THE *PICCOLO* ONCE IT IS WITHIN SATURN'S ATMOSPHERE. THE PROGRAM LOADED ONTO IT WILL EXECUTE AUTOMATICALLY AFTER YOU DO SO.

FAIL, OR REPLY TO THIS MESSAGE, AND OUR ARRANGEMENT WILL BE NULLIFIED. YOU ARE MORE THAN YOU KNOW, KALE DRAYTON. TRASS GUIDES YOU.

FROM ICE TO ASHES—R

"What program?" I whispered, as if anybody could hear me. I leaned back against the rocky wall of my hollow. I don't know why I was surprised, but I was hoping for more of a direction than that.

My hand-terminal made a strange squealing noise, as if answering me. The screen flickered, and a new icon appeared in the corner of the flat screen: an orange circle set against a white background. I attempted to open whatever the strange program was, but it was encrypted and, again, well beyond my ability to slice.

A program... I didn't have to sneak a bomb or a weapon onto the *Piccolo* but merely upload whatever the program was, and my mother would be free. Of all the unlawful tasks I'd ever been asked to perform, this one seemed perhaps the most innocent. The only sneaking around required would be to make sure nobody examined the hand-terminal too closely on my journey to Pervenio Station, which I didn't think would be difficult, since the device operated the same as any other hand-terminal.

Yet, as the tiny orange circle stared at me like an all-knowing eye, I couldn't shake the feeling that the program was more than what it seemed. A similar symbol had been painted on the hatch of Dexter's shop where I found him dead.

I put the device down and exhaled. It was too late to turn back. I could've reported the message before I responded, but now I was too guilty to avoid imprisonment if I were caught. I closed my eyes and pictured my mother's face, her sallow flesh pulled so taut that she was beginning to look like a skeleton, and I knew I'd made the only decision I could.

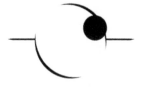

EIGHT

Scanners. Why do there have to be scanners?

The morning after meeting with Captain Saunders and getting my job back, I waited in line at the Darien Docks to board a shuttle bound for Pervenio Station. Getting onto any inter-Ring Shuttle off Titan required passing through heavy-duty security scanners and decon-chambers.

They existed between the Upper and Lower Wards, but while I'd been nervous passing through them with the hand-terminal, those scanners were focused mostly on ensuring nobody had unlicensed weapons or explosives. Since the last time I'd taken a shuttle, however, state-of-the-art scanners had been installed in the docks, I presumed because of all the recent trouble on Titan. Being Pervenio-made meant that they were the finest in the solar system, and they were integrated fully with decon-chambers for the sake of efficiency. Not even Earthers could avoid full inspection. That meant Pervenio officers were going to directly examine all my belongings while I was being cleaned. I wouldn't even be there to provide an explanation for the mysterious program on my hand-terminal if they noticed it.

My throat got so dry I could hardly swallow. For years, I'd made a living breaking laws, but they were never serious enough to get me spaced had I been caught.

The Earthers waiting at the shuttle's designated hangar went first—only they could afford the best seats—but I was next in line. Another failed attempt to see my mom before I departed had forced me onto the last possible shuttle that would reach Pervenio Station in time for the *Piccolo*'s departure. In my rush, I'd hurried to the front of the Ringer passengers. I regretted it immediately. The teams monitoring the security equipment probably would've been listless by the end of the line. Now I would have their full attention.

I aimed my gaze straight ahead and tried not to panic. Sweat poured down my forehead. Thankfully, the warm temperature inside the metal-clad hangar had every other Ringer sweating too. My flaring nostrils or twitching fingers probably weren't much of a help, though.

"Next," a voice called out.

I could picture officers breaking into the decon-chamber while I stood naked and alone, their batons cracking me across the head before they cuffed me and dragged me away.

"Next!" the officer in front of me grunted. "Pay attention, Ringer! We're on a schedule."

It was my turn. I murmured "sorry" to him and handed him my ID card. He scrutinized it, and me, for about a minute before returning it and ushering me into the decon-chamber. It was much bigger than the one at the quarantine—more indus-trial. They were never my favorite things to step into, but typi-cally, I only had to worry about my body coming up clean.

The din of the waiting area was silenced as the vacuum-sealed chamber closed behind me. The only sound other than the rapid thumping of my heart was the soft, melodious hum of high-end electrostatic cleaners powering up.

"Clothes and belongings," an automated female voice requested. A panel in the wall beside me folded open, revealing a chute.

I placed my travel bag in first. It contained only clothes and sanitary products. I removed my shirt next, just to buy myself time, and then my gloves and mask. With nothing left but my pants, I dipped my hand into my pocket, feeling my pulse in my fingertips as I did. I slowly withdrew the hand-terminal. I think I was closing my eyes during most of this, but I peeked through my lashes once to notice that the enigmatic icon on the screen was no longer orange. I don't know when, but it had become blue and filled with green to resemble a normal Solnet icon.

I stared at the hand-terminal for a few seconds, confused, then realized I probably looked suspicious and dropped it in the chute. It struck the bottom so hard, I was lucky the screen didn't break.

I attempted to shrug it off and act casual before undressing all the way. When I was finished, I was directed to the center of the chamber, where the decontamination process initiated. The procedure was similar to the one in the Q-Zone, and the blowing air along with the tingling beams dried the thick layer of sweat on my back. Every second I stood there felt like an hour, until a voice announced I was clean and my belongings reappeared by the exit. I'd never been so thrilled to hear the word "clean," though for all the wrong reasons.

I threw my clothes back on before anyone decided to change their mind. I was still snapping my gloves over my wrists when I exited and hurried toward the docked shuttle. An officer at the entrance gave me one final check with a scanner, even though he let an Earther ahead of me walk right on by, and then I was through.

My assigned seat was in the last row of the ship. Ignoring the glowers of the dozens of already seated Earthers, I shuffled down the aisle. I stowed my bag below the cushion and fell into it.

The heat and my nerves had me panting uncontrollably. My sanitary mask at least helped stifle the sound so that the other passengers wouldn't think I was having a panic attack. I stretched open my pocket and glanced inside at the hand-terminal. Nobody sat near me yet, but I wasn't going to take any more risks.

The icon was orange again.

"Kale Drayton!" someone exclaimed and slapped me on the shoulder.

I yanked my hand out of my pocket too fast, banging it against the seat in front of me. It hurt like hell. Two years on the gas harvester really had made me forget everything I'd learned in the Lowers about acting cool when I was up to no good. I glanced up and saw Desmond's toothy grin.

"Don't tell me you got a job on the fuckin' station?" he asked. He stored his bag and plopped down beside me. Considering my luck, I don't know why I ever expected to be seated next to anybody else.

"Nope," I replied, struggling not to show how much pain I was in. "Decided I'd give the *Piccolo* another chance."

"Is that right? I'm surprised that mud stomper Saunders took you back. He whined like a child when he asked me to try and help him find some new recruits."

"Yeah, well, he did."

"Trass, what crawled up your ass?" Desmond shifted in his seat to get more comfortable, purposefully jutting his bony elbow over my armrest.

I nudged him back. "Sorry. It's hot in here."

"As usual." He leaned his head back and closed his eyes. "You missed a hell of a time the other night. Your girl got drunker than I've ever seen her. Mentioned you a few times too. She seemed pissed you were leaving."

It was hard to know when he was bullshitting. I figured this was one of those times based on how I'd seen her acting at the Foundry. I grunted in response and turned my head toward a narrow viewport to try to take a nap. Desmond thankfully didn't bother me much after that. It was an eight-hour flight through zero-g to Pervenio Station, and the shuttle wasn't going to get any cooler. I figured he was saving his latest wisecracks for the four months we'd be sharing a dorm.

Unable to sleep, I gazed through the shuttle's viewport out into space for most of the flight. No stars were visible, since by then, Saturn constituted the entire view and was cast in shadow while it eclipsed the sun. I could, however, see the glimmer of the planet's blade-like belt of rock and ice, illuminated by the bright lights of Pervenio Station. It was built into one of the planet's tiniest moons, located along its inner ring. If Titan was the heart of the Ring, the station was its brain, directing everything that happened on Saturn's many moons and settlements.

People said it was the largest station in all of Sol. Almost all transport of goods from around the solar system ran through the many docking chutes poking out of the rocky exterior, along with most of Saturn's gas-harvesting and ice-hauling industries. Those were what had allowed Pervenio to grow into the largest corporation in Sol. Others had smaller stations and colonies located on the Ring, but it was only with Pervenio's permission, and getting that cost a pretty credit.

Captain Saunders liked to boast that the *Piccolo* was his, passed down through his clan-family to those who were worthiest, but everybody who'd served more than a shift and seen all the faded corporation logos on board knew that wasn't true. Pervenio just didn't care much about its antiquated harvesters anymore and rented them out. They operated slower, took in less gas, and required more of a workforce.

"We will be arriving at Hangar 13 on Pervenio Station in fifteen minutes," an automated voice announced throughout the cabin. I could hardly hear it over Desmond's incessant snoring. "Please ensure your restraints remain fastened."

Most of the passengers, including myself, already had theirs on. We were in zero-g, after all, and the security officers on board didn't take too kindly to people floating around the cabin unless they had to use the restroom. The warning only existed because there was always the danger of the shuttle banging into a rock or some debris as it gradually descended over Saturn's inner rings toward the station.

After once again preventing Desmond's arm from slipping into my area, I leaned closer to my viewport to watch as we grew nearer. An ice hauler blinked around a frozen rock a few hundred kilometers to the shuttle's side, and another one beyond that. Many more haulers existed than gas harvesters, since they were almost entirely automated. There were fewer potential hazards to account for outside of Saturn's erratic atmosphere, where they operated. Communications within it were spotty at best, limiting updates from the stations monitoring the planet and the ability to exclusively automate systems.

New-age gas harvesters circumvented that by skirting the very fringes of Saturn's atmosphere and depositing balloon-like vessels to sink through, fill with gas, and rise back to be retrieved. They worked well, but nowhere near as efficiently as the gas harvesters like Piccolo that went deeper. They required skilled, hands-on navigators like Cora to avoid unpredictable storms and locate concentrated pockets of the vital gases we were after. Honestly, I didn't understand how Cora managed it all.

Cora... For the first time since accepting R's offer, I realized that I was going to be uploading the mysterious program into *her* command console. The captain oversaw the ship, sure, but she controlled navigation. Though the thought of spending time with her again was the single bright spot in this whole ordeal, she was the last person I wanted to be forced to lie to.

I didn't have a choice. I had to get the job done, like old times. The stark curtain of blackness beyond the glass made my reflection clearer than usual, and all I could see in my yellow-brown eyes was the mother I shared their color with. Her condition deteriorated rapidly. She couldn't have long.

My reflection vanished when the shuttle slipped into one of Pervenio Station's airy hangars. The ship tilted vertically ninety degrees until it was able to land atop the very airlock it passed through. Pervenio Station, and what was left of the moon it invaded, had been provided additional spin when it was built to generate a stronger centripetal force. The floors of all its inhabitable spaces were located on the inner face of the exterior shell to take advantage of that.

A familiar force tugged on my body as soon as the ship touched down. The simulated g conditions on the station were relatively similar to Titan's, and after hours in transit, they were much appreciated. My restraints came undone, and a security officer began escorting passengers out of the shuttle. Earthers went first, since they were in the front, and the pack of masked Ringers followed soon after.

Desmond and I were in the last row and had to wait until everyone else was off. I nudged him awake. We didn't have much time to waste, considering the *Piccolo*'s hangar was located clear across the station.

"What's your rush?" Desmond asked, yawning. He rubbed his eyes and got to his feet as leisurely as one could possibly do so.

"The *Piccolo*'s scheduled to leave soon," I said. I sprang up once he was finally ready and grabbed my bag. I stayed right on his heels as he moseyed down the aisle.

"Relax. You think Saunders will leave without us there? Crew is light as it is."

"I'd rather not risk it."

He sighed. "Dammit, Kale. Have you ever broken a rule in your life?"

I would've grinned if I hadn't been so nervous. I didn't talk about my past life much. I'd found that the best way to leave it behind was to pretend it'd never happened. What he didn't know was that the only reason I was eager to get on the *Piccolo* was to escape the prying eyes of security. Though the armed presence would be greater, there'd be no more decon-chamber scanners to pass through after we disembarked.

"Can we just get there and then argue?" I asked.

"Fine, fine, quit your whining," he said. "You just can't wait to see Cora, can you? Me neither." He smirked and picked up his pace as if he expected me to smack him. I'm not going to lie —I wanted to. But at least he gave me something to worry about other than what was in my pocket.

"Relax," he said as I sped up to catch him. My cheeks were probably fluorescent pink. "I met a girl back in Darien during our last break. I tried as hard as I could, but Cora's all yours."

"She's not mine," I grumbled.

"Have I ever told you you're a damn idiot?"

I took an exasperated breath of the station's warm, stale air. "Plenty."

The similarities between the docks of Pervenio Station and those of Darien didn't extend beyond the fact that they were both packed. The former wasn't a place to go shopping. Hangar bay after hangar bay was positioned on either side of a gracious concourse. The only breaks were for eateries and bars catering to the station's tremendous workforce. I'd visited a few before and after shifts, but the moods of the mostly Earther patrons were exactly what you'd expect: gruff, exhausted, and wary of my kind.

Desmond and I passed one bar that had the words NO GLOVES OR MASKS PERMITTED ON PATRONS posted on the door. Earthers tried to be clever about keeping my people out of certain places without outright saying NO RINGERS ALLOWED. With glasses at the bar passed between Trass knows how many uncovered hands, there wasn't a chance in hell I'd ever go in.

As in the Uppers, the views from the main concourse were spectacular. Translucencies were cut into the passageway's floor at a downward angle to reveal Saturn's rings. Seeing them extend away from me on a horizontal plane almost made them feel artificial.

We had to take the tram-line crisscrossing the tiny moon to reach the *Piccolo*'s departure hangar. Since Desmond and I had been the last to get off the shuttle from Titan, the first tram was full, making us later than I'd thought. Security ushered us into our seats when the next tram finally arrived after twenty more minutes.

The tram-line was closer to a lift than a train, since cutting through the spherical station from where we were standing meant going straight up. Every seat in the car was arranged horizontally, with our backs facing the floor. Halfway through the moon's core, the car flipped 180 degrees so that we'd be right side up on the other side upon arrival. I remembered puking the first time I took one and having it whipped right back in my face. That was when I learned that the center of Pervenio Station had no gravity. It was also the first time I had the pleasure of meeting Desmond. He'd been delighted not to try to hide his amusement.

The *Piccolo*'s hangar was a short distance from where we were let off. I was relieved to find the ship still docked. Security scanned our IDs and checked our bags, then added us to the departure ledger before allowing us to pass. That part wasn't stressful, but I was glad to be through. Security checkpoints had become so ingrained in my life that I hadn't really noticed how many there were until I'd had something to hide. It was like a tremendous weight being lifted off me.

Captain Saunders waited directly inside, foot tapping. At first, I was worried, then I noticed that the *Piccolo* was still being loaded with supplies. Members of the crew rolled containers filled with food and other necessities into the cargo hold. Others carted cumbersome cylindrical canisters meant for transported harvested gases to the ship's cold storage.

The *Piccolo* currently had a total crew of forty-one, with pretty much an even split between Ringers and Earthers. My last time aboard, it was forty-three, but things changed shift to shift. I recognized most of the faces save for a few new members of the maintenance crew, like me. We did everything from cleaning harvester canisters and tanks to making minor repairs. Then there was a handful of overseeing mechanics, including the head one, security, a few engineers, a doctor, and a chef who seemed unnecessary considering the slop he served. I didn't spot Cora, but the ship's engines rumbled, so she was probably already at her post running through checks. She was the only Ringer with a position above maintenance.

"There you two are," Captain Saunders remarked without averting his gaze from his busy crew.

"Sorry we're late, sir," I said.

"Not your fault," the captain groused. "Pervenio security has everything backed up more than usual. We had to wait for them to sweep the entire ship before we could start loading. Like anyone in Sol gives a damn about the *Piccolo* but us." The captain turned to Desmond and me. "Get hauling—we're only waiting on a few more. Cora's had the engines prepped for hours already. Waste of damn time."

"Yes, sir," I said.

Desmond glared at me for a moment as we set off toward the *Piccolo,* and then sighed. "'Yes, sir,'" he mimicked.

I ignored him.

The *Piccolo* was exactly how I remembered. Its tapered hull was designed to slash through heavy winds and looked to have experienced far too many storms in its time. A patchwork of plates and fist-sized bolts coated the exterior, all with varying degrees of corrosion and piss-colored stains from being pounded by Saturn's sulfuric atmosphere. It was impossible to tell what was original from when the ship was constructed, years before the Great Reunion had even happened. Its flanks were what inspired its name, as they had the appearance of an ancient woodwind instrument. A line of vertical ducts ran down either side, interspersed with the massive pumps used to siphon gas out of Saturn's atmosphere. Tubes extended from them and ran across the hull, able to be extended and reeled to reach gas pockets. They led to the harvesting bay, where gas was refined and sorted before being carted to cold storage in the belly of the ship.

At the front end, a glassy bulb popped out like the eye of an ancient insect. It housed the command deck, where I knew Cora waited anxiously to put her navigating skills to good use on the decades-old command console. The nuclear-thermal engine with auxiliary ion thrusters stuck out the very back. While most ships used ionic impulse drives these days, anything heading into Saturn needed extra thrust. Stubby wings flanked it, which alone wouldn't accomplish much if the engines failed while in the midst of Saturn's impressive winds. It was a long plummet to the planet's core, where the pressure would crush our bones into dust before the ship itself gave out. The captain often reminded us of the horrific story of the *Sunfire,* a gas harvester, which nearly three years ago had inexplicably lost power to its engines and disappeared down there, never to be heard from again. It was his way of ensuring that nobody slacked off when it came to keeping the engine core in optimal condition.

"You two, let's fuckin' move it!" John shouted from his position at the base of the ship's entry-ramp. Seeing him made my heart skip a beat, but the fact that he was just pointing in our direction and not charging me meant he still didn't know I was the one who stole his hand-terminal. He was in an exceedingly grumpy mood, however, and I figured it was because of the loss.

"Ship ain't gonna prep itself," he said, "and I don't feel like hearing that bitch complaining that we had her keep the engines on too long."

"Why're you standing around, then?" Desmond asked.

John grinned, a wad of synth-tobacco in his mouth making his lower lip bulge. He crossed his arms so that his biceps bulged out of his boiler suit's short sleeves. On either side of him, the two other burly Earther members of the *Piccolo* security team who'd been with him in the Sunken Credit did the same. They made sure that scuffles on the *Piccolo* didn't last long... when they weren't the ones starting them.

"I'm so glad to see you again, Desmond," John said. "Should be a fun shift." He spat at our feet.

I noticed Desmond's hands ball into fists, but I grabbed him by the arm and pulled him onto the ship. The XO was looking for any excuse to fight and get Ringers stuck on a shift keeping the boiling-hot engine room squeaky clean. He glared at us until we were all the way onto the ship.

"Wait until we're in Saturn, at least," I said.

"I'm going to kill that man," Desmond seethed.

"Well, wait until I'm asleep, then."

We dropped our bags off in the Ringer dormitory. Desmond was greeted in the hallway by his close friends Lester Cromwell and Yavik Vanos. They'd been in the Foundry the night before too. The three of them liked to pretend they oversaw the Ringer members of the crew, with Desmond as their ringleader. Lester had an even sharper tongue than him, and the narrowest, most hawkish face I'd ever seen. Yavik wasn't bad on his own but was frequently too high on foundry salts to do anything but go along with everything the other two did. His skin was a medium-gray hue because his ancestors apparently came from a place on Pre-Meteorite Earth where people were all brown-skinned.

"What took you so long?" Lester asked. "Thought you were coming up with us. That mud stomper, John, is in rare form today."

"I had business," Desmond answered succinctly. "Let's go."

I listened to their footsteps fade down the hall before taking a second to change my gloves; they had the filth of Darien and Pervenio Station all over them. After I did, I glanced into my pocket at the hand-terminal, where the mysterious orange circle remained.

After finding out about my mother, I never thought I'd be back on the *Piccolo,* yet there I was. The first step of R's task was done. Now it was time to help get the ship moving.

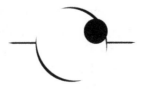

NINE

WHEN THE *PICCOLO* ENTERED SATURN'S UPPER
atmosphere, all the Ringers, including me, were issued a g-stim
injection. The chems helped our muscles and organs endure the
Earth-like g conditions, where even breathing could be strain-
ing. The ship's doctor oversaw dispersing doses every morning
so that we wouldn't deplete the ship's Pervenio-issued supply
before the shift was up.

I was then immediately assigned to work in the harvesting
bay. No time to check out the command deck or say hi to Cora. I
wondered if she'd even heard I was back.

The harvesting bay was the largest open space on the vessel,
and while the floors, walls, and ceilings matched the ship's worn
exterior, all the equipment inside was kept squeaky clean. The
overall harvesting process seemed relatively simple, ignoring the
myriad technical aspects I didn't need to understand.

Vacuum chambers lining the wall were switched on and off
by the navigator, and Cora siphoned gas out of Saturn's stormy
skies when she located a pocket composed of the valuable ones.
Pervenio had no interest in most of the elements that made up
Saturn's atmosphere, so the vacuums emptied their stores

through a series of thick pipes into towering, noisy vats. Chemical reactions of some sort took place within them to filter the valuable gases into spherical tanks. The largest ones were labeled for helium-3 and deuterium. Those two rare gases, among a few other lesser ones, were what drove fusion cores and interplanetary engine systems. Basically, they were what made the Ring so desirable for Pervenio. Jupiter couldn't compete when it came to their abundance. Another one of Darien Trass's brilliant foresights in choosing Titan to run to.

Much of the harvesting procedure was automated up until storage, and apparently, the newer harvesters had that almost entirely mechanized as well. Engineering staff monitored the systems to make sure levels in every storage container remained at an acceptable level, so that we weren't all blown to bits. Maintenance men like me were there only for conveyance and cleaning. Anything that interacted with the gases had to be kept as spotless as a Ringer's body. Otherwise, like the captain always said, "We'd join the *Sunfire* in being eternally crushed by Saturn's core." Every once in a while, the tanks and vacuum chambers were emptied, and I had to climb in to rub them down too.

It took only an hour of scrubbing the grime out of harvester canisters for me to fall back into my old routine. Prep a canister, wipe the sweat from my brow, and pass it over to a stronger Earther, who would have it inspected by the head mechanic before carting it down to cold storage all the way on the other side of the ship. Keeping a stockpile of flammable gases as far away from humans as possible was the first rule of gas harvesting.

The work was mind-numbing. As I scrubbed, I often found myself thinking about how I could've successfully robbed Tanner Saunders. My duties rarely differed from what the Ringers cleaning the restaurants in Delora's Upper Ward did. It was high-stakes cleaning—a lack of attention could taint an entire haul or potentially result in a fiery eruption—but it was cleaning nonetheless.

John liked to remind us how cleaning was a job fit for Ringers, that our long arms and slender fingers allowed us to reach impossible places. I couldn't deny that might be true, but I welcomed every chance to switch things up. Earther maintenance staff got to do all the lifting and carting, since Earth g conditions made things heavier and made us tire more rapidly no matter how strong the g-stims were.

Sometimes, however, equipment throughout the *Piccolo* would malfunction, and I'd have an opportunity to actually repair something. The *Piccolo* being old as it was, that was a common occurrence. But there were a dozen other workers to compete with, as well as the grumpy Earther head mechanic, Culver, who chose who got to do what. The captain tried to make sure the work was spread evenly to keep us all focused, but an Earther was likely to choose his own as often as he was permitted. That was simply the way of things.

After a few hours of sweating in the harvesting bay, I'd have given almost anything for a chance to roam the ship's halls and perhaps catch a glance through a viewport at Saturn's blustery, ruddy sky. Except for the Ringer dorms, the ship was kept at a balmy seventeen degrees Celsius, but all the working machinery in the harvesting bay made it the second-hottest area outside of the engine core room. The g-stim kept my heart from giving out, but it did nothing for the heat.

"Hey, Drayton, keep that hand moving!" Culver shouted from across the room. He leaned on a cane, his pebbly eyes glaring in my direction. The wrinkles striating his face seemed to deepen every time I saw him. A scraggly white beard used to cover a lot of them, but it was no longer enough.

I nodded, without the energy to raise my voice. Desmond

snickered beside me. We were both on harvesting canister prep, right next to each other yet again.

"Gotta love that man," Desmond said under his breath.

"Do you have something to say about everything?" I groaned and dipped my hand farther into the canister I was prepping to receive a new haul.

"I'm not the one who got caught daydreaming. Must really make your heart ache when you get in trouble like that, Earther lover. Must make you want to give old Culver a hug and say sorry."

"Why the hell are you even here?"

"You two—enough!" Culver hollered. "Get working, or I'll have those masks replaced with muzzles."

Desmond muttered something under his breath, so softly that I couldn't hear him over the machinery. Then he whispered to me: "Same reason as anyone else. Credits. Trass damn them. Didn't exist on the Ring until the Earthers arrived, you know. All we cared about was making things better."

I hushed him. The rag in my hand ran across the bottom of the canister, scraping off a profuse layer of grunge. Even through my sanitary mask, the smell was foul, like sulfur mixed into a cesspool.

"That was when people like us were judged on skill alone," Desmond continued all on his own. "You probably would've still been right where you are, but I could've been a king."

"Or a jester," I muttered.

"What was that?"

"Whatever you say," I said a little louder.

I removed my hand from a freshly cleaned canister and handed it over to an Earther. It was marked DEUTERIUM, so he carted it over to the matching tank and hooked it up to a nozzle. He raised a thumb to an engineer, then a series of green bars on the side of the canister lit up. The worker detached it once they were filled.

"All right, navigation says this pocket's been emptied out!" Culver announced a short time later. I heard his cane clicking as he shuffled into the center of the room so everyone could hear. "Chow time!"

Everyone exhaled in relief and stopped what they were doing.

"Finally," Desmond said. He purposefully nudged me with his shoulder on his way by. "I'm starving."

At least that was something we could agree on. Not sure why, but cleaning up filth had my stomach rumbling. I just had to clean my gloves first. They were so filthy it looked like I'd been sloshing around in a Martian sewer.

I stepped up to the chef's counter in the galley, and he slapped a pile of food down into my bowl. It was just lumpy, colorless goop, but it contained all the necessary daily nutrients. Or so we were told, and it didn't look any worse than most of what I'd grown up eating in the Lowers. I filled a cup with murky water from a leaky nozzle at the end of the line and then turned to find a seat.

The galley was small compared with the harvester bay. Its exposed ceiling was low enough for me to hear the constant buzzing emanating from a series of bundled circuits and ducts. The tiled floor was permanently stained.

Two long tables were set on either side of the room, each flanked by rusty benches. Ringers wearing gloves and sanitary masks stretched down to their necks sat at one of them, and Earthers at the other. Even if some Earthers and Ringers were friends, it was like an invisible line split the galley in half.

Nobody dared to even think about crossing it. That was the quickest way to incite a fight.

I turned toward the Ringer table and spotted Cora. It was my first sight of her since I'd boarded the ship. The only times she ever got off navigation duty was to eat and sleep, but she was always kept on call. The *Piccolo* had an autopilot setting and other crew members who knew the basics of flying, but if there was even the hint of a storm, she was summoned no matter what she was doing.

As usual, she sat at the very end of the table, with an extra-wide space between her and the nearest person and nobody across from her. Some of the Ringer crew felt she was a risk because her strengthened immune system meant she might be carrying something. This ensured, along with her rank, that there was never any real danger of unwanted advances when Ringers drank not far from her bed in our shared dorm. It also served to make her even more intimidating to me.

The inherent risk involved in falling for her was real. In our dorms, she was even required to wear a mask and gloves. I never thought about it much, but visiting the Q-Zone countless times has a way of making someone view even the tiniest details differently. Paranoia had become second nature.

But that wasn't enough for me to let her eat alone. I headed to the seat across from her, knowing from years of observation that she was neat enough for me to be perfectly safe unless I shared her spoon. As I sat down, she didn't even bother to glance up from her meal.

"I told you he was back," Desmond said to Cora. He sat on the same side as her, though with a solid meter of empty space between them.

"Yep," Cora answered, still not looking up. She was always fairly timid, but this seemed different. I guess I should've expected her to be angry that I'd planned to leave the *Piccolo* without telling her.

"Couldn't stay away," I said, smiling at Cora. She said nothing and continued to eat.

"Of course you couldn't," Desmond replied. He raised a spoonful of the goop toward his mouth, then stopped and stared at it dejectedly as he allowed it to drip back into his bowl. "I should've jumped at one of those openings for work with Venta Co when they started construction Europa Colony a year back. Open call to anyone with the credits to get there. I hear they serve fresh greens every day. Imagine that?"

"You should go, then. I'm sure they're still building." I pulled my mask down to my chin and shoveled a spoonful of the goop into my mouth. It was pretty much tasteless and took less work to force down my throat than ration bars.

"Can you afford passage that far?"

I didn't respond.

"Exactly," Desmond said. "So why *did* you really decide to come back, Kale?"

"Like you said earlier: I needed the credits," I said.

"No, no, that's not it." Desmond grinned in Cora's direction. Luckily, she was too busy trying to ignore me to notice. "I bet that shit Saunders offered you something. Ringers dropping like sick flies and he gets a sure hand back."

"Nope." I shrugged. "I just realized there wasn't anything better."

"Oh, c'mon." Desmond reached over the table and prodded my arm. "I bet he promised you he'd make you head mechanic one day." He snickered. "Told Lester that once too, and Yavik." His two pals sat on the other side of him, nodding in unison and holding in laughter. They were low-level maintenance men as well.

My pale cheeks blushed as much as they could.

"Trust me," Desmond said, his voice purposefully elevated so that the whole room would hear him. "Nobody's getting that job until the old man kicks the fucking bucket!"

"Watch your mouth, skelly, before I shut it for you again!" John hollered over in response. "I'm sure our lovely Cora is dying to see a show."

Desmond slammed his fists on the table and jumped to his feet. Cora dropped her spoon and finally looked up, our gazes meeting for the first time. That was the only reason I stayed quiet despite that word getting my blood boiling.

"What the hell did you just call me, mud stomper?" Desmond growled.

John rose to his feet beside the two members of his security team. I'd seen my share of fights growing up in the Lowers, so I knew when one was about to happen. I was usually smart enough to avoid exchanging blows with an Earther, though. They were physically much stronger, especially under the grueling Earth-like g conditions of Saturn's upper atmosphere.

"Your big ears didn't hear?" one of the guards next to him said. "He called you a Filthy. Fucking. Skelly."

Before Desmond could react, the last months' worth of troubles swelled up in me. I didn't care if Cora saw. I sprang across the table and crashed into the guard. It wasn't enough to knock the broad-shouldered Earther over, but it was enough to make him reel.

Desmond backed me up and swung at John. After a few seconds, nearly everyone in the galley joined in, which was pretty much the entire crew minus Captain Saunders and the doctor. John and his security team kept their batons sheathed; they had no interest in wrapping things up promptly. Old Culver was even brave enough to throw a few punches before his people pulled him away. In the middle of it, something hit me so hard in the gut that I keeled over. That was when I saw her.

John had escaped Desmond and torn Cora out of her seat, her head banging against the floor. Typically, she was left out of scrums. Not because she was one of the few women on board, but because her job was more crucial than any other and she was the best at it. Injuring her was the fastest way to get onto the captain's shit list. I knew that had to make the Earthers jealous, and I saw that jealousy written all over John's face as he hunched on top of her. A messy brawl was the perfect opportunity for him to sneak in a shot to relieve his envy.

My instincts kicked in. I scurried along the floor and snatched a baton off one of the guards' belts. John had her by the throat and said, "Maybe the cap'n won't favor you so much if I bust your pretty—"

I cracked him across the side of the head before he could finish. With a weapon, it didn't matter how weak I was in comparison to him. He toppled over, blood splattering onto the floor. I grabbed Cora by the wrist, heaved her to her feet, and yanked her out of the fray. I took a few hits in the side along the way but somehow kept my balance.

I managed to get her to the wall by the galley's exit, hidden behind a rack for trays. We stood there, panting and watching the brawl. It was impossible to tell whose fist was whose anymore. But it wouldn't be long before we were spotted and dragged right back into it.

The clacking of heavy footsteps suddenly echoed from outside in the *Piccolo*'s corridors. "Enough!" Captain Saunders roared as he stormed in with a pulse-pistol in his hand. He shot at one of the empty, overturned tables and everyone, including me, froze. "Next one will go through the head of whoever throws another punch."

Anyone still standing took a step back. The captain moved

farther into the room, and then Cora tapped me on the shoulder and gestured toward the hallway. With all the groaning and people twisting off tipped furniture, she was easily able to slip behind the captain out of the room without anyone realizing. I followed her, no questions asked.

"I'm tired of this," the captain continued. "I don't want to have to hire a real security team, but if this keeps happening, I damn-well will!"

"But, sir—" I heard one of John's security members reply.

"Quiet! Any damage is coming out of your paychecks. Start cleaning, boys!"

I followed Cora down the corridor until I couldn't hear the captain anymore. "What're you doing?" I whispered.

"We have to get you to the command deck," she said. "I'll say you were eating there with me the whole time. None of the Earthers will know who swung that baton."

"I don't think anybody saw or we wouldn't have gotten out."

"Do you want to risk it?"

Brawls weren't uncommon during recreational hours, but hitting the XO with a weapon wasn't how they typically ended. Even if I was protecting the navigator, Captain Saunders would have to make an example of me if he ever found out. That meant engine room maintenance duty at the very least, if John didn't kill me first.

"Right," I said, swallowing. "Good plan." Being around her almost made me forget the reason I was back on the *Piccolo*. I'd been wondering what my excuse for getting into the command deck was going to be, and now I had it.

"I guess this makes us even?" I asked, trying not to dwell on it.

"Nope," she said. "Or did you forget I pulled you out of another clash in Darien? You seem to attract them."

"Yeah..." I glanced over at her. Her long hair made it impossible to tell, but I knew there had to be a bump on her head courtesy of John. "Are you okay?"

"I'm fine. You shouldn't have hit him like that. John's all talk."

"Didn't look like that to me."

"He's just jealous. He was the navigator before I was brought on, and almost got the *Piccolo* torn to pieces. That's all it is." She glanced back over her shoulder and then sped up. "We have to hurry—let's go."

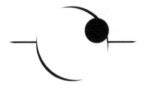

TEN

I DIDN'T GET TO FREQUENT THE *PICCOLO*'S COMMAND DECK much; it didn't often get messy enough to require cleaning like the rest of the ship. Cora's ID card got us in, and the blinking lights and green-text-filled view-screens of the consoles wrapping the circular space greeted us.

The room was about ten meters in diameter, with a transparent dome arcing over the top and front. The atmosphere of Saturn was visible beyond it, whipping about in amber hues.

Cora took her spot at the command console and canceled auto-pilot. I sat beside her at a less important-looking console. Every bit of tech in the command deck was so simultaneously dated and complex that it all appeared foreign. It took seeing the command console and its innumerable buttons, along with a series of screens filled with information, for me to realize I wasn't even sure where to connect a hand-terminal to it.

Cora's slender arms extended over the console and her fingers danced across the keys. She didn't just move fast. There was a grace to it that I hardly thought could be possible in the act of typing.

She stopped and looked at me. "Thank you," she said softly.

"For what?" I asked.

"John. I didn't say it before."

"Oh, that. Don't worry about it. Like you said, I'm sure he wouldn't have done anything. Everyone's just on edge."

"Everyone's always on edge. It was the same before you got here. Someone mouths off and someone else decides they've had enough."

"Makes you wonder why Captain Saunders even bothers hiring people like us."

"Like *you*—remember?" She pointed to her mouth and lack of sanitary mask.

"You're one of us, Cora. Can't change that."

The flickers of a grin showed on her face for a fraction of a second before vanishing. I couldn't think of a time when she'd truly smiled, with no reservations.

She turned her attention back to the command console. Something was clearly on her mind, but she remained silent. I took the opportunity to lean back in my chair and stretch my aching arms. To be honest, I was more grateful for her saving me from the cleanup job in the galley than anything else. When we left, food was spilled all over and barely a piece of furniture seemed to have survived being toppled.

I studied the command console. Circuits ran up underneath it to provide power and Trass-knows-what-else. They weren't what I was searching for. As with any console, there had to be a slot to plug in a hand-terminal to transfer data in case connection to Solnet wasn't possible. A number of different ports along the front might have been able to fit it. Or break it. I couldn't read the labels above them from my angle. I peeked at my hand-terminal to figure it out and then leaned in to get a better view of the equipment.

"Another new hand-terminal?" Cora asked. I retreated immediately and was relieved to find that she'd been busy studying Saturn's current meteorological charts when she'd said it. She seemed distracted.

"What?" I shoved the hand-terminal back into my pocket. "Oh, not exactly. That new one couldn't be fixed so I went back to my last model. Old, but it does the trick. Venta's tech is always reliable, even if it's weaker."

She grunted in agreement. It was only then that I realized she wasn't really working. She aimlessly rifled through atmospheric data, but that was it. Something had her distracted.

"Kale," she said, almost in a whisper.

"Yeah?" I asked.

"Is everything all right?"

"What do you mean?"

She stopped typing. This time when she turned to face me, she rotated her entire seat. "You've been here two years, and you've never been the one to start a fight."

"I didn't start it," I groused. The way that John and the other guard said the word *skelly* repeated over and over in my head. They'd asked for it.

"You know what I mean."

"It was nothing. I just don't like that word. 'Skelly.'"

"He's used it before. It's just... I've never seen you like that. So angry. Something happened to you during the last shift, didn't it? Same thing that made you want to quit."

"Is that what this is about?" I questioned, getting defensive.

"No!" She sighed. "Never mind."

Her gaze fell back toward the console. The most words we'd ever exchanged, and again I was blowing it. If she was going to make saving me a habit, I at least owed her a bit of truth. I slid my chair closer. This allowed me to figure out which port was labeled for hand-terminal intake, but that was no longer my focus.

"I wanted to tell you, Cora," I said. "I just didn't know how. I thought I had to stay on Titan. I... My mother—"

"Is sick," Cora finished for me. She turned back and stared into my eyes. Straight into them.

"How did you know?" I asked, brow furrowing.

"I can hear it in your voice." She reached out slowly and placed her hand on my arm. The hairs on the back of my neck stood on end. "I can see it in your eyes. The helpless feeling. I'm so sorry."

My lower lip began to tremble. I bit it so that Cora wouldn't see my sanitary mask moving with it. Before long, my eyes welled with tears, and I couldn't stop them. All the emotions I'd been struggling to bottle up came gushing out of me. The only thing I could manage in response was to murmur, "Thanks."

"I understand," she said. "I lost mine to that place right after I was born."

Based on the way she looked, I knew, as did everybody else, that her mother had been forcefully impregnated by an Earther, but I'd never asked her about it. Because she was born alive, I'd figured that her mom had survived as well. Apparently, I'd been wrong.

"I had no idea," I said, finally able to compose myself enough to speak. "I didn't know my father for very long, but I always had my mom at least. I can't imagine growing up alone."

"Not really alone. The Darien Lowers' orphanage took me in for a while, but they were even more crowded than now, and I was lucky to get crumbs from the other kids. Once I grew enough for everyone to realize what I was, they eventually had to kick me out for my safety."

So not alone, but hardly noticed, then noticed for all the wrong reasons, and, finally, abandoned. It helped explain why she was so timid.

"Ringers kicking out Ringers," I said. "That's awful, Cora. And we wonder why we are where we are."

"It was a long time ago. I'm just glad I grew a little taller than the others and am good with tech. Most kids leave the orphanage and wind up right back on the streets. I was at least able to get a job at a busy coffee shop in the Uppers. One day, Captain Saunders saw the way I worked the register and took me in. I've been here ever since."

"You did it the right way. I—" I considered telling her the truth about who I was before the *Piccolo,* but after everything she'd been through, she should've been the one to turn to the shadows for answers. What was *my* excuse?

"I wish I'd found this ship sooner," I said. "Maybe then I'd have enough credits saved to get my mom what she needs."

Cora frowned. "They say it's getting better in the Q-Zones, but from what I hear, getting the right medicine is harder than ever."

"Try impossible. It might not seem it after what you went through, but you're lucky you don't have to worry about getting sick as much as we do. If I were you, I'd do whatever I could to keep your list of friends short, so you never have to step into one of those places."

Her hand slid down my arm and fell to rest over my gloved one. "Don't say that. I may feel lost sometimes, but I know what I am." For once, she smiled fully at me. The sight made Saturn's rings seem like a cheap sideshow. "As a fellow Ringer woman, I know your mother will make it," she said.

I half-laughed, half-sniveled. "You sound so sure."

"Mine fought through sickness long enough after an Earther took her against her will to give birth to me. We're stronger than they think we are, Kale."

"I hope you're right."

"I am."

We held each other's gaze. I'd never been so near to her. She was shorter than me, so I could feel her warm breath against my neck. It probably smelled like the grub she'd just eaten in the galley, but to me, I might as well have been in a garden.

"Drayton, what're you doing up here?" somebody asked crossly.

Our heads snapped around instantaneously, and Cora reeled her hand away from mine. Captain Saunders stood in the command deck's entrance. He appeared exhausted.

"Captain!" Cora exclaimed before I could answer, which was probably a good thing, since I had no idea what would have come out of my mouth. Heart-to-hearts with Cora were new territory for me. "Sir... I... Kale and I were just catching up."

"You know the rules, Cora," he said. "No maintenance allowed in here without my permission."

"S... sorry, sir."

"Don't let it happen again," he warned, his glare boring through her. Then his countenance lightened, and he leaned on my chair. "You two missed a hell of a mess down there."

"What happened?" I asked. I peered at my outfit. A few spots of blood stained my hip. I covered them with my hand.

"Same shit as always," he groaned. "Both our people seem intent on tearing my ship to pieces."

"Anything I can help with, sir?"

"Not anymore." Saunders leaned over the back of Cora's chair. "Anything looking promising out there?" he asked her.

Cora turned her attention back to the ship's myriad atmospheric readouts I could never in a million years understand. "There looks to be a potential Deuterium pocket a few thousand klicks south of here," she replied. "It'll be a little bit of a dive."

"Good. Break's over then. Let's get back to work."

"Yes, sir," Cora and I said simultaneously. We both stifled a grin as we caught each other's gaze one last time.

I then hopped to my feet, and only when I reached the exit and heard Cora hammering away at the *Piccolo's* controls behind me did I remember the main reason I'd needed to be in the command deck. I'd been right there, the hand-terminal slot within reach so I could plant the device for R, and I'd missed my chance.

Cora was right, as usual. Soon after I reported back to the harvesting bay, the *Piccolo* struck gold with a major gas pocket located outside of any devastating storms. A fully-manned harvester like the *Piccolo* couldn't afford to miss any like it and make a profit. Four hours straight of canister prep and tank cleaning ensued, all while listening to Culver holler. Everyone who could work after the brawl was tired and sore. A few others had to head down to the med bay for treatment. Faces had bruises and scrapes. I probably had one or two of my own, but none of the metal walls were polished enough for me to tell by reflection.

Desmond's right eye was so swollen he could hardly see through it. He didn't say a word the entire time we worked next to each other. At first, it was a relief, but toward the end, I found it eerie.

"All right, boys," Culver announced after many tireless hours. "Pocket's pressure is low and a big storm's rolling in. Time for us to head up, so you're done for the day. Get some sleep."

We filed out lethargically. My arms and legs burned with soreness. My chest was so tight from being deeper in Saturn's Atmosphere that it felt like I was pulling each breath. I couldn't wait to get to the Ringer dorms and feel cool air against my filthy skin. The first days working under Earth-like g were always the toughest. It didn't matter how many shifts I'd served or how recently I'd received a g-stim—my body never got used to it.

"Where the hell did you run off to back there?" Desmond said into my ear once we reached the ship's corridor.

"Back where?" I said.

"Don't play stupid."

"I'm not in the mood, Des." If growing up as a pickpocket had taught me anything, it was that there were times to run. For someone who loved fights as much as him, I could only imagine what he thought about any man who did that.

He pushed me against the wall. The rest of the crew continued walking by. "I saw what you did, Kale," he whispered.

"I don't know what you're talking about," I said.

"To John."

My eyes widened. I grabbed him by the shirt and pulled him close so that I could be as quiet as possible. "Did he see?" I asked.

"If he did, he won't remember after that hit. He's in the med bay, probably with a bandage around his head."

"Anyone else?"

"No mud stompers anyway. No way you'd be here right now otherwise. Lucky for us, they think we all look the same."

I released him. "He was going to—"

Desmond shook his head to silence me. "I saw." He patted me on the shoulder and smiled with pride like a father watching his son take his first steps. "I didn't know you had it in you."

"There's a lot you don't know," I said, shaking off his hand and continuing on my way through the corridor. He kept pace with me.

"Damn, Kale, what is it with you? Can't take a joke. Can't take a compliment."

"Just keep it down, okay? I don't want engine duty."

"Engine duty? They'd probably put you through an airlock for that. 'Assault with a deadly weapon,' I think they call it. Might've been worth the punishment for putting that mud stomper down."

I swallowed the lump forming in my throat.

"Relax." Desmond slapped me on the back. "Captain's too pissed at John for letting that get out of hand to care who it was. Your secret's safe with us."

"Us?" I asked. He ignored me and walked on ahead into the Ringer dorms. I wanted to follow, but my legs stopped working. Desmond was the last person I needed holding a secret over me, especially one that could get me killed.

As I stood still, I noticed the two members of John's security team down the corridor. They were helping him out of the med bay, each one holding a burly arm. Desmond had been right about the bandage. Mom would have slapped me for feeling proud, but after robbing his hand-terminal and gifting him with a concussion, I had finally given John what he deserved.

The ship's medical officer, Dara Orsini, was with them, probably explaining how John should be careful not to be too active. Doctor Orsini, a middle-aged Earther woman, was easy to deal with because she didn't talk much, but she wasn't capable of much more than setting a broken bone. The only way to wind up serving as a nurse on an old harvester like the *Piccolo* was to flunk out of every important medical training university in Sol.

They walked directly toward me. I didn't move.

"Out of our way, Ringer," one of them ordered, finally convincing me to step to the side. John and the others eyed me warily as they passed, but nobody said anything else. If any of them had seen me strike him, that wouldn't have been the case. I breathed a sigh of relief and entered the Ringer dorm.

A minimal decon-chamber was constructed around the

entrance. It didn't require a full strip down, but electrostatic cleaners tickled me before I was allowed in. Cold air blasted through noisy air recyclers directly above as the entrance sealed behind me. The sweat on my brow dried almost instantly. I could've fallen asleep right there.

The Ringer dorms were as unimpressive, as one could imagine. A rec room on one end had some areas to sit and watch an obsolete view-screen. The only entertainment it had programmed on it were a few dated shows, the best being about an explorer traveling to the more desolate parts of Earth. Another featured a female modeling ring on Mars, which was less awkward to throw on when Cora wasn't around. She outranked everyone in the room and barely talked to any of us, so the crew was basically surrounded solely by men for months, leaving us with certain... needs. As a result, most of us had seen every episode of that show. The others would talk about their experiences with girls as we watched. I'd stay quiet.

We mostly kept it set to the Ring-wide newsfeed, though. Reception on Saturn was awful, so the image was grainy and the sound quality poor, but occasionally, the Ring's laser-relays shot us a few minutes of service to figure out what was going on around Sol.

The most cherished feature of the dorms was the bar tucked into the corner. Desmond and the others were already crowded around it, getting a head start on knocking themselves out. The cabinets below stored the cheapest forms of synthahol one could buy—if that was what all of it even was. I'd tasted an unmarked bottle once that made my throat feel like I'd swallowed fire. There wasn't any potable water to wash it down either. That was reserved for the kitchen and communal showers.

Cora sat alone on one of the rec room's grime-stained couches, wearing a sanitary mask and gloves as was required of her in the Ringer dorm. Our gazes met momentarily before I took a seat next to her. A story on the newsfeed about the status of a Pervenio-owned asteroid mining colony called Undina flickered on, sound and picture coming in and out. Apparently, they'd experienced an airlock failure a few months back, causing dozens of deaths and an entire sector to be devastated. It cut out completely before reports about the reparation status started.

"There he is!" Lester shouted over from the bar, his words already slurred. "The conquering hero has returned!"

He plopped down next to me and presented me with one of the two glasses in his grip. It was filled with something green, and the smell was so sharp it stung my nostrils. I pushed it aside as politely as I could manage. It might've felt good to calm my nerves and unwind, but I needed to stay focused if I wanted to figure out how to get my hand-terminal back to the command deck unseen.

"And here you thought he loved those mud stompers," Yavik added from the bar. He stood next to a broadly grinning Desmond. Most of the Ringer crew crowded around them.

"Always knew he had potential," said Desmond. He took a long sip of his drink, his face scrunching as he forced it down his throat.

"And look." Lester leaned over me and pointed to Cora, his drinks spilling onto my lap. His breath reeked. "He's even won over our dear Cora!"

Cora glared past him, right at me. It was obvious by her expression that she thought I'd spent the entire working shift boasting to the crew. She looked appalled.

"I didn't..." I whispered, shaking my head at her.

She turned away, got up, and headed off to her bed. A narrow hall with bunks stacked on either side was adjacent to the rec room, but that wasn't where she slept. Her bed was in a nook on the other side of the room, where an unused kitchen was located. A makeshift door latched to the wall separated her from the rest of us.

Suddenly, I felt silly for telling her that she was one of us when the divide was so clear. I used to like to pretend she had her own area because she was a different gender and rank, but that was just naïve. Of all the times I'd seen her disappear behind the curtain, it was only then that I finally understood why she was so quiet. It wasn't because of what had happened with her parents, but because she must've known she was destined to be alone. Earthers were skeptical of her, Ringers accepted her as a person, but neither would want her by their side. She was in a quarantine of her very own.

"Never any fun with her," Lester groaned. He leaned back and took a sip from one drink and then the other.

"Leave her alone, Lester," I said.

"C'mon, then. Prove me wrong. Get in there and let us know for once what hybrid tastes like."

"I said leave her alone!" I slapped one of the glasses from his hand. It hit the wall and synthahol splashed everywhere. Before I knew what was happening, I had him by the collar, my fist clenched.

Desmond moseyed over and wrenched himself in between us. "He's just messing around," he said to me. He peeled my hand off Lester and lifted him from the couch. Then he told him, "Let Kale have his day."

"You two deserve each other," Lester growled. He downed the rest of his remaining drink and then cackled all the way back to the bar. Yavik dumped a small pile of foundry salts he'd somehow smuggled through security onto the countertop.

I stormed out of the room to my bed and took a seat without another word. I was too tired to waste any. The work, my mom, the crew, Cora—I was more exhausted than I could ever remember. I zoned out the racket of the people enjoying their time off and lay down. Doing so helped ease my sore muscles, even though the mattress was so flimsy I could feel the frame beneath, and my pillow barely had any fluff left to it. It was like sleeping on a cloth bag filled with Titanian sand.

I burrowed the back of my head into the bed and stared forward. I had a straight view of Cora's door, and I couldn't help but notice her pale feet through the open bottom. Her clothing dropped to the floor around them. It felt wrong looking, even though I couldn't see anything more than her lower calves, but as I began to avert my eyes, I noticed something hanging out of her crumpled pocket: her ID card. The same card that was able to get us into the command deck at any time.

Soon, everybody would be drunk or high and sleeping for what passed as a night on the *Piccolo*. It was time for me to do what I did best. I could grab Cora's card, sneak to the command deck, and be done with it. Whatever happened afterward, I'd take the blame. She'd probably help me if I explained the situation, but I didn't want her involved. Maybe we could never have anything real, but I owed her.

I turned my head toward the wall and kept my eyes open. My first task was managing to stay awake until nobody else was.

Not falling asleep wasn't overly challenging. My body was drained and my eyelids heavy, but at a certain point, the *Piccolo* entered the storm Culver warned us about. Had it been worse, Cora would've been roused to take control and divert us from the course she'd plotted into the autopilot, and my whole plan would've been ruined. But that was why the ship ascended to shallow atmosphere during off-times.

Still, this storm was still enough to have the ship's hull shaking, and in the Ringer dorm, that meant all the exposed pipes rattling. Drunken Ringers also had a penchant for snoring.

Together, there was enough noise to keep me awake and then to cover my movements.

I slowly flipped my body over. What little light remained emanated from the corridor outside, so it was difficult to see. I slid my legs off the bed and lowered my feet without a sound. My head was groggy, but lying down had rejuvenated my limbs.

I shuffled along, weaving through a forest of lanky arms and legs hanging from the upper level of bunks. A tremor from the storm caused a hand to land on my shoulder. I think it belonged to Lester, but he was so far gone that I was able to remove it while he kept on snoring.

I reached Cora's divider and knelt. The other side was silent as she slept, and her clothes were right where I'd seen them earlier.

I took a deep breath, started to reach under the door, and stopped. I was clearly one of the few people on the *Piccolo* in which Cora had even a fraction of trust, and I was about to break it. I was betraying my mom's trust too. I told myself that they'd both understand. A lie, probably, but unless I planned on including Cora in R's mission, or sneaking into the captain's quarters to get his ID, it was the only way.

I shoved my hand in farther before I could second-guess myself. My stringy arms may have helped with cleaning, but my long fingers were built to dig into pockets. They brushed against her clothes, where I fished around for a few seconds before I found the card and slowly drew it out. When I pulled back my hand, it sat in the center of my palm.

I took another deep breath to steady myself. When I was sure Cora hadn't been roused, I stood and made my way to the dorm's sealed exit. I remained extremely cautious: Lurking around the ship when shifts were all done was forbidden for Ringer maintenance crew.

A swipe of Cora's card over the control panel got it open in a hurry and bypassed the decon-chamber. I peered around the corner. The lights were dimmed, but I spotted one of John's security team patrolling the central corridor about thirty meters up ahead. He faced the opposite direction.

I slipped out of the room. The door closed behind me, but the storm covered its *whoosh*. I stayed low as I crept toward the guard. I had to stay beneath the viewport on the door to the Earther dorms. As I got closer, I heard the guard chuckling. He was watching something on his hand-terminal.

Again, I wasn't surprised by his lack of vigilance. There was nothing to steal on the *Piccolo,* especially since we still had months left with each other. No reason for anybody to purposely damage any equipment either. We were each paid off a percentage of the gas we harvested, after all.

A left at the central corridor would take me straight to the command deck, but the guard stood directly in the middle of it. Knocking out an Earther without a baton and a running start wasn't going to happen, so I searched the walls for something to throw. I spotted a cluster of pipes, and one of the joints was filled with rusty screws.

I located the loosest nut that could be removed without a wrench. The pipe wouldn't miss it; ship parts often came loose during storms. I took the nut and flung it into the central corridor so that it bounced off the wall and deflected in the direction opposite where I needed to go. The clank was loud enough to draw the guard's attention.

He turned to check it out. I slipped behind him like a ghost and moved as quickly as possible, not bothering to look back. No other branches or nooks lay in my path to hide in, just a short, straight shot to the command deck. If he saw me, he saw me, and there would be nothing I could do but outrun him. He didn't.

I reached the locked entrance, breathing heavier now, and leaned against the side wall. Another swipe of Cora's card and I was through. The *Piccolo* was presently on Saturn's dark side, so all I could see through the transparent dome were pale lines of gusting wind. The command console bathed the room in a greenish aura. Controls flickered and beeped.

I took a seat at the console and fetched my hand-terminal from my pocket. The orange circle glared up at me, judging me with its silent fury. I would be as glad to get rid of it as I would be to complete my end of the deal.

With my free hand, I located the slot beneath the front panel to insert the device. I closed my eyes, not sure of why I was so nervous. I inhaled slowly to keep my fingers steady, and placed it in. A soft chime indicated that the connection was established. After all the irritation, I half-expected there to be fireworks, or at least a message thanking me, but there wasn't. A field of text popped up on a tiny screen above the port.

UPLOAD IN PROGRESS... PLEASE DO NOT REMOVE DEVICE...

That was it. I would've cheered myself if the result wasn't so anticlimactic. I leaned back in the chair and waited. R wasn't clear on what to do next.

The metal structure of the dome whined and stole my attention from the console. The storm outside strengthened, or at least it seemed that way to me. If it got bad enough, Cora would be forced back on duty. I had no idea how long the update would take but knew that if I got caught up here, I'd have some serious explaining to do. As it was, I doubted anybody would realize the device was inserted unless they were trying to connect one of their own into the same port.

I had to get Cora's ID back to her. I was fully prepared to

take responsibility if I got caught, but that wasn't the plan I preferred. Everything I'd done was to save my mother, and I planned on actually getting to see her again, without glass in the way. Maybe, after all the progress we'd made, I could even convince Cora to come with me next time.

I eyed the screen for a few more seconds and then left the command deck behind. I hoped I wouldn't be back soon.

The guard in the hall had returned to watching his hand-terminal without bothering to move from the spot where the nut landed. I snuck back past him easily and was in the Ringer dorm in less than a minute. The door resealed behind me like I'd never left. With Cora's card in my hand, I approached her door. I was just about to return it, when I heard her.

"Kale, is that you?" she whispered softly like she'd just woken.

I suppressed a shriek as I slipped and fell onto my rear. Somehow, I was able to keep the card in my grasp and return to a crouch so that I could hide it behind my back.

"Kale?" she said.

"It's... it's me," I stuttered.

She unlatched her door and cracked it open just enough for me to peek inside. She sat on the end of her bed, a thin sheet drawn across her body. She didn't appear angry, just tired.

"Cora, I didn't mean to wake you. I just..." I sighed. I had no idea what to say.

"It's okay." She waved me closer so that we could whisper more easily. I found moving far more difficult than connecting the hand-terminal had been. My legs felt like they were submerged in wet concrete. Somehow, I managed to drag them forward a few steps before I remembered her card was still in my possession. I rotated my hand to face away from her.

"I'm sorry I reacted that way earlier," she said. "I know you wouldn't have told them."

I exhaled so loudly I sounded like a leaky gas pipe. She didn't see. "Don't worry about it," I said as I got closer, keeping the card out of sight. "They just don't know when to stop."

"If anyone else found out—"

"They won't." I kneeled beside her bed, slipping her card back into her pocket unseen as I did. "None of them would say a word to an Earther."

"I'd defend you if they did. All the captain cares about is the *Piccolo* running smoothly."

"I don't deserve that." A sinking sensation in my stomach over what I'd just done made me feel nauseous. I went to stand. Her cold fingers gripped my arm to stop me.

"Yes, you do," she said.

I regarded her, confused. With her other hand, she reached for my sanitary mask and pulled it down just enough to reveal my lips. She leaned toward me, stopping a few centimeters away. Her silvery hair tickled my face and caused goosebumps to cover my entire body.

My breathing stopped. My eyelids were probably drawn so wide that it looked like I'd stumbled upon a dead body.

"I'm clean, Kale," she whispered. "I promise. You'll be okay. I... I want this. I have for a long time."

I couldn't manage words. Only a nod so subtle she wouldn't have been able to see it if we weren't so close. Her lips pressed against mine, and before I could control it, my arms were wrapped around her. I longed to remove my gloves so I could feel the smooth camber of her bare back.

We didn't make sense. It wasn't safe. But in that moment, everything else in the world, all my problems, faded away.

ELEVEN

A VIOLENT TREMOR STARTLED ME AWAKE. MY EYES snapped open, and I searched the darkness. I wasn't sure what was a dream and what wasn't, but when I felt my arm draped over another body, I remembered. Cora and I were squeezed onto her bed. Neither of us wore anything. Not even a mask or gloves.

I touched her arm just to ensure she was real. She was still fast asleep, her head resting on my chest. I never wanted to move.

Another tremor, this one more intense than the last.

"What's that?" Cora yawned.

As I started to answer, the *Piccolo* lurched to the side. We were tossed out of the bed. Cups and other equipment slid across the rec room floor, clamoring against the walls like cymbals. The groans and confused shouts of the stirred crew filled the room.

Cora and I peeled our tangled bodies from each other. My shoulder stung from crashing against the floor. She'd landed on me, so she was fine.

"Storm?" I groaned. If it was, it was the worst I'd ever felt.

Usually, short-range scanners picked up a bad one before the *Piccolo* wound up too deep and Cora was woken to alter our heading.

"Must be," she said.

She grabbed her clothes and stood, fully naked. I couldn't believe my eyes. I felt like I was seeing the stars for the first time again. She caught me staring and giggled.

"Are you going to sit there, or are you going to help?" she asked.

I don't even want to imagine how much I blushed. I jumped to my feet and fumbled around with her boiler suit's loose sleeve as I tried to get it on her. Once I did, she zipped up the outfit and faced me.

"Cora, I—" I said before she placed one of her slender fingers over my mouth.

She smiled. "Find somewhere to sit in case this gets worse," she said. "We can talk after."

The smile I returned grew wider. It was beyond my control, like I was intoxicated. When I didn't say anything, she just giggled again, planted a kiss on my cheek, and hurried through the curtain.

I stood with a goofy grin on my face for a few moments before deciding to get dressed myself. I had to sit down on the bunk to do it, and not because the ship was shaking. After the worst tremor, it'd almost entirely stopped. But my legs were wobbly, in no small part due to the best night of my life.

I finished dressing and sat up. The weight of my boiler suit felt off without the compromised hand-terminal in my pocket. I wondered if it'd finished uploading the program, which I assumed was going to somehow tap into the captain's credit account and rob him. Something like that at least. I didn't care. If someone found it, I decided I'd say I left it up there by accident while I was with Cora. Everything had gone perfectly, and my mom would have no choice but to forgive me for what I'd done after it got her out of that hellhole.

On the other side of the divider, the Ringer crew ran amok trying to figure out what was going on. The standard protocol for a storm was for Cora or the captain to announce over the ship's main com-system whether or not we needed to strap down. The speakers remained silent. I could manage to think of only one thing other than a powerful storm that could knock a ship the size of the *Piccolo* around like it was a pool ball—one of the dual engines blowing out. Of course, that would also have involved us taking a nosedive straight into the heart of the gas giant to join the *Sunfire,* and the force of gravity tugging on my body hadn't gotten any stronger to indicate that had happened. The ship seemed to be flying as steady as it was when there was no storm at all.

I slid forward and rested my feet flat against the floor. It vibrated gently, like it always did from the ship's engines. I placed my hand against the wall, and it felt the same there. The worst storm I'd ever experienced on the *Piccolo* also seemed to have been the shortest.

I stood and took a step toward the curtain. I stopped when I realized that I was about to walk into a crowded rec room directly from Cora's bed. I'd never hear the end of it from Desmond and the others. It was better to stay put and wait it out...

A crack rang out, so loud it resonated in the pipes. It sounded like a piece of the *Piccolo*'s wing snapping off. The ship dipped again, throwing me forward through the curtain and onto my chest. Red disaster lights along the edges of the ceiling and floors flashed on. Shrill emergency alarms began wailing.

I sprang to my feet and bolted toward the dorm's exit. It should've been sealed, but it was wide open, decon-chamber and all. Desmond managed to get to his feet swiftly enough to catch up with me.

"What was that?" he shouted over the alarm.

"I'm not sure," I said.

We emerged into the hallway. A crowd of Earthers gathered outside of their dorm. Culver lay in the center of them, howling in pain.

"What happened?" I asked one of the security guards. When he looked at me, I realized he was the one I'd snuck past earlier.

"Whatever that was tossed Culver into the wall," he replied. I leaned in to get a closer look. Culver's leg was twisted, a sharp piece of his tibia poking through a bloody gash just below his knee.

"Step aside, Ringer!" the guard growled.

"Screw them," Desmond hissed.

A series of bangs rang out from the direction of the command deck. They were softer than the one that had preceded the ship's staggering, but they sounded like gunshots, and not just from a single gun.

"Cora!" I yelled. I sprinted as fast as I could toward the central corridor, Desmond right behind me.

We popped out into the intersection and saw Captain Saunders sprinting toward us from the command deck. Cora was behind him, the g conditions slowing her down, but he had one hand around her wrist to help pull her along. With the other, he fired his pulse-pistol blindly over his shoulder. Two other Earthers ran alongside them. One was promptly struck in the back by a spray of automatic rounds and toppled onto his face.

Bullets whizzed by Desmond and me. I was just able to grab him and heave him back behind the corner as one zipped by his ear like an angry hornet from ancient Earth. He was in shock, and soon after, when the captain and Cora joined us around the corner, they were equally shaken. I grabbed Cora and pulled her close, but she couldn't focus on me. Her eyes were glued open. Captain Saunders clutched the handle of his pistol, hands shaking. The other Earther hadn't made it.

"Captain, what the hell's going on?" Desmond asked, his voice cracking.

I would've asked the same thing if I could have mustered the words. Almost getting shot had my heart pounding, but seeing Cora so near the same fate had my legs faint. As I held her, I found that she was helping me stay upright as much as I was her.

"They came..." Captain Saunders panted. He sounded like he'd just run all the way around Pervenio Station. "They came through the viewport on the bridge. Fired right through the glass." He paused to breathe again and then popped his pistol around the corner. "Bastards!" he yelled as he fired off more shots at whatever was down the hall.

"Who?" Desmond questioned.

"I don't know! They're in heavy armor and tinted visors. Three of them, I think. Got automatic pulse-rifles too."

"Do we have any weapons?" I asked with urgency as the heavy footsteps of the attackers drew nearer. I knew it was a stupid question, but it was the first thing that popped into my head.

"This is a harvesting ship—what in Earth's name do you think? This and some batons are it." Captain Saunders gestured toward his pistol and then reached out to fire another shot. His features darkened when he heard the click indicating that the clip was empty.

"We should get everybody we can into the harvesting bay, then," I said.

"Run?" Desmond said. "That's just like you, Kale. We've got numbers."

"Yeah—and fists."

"Kale's right," Cora addressed the captain meekly. "We can lock the blast door down from the inside."

Captain Saunders didn't wait for any more opinions. "You heard her," he said. "Let's move!"

He sprinted back down the straight corridor toward the galley. Desmond grumbled something before following. I glanced back into Cora's eyes to make sure she was ready. Every echoing footstep of the nameless invaders seemed to be making her shudder. She forced herself to nod, and I did the same before we fled.

"Everyone to the harvester bay!" Captain Saunders shouted as he ran past the dorms.

"What is it?" an Earther roaming the corridor asked.

"Emergency protocol! Let's move, move!"

Ringers and Earthers poured out of their respective dormitories ahead. They stared at what was behind us, and I didn't need to turn around to know our assailants must have rounded the corner. The faces of both races filled with dread before they all started sprinting down the hall. Three Earthers tried to help Culver up, but two of them were the ship's security guards. They decided to drop the head mechanic and fell in behind John toward the harvester bay as soon as he exited the dorm. That left only one Earther with Culver, and we all blew by them.

The deafening clatter of pulse-rifle fire erupted, making the pipes running along the metal walls rattle and clang. Culver cried out in pain and collapsed with a thud. I didn't risk looking back. I was slow under Earth-like g, and Desmond and Cora weren't much faster, but they'd been working on the *Piccolo* longer than I had. Scrubbing canisters and controlled lifting we could handle, but Ringers weren't built for sprinting while on

Saturn. Plus, there'd been no opportunity to receive my standard-issued morning g-stim before getting to work.

The next turn in the passage led to the harvesting bay. It was a long, straight run away, especially with bullets peppering the walls and ceiling behind us. Even with the alarm continuing to cry, they were all I could hear. Hisses and snaps. Instruments of death all around me. I hadn't pushed my legs so hard since the time my mother had caught me running foundry salts for Dexter when I was ten.

The captain yelped and smashed into the wall ahead of me. Turning my head to see what happened couldn't have wasted much more than a millisecond, but it was enough of a hesitation for me to be hit as well. A bullet clipped the meaty part of my thigh, causing me to trip. I would've smashed my head on the floor if Desmond hadn't caught me and dragged me to safety around the corner.

"You okay?" he gasped.

Exerting myself in high g had my heart racing so rapidly I thought my chest was going to explode. I could hardly breathe. My muscles burned like I'd been dipped in a vat of acid. Cora kneeled over me and frantically checked my injured leg. I couldn't see straight enough to decipher her reaction to what she saw.

"There's no blood," she said. She was nearly as winded as the rest of the Ringers were.

I rubbed the area of the wound and brought my fingers close to my dizzy eyes. My leg hurt like I'd been hit with a hammer, but there was no blood.

A flurry of bullets struck the back wall of the adjacent hall. I forced myself to focus, and that was when I noticed that many of the bullets were bouncing back onto the floor. They were rubberized, flathead rounds, used on ships in space to prevent piercing the hull, or during riots when security didn't want to kill anybody. Luckily, the bullet that'd hit me had done so in one of the few places on my slim Ringer body where there was some extra meat; otherwise, it might've shattered a bone.

"I'm fine," I said, still catching my breath.

"Good," Desmond said. "We're close." He grabbed my arm, groaning as he tried to lift me.

I pulled away and peered back around the corner as furtively as possible. Captain Saunders slumped over a cluster of conduits. His bloody head rested against the wall, and he wasn't moving.

Beyond him, three attackers clad in heavy, powered armor marched down the hall, pulse-rifles in their hands. Half-sphere helmets enclosed their heads, with tinted visors that made it impossible to determine who they were. I tried to see what color the suits were to get an idea of what faction they might belong to —Pervenio, Venta Co, pirates—but the ship's emergency lighting was too red to allow me to tell.

"Would you come on!" Desmond implored.

"Kale, what are you doing?" Cora asked. "We have to go."

I knew I should listen, but just then, the captain's eyelids fluttered. Because his fall hadn't been stopped by human arms, he'd been knocked unconscious, but he still was breathing.

It seemed wrong to leave him out there with a faceless death squad bearing down on him. While I was trying to decide what to do, a hungover member of the *Piccolo*'s crew who'd been left behind stumbled out of the Ringer dorms right in front of the attackers. He didn't make it far before a bullet caught him on the hip and sent him twisting through the air and into the wall.

The distraction was exactly what I needed. I fought every survival instinct in my body, held my breath, and plunged into the hall. I threw my arm under the captain's broad shoulder and hauled him backward. The Earther's body was heavy, especially while I was dealing with overstrained muscles and an injured leg I could hardly put any weight on. I was fortunate we didn't have to get far. By the time the attackers noticed what was happening, I'd dragged him to safety.

My leg suddenly gave out, and I staggered along with his body toward another wall. I was cramping all over. Breathing hurt so badly it felt like someone inside of me had a knife to my ribs. I moaned and grasped at my chest.

"Kale!" Cora yelled. She lunged forward and caught me. Captain Saunders slipped from my grasp, but Desmond reluctantly placed his arm under the captain's shoulder to keep him upright.

"He wouldn't have done the same for you," he remarked.

There was no time to catch my breath. Cora and I joined Desmond in carrying the hefty captain, and we set off toward the harvesting bay together. Our three exhausted pairs of legs were going to have to do. Up ahead, I could see that the harvesting bay doors were open, but under the emergency lighting, it'd be impossible for anyone inside to tell who we were until we were closer. None of us had the energy to call out over the alarms.

The attackers were just coming around the nearest corner when a group of Earthers finally recognized us and ran out. I'd never been more grateful for them. Their strong arms grabbed hold of all of us and took the weight of the captain off our limbs. Bullet fire clattered again right before we were heaved into the harvester bay. The blast doors sealed shut behind us, and the ship's alarms grew quiet.

Everyone in the harvesting bay stared while Cora, Desmond, and I crumpled to the floor, wheezing. I was relieved to finally give my legs a rest, but it still pained me to breathe. Cora was behind me, her arms wrapped around mine to keep me from tipping all the way onto my side.

A relatively equal split of Ringers and Earthers were

present, only twenty or so altogether. The rest were either caught in the carnage outside, lying somewhere wounded, or dead. The Earthers who'd taken Captain Saunders from us carefully laid him on the floor in front of Doctor Orsini, who used a pile of dirty harvester rags to prop up his head.

Captain Saunders wasn't exactly a friend, but we'd known each other for years. I couldn't ever remember seeing him vulnerable. Blood trickled down the ends of his hair from a gash on his head, and Doctor Orsini used the cleanest cloth she could find to wipe it off, her hands trembling.

"He's still breathing," Doctor Orsini said.

"What happened?" John questioned, glaring in our direction. He sat near the captain against a rack of canisters, bandage still wound around his head.

"He got hit," Desmond replied.

"You see who they are?"

Desmond shook his head.

"Soldiers, I think," Cora said.

"Heavy armor... guns..." I panted. I pulled up my pants leg to reveal a welt the size of a cherry on the back of my calf. "They're using nonlethal rounds."

"Makes sense," John said. "They don't want to blow us all to bits."

"Or they want us alive," I said.

"For what?"

All I could manage was a shrug. I had no idea if or why they'd want that. Worst-case scenario, I'd heard rumors of a black-market slave trade that went on in the asteroid belt, where even the most influential corporations of the USF had trouble governing, and it could've reached Titan. Best-case scenario, our cold storage was being robbed of any gas we'd harvested, and our robbers were kind enough not to kill us, though any group smart enough to locate a ship in the middle of

Saturn's stormy atmosphere should have been smart enough to wait longer than a few days into a harvesting shift to hit it for that.

"Des!" Yavik yelled. His eyes were bloodshot from a night of sniffing salts. He shoved his way toward Desmond, pushing aside the Earthers. He offered to help his friend up, but Desmond seemed content on the floor.

"Lester?" Desmond asked.

Yavik frowned. "Too hungover to get up," he said.

Desmond didn't have a response.

"We've got to message for help," John said. "Cora, are you okay?"

For a moment, it sickened me to think that he was pretending he cared about her after what he'd attempted in the galley, but then I remembered that, as XO, he was in charge with the captain unconscious. He needed her. Nobody else with enough knowledge of navigation or communications appeared to have made it.

She nodded.

He gestured toward a control console that secondarily governed the harvesting machinery in case of malfunction. "Good. Get onto that control console and..." He lost his train of thought. His mask of composure slipped away, and it became clear he was as petrified as the rest of us. "See if you can contact anybody. Pervenio Station, another harvester, hell, a luxury cruise liner—anything!"

"I don't know the com-systems that well," she replied.

He pounded on a canister. "Just do it, dammit!"

If I wasn't still so exhausted, I would've said something. Cora gave my arm a squeeze to make sure I didn't.

"It's okay," she whispered, smiling at me. It was a frail smile, barely noticeable, but it was enough to calm me. She released me and was helped over to the console by one of the less tired crew members. Once she was there, her fingers fluttered across the keys.

"How does it look?" John asked.

"Not good," she replied as she continued to anxiously type away. "There's another storm passing, and they've infiltrated our systems from the command deck. Main communications are down if we can even get something out with all the interference. It'll take some time to find a workaround."

"Get it done."

"I didn't sign up for this," said a Ringer sitting with his arms around his knees by the harvesting tanks. He was new to the *Piccolo*.

"None of us did, yet here we are," Desmond said. He finally accepted Yavik's help up. "Never thought I'd die with a bunch of stinking mud stompers."

"Why don't you come say that to my face!" one of the Earther guards barked.

Desmond stopped and turned around. He still breathed so heavily I could see his chest heaving, but that didn't stop him from jumping at a chance to fight. "Gladly," he said. "Then I'll toss you out to those fucks. Bet the cap'n will do the same to us once he comes to, just to save his ass."

"Watch your mouth, ghost!"

"Quiet, all of you!" John ordered. He used a rack of canisters to pick himself up. "Captain's out, which means I'm in charge. Both of you, all of you, get to barricading the blast door just in case. It might hold long enough for Cora on its own, but if it doesn't, we need to buy time. I don't feel like dying in here with *any* of you shits."

Realizing he was right, everyone who was standing hopped to. I was still too tired to move, and my gaze left Cora to scan the room.

"The only equipment that's mobile are canister racks," I

gathered the energy to say. "But they're wearing powered armor out there, so it'll only stop them for a few seconds, and tire us out."

"So what would you have us do, Drayton?" John said. "We've got nothing to fight back with. Pervenio is our only shot at rescue."

"I'm saying we figure out what they want. What if Cora can't get a message out? They're not killing us, so maybe we could just give it to them."

John stormed toward me. Instinctually, I slid back along the floor until the wall stopped me. "The captain thanks you for getting him here, but right now, I'm giving the orders," he bristled. "If you got any *actual* ideas then, by all means, tell me. Otherwise, shut the hell up and start emptying those racks so we can move them!"

Desmond appeared in front of me from out of nowhere. "Move the shit yourself," he said to John. "We're not wasting any more of our time listening to you." He gestured for Yavik, and together they helped me up. They walked me past the XO, to the area around the console where Cora was working. One by one, all the other Ringers stopped working on the racks and followed our lead.

John's fists were clenched. Who knows what he would've done if he wasn't injured and terrified, but his cheeks turned bright red before he rubbed the wound on his head and exhaled. "Captain's gonna hear about this when he wakes up," he growled. "You'll all be scrubbing the engine for the rest of the shift!"

"Haven't you heard?" Desmond said. "Shift's over."

Nearly a half hour passed in silence; I couldn't be exactly sure without a hand-terminal and didn't bother asking. Barely a soul had spoken since Desmond's last words. All I could hear was the steady rattling of worn air recyclers, the heavy breathing of twenty or so frightened people, and the constant clicking of Cora's busy fingers as she tried to save us.

So far, she had no luck broadcasting our need for assistance. Sweat poured down her forehead and arms. I thought about walking over to encourage her a few times, but I didn't want to distract her, and my leg was too sore for me to get up. Watching her and wishing for her to succeed was the best I could offer.

John and the Earthers had emptied the canister racks and shoved them in front of the blast door, so they were drained as well—all to buy us maybe a minute if the attackers were able to slice through the blast doors. In the rare case of toxic gas leaks, the harvesting bay was able to be sealed from either side. We'd secured it on our end, which meant that only Captain Saunders's override code was supposed to be able to open it from the corridor.

The captain was conscious again, but he hadn't uttered a word since coming to. I caught him staring at me a few times, but every time I did, he looked to the ground as if he were ashamed. I'm guessing one of the Earthers had informed him of who'd gone back to save him. It was the least I could do for the chance he'd given me, but I'm sure if I were a captain, I'd want to be the one saving my crew and not the other way around.

Presently, he was as useless as any of us except for Cora, and likely suffering from a concussion like the hotheaded XO sitting beside him. They were the only two people on the ship with leadership experience, and the XO had already alienated half of the remaining crew.

"Who raids a harvesting ship this old?" Doctor Orsini asked from across the room, breaking the unsettling silence. Everybody glared at her as if she'd just fired off a gun. Everybody except me. Hearing those words caused me to remember my initial thoughts upon receiving R's message back on Titan.

My breathing hastened. It couldn't be connected.

"For gas stores, I reckon," another crew member responded, motioning to the dozens of canisters standing all around him.

"This early in the shift?" said another, echoing my sentiments exactly.

Desmond sat up and glanced in Captain Saunders's direction. "You finally insult the wrong person, Cap?" he said.

"Shut it," John growled so that the captain didn't have to waste the energy projecting his voice across the harvester bay.

Desmond grinned but didn't respond.

"Maybe they got what they wanted from cold storage and left," Yavik said.

"Kindest pirates I've ever heard of if that's the case," someone else added.

"Enough," Captain Saunders groaned. "You're all giving me a headache. Let Cora keep working. Anything yet, girl?"

"Nothing," she responded softly, too focused to worry about if anyone could hear her. "I'm locked out of everything. Every time I find a way through, they have a counter."

They conversed back and forth with technobabble I couldn't follow. R's message repeated in my head. If this really was connected and I'd invited our invaders on board, what could they want?

"Hey, Kale," Desmond said, snapping me out of it. He was slumped against the harvesting vats beside me. He had his eyes closed, but he wasn't asleep. He was just resting, preparing for the fight we all knew might be imminent.

"What?" I asked.

He held out his palm. A Red Wing Company g-stim pack lay in the center of it. "Here," he said. "I'm tired of listening to you wheeze."

"Whe—" I lowered my voice. "Where'd you get that?"

He nodded toward Yavik. "He's always got an extra stash to take the edge off. C'mon."

I looked around as if it mattered we were breaking the captain's rules, then grabbed the stim and jabbed it into the side of my neck. In seconds, it felt as if there had been a belt tied around my lungs that was now loosening notch by notch.

"There you go." He slapped me on the back and slid closer. "I saw you," he whispered directly into my ear, playing his guessing games with me once more.

"Saw me?" My heart skipped a beat. He couldn't have seen. Nobody saw. Was I about to be blamed for this?

"Getting up out of her bed," he clarified. "Thought you'd be able to hide it from me in the chaos, but I think I have a knack for catching you." He turned to face me and smirked.

"Oh, that," I replied, trying not to let my relief show.

"Lester will shit himself if he ever finds out. I never thought it'd actually happen. Never thought I'd be jealous of you either."

"Why? You've got a girl back on Titan, don't you?"

He hesitated, and his lips twisted. "Yeah... sure I do... but not one like her. You're braver than I thought."

I peered over at Cora. Even considering the circumstances, she was as stunning as ever. Watching the way the muscles on her slender forearms tightened and untightened as her fingers flew across the console's controls quieted my mind for a few much-needed seconds.

"At least one of us had a last night to remember," Desmond said.

"We're not going to die," I said, mostly to reassure myself. "She'll find help. They don't even want us de—"

"Trass!" Cora exclaimed. Everyone's attention fell on her. In two years of knowing her, I'd never heard her raise her voice so high.

"What?" more than a few members of the crew, including myself, asked in unison.

"They're diverting power from the ship's systems. They're..." She backed away from the console, her eyes gaping in horror as if she was about to faint. I used Desmond's shoulder to get to my feet and limped over to her. The screen blinked and was cluttered with indecipherable strings of code.

"What is it?" I asked.

The *Piccolo* answered me before she could. The room's air recyclers hummed loudly for a few seconds and then clicked. The attackers had reversed the harvester bay's oxygen supply, sucking it out of the room. It was an emergency protocol to be used in the event of a fire.

"What's happening?" voices questioned.

"Cora, stop this!" Captain Saunders ordered.

She threw herself back toward the console, carrying me with her. I could feel her arms trembling as I held them, or maybe it was my hands. Probably both. Everything she tried was received by an error message.

My body started to feel warmer. The current of air flowing through the ship had never been noticeable to me until then, when so much of it had been sucked away.

"C'mon," Cora said to herself. "Work!" She banged on the keys, and the screen went black. The sound of the rest of the room's machinery losing power hung on the stale air. Even the red emergency lights finally switched off, drowning us in complete blackness.

"Was that you?" I asked.

"No..." Cora whimpered. I felt her head fall against my chest, her hands against my back. "I couldn't stop them... I couldn't..." She sobbed, and we fell to our knees together. I withheld my tears. We needed to control our breathing, or we'd suffocate even more quickly.

It was hard to hear what anyone else was saying. Curses and frightened shouts echoed. Crew members ran for the blast door, the thinning air causing them to forget that they weren't safe on the other side of it either.

"It's sealed!" they shouted.

Of course it was. Without power, there was no way to get it open.

I held Cora close. I'd have given anything to look upon her face again. It was too dark to even see her nose as it grazed mine. I could only feel her tears on my cheeks.

"Just breathe slowly," I said.

"I wish I'd been with you sooner," she sniveled.

"Me too," I answered. The words slipped through my lips as little more than a whisper. My head was getting lighter and lighter every second.

"I don't want to die... Kale."

For two years, I'd dreamed of hugging her. I'd dreamed of kissing her and lying by her side. Now I'd done all of that, and it'd be the last thing I ever did. We were all going to die.

TWELVE

A FLICKER OF LIGHT. THE THRUM AND TICKS OF POWER being restored. At first, I thought I was dead, that those Earthers who clung to the religions of the old world were right and there really was a realm my spirit went to after death. I'd always believed that when I was cremated, and my ashes were released into the winds of Titan, as was Ringer custom, I'd become a part of our moon's icy winds. Drifting for all eternity and watching over my people.

I was doing neither. Breathable air rushed down my throat, inflated my lungs, and I gasped. In my arms, I felt Cora do the same, her chest lifting my hand as I squeezed her tight. The room was filled with the sounds of others having the same reaction. We were alive... at least for the time being.

The halogen lights in the harvesting bay grew brighter, and I realized the blast door was wide open. The canister racks stacked in front of it had all been shoved to the side except for the one currently being moved by an attacker. John's great wall, brushed aside like a pile of infected laundry.

I wanted to grab Cora and run for cover behind anything I could find, but I couldn't convince my legs to cooperate. My body was still too fatigued from oxygen deprivation to speak comprehensibly, let alone move. The rest of the crew was in the same position. Reversing the air recyclers was a perfect way for whoever the attackers were to avoid a fight. I just couldn't understand what they wanted.

And then I saw it.

An attacker finished sliding the last rack out of the way and turned to face us just as two others entered the room. My vision was getting less blurry, and under the blooming light, I could better see the details of their armor. All three suits were identical and bulky enough to make it impossible to tell where their wearers might've originated from. They were entirely white except for their tinted visors and one other feature: a pale orange circle in the center of their chest plates.

My jaw dropped. Doctor Orsini regained her strength quicker than the rest and scrambled for cover. One of the attackers promptly shot her down. The flat-head round didn't kill her, but getting hit that hard in the gut at close quarters had her curled up on the ground desperate for the air she'd only just regained.

"Bastards!" another Earther yelled. Not only were the Earthers closer to the door, but their stronger muscles allowed them to recover sooner. Four of them pounced at the attackers. What proceeded happened so fast that it was hard to tell who was who, though I was sure that while John's two-person security team joined the defense, he stayed put like the coward he was. The captain struggled to rise but wasn't able to move speedily enough.

Two of the Earthers were taken out at the legs. Another landed a punch against one of the attackers but probably broke his hand against the armor before being smacked into the canister racks. The fourth was grabbed by the throat and slammed to the ground so hard the metal floor caved.

Before anybody else could move, the captain was heaved to his feet and placed at gunpoint. The attacker holding the rifle switched out the clip on his or her pulse-rifle for another. John was next to them, crouched like he was finally preparing himself to join the fray, but remaining still.

"The next rounds are live," the attacker with the captain said. A distortion device rendered the voice too deep to be natural or infer gender. It resonated over the cavernous silence of a crew too tired and too terrified to move.

"Do it," Desmond said after the longest seconds of quiet in my life. "See if we care."

The other two attackers switched their clips as well, each taking aim at one side of the room. I positioned my body in front of Cora, and then all my muscles tensed. Nobody fired, but the message was clear enough for even Desmond to hold his tongue.

"What do you want? Gas?" Captain Saunders rasped, the gun barrel pressed against his bloody hair. "We have nothing else of value here."

"Value is a relative term," the attacker replied.

"We'll give you whatever it is."

"What we want, you cannot give."

"Then just leave, whoever you are!" John yelled.

The attacker doing all the talking turned his or her attention away from the captain and stepped toward the center of the room. It was impossible to see any eyes through the visor; however, I couldn't help but feel that he or she stared directly at me.

"We are the will of Titan," he or she said. "Comply with our demands, and you may survive this."

The speaker exchanged a series of calculated hand gestures with the other attackers. It wasn't just military signals either. I could tell from experience that they were communicating in sign language. That had me believing they might be Ringers.

Deafness had essentially been eliminated on Earth, with its advancements in the areas of genetics and affordable surgical options, so it was a dead language for Earthers. But signing had been a huge part of how we communicated in the early days of the Ring, when we were founding our colonies from the inside of protective suits. Having an entire construction crew chattering over in-helmet com-links could be confusing. Most Ringers weren't fluent anymore, and I basically knew only the few words and phrases I remembered from school, which came in handy as a thief trying to remain as discreet as possible. The attackers were so fluid with it that the only word I recognized was *live*.

"Who are they?" Cora whispered, the terror in her voice palpable.

I don't know, but I think I invited them here, was what I wanted to say. I settled on simply "I don't know," which was still the honest truth. Them being Ringers was really an educated guess. Any Earther could learn sign language if they had the time or the desire to put on a mask and make my kind appear culpable. The only thing I could be sure about was that they were professionals, and they weren't messing around.

"Stand," one of the other attackers said to all the Ringers in the harvesting bay as he or she approached us. Another said the same to the Earthers across the way.

We all complied.

The attacker's head rotated so that his or her visor aimed directly at Cora and me. My stomach knotted. Her fingers dug into my side and mine into hers.

"Apart," the distorted voice ordered. "Show your hands."

We hesitated.

"Now," he or she demanded.

"It's okay," I whispered to Cora. "It's okay." It took all my willpower to pry my hands off her, but I did so and made sure to position myself in front of her as I raised them. I couldn't even feel if they were quaking anymore, they'd been doing it for so long.

"Form a line at the door," the attacker said. "The order is irrelevant."

"For what?" Desmond questioned. "I'm sick of this. I won't be marched away willingly to be used like a sack of meat if that's what this is!"

"Me... me neither," Yavik nervously agreed.

Again, I wished Desmond could just keep his mouth shut. The attacker promptly stormed over to him and raised his or her pulse-rifle so that the barrel pressed into the center of his forehead.

"Failure to comply won't be tolerated," he or she threatened.

The attacker's finger pulled the trigger halfway, and Desmond's expression was ripe with a level of apprehension I didn't know he was capable of. I could see the lump in his throat bob.

I willed him with my thoughts to stay quiet. It was better to be a slave, if that was what was coming, than a stain on the floor. Ringers were no good in underground brothels, considering our immune systems, so if we were being acquired for work, the worst place I could conceive of that we'd be placed was some hollowed-out asteroid mine. The Lowers weren't much different.

"Listen to them," I said. "If they wanted us dead, they'd have kept the air off." I limped toward the blast door, checking to make sure that Cora followed. She did. I held her gaze as we walked.

"Back to your old obedient self, are you, Kale?" Desmond said through clenched teeth.

I wasn't foolish enough to respond. Cora and I found a spot

behind the Earthers, who reluctantly formed a line at gunpoint. I made sure she was in front of me.

Most of the Ringers followed me, and once Yavik decided he'd rather live a little bit longer, so did he. Only then did Desmond finally lower his shoulders, sidestep the rifle, and mope toward the door.

I exhaled. He was a pain in my ass, but I didn't want to see him die. I didn't want to see any of the crew die. Not even John, who took his rightful position as second in line behind the captain. "We're complying," Captain Saunders said, mustering his most authoritative tone. "Just tell us what's happening, and we'll continue to. Nobody has to get hurt."

"Judgment, for your benefactor," the attacker near the head of the line said.

"Where are you taking us?" John asked. He could barely squeak the words out.

None of the attackers answered. They signed something to one another and then spread out at equal intervals along the line, guns still raised. "Time to move," one of them ordered; it was impossible to tell which, maybe all. The unnatural voice seemed to be coming from all around me. "Move!"

They simultaneously cocked their rifles. Everyone did what they were told. I had to look down just to make sure I didn't trip over my feet as I started walking. After a few steps, I reached out without thinking about it and placed a quaking hand on Cora's hip. Maybe it was to reassure her, but it was probably more for my own sake.

"Hand," the nearest attacker warned. I pulled it away immediately. Cora shuddered. As I looked up, I couldn't help but stare at the orange circle on the attacker's chest. The same circle that had been there when I found Dexter dead. The same circle that had nearly given me a heart attack as I transported it through the heart of Pervenio Corp.

"Yup, I should've never taken a job on this ship," Desmond grumbled. He walked directly behind me. "Had a good thing going, running food down from the Uppers. Barely any *all-important* credits in it, though."

I shushed him.

"I'll be quiet when they put a bullet in my brain," he said.

"I'm sure they'd be happy to," I answered.

Before he could say anything else, the nearest attacker slammed me in the gut with the butt of a pulse-rifle. I'm sure it wasn't as hard as possible, since wearing a powered suit, he or she could have ruptured my organs, but it was enough to knock the wind out of me and drop me to a knee.

"Kale!" Cora yelped. She went to help me, but the attacker grabbed her and forced her back into place. I was lifted next.

"Move quietly," the attacker demanded and shoved me into line.

I guess there was a shred of decency in Desmond because that got him to shut up in a hurry. Cora glanced back at me over her shoulder, tears dripping down her flushed cheeks. I forced a crooked smile and continued to limp, now also hunched over from the throbbing pain in my stomach.

We were led to the compartment outside of the *Piccolo*'s starboard docking airlock. It was little more than a wide hallway. Benches ran down the sides with empty exo-suits hanging over them in case of exterior repairs. The airlock was at the far end, from which a shaft extended to mate with stations or ships that didn't have a hangar large enough to fit the entire vessel.

The half of the *Piccolo*'s crew that hadn't made it to the harvesting bay were already there, sitting on the benches under the guard of a fourth faceless attacker. Most of them were bruised and bloody. There was an order to it: The obvious

Ringers sat on one side and the Earthers on the other. All of them appeared too exhausted to be afraid anymore. I couldn't imagine what they'd gone through while we hid in the harvesting bay.

"Lester!" Desmond shouted. He was promptly grabbed and thrown back into line after an attempt to run to him. Lester was the nearest seated Ringer. He turned his head, his eyes groggy from a hangover and ringed by dark bruises. He looked like a man resigned to his fate.

The attackers stopped us and then signed to each other. *Test* was one of the words I thought I recognized. The attacker who led us seized the captain, and then the one who'd awaited us at the airlock withdrew a long, detachable needle attached to some form of scanning device.

"What the hell is that!" the captain yelled and tried to shake free. He was silenced by the barrel of a gun against his head. They restrained him and plunged the needle into his right arm just below the shoulder. He moaned until it was all the way in, down to the bone, and the scanner beeped. The captain was then placed on the Earther side of the hall, and a new, clean needle was screwed into the device. That settled where the attackers were from. Only Ringers would care about being hygienic during a raid.

It went on like that down the line. Some fought, most didn't risk it. The first bunch were all Earthers, then there were a few Ringers interspersed who'd followed the orders to get in line ahead of me. They were placed across the hall adjacent to Lester.

I was in the back half of the line, and by the time it was Cora's turn ahead of me, it was easy to figure out what they were scanning. They wanted to be sure of everyone's origin by going deep enough to get a bone density reading. Sometimes newer-generation Ringers could be hard to identify, or there were tall

Earthers whose families had spent too much time in their lives on asteroid mines. Other Ringers, like Yavik, for example, had brownish-gray skin even though they displayed all the other physical traits of Ringers. But bone density was the key. Even the oldest Earther offworlders had only endured the low gravity beyond Earth for a handful of generations. The frail skeleton of someone with lineage dating back to Trass's first settlers was impossible to replicate. Sanitary masks usually made it easy to tell without need for tests, but many of the *Piccolo*'s Ringer crew were missing theirs.

I reached up to my mouth, only then realizing I'd forgotten mine during all the chaos. As I did, the attackers pulled Cora forward. She shrieked a bit but managed to stay calm. My skin crawled as the needle sank into her arm. I tried but failed to catch a glimpse of the information that popped up on the scanner after it beeped. She wasn't sorted as easily as the others. Some signing was exchanged, and one of the words was *Earth*.

"She's one of us," I stepped forward and attested before I could second-guess myself. Seeing the rows arrayed before us, I realized that the Earther she'd be sitting next to if she was sent to that side was one of John's security team. If we were all going to die, I wasn't going to let her do it away from the people who accepted her.

A rifle was immediately pressed against my back. Cora mouthed the word "No" to me, her eyes bright with concern.

I swallowed hard and repeated myself. "She's one of us."

They grabbed my arm, and the long needle stabbed into it without warning. I winced. It felt like a sharp string of ice burrowing into me, and finally a stinging pressure on my bone that lasted for half a second. The needle slid out, along with a tiny smidge of blood, and when the scanner beeped, two of the attackers crowded around the results. They signed to each other. I didn't catch any of their words, but Cora was placed on the Ringer side, and me right beside her.

"I told you, you're one of us," I whispered to her.

I saw her lips twitch a bit, as if she wanted to smile but couldn't. It was enough for me. Our hands brushed, but I didn't dare hold hers while we were under watch. I'd already been defiant enough.

Desmond arrived beside me shortly after, and the rest of the scans went relatively smooth, minus all the cursing being thrown at the attackers. With everyone sorted, one of them slowly crossed the room and stopped in front of the docking shaft airlock's controls. He or she began typing into them.

"Well, here we are," Desmond said to me. "Nowhere to run now."

I hushed him, for what seemed like the thousandth time.

"What now?" Captain Saunders addressed the attackers. "We've done everything you've asked."

The inner seal of the airlock opened, and the attacker there turned to face us, Earthers and Ringers split on either side of the hall. The lines were drawn, with no shades of gray. The other three attackers arrayed themselves between the rows, rifles armed.

The attacker by the airlock gestured into the open chamber. "All Earthers get in, and you will be spared pain."

Every member of the *Piccolo*'s crew looked up, confused and petrified. The airlock led to only one place, and no human could survive out there no matter what race they were.

"Get in," the attacker repeated.

Being at gunpoint convinced some of the Earthers to listen, but Captain Saunders held out his arms to stop them. He used the shoulders of the men at his sides for support and lifted himself onto his chair until his face was level with the attacker in front of him.

"None of us are getting in there," he growled. "I think it's about time you all got the hell off my ship!"

Without hesitation, the attacker by the airlock aimed at the captain and shot him in the stomach, with a real bullet this time. A cloud of red sprayed onto John. The captain howled in pain and lunged for the attacker's rifle, but nobody else moved; we were too shocked. The attacker ducked out of the way, grabbed Captain Saunders by the collar, and hurled him down the hall. He went skidding to a halt right by my feet.

"Captain!" I hollered. I slid down from my seat and went to press my palm against his wound before realizing I had no gloves on. Cora pushed my arm away while I hesitated and did it herself. Blood bubbled in his mouth as he labored to breathe. An attacker lifted us away from him and forced us back into our seats.

"He made his choice," I was told by the attacker holding a gun in my face. "Make yours."

I remained as still as possible, but my entire body quivered. Cora struggled to stifle her tears, staring at the writhing captain, completely aghast.

"Don't do it," Desmond said to us, his voice cracking. "He isn't worth it."

"Get in," the attacker by the airlock ordered the Earthers once again. This time, he or she didn't wait for them to follow orders. Culver was the first one in line, and his untreated broken leg had left him barely conscious. The attacker hoisted him up and dumped him into the airlock.

One by one, the rest were forced in. Some fought, others couldn't manage to, but none of them could stop it.

"What is this?" John stammered when it was his turn to be placed. "Don't do this! I'll do anything!" He was grabbed by the neck and flung into the airlock, slamming against the outer seal.

"Don't do this!" He scrambled to his knees and toward the exit, but another Earther was promptly thrust into him.

"Kale... what's happening?" Cora asked.

She wasn't stupid, so I knew that she had to know the answer. She just couldn't comprehend it. I didn't want to either. I wanted to hope that these faceless Ringers were just trying to show that they were serious, but only Earthers filled the airlock. I didn't know what to say. Even Desmond, who'd no doubt heard her, remained silent. I kept hoping that I was going to wake up in Cora's bed after a bad dream. That this was my nerves getting the better of me following the fear I'd felt while saving my mom in the command deck.

The last Earther was forced in, and then the inner seal of the airlock shut with a hiss. A circular viewport in the center allowed me to see the terrified Earthers within. The chamber was so small they were piled on top of one another.

The attackers lowered their weapons, as if they were confident that none of us Ringer members of the crew would do anything rash. Apparently, they were right. It was like I was back in the Q-Zone across from my mother—totally helpless. I heard the captain coughing but couldn't tear my gaze from the airlock to look down at him. Suppressed sobs emanated from either side of me. More of my own tears gathered in the corner of my eyes.

"Stop this," the captain gurgled.

The attacker in front of me ignored him and withdrew a familiar-looking hand-terminal. The one I'd placed in the command deck. Mine. He or she set the device to record and aimed it at the attacker standing by the airlock. I hadn't noticed it on the way in, but a wire stretched away from it, across the floor, and toward the command deck. The other attackers positioned themselves so that they weren't obstructing the view. A bit of signing was exchanged, and then the attacker by the airlock counted down from ten on his or her armored fingers.

The Earthers trapped inside the airlock grew even more hysterical. Their voices were muted by the seal as they pounded on the viewport. I'd served beside many of them for months, if not years. John's face was in the center, and as much as I despised him, seeing him so scared... I couldn't bear to watch.

"You must watch," an attacker said to me, a hand turning my cheek. I couldn't fight its augmented strength, and as I was compelled to look back toward the airlock, I felt Cora's fingers threading through mine. They were ice-cold, trembling, and covered in the captain's blood. At that moment, disease was the last thing either of us was worried about. We needed each other. She squeezed, and I squeezed back. A day ago, I would've been thrilled by her attention; now I wished she were nowhere near me, nowhere near this nightmare.

"Please, don't do this," I whispered through quaking lips.

The attacker leaned over until his or her visor was only centimeters away from my face. "Take solace in knowing that they will not suffer, Kale Drayton."

Everyone else was too focused on what was happening to hear the words. Like R, the attacker knew my name. My throat went dry. My heart had been racing more often than not ever since the message came through, but at that moment, it felt like it'd completely stopped. I could no longer deny that what was happening was connected to me.

"We are descendants of those chosen by Trass—Titanborn," the distorted voice of the attacker by the airlock addressed the recording hand-terminal after the countdown finished. "We tire of being owned; of rotting in your Q-Zones as you suck our home dry. Retribution is coming. This is what happens to those who steal from our Ring." The attacker placed his or her hand over the airlock controls. "From ice to ashes."

I wanted to scream for them to stop, but nothing came out. The attacker keyed a command on the controls and sentenced every Earther to death without even a second's hesitation. The outer seal of the airlock blew open, and the winds of Saturn silently whipped in to heave them all out.

THIRTEEN

In seconds, the faces of the Earther members of the crew were gone, and I was left gawking at the *Piccolo*'s empty airlock. The muffled whistling of the wind beyond the seal was all I could hear. The breathing of every Ringer around me seemed to have ceased.

And then, a hand fell on my arm. I was looking past Cora, so I knew it wasn't her, and the grip was too strong to be Desmond's. Before I knew it, an attacker heaved off my seat and slung me over his or her armored shoulders.

"What are you doing?" I yelled, though I was in such deep shock, it was closer to a yelp.

"Put him down!" Cora shouted once she realized what was happening. She clutched my hand and pulled. The attacker who'd grabbed me pushed her away with ease.

"He's coming with us," he or she said.

"Put him down!" Cora repeated. She sprang forward, and this time, the attacker holding me seized her by the throat.

"Let her go!" I hollered. I swung my arms and kicked my feet, but each blow slammed futilely against armor as unbreakable as stone. It was like an infant throwing a tantrum because it needed to be fed. Helpless, yet again. "Don't hurt her!"

"You pieces of shit!" Desmond growled. He pushed off the wall and dived forward, slamming into the thighs of the attacker holding me. Armored or not, he or she staggered from the force of Desmond's blow. I dropped to the floor, and if my body was sore before, it was even more so after plummeting a few meters onto my back in Earth g.

Cora fell free as well, landing on her feet and hurrying over to me. "Kale," she gasped, her voice hoarse from being choked.

Another of the attackers charged us and smashed Desmond in the face with the butt of his or her rifle before he could do any more damage. Blood squirted out as Desmond's nose cracked audibly, and he toppled on top of Cora and me.

Disoriented, I groped to try to find which arms belonged to Cora. I turned my head and saw Captain Saunders right in front of me, eyes closed. The corner of my mouth was submerged in a pool of his blood, and without my sanitary mask on, the metallic-tasting liquid seeped into the cracks in my chapped lips. I gagged.

"You idiot!" an attacker barked. "He isn't to be harmed."

A strong hand reached into the mess of tangled, blood-soaked limbs I was trapped beneath and dragged me along the floor. Cora grabbed my ankle.

"Let him go!" she screamed. She was torn off me and pulled along the bloody floor in the other direction. Again, I was lifted over an attacker's shoulder, too sickened and in pain to even attempt to squirm free.

I caught a glimpse behind me as the upper half of my limp body swung. Desmond covered his nose and writhed in pain next to our unconscious or dead captain. Almost every Ringer capable of moving had risen to their feet to stand beside Cora, with Yavik and Lester at the front, hardly able to stay upright.

The mix of terror and rage on their faces was unlike anything I'd ever seen before. I was no Earther; friend or not, I was one of their own. They were done watching.

Three attackers stood across from them, aiming their rifles.

"Don't..." I groaned.

"You said nobody would be harmed," Cora whimpered. Her clenched, red-stained fists shook.

"He won't be," the attacker holding me said. "Neither will any of you if you stand down."

"Listen to them," I said. "Please... Cora."

She stared into my eyes, and I could barely recognize her underneath her blood-drenched face and hair.

"Please," I said. "Don't."

The attackers slowly backed away, keeping their rifles aimed. I twisted my head around as I was carried, and didn't let my gaze leave Cora's, begging her with my expression to stay put. I didn't know what was going to happen to them, but it was a better option than them being mowed down with no other witness but me.

"Take the captain," an attacker ordered. Another stepped forward to grab Captain Saunders's wounded body and sling it over his or her shoulder.

"I'll kill you!" Desmond roared. He crawled at the attacker but couldn't get far on the slick floor. His face was so red he looked like a creature out of a nightmare.

Yavik and Lester hurried to help him to his feet, but the guns kept them at bay. The attackers continued to retreat, and once we were around the corner, they started to jog. My ribs dug into a plated shoulder as I bounced up and down repeatedly.

Eventually, they placed me down gently. I found it difficult to focus, but I recognized the sealed entrance of the command deck beside me. The attackers were having a discussion in sign language. One removed his helmet. He was a Ringer man, with graying hair and weary features.

"Where are you taking me?" I moaned.

"Fear not, Kale Drayton," the unmasked man said. He removed his armor with the help of the others. Beneath it, he wore a white boiler suit, similarly marked with an orange ring on the torso.

"Please, don't hurt them."

The man kneeled and placed a hand on my shoulder. His fingers were surprisingly weak without his powered armor on, just like those of any normal Ringer. "By the time the *Piccolo* reaches Pervenio Station, we will all be heroes. Soon, you will be too."

Before I could answer, the other attackers lifted me. One wiped Captain Saunders's blood off my mouth with a clean rag while another extended my arm. I noticed the same device they had been using to analyze our bone density earlier, only this time, a syringe was attached to the end. I flinched.

"Relax," a distorted voice said. "It's antibiotics, and Trass knows what else. The last of what we've got."

The icy metal needle pricked a vein on my neck and injected me with the medicinal concoction. Once the syringe was emptied of every last drop, they emptied my pockets, which carried nothing but an ID card and some garbage, and forced me into the discarded armor of the unmarked attacker, like I was their plaything. I didn't have the energy to resist.

My legs and arms fit in snugly, as if it had been designed with me specifically in mind. Short pins stuck into my back and chest on the inside. After their initial pinch, my lungs and heart suddenly felt at ease, as if I were back on Titan. The helmet went on last. I could still see and hear through it, but the sounds of the world around me were softer now.

"You will never be forgotten, Joran," one of the faceless

attackers said to the unmasked man.

The distortion was gone, revealing the voice of a woman.

"Only not by you," the man she called Joran said. His tone was gentle, almost tranquil in nature.

"You might need this." The female attacker handed him back his pulse-rifle. He hesitated for a second before nodding and taking it. "For Titan, my brothers and sister."

"For Titan."

An arm wrapped around my newly armored body and guided me in front of the sealed entrance to the command deck. Another attacker picked up a weathered respirator mask lying beside the door and placed it over the captain's mouth. He or she also hugged his body with a shiny, ruffled blanket. Joran then raised the hand-terminal I'd smuggled aboard and keyed some commands.

"Hold on to something," the female attacker said to him, "and place the fear of Trass into their hearts."

I had to turn my entire torso to look behind me while wearing the armor. Joran fought back tears, watching us longingly. His fingers hovered over a key on the hand-terminal. Over his shoulder, I spotted Cora standing at the other end of the hallway. Her hair was strung across her tear-and-blood-stained face. I couldn't manage words, so I reached toward her with the aid of the powered armor wrapping my arm. I wanted to stroke her soft cheek one last time and tell her to survive.

"From ice to ashes!" Joran bellowed. He tapped the hand-terminal, signaling the command deck's entrance to open. My body was swiftly tugged through by a powerful change in pressure. In the seconds before it caused me to faint, I saw that the transparent dome of the command deck was splayed open and exposed to Saturn. The dark mass of another vessel loomed above, with me, the armored attackers, and Captain Saunders's body being pulled toward it by Saturn's unrelenting wind.

FOURTEEN

My eyelids blinked open. My gaze darted from side to side. Cold air brushed against my cheeks, colder than it ever was even in the Darien Lowers. I could see my breath escaping the now-open visor of the armor the *Piccolo*'s attackers had forced me into.

I sat upright on a bed that looked like it'd endured at least a dozen wars. The room surrounding me bore a similar character. The amount of corrosion on the walls made the Ringer dorms on the *Piccolo* seem brand-new. Clusters of pipes were bent or broken. Panels of the grated floor were flat-out missing. The air recyclers ticked as if someone were sitting in the ducts bashing them with a wrench.

I turned my body to see if anybody was behind me. The powered armor didn't dull the unrelenting soreness irritating every part of my body, but it allowed me to operate my limbs with minimal effort. There was, however, a new pain affecting me: my eyes felt like they were being tugged on from inside my skull, and the result was a pounding headache.

"He's awake," someone said. "Finally. A mouthful of Earther blood—that's a new one. You're lucky he's still clean."

"He's stronger than he looks," answered somebody else.

"Who is that?" I yelled nervously. My gaze snapped toward the room's entrance, but it was sealed. Nobody was around me, and it took a few seconds to realize that the voices had emanated from a view-screen built into the wall above my bed.

At first, the only thing on the display was the fuzzy image of an empty chair. Then the lower part of an attacker's white armor passed by, and a chill ran up my spine. I scrambled backward on the bed as far as I could go, until I could feel the room's corroded wall wilting under the strength of my suit. That was when I noticed a slight but unceasing vibration all around me—the familiar reverberation of nuclear-thermal engines powering a ship through Saturn—and remembered what had happened before I passed out.

"W... what's going on?" I stammered.

An attacker silently sat in the chair, visor raised like mine. The grainy image and general murkiness of the room on the view-screen made the face difficult to perceive, but I saw nothing out of a nightmare, no demon with flaming red eyes. Only a female Ringer, same as any other. Or at least that was what I thought until she leaned forward into a field of light bright enough for me to regard her in detail.

She had stark black hair, trimmed short around her ears in a way that framed her pale features. Her hazel eyes spoke of two lifetimes' worth of experiences, even though she didn't appear to be older than forty. She might once have been beautiful, however, the left half of her face was mottled by a patchwork of gruesome scars, from her jaw all the way up to her hairline, like an explosion had gone off right next to her and she'd somehow survived. A portion of her left cheek was missing entirely, revealing the muscle and sinew beneath, along with a few of her yellowed teeth.

I was wrong. Demon she wasn't, but she could've easily

been the invention of a nightmare. "Relax, Kale. You are safe now," she said. "Healthy, no thanks to my crew." Her voice was so gravelly it would've been easy to mistake her for a man, and the way her open wound stretched and contracted as she spoke made it even harder to look at.

"How do you know my name?" I questioned.

"We see all of Titan. You are Kale, son of Katrina and Alann, born in Darien, Titan, in 2315 and a resident of Level B2 of the Darien Lowers. With your mother struggling to support both of you, you turned to thieving to make life a little more manageable."

My hand slipped off the surface of the bed. I sank backward. "Mom..." I whispered. Memories of the last time I saw her aggravated my thoughts and made my head pound even worse.

"The first crime your mother found out about was when you ran salts at the age of ten for a vile Ringer named Dexter Howser," the woman continued. "At the age of sixteen, you were arrested for breaking into the residence of your mother's former employer and were forced to a life of honest work aboard the *Piccolo*. Now, we are here. Shall I continue?"

"Whe—" I wheezed. My throat was raw, and I needed to gather my breath to speak coherently. "Where is here?"

The woman spread her arms offscreen in an exaggerated motion, as if we'd just stepped inside the awe-inspiring ruins of some ancient palace. "Welcome to the gas harvester formerly known as the *Sunfire*."

Hearing the name of the ship made my eyes go wide for a few seconds before the unusual stress being inflicted upon them made me blink.

"The name is familiar?" she asked.

I nodded as best I could. There wasn't much room for my head to move inside of my helmet.

"Yes, who could forget the tragic story of the *Sunfire*, even after all these years?" she said, seeming amused. "The engine malfunction that caused a harvester to be consumed by Saturn. At least that's what Pervenio Corp assumed happened when we disappeared and were never heard from again. They never considered that, perhaps, we didn't want to be found."

I propped myself up to try to get a better look at her. As far as I could tell, she was as much a stranger as the bed I sat on. There was no way I could've ever forgotten those scars, even if we'd run together in the Lowers only once. Squinting at her didn't help my sore eyes at all, and the pain grew so intense that I groaned and had to squeeze them shut.

"We're deeper into the atmosphere of Saturn than any person born on Titan ought to be," she said. "The suit will ensure that your body remains upright, and your lungs don't collapse, but it can't help with everything." She pointed toward the counter beside my bed where a g-stim rested that I only then noticed. The emblem of Venta Co—a series of three overlaid Vs —was imprinted on the pack. "In time, your eyes and head will grow more accustomed to the stress. That will help."

I stared at the stim but didn't budge.

"It's just a g-stim," she insisted. "More potent than the ones your captain provided. Like how we made them to be all those many decades ago."

I remained still, and eventually, she sighed. "If I wanted you dead, you wouldn't be here, so you might as well get comfortable."

I turned squarely toward the screen and growled, "Tell that to the people you murdered!" Shouting exacerbated the pain behind my eyes and forced me to lower my voice. "Why did you do it?"

"Justice." She grinned, the deformed side of her face crinkling to give it a ghoulish quality.

"For what? Who are you?"

"I am Titanborn, just like you and the portion of your crew that was permitted to live."

"That isn't a name."

"It's been a long time since my name was relevant. Officially, I am dead, but you may call me Rin."

My nervousness was ousted by a long-suppressed rage festering in my gut. Her name had to mean only one thing. "It's you, isn't it? R?" I asked.

Again, she grinned, even more impishly this time.

I sprang to my knees and clutched the view-screen's paper-thin frame. "My mom," I said. "You promised you'd help her. Is she all right? Tell me!"

"You fulfilled your end of the bargain. Your beloved mother is on the road to recovery. She'll never see the inside of a Q-Zone again."

"Let me talk to her."

"Communication with Titan is impossible where we are. My word will have to do for now."

"You're lying!"

"You've done well, Kale," she said calmly. "Take the stim. When you can think clearly, we will talk."

The feed cut out and the screen went dark. "Show me her!" I screamed. I didn't care how much it hurt my head. I punched the wall, my suit-powered fist denting the wall so deep it almost split open. "What the hell am I doing here?"

The exertion caused the discomfort behind my eyes to flare up worse than ever. I lost my balance and fell backward off the mattress. It felt like someone was dragging the dull edge of a rusty knife in a circle around the inside of my skull. A bullet to the head would've been a mercy, though one my captors seemed incapable of.

"What do you want with me?" I panted. Nobody answered.

I reached through my open visor and pushed on my temples

to try to drive the throbbing pain out. It didn't help much, but it focused me enough to be able to twist my body to face the g-stim. Without the suit they'd shoved me into, I probably wouldn't have even been able to move. The pill appeared harmless, like the ones we took for shifts on the *Piccolo,* only with Venta Co as the manufacturer. Rin, R, whoever she was, was the only person who could answer the countless questions swarming around my weary brain, the least of which was where the fuck we were. I'd held up my end of the deal. I needed to know for sure that my mom was okay.

I reached out and snatched the g-stim. My powered fingers caused the pack to compress slightly. I'd have to get used to my newfound strength. I stared at it for a few seconds until my eyes were too strained to focus.

Rin was right about one thing: if they wanted to kill me, they'd have done it already. If they wanted slaves, they would've taken every member of the *Piccolo*'s crew. Instead, they'd murdered half of us and did Trass knows what with the rest. Cora, Desmond, and the other Ringers were all alive when I left. Rin knew where.

I jabbed the pack into my neck and pushed down to cue the injection. I got to my feet slowly and fought an oppressive sense of vertigo all the way to the door. It slid open for me automatically, as if I was never locked in.

If I wasn't a prisoner, what was I?

No one greeted me when I exited the room into an area that passed for dorms. Nobody was in sight. The only sound was the rhythmic ticking of the faulty air recyclers and the constant clacking of every part of the ship that wasn't battened down, as if angry spirits hid within the walls, shaking the pipes. My suit helped me maintain balance, but I had to walk only a few steps before I realized that without it I'd be rocked side to side after every step by winds more severe than what the *Piccolo* had ever endured.

The *Sunfire*—if that was really where I was—had a layout like the *Piccolo*'s. It made sense, considering they would've been manufactured around the same year, based on the reports about the crash. I spotted remnants of Pervenio logos all over the walls, though the ones that weren't entirely tarnished appeared to have been aggressively scratched away.

I passed a door with char-marks surrounding the frame. A heap of spare parts and scraps blockaded it, with no way through without a wrecking ball. Then I reached the ship's central corridor, where my path split. To my right, toward the engines, it was dark as a Titanian night. To my left, the lighting was barely functional, the fixtures seeming like they'd been through numerous rounds of makeshift repairs. Down a way, in that direction, the command deck's entrance remained wide open, glowing like a beacon.

I headed toward it. I didn't feel afraid, though I'd spent so long being in a state of alarm that I wasn't sure if I still remembered what normal anxiety felt like. I did know that my head was starting to feel clearer and that my every stride was being fueled by anger.

Once I was only a few meters outside, I spotted the attackers of the *Piccolo*. They weren't carrying guns or wearing dark visors. They weren't signing or distorting their voices as they plotted their next sinister move. The three of them lounged around a command deck, not unlike the *Piccolo*'s, chatting like nothing was wrong. Rin sat on one side, chomping on the last bits of a ration bar. She had to use the right side of her mouth so crumbs didn't spill through the gap in her left cheek.

Another attacker sat at the navigation console. That too was reminiscent of the *Piccolo*'s, though like the rest of the ship, it had clearly borne more than its fair share of crude repairs. The middle-aged navigator's face wasn't disfigured like Rin's, but he had a densely bearded chin.

Knotted black hair fell to his shoulders, and it was obvious it hadn't been properly washed in a long, long time. A blithe smirk crossed his face as he noticed me approaching.

To his right sat both the grimmest and oldest of the trio. His lips drew a straight line, accentuated by his long jaw. He had to be pushing fifty and had already lost every strand of his hair. Wrinkles creased his soaring forehead, so deep that they seemed to belong on an Earther's face. In fact, I realized that all three of them were wrinkled more thoroughly than most Ringers of their ages, the result of being stuck in g conditions pushing Earth's for a long time, I guessed. But how long? The *Sunfire*'s supposed crash had occurred three years earlier.

"There he is!" the navigator exclaimed once I entered the room. "Thought you'd never wake up after the scare we gave you, kid."

Something about his comment pushed me over the edge. Perhaps it was the way he said it, like the universe was one big punch line. Perhaps it was seeing them all relaxing like *their* worlds hadn't changed. More likely, it was a combination of everything.

I charged at him, hand reared back to crack him across the jaw, but I was clumsy in my new suit, and he easily evaded the blow. Rin and the grim Ringer grabbed hold of me just before my fist crashed through the navigation console. The three of us stumbled backward, with only me falling onto my ass, while they held my torso upright.

"Whoa, now!" The navigator chuckled. He snapped right back into his lounging position and carefree expression. "Someone angry?"

Curses shot out of my mouth so fast, I'm not even sure what

I said. I lunged at him from my knees, but Rin didn't allow me to get far.

"Shut it, Hayes!" she snapped. In person, her voice sounded even stranger, with the hole in her face clearly affecting her speech. I could hear the soft, watery clicking of her tongue against her gums after every hard consonant. "Or do I have to remind you of your first day after the captain went?"

Hayes scowled, shook his head, and crossed his arms.

"Thought so," Rin said. "Now go get Kale something to eat."

"Rini," he protested.

Rin's glare bored through him. It made the grimace Captain Saunders wore when he was irritated seem like a smile. "That's an order."

Hayes hopped to his feet and performed an embellished bow. "My lady," he said before sauntering around us.

"You'll have to excuse Hayes," Rin said. "So many years away from home have corroded his manners, if he ever had them."

"All the years around you, beautiful!" he shouted back, his voice echoing through the vacant corridor outside.

"Years?" I asked.

"I'm sure you have questions," Rin said. "As long as you promise not to break apart the command deck if we let you go, I'll answer whatever I can."

"You won't space me?"

"Not if I can help it."

I nodded, then realized my head was covered by a bulbous helmet and she was at my side. I bowed my entire torso forward instead.

They heaved me to my feet and set me into one of the chairs wrapping the command deck. Rin sat across from me in the one Hayes had vacated. Like her voice, her face was somewhat different than it'd been through the video feed. There was a warmth to her eyes, the kind someone bears when they see a friend or loved one after a long absence. It caught me so off guard that my desire to grab her by the throat and demand the truth was stunted.

"By Trass, you've grown," she said. "You look just like him."

"What are you talking about?" I asked.

"You really don't remember? I guess your mother did all she could to get rid of us."

My mind started racing, wondering how long Rin had been watching me, trying to think of all the times I might've felt someone lingering in the shadows to my side. I was at a loss for words. I studied her now that my eyes were feeling better and tried to picture her without the scars mutilating half of her face.

And that was when I remembered...

I was barely four years old, tall for my age, even for a Ringer. My head reached my mother's chest. I stood beside her, gazing up at her inquisitively. Tears filled her eyes, accompanying a look of conviction on her face that as a child I mistook to be purely sorrow.

Few areas of the Darien Uppers existed that were as dark as the world below, where we came from. We were in one of them. A morgue, a funeral home—it was a little bit of both. It was the Darien Hall of Ashes—where Ringers went to say goodbye to their loved ones. It was essentially a long, low hallway lined in stark panels, with a series of glass-topped tubes poking out along the exterior side.

Earthers traditionally buried their fallen in caskets beneath the ground, whether it was on their homeworld, or Mars, or some asteroid somewhere. My people released the ashes of their burned dead into the winds of Titan. We'd done it that way since the days of Trass's first settlers.

My mother held a transparent, spherical container filled with what looked like dust. I was too young to understand that it was all that remained of my father.

"Kale, come here," she said to me.

I shuffled forward. Six extraction tubes lined the wall, and a few other families were clustered beside them. I knew from watching them that I was supposed to be sad. They sobbed as they passed around their crystalline spheres and whispered to them.

"Here." She handed me the container. It was as light as a helium balloon and slightly pliable.

"I thought you said he'd be here," I said.

She kneeled and looked me straight in the eyes. A sanitary mask covered half of her face, but she was still young, with not a strand of gray in her hair. "He's in there now, Kale. I know it's hard for you to understand, but he's gone."

"Does that mean... he's dead?"

She nodded solemnly. "Yes. He's going to be a part of Titan now, and it's your job to get him there." She opened the lid of the tube and gestured to the vessel in my hands.

I rotated the sphere, watching ashes tumble. My eyes were pressed up against it, wondering how they were any different from the dust that gathered daily in the hollows of the Lowers.

"So I won't see him anymore?" I asked.

"No, Kale, not anymore. But he'll always be looking after you. I know he wished..." She paused, having to gather her breath and wipe her eyes before she could continue. "I know he wished he could've seen you one last time, but he...he couldn't."

"But he said he would be there for my birthday!" I protested. "He promised!"

"Well, he won't!" she snapped.

I doubt it was her intention to make me cry, but I did anyway. She wrapped her arms around my head and drew me close, kissing me on the forehead until it was raw.

"He's gone, sweetheart, okay?" she whispered. Her lips were trembling. "I know it's hard, but we just have to say goodbye."

"I don't want to," I sniveled.

"Some things are out of our hands." She took the sphere from me and raised it toward the ceiling. Then she closed her eyes and took a deep breath. "We surrender this soul unto the winds of Titan. May he forever watch over those chosen by Trass."

She lowered the sphere into the tube. It slid in perfectly without falling all the way through. "From ice to ashes," she said. Then she struck a command on a nearby control panel, and the sphere was sucked through the dense Darien enclosure toward a tiny pinpoint of light. I didn't know how the process worked at the time, but it would emerge into the sky and rise through the thick atmosphere of Titan. Once it reached a high enough altitude, the change in pressure would cause it to pop like a balloon, sprinkling the ashes into the clouds.

My mom stepped back, her hands still trembling out in front of her as if she'd just accomplished some incredible feat. Her thousand-meter stare was aimed at the tube.

"Where did it go?" I asked.

"Into the sky," she said. She leaned over and clasped her hands over mine. "Your father loved you, Kale. He may not have known how to show it well, but he did. He wanted you to promise something after he was gone. It's very important."

I nodded hesitantly.

"Remember him always, but never be like him," she said. "Ever. Do you understand?"

I searched the room, unsure of what to say. My father and I weren't very close, though that was only because I didn't see him much before he was gone. My mom said it was because he worked late into the nights thieving and conning—doing whatever it took to scrape by in the Lowers. On the rare occasions he'd visit us in our hollow, I'd get so excited that I couldn't turn off my smile.

My mother always sat in the corner, observing quietly as he performed magic tricks with ration bars for me or as we watched the newsfeeds on our tiny view-screen. After a few hours, he'd be gone, and then it'd be weeks, sometimes months before I saw him again... until the day she told me he was shot while trying to rob a wealthy Earther.

"Okay, Kale?" my mother repeated, grabbing me by the jaw to regain my attention.

"O...okay," I stuttered.

"Good. You're being so strong, Kale." She smiled through her tears and planted a kiss on my cheek. "Now, my boss let me have some lettuce from the gardens to take home tonight. How does that sound? I think we could both use it."

My eyes lit up. "Real lettuce?"

"Yup. The real thing."

I bobbed my head enthusiastically, and she gave me one last kiss before we started off. I can't recall whether either of us looked back toward the tube my dad's remnants were slurped through, but when we reached the exit, a woman stood in our way. Rin, minus the burns.

She was strange to me even as a child. The skin on her youthful face was smooth and unmarred, but her eyes brimmed with ire.

"This isn't right, Kat!" Rin said, taking no effort to mask her resentment. "Kale is his son too."

"I didn't make this decision alone," my mom answered.

"Like Alann would've said no to you?"

My mom grabbed Rin by the collar. "I won't risk him being discovered," she whispered sternly.

"You'll toss him aside just like that, then? You learned well from that Earther master of yours, didn't you?"

My mom slapped Rin across the face so hard that the skin on her pale cheek went red on the side where one day it would no longer exist. Rin didn't back away.

"I'll always love your brother, but I have to do what's best for our boy," my mom said. "It's no life for him."

"And what about what he wants?"

"The decision's been made, so honor it and stay away from my son!" She grabbed my hand and pulled. "Let's go, Kale."

"You're a coward, Kat!" Rin hollered. "Always will be!"

My mother ignored her and tugged me even harder, but I stared back at the woman, at Rin, who watched us with revulsion until we'd vanished into the crowds of Darien.

Their exchange meant little to me as a child. I'd barely understood what I was doing in the Hall of Ashes. But now, as I stared at Rin's disfigured face, I didn't need her to say it for me to realize what she was.

"You're..." I began.

"Your aunt," she finished for me. "Your mother told you your father died trying to rob an Earther when you were four." She scratched a patch of shiny burn scars on her upper cheek before her piercing gaze shifted to look straight at my face. "She lied. You are more than you know, Kale Drayton."

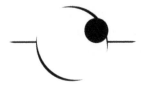

FIFTEEN

"My dad's alive?" I asked, hardly able to believe the words escaping my mouth.

The half of Rin's lips that weren't deformed drooped into a frown. "He was... until roughly two months ago on Earth, when he gave his life distracting a collector on M-day so we might have a chance at more than just surviving."

The momentary high I felt over learning about a fifteen-year-old miracle swiftly faded. My heart sank. "But I saw his ashes go to the sky and... and so did you. You were there."

"All a lie concocted by him and that mother of yours to keep you safe," she said. "There's a lot you don't know, Kale."

I hopped to my feet and pointed at her chest. "And I'm supposed to believe you? I watched you murder all those people on the *Piccolo*."

The grim, silent Ringer sitting beside us rose to his feet as well. He looked like he might have ripped me apart if Rin didn't hold her arm out in front of him.

"'Murder,'" she scoffed. "There isn't a single Earther out there who wouldn't put a bullet in your head if it meant them surviving or stuffing their wallet. The truth is that your father was a hero, and he believed in Titan. Like your mom, he didn't want his life for you, but now he's gone. I'll be damned if I let you become another cog on a gas harvester. Working for *them.* Handing the Ring over to *them,* one day at a time. Believe me or don't, but it's time you knew exactly who you are."

After spending a few seconds in disbelief, I leaned back in my chair. The grim Ringer did so as well. I had no idea what to say and was grateful when Hayes reappeared behind me, allowing me some time to compose myself. He dropped a ration bar onto my lap.

"Here you go, your highness," he said, his voice dripping with sarcasm.

"Thank you, Hayes," Rin said. She stood. "You can have the controls back. I'd like to speak with Kale alone."

Hayes shimmied around us effortlessly to return to the ship's navigation console, remarkably nimble for someone clad in a bulky suit of powered armor. He stopped in front of Rin and took her by the shoulders. "Go easy on him," he said, smirking.

Rin let him by without comment, but to me, she said, "Walk with me. Your muscles can use the exercise." She nodded in the direction of the quiet Ringer. He grunted in response. Given the option of staying with him and Hayes versus going off with a woman I at least had a vague memory of, I chose the latter.

"He doesn't talk much, does he?" I asked after I caught up with her.

"Gareth?" she said. "No. Our former captain made sure of that when he sliced out his tongue. Used to be impossible to shut him up before that."

"Oh..." I instinctually rubbed my tongue against the back of my teeth to remind myself it was still there.

"I know all of this is a lot to hear, Kale. It wasn't fair of them to keep you in the dark."

I stopped. "'A lot to hear?' You want me to believe that my mom was lying for all of these years; that my dad, your brother, was running around Sol for my entire life and never once tried to contact me?"

"Oh, he wanted to. And if Katrina weren't so damn stubborn, he might've."

"Stop talking about her like that!"

"Sorry... old habits." She placed her hand on the back of my armor and urged me forward. "He stayed away like he was supposed to, but that doesn't mean he forgot. Your dad was no paltry thief, Kale. You think you survived getting out of that life because you're lucky? He was watching, every step of the way. Nobody in the Lowers would dare hurt you with him around."

"Are you saying he was a fence?"

"You really have no idea?"

"Why don't you just tell me whatever it is you want to tell me."

"Soon. First, let me show you that your pretty mother is safe and sound, and then you might start trusting me a little. There's no point in wasting my breath."

"That's a good start."

She led me back toward the room I'd arrived in. We turned before reaching it into what I assumed had been one of the *Sunfire*'s rec rooms. There was a couch, its fabric covering almost entirely frayed down to the metal frame, a view-screen, and nothing else but empty space.

"Like I said earlier, there is no way for us to contact anybody on Titan from this deep in Saturn, but Rylah was able to send an update before the plunge. She figured you might not be big on talking until you could see your mother."

I choked back a moan of frustration. "Who is that now?"

"You found that hand-terminal in her office. My half-sister."

I recalled the stunning woman in violet back in the

Foundry. I should've known better than to think she'd left her door wide open by accident, considering what she had hiding inside. What kind of thief was I, being played so obviously?

"Of course she is," I groused. "Any more lost family members I should know about?"

"No relation to you, actually. She got the looks and the brain, we got the bloodline. Lucky for her. Amazing what she did with the hand-terminal, though, isn't it? I forgot to ask if you had any trouble getting it through security."

"None," I said. "My mom?"

"Right."

Rin switched on the view-screen and shuffled through a few recordings before selecting one. The time stamp was from a few hours earlier, and I fell to my knees in front of the screen when I saw what was on it. The feed was so rife with static that hearing anything was impossible, but my mother sat upright on a medical table, in a cavern that looked nothing like her Q-Zone room.

"We had her extracted the moment you left Titan," Rin said. "She's in the capable hands of our own doctor, receiving treatment."

I assumed she had to be talking about the woman standing in front of my mom, inspecting her eyes and throat with a flash-light. She faced the other direction, so I was able to see only the curls of her red hair, but she was shorter than your average Ringer.

I slid across the floor on my knees until the screen was an arm's length away. The recording wasn't long, only a handful of seconds of my mom undergoing inspections, but there was no question that she looked healthier already. An IV was still plugged into her arm, but her rashes were healing and her eyes bustled with renewed vigor. My fingers ran across the screen.

"She had something called strep," Rin said. "She's going to

be fine now, thanks to you. We'll make arrangements for a new identity so that she can avoid any trouble."

The sight brought a smile to my lips that I was grateful my helmet kept Rin from seeing. "Will I ever be able to see her again?"

"Returning to Titan will be difficult for some time. We have more important issues to deal with."

"'More important?'" I whipped around, my cheeks hot with anger. "She's supposedly your sister-in-law, for Trass's sake! You should've helped her the moment they stuck her in there!"

"I did. Arrangements had to be made. With Alann—your father—gone, I had to make sure you weren't harmed. And unfortunately, you went right back to that ingrate Dexter Howser. Who knows what he was planning on doing with you. We had to intervene."

"I can handle myself. You didn't have to bring me here or make me watch you kill those people!"

"I had no choice!" Rin said, raising her voice for the first time. Her jaw stretched so far I could see an entire row of teeth through her wound. It shut me right up. "Don't you understand? You're not just some kid from Darien. You're not the worthless son of a thief and some Earther's slave-bitch. You're the blood of Trass!" She pounded her chest plate. "We didn't die off after the Great Reunion, Kale. We hid. Your father, you, me—we're his descendants. The last of his line."

My mouth froze. I had to sit on the couch, or I would've fallen, suit and all. It was the most ridiculous claim I'd ever heard. Rin panted, and before either of us could do anything else, Hayes burst into the room. Gareth leaned against the wall by the door.

"Rin, it's happening," Hayes said excitedly.

"Don't you have a ship to pilot?" Rin bristled.

He waved his hand dismissively. "It's on auto. I bounced our reception off a luxury cruiser passing above us to capture this off the Ring-wide newsfeeds. Look at this."

He switched the view-screen over to the feed. It was grainy but clear enough to understand what we were looking at. The ticker at the bottom read URGENT: ATTACK ON THE *PICCOLO,* and the reporter in front of the camera stood in a hangar on Pervenio Station. Her voice went in and out. Not that I could focus anyway, considering the news about my father. The only thing I heard was that Director Sodervall was going to be addressing the Ring in a matter of hours.

In the background sat the *Piccolo,* its aft torn asunder. Pervenio security officers surrounded it, and one by one, members of the Ringer crew were escorted off the ship. They weren't being treated like victims. I saw Yavik, Lester, and Desmond, nose still bleeding, amongst all the others. Sweat poured down their faces. Some of them needed help walking. The one person I didn't spot was Cora. That fact finally earned my full attention.

The reporter said, "Early reports say that one of the same Ringers responsible for the horrific video being circulated throughout Solnet attempted to accelerate the *Piccolo,* a gas harvester loaded with flammable gases, into Pervenio Station. While there is no word on who exactly he was, two heroic Pervenio Collectors thwarted the attack and were able to detain the surviving members of the crew."

"You said they wouldn't be harmed," I said.

"Relax, lover boy." Hayes playfully thrust his hand past my face. "Deception. Joran was going to stop before anything happened. We merely wanted to show them that they aren't safe, even in their station."

"Quiet, Hayes," Rin ordered.

He leaned in next to the side of my helmet. "They'll think that all this was our endgame," he whispered, "and bring that hand-terminal of yours right into their security headquarters to be analyzed, just like we want. It'll provide us with a brief opening into their systems when they do, thanks to that gorgeous sister of Rin's."

"I said quiet!"

Hayes hopped away, snickering. I stared at the view-screen. Someone was being carried out of the ship on a hovering gurney. I slid as far forward on the couch as I could. Lousy feed and all, I confirmed it was Cora. Her head was propped up, and she wore a pained grimace, no doubt due to the brace wrapping her arm, but she was alive. A few more Ringers being treated for minor wounds followed behind her. Then came a body bag.

"Those mud-stomping bastards!" Hayes growled.

"From ice to ashes, Joran," Rin said solemnly. Gareth stepped over and placed a comforting hand on her arm.

"They'll pay for this."

"He knew what he was volunteering for. We can only hope he took some of them out first."

Gareth nudged Rin so hard I could feel her armored shoulder tap mine. He pointed at the screen, and I followed his finger, finally able to avert my focus from Cora. Strolling out of the *Piccolo* last was a pair of men in Pervenio armor who were two peculiar-looking officers. One was an Earther with a graying beard and hair, an iron glower, and a pulse-pistol dangling from his hip. The top part of his armor was removed, revealing a faded brown duster. The other was taller and lean, an offworlder in his twenties most likely, with a strange yellow-colored lens apparatus stretching over his right eye.

"Collectors," Hayes said. "Guess that video made us more popular than we thought."

"They'll be taken care of," Rin grunted. The feed switched over, and the stern face of Director Sodervall appeared onscreen, ready to address the Ring. "Turn this off. It's time we all rest."

"But the director—"

"Off."

She powered the view-screen down herself and stood. Without another word or even a glance back at me, she left the room, clearly affected by the death of one of the men under her command. Gareth snorted and followed her.

Hayes plopped down onto the couch beside me. "You get used to her," he said. "She isn't all bad." He patted me on the back and held out the ration bar from earlier. "You forgot this, by the way."

"What will they do to them?" I asked as he dropped it onto my lap.

"Who?"

"The crew of the *Piccolo*."

"That what you're worried about?" Hayes said. "They'll lock 'em up on the station for a bit while they try to figure out what happened. Standard procedure."

"Standard? I've heard about how they interrogate prisoners in that place. You're all so worried about our people, why'd you leave them on the ship to be taken in?"

"We don't have the supplies for 'em. The *Sunfire* would fall apart faster than it already is. Would you rather us all starve here together, or let them take a few lumps before Pervenio realizes they don't know anything?"

"I..." I bit my lower lip. I'd traded my mother's freedom for the imprisonment of the woman I loved. Whether or not Cora knew anything, Pervenio Station's cells were infamous for a reason. They'd try whatever it took to get answers out of her and the others before they set them free.

"Kid, eventually, you got to realize that this was going to happen with or without you," Hayes said.

"I'm sure you know that's not true."

In my peripherals, I noticed Hayes's brow furrow. "She told you, didn't she?" he said. "Pretty crazy, isn't it?"

"Do you all really expect me to believe anything she told me?" It was insane. Trass was a genius, a brilliant scientist and inventor who'd constructed the ark that would carry human beings farther through space than ever before in only a handful of years, under the pressure of impending Armageddon. Me? I was a reformed thief who couldn't even save his mom from sickness on his own. Sure, I could repair a faulty harvesting vacuum or a flickering light, but I was far from a genius.

"Personally, I don't care as long as it gets the job done," Hayes replied. "I didn't believe her either when we first met, but she can be very convincing."

"We'll see about that."

"Your pop worked hard to keep the lot of you hidden from Pervenio. Seems like as good an indication as any that that's what you all are. Wouldn't do Pervenio Corp any good having a bunch of Trass's running around after they took over."

"You knew him too?"

"Nah. Alann let very few people actually know him, but I'd see him around before I got stuck here. This, all of this—the Children of Titan—he helped start it."

"So that's what you're calling yourselves?" I said, making no effort to mask my disdain.

"Look down, kid." Hayes tapped the orange circle printed on the chest plate of my armor. "You're one of us now. Better get used to it."

"Shoving me in your armor doesn't make me one of you."

"Do you think I asked to be trapped on this piece of junk for three years either? It sure as hell would've been easier not to have been born a Ringer. But let me ask you this: If you'd known you'd wind up here, if you'd known everything that would happen, would you have said no to helping your mom?"

The question gave me pause, and as soon as he noticed that, he grinned. I wanted to be irritated by his reaction, but I couldn't because I knew he was right. I would have done it all the same, and if I didn't, it would've been Cora or Desmond, or some new Ringer crew member I'd never met before forced to do their bidding. Rin didn't seem like the type of woman who'd give up easily.

"Exactly!" Hayes said. He hopped to his feet. "Now, what do you say we cheer you up a bit. We've got a gift for you. I swear on your great-however-many-times-grandpa, you'll love it."

"I'm not—"

"Won't accept any 'nos.'" He yanked on my arm, his powered suit easily providing the muscle to haul me upright. "After three years with those two, no way I'm dealing with another sorry sack. Oh." He bent over, picked up the ration bar, and shoved it into my hand. "And would you eat the damn thing already? You pass out, and it'll be my ass."

With that, he left the room. I guess I was starving because once he was around the corner, I ripped open the wrapper and shoved half of the bar into my mouth. Chicken soup-flavored, it tasted like heaven. I scarfed down the rest and hurried to catch up with him, struggling to match his strides. He was far more accustomed than I to walking in these suits.

"How have I never heard of your group... organization... whatever it is?" I asked, still chewing.

"Outside of Pervenio higher-ups, few had before the recording we sent out on the *Piccolo*," he answered. "For decades there've been factions of Titanborn protesting for more rights, with names and fancy leaders. Pervenio and his hound Director Sodervall put them all down. Unlike them, the Children of Titan aren't a group. We're a symbol. We're everywhere, and nowhere—operating out of sight. Cells functioning on our own terms. This is just one of many, kid. Few of us know of each other, even fewer have seen each other, but we all know what we want."

"And what's that?"

"Our home back."

A difficult sentiment to argue with. Every Ringer dreamed of what it might've been like to live before the Great Reunion, when our chief concern was how best to work together to acquire the resources we needed and build a prosperous, peaceful civilization. The new, better Earth Darien Trass had dreamed of. We never considered going back, and it wasn't only because Titan's atmosphere was often too stormy to see through. Even once we discovered that Earthers had survived a century after the Meteorite hit, we were happy to let them rebuild on their own and fight each other for control, until Luxarn Pervenio's father showed up on our doorstep and we foolishly invited them in.

"Do you know how many Titanborn are living throughout the Ring?" Hayes asked after a few seconds went by without me responding. "And I don't mean one-generation offworlders from Earth. I mean real, genuine men and women with roots dating back to before the Great Reunion."

I shrugged.

"Roughly two-point-three million by census," he answered. "Probably a couple hundred thousand more illegitimates. Hasn't grown in decades because of our damn immune systems, but it hasn't fallen much either since the plague's effects leveled out. Just like Trass never thought the people we left behind would eventually enslave us, Earthers never figured their arrival would drive us to focus on settling down with a good mate and popping out baby Ringers."

"Just so they can get sick too," I grumbled.

"You're not listening. By blood, we outnumber the Earthers here three to one, probably more. Eventually, new Earther immigrants will close the gap like Pervenio wants, but if we can make them fear this place too much to dig out of the mud on Earth and drag their asses over, if they choose to go to a Venta Co colony at Europa instead, or Mars, then guess what?"

"It gets better."

"It does indeed. But if we don't change anything, eventually, there won't be anyone to remember the days before they arrived and the home *we* built. We'll be offworlders, the same as any others, throwing our lot into the Departure Lottery just to feel like we're worth something."

He turned down a branch in the hallway, and as I followed, I realized, based on my knowledge of the *Piccolo,* where we were headed. We were at the starboard airlock wing. This hall was flanked by similar rows of benches, only there were no empty exo-suits hanging on the wall. The inner seal was closed.

I froze.

"Don't worry," Hayes snickered. "I'm not going to shove you out." He keyed a command to open the inner seal, and sitting inside the airlock was Captain Saunders, his wrist cuffed to a pipe. His skin was whiter than any Earther's should be, and his whole body was drenched in sweat, even though he was shivering. A torn shirt was tied around his torso, covering a gunshot wound.

"Captain Saunders!" I exclaimed and scurried over. His head slumped to the side as he wheezed. Judging by how red the floor around him was, he'd lost a lot of blood. I nudged him, but his eyelids only fluttered, and he groaned something inaudible.

"What the hell are you doing to him?" I questioned.

"Figured we'd save the worst of them for you, Mr. Trass," Hayes said, grinning.

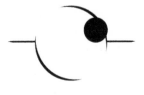

SIXTEEN

Hayes wasn't pleased when I asked him to show me where the ship's water stores were so I could retrieve some for Captain Saunders, but he reluctantly let me do as I pleased. That was the first time I began to consider that maybe he and Rin were telling the truth about who I was. No doors were locked for a Trass. The thought was so unbelievable it almost had me amused. Almost.

The *Sunfire*'s galley was barren. Cabinet doors hung loose and tables were tossed about, stained with blood and corrosion. It was like I'd stepped into a time machine and emerged on the *Piccolo* years after it being abandoned. A pallet filled with ration bars like the one I'd been given earlier sat in the corner, along with a few small tanks of water. All of it bore Venta Co markings, and while I wasn't sure how they got the supplies onto the *Sunfire,* there was no doubt they were how Rin and her skeleton crew had survived for so long. Some expiration dates were after the *Sunfire's* supposed disappearance. I wondered if Venta knew they were backing a public execution, all to stick it to their corporate rivals.

I filled a cup with water for the captain before realizing how dry my own throat was. I downed three cups, then saved one for him. With the Venta g-stim diminishing my soreness, I also found that I was starving. I stuffed another ration bar in my mouth and grabbed two more just in case. Nobody stopped me. Hayes returned to the command deck after he saw what I was up to. Gareth stayed to watch my every move, but despite his hawkish glare, he kept his distance.

"Hey, Captain," I said as I approached the airlock, water in hand and focused on ensuring I didn't crush the cup with my unnaturally strong grip. I kneeled beside him. "C'mon, you need this."

He was barely conscious. I grabbed his jaw and pried open his mouth enough to pour some water inside. Most of it dribbled down his chin, washing the blood away, but some of it got in. He coughed, and I held his mouth shut so he wouldn't spit it out before I forced in some more. When it seemed he'd had his fill, I yanked on the cloth wrapping his torso and dripped some into the area of his wound. He moaned and pushed at my arm, but with my suit on, he couldn't fight me off. I continued cleaning him until the cup was empty.

"You'll thank me for that," I said.

I noticed the whites of his eyes peeking through a narrow crack in his eyelids as his head turned to face me. He shivered again. The *Sunfire* was cold, even for Ringers, so I couldn't imagine how he must have felt. I got back up and returned to the room I'd first awakened in. All I could find was a ratty blanket, but I knew it was the best I'd get. I couldn't risk letting him borrow any of my clothes. After falling face-first into a pool of his Earther blood, I was lucky I wasn't already covered in rashes and vomiting, even though for once in my life, a trip to quarantine was the least of my concerns.

When I returned to the airlock, I lay the blanket over his shoulders. He grabbed the ends, crossed his arms, and failed in an attempt to whisper. Then his head drooped back against the wall, and he passed out. So I waited for an hour, maybe two. I waited so long that I started to doze off...

I stood in front of a transparent divider. It was similar to the one in the Darien Q-Zone that separated my mother and me. One by one, a crowd of people on the other side turned to reveal their faces.

First, I saw John, a bandage wrapped around his head. Then came the other familiar faces of the *Piccolo*'s Earther crew, until Captain Saunders appeared. Blood leaked out of a widening hole in his stomach as he stood.

"Help us." I could hear their muffled cries, but there was no intercom through which to reply. Lester parted the crowd and limped toward me, bruised and bloody. Yavik arrived next to him, along with a few more recognizable Ringers. Desmond approached last, only he wasn't alone. He took Cora's hand as she wept.

"You did it now, Kale," he sneered.

"Why did you do this?" Cora sniveled. It was hard to hear her over the constant repetition of the Earthers asking for help.

"Cora," I said and placed my hands against the glass. "Cora!"

Someone touched my shoulder. I turned to see my mother standing beside me, completely healthy and wearing a bright smile. Finally, I was on her side of the divider.

"Don't watch, Kale," she said with a calming presence. "It'll all be over soon."

I looked nervously between her and the entire crew of the *Piccolo*. Desmond cackled. The captain cursed me as his belly opened farther. Cora peered up at me through the bloody fingers covering her face, heartbroken.

An obnoxious klaxon blared. My mother took my hand. Then, the back wall of the room the crew was in whooshed open, and their screams were squelched as they vanished into blackness.

"Cora!" I shouted as my eyes sprang open. I was panting, the salty tang of sweat on my lips as more dribbled down my face. I searched from side to side and discovered Rin beside me. The ghastly nature of her face shocked me once again now with the brighter halogen lights of the airlock beaming down on her. She held a cup of water.

"Relax, Kale," she said. "It was only a dream."

I sat up and wiped my brow. "I was hoping all of this was," I said.

"So did I." She crouched beside me and glared at Captain Saunders. He continued to shiver and clutch the blanket tightly against his chest. "You can try to help him as much as you want, but it isn't going to change anything that happened."

"What are you going to do to him?" I asked.

"Like Hayes told you, that's not up to me," she said.

"Maybe we are family, but I'm not a murderer."

"It'd be a mercy at this point. There's nowhere else for him to go but out the hatch. Aren't you tired of being called 'Earther-lover?'"

"Water..." Captain Saunders croaked. He pawed at Rin's leg, his arm barely able to move.

"You want this?" Rin regarded him with disdain. She tilted the cup in her hand and slowly allowed it to drip over the rim onto the floor.

"Stop! Just leave him alone." I grabbed the cup from her and held it under his mouth. He struggled through a few sips alone before I had to support his head to help.

Rin snickered and sat against the wall across from me. She poked him in the head, watching with delight as it caused his entire body to tip.

"Fine," she said. "If you can tell me one reason your captain deserves to live, then I'll happily pilot this ship straight to Pervenio Station and turn myself in."

I took a moment to think, and then said, "He gave me my first chance. Got me out of the shadows."

"Please. If your father wasn't who he was, you would've never escaped your life of thievery on Darien alive. Saunders helped you? He enslaved you. You broke into his clan-brother's residence and got caught, so he made you work it off for a year, even though nothing was stolen. Then he started paying you like he does the other Titanborn members of his crew and made you feel as if your life had changed. Brought you the joy of credits. The Earthers working next to you make double your wage, at least, but it's more than you could ever earn legally in the Lowers, so that's fine. Why should we be treated the same as our brethren from the homeworld?"

My hands tightened into fists. I wanted to scream at her, but I restrained myself. "Did you bring me here just to have somebody new to lecture?" I said.

"No," Rin said. "I want you to stop blaming the universe for how our people live and start blaming the Earthers. He's the same as any of them. All that matters to them is the profit margin and let anyone who stands in the way of it rot in quarantine. They'll make bastards out of us all."

"And 'kill as many as possible' is the only answer you could come up with? Trass wouldn't have wanted this."

"Trass died thinking Earth was going with him. 'He gave his life to give us the Ring.' How thrilled do you think he would be to see how they've corrupted his vision? Robbed it of its very soul."

"You tell me," I said. "You're the expert on him."

She bit her mangled lip, then sighed. "Do you want to know how I wound up on the *Sunfire?*"

I glared at her but said nothing. She must have taken that as a "yes," because she began telling the story anyway.

"Your dad spent his whole life running," she said. "Director Sodervall and his employer never stopped hunting the descendants of Trass after the Great Reunion. They knew we weren't all gone, not yet. Alann struggled to hide us every step of the way. My name changed countless times. He didn't want that for you, and neither did your mom. So we hacked the system and gave you a dead father with the name 'Drayton.' Years later, Alann grew tired of having to look out for his little sister too. He decided that I should hide on a gas harvester, out of sight, until the Children of Titan were ready to make a real difference.

"The crew of the *Sunfire* were the ones eventually meant to be placed in the airlock and evacuated for all the Ring to see. You were never meant to be involved. But the *Sunfire* had a captain just like this one. He liked to prey on the Titanborn women he hired. Put a little bonus into their paychecks after he took them, and then toss them away if they got sick. For the first few shifts, I was a good girl following her brother's orders. I met Hayes, Gareth, and Joran, and we helped harvest tons of gas in the name of Luxarn Pervenio. And every night, I or some other poor Titanborn woman, would be escorted away to the captain's room and he'd have his way.

"He wrapped up his pathetic excuse for a cock just so he could keep us around, but it was a miracle I never got sick. Trass blood is stronger than most. Eventually, I couldn't take it anymore. I drove a blade into his neck, and that was the end of it. The ship's security helped me earn this in the riot that followed." She pointed at the grisly burns maiming her face. "The few left on this ship are the only ones who survived, and we took the *Sunfire* for ourselves. That was when I decided I was tired of following orders. My sister was our eyes and ears on Titan, so I became our eyes and ears on Saturn. Waiting. Watching."

"Getting help from Venta Co," I added. "An *Earther* corp."

"Your dad was stubborn until the day he ate a bullet, but he wasn't about to let me die for failing him. He spent years brokering an agreement with the only company that had the means of getting supplies to a ship that didn't exist. Their medicine probably saved your life back on the *Piccolo,* so I can't say I regret it. We do what we have to for survival, and in the end, it'll be their mistake. If Venta Co wants to watch their competition burn so badly, then they can all burn together."

"I'm sorry, Rin, but just because your captain did that to you doesn't mean Saunders is the same. He doesn't deserve to suffer like this."

She stood and said, "Then end it for him. Or don't. Your choice put him here, after all. Just know that you're wrong. He's exactly the same. They all are. Just ask him. Ask him about Cora."

I grabbed her armored wrist and squeezed. "What about her?"

"You want to save him, get him to tell you why he named her navigator over an Earther." She stared toward the airlock's outer seal for a moment, as if she saw something there, then ripped her arm free and stalked away.

"What about her!" I yelled, running after her.

Rin whipped around and grabbed me by the throat, so swiftly that I couldn't even muster an attempt at evading her. She looked like she was ready to snap my neck in two.

"Cora!" she bellowed. "Your mother! Do you ever tire of worrying about other people? You're the only one here now, and you have a more important role to play than anyone on Titan has had for generations."

"I... I still don't understand what you want," I stuttered.

"I'm trying to be patient with you, Kale, but you're as stubborn as he was."

"I wouldn't know."

Rin released me. Her scowl softened. "Do you love Titan?" she asked.

"Of course. It's my home."

"Do you hate Earthers?"

"Only some of them." Her eyes narrowed. I held strong. "That's the honest truth."

"Do you hate Pervenio Corp, then?"

I thought back to all the moments dealing with security in Darien—being shocked, shuffling into the Q-Zone, my hollow about to be repossessed, Director Sodervall inspiring a riot in the Uppers all around me.

"Yes," I said. "I do."

"Then follow me."

Hayes was already in the command deck when we arrived. The *Sunfire* juddered more than usual, and beyond the viewport whipped a windy haze so dark and thick that it was as if a black hole had swallowed us.

"Strap in," Hayes said. "We're entering a bad one."

The *Sunfire* lurched, hurling my body to the side. Gareth caught me and planted me in a seat. He strapped me in before he and Rin headed to seats of their own.

"Storm?" I asked.

Rin nodded. The structure of the domed viewport rattled so loudly I thought it was going to shatter. Lightning coruscated all around us, bolts the length of Pervenio Station. My heart started racing.

"Hayes, do you have the director's address saved up here from earlier?" Rin asked.

"Sure," he said. "Why?"

"We're going to show Kale."

"Oh, c'mon, Rini. He isn't ready yet."

"Neither were you when I stuck Captain Sildario."

Gareth signed something to Hayes, who rolled his eyes.

"That was different," Hayes said. "This is—"

"Show me," I cut him off. All three of them faced me, surprised to hear my voice. The *Sunfire* quaked, and I clutched my chair's armrests so tight they dimpled. I swallowed hard. "Show me."

"You heard him," Rin said.

Hayes grumbled something, but he signaled one of the command deck's small view-screens to switch to the grainy newsfeed from earlier. Director Sodervall's face appeared on it, lines of exhaustion creasing his old face. He sat in front of a viewport looking out upon Saturn's dazzling rings and a handful of its many moons.

"People of the Ring," he said. Hayes had to blast the volume because the storm was so loud. "By now you've all heard of the horrible fate which befell the *Piccolo* and its loyal Earther crew members. I speak to you now, not as your director, not as the Voice of the Ring, but as one human making a solemn promise to others. The terrorists behind this attack will pay for their crimes. They call themselves the Children of Titan, but we are the people of Titan. Together, we have all helped the Ring thrive! One cowardly act will never thwart all that we have accomplished.

"I am asking—begging for your help in bringing the man responsible for the unwarranted slaughter of twenty-one innocent members of the *Piccolo's* crew to justice." An image popped up next to the Director's face. It was a cropped view of the Uppers during the riot his address about the Departure Lottery incited. Framed in the center of it, I saw myself, and behind me, the plants surrounding the Trass memorial were up in flames—a ring of crackling orange framing my head.

"He is Kale Drayton," Sodervall said. "An eighteen-year-old male from level B2 of the Darien Lower Ward. We believe he was also behind a riot that took place not two days ago in the Darien Uppers and cost the lives of two veteran security officers. Consider him armed and extremely dangerous.

"But he is not alone. People in league with these terrorists can be anywhere. Working beside you. Living beside you. Any accurate report of suspicious behavior will be handsomely rewarded. Anyone who is able to provide information leading directly to the arrest of Kale Drayton will personally receive one hundred thousand credits from the account of Luxarn Pervenio. It is time for us to take back the Ring from lawlessness! Lastly, anyone caught replicating the symbol of the Children of Titan anywhere in Sol will be punished by the fullest extent of USF Colonial Law.

"Your safety, no matter where you or your parents were born, is our utmost concern. The fight to ensure our survival rests in all of our hands."

The feed cut to static. My jaw hung open. Rin could have been lying about everything she'd said since I woke up on the *Sunfire,* but I'd just watched an address issued by the Voice of the Ring. It wasn't a doctored video, it was his voice.

"They think it was me?" I muttered.

"The only Ringer who didn't return," Rin said. "Half a crew that didn't see you die. Even we weren't expecting Sodervall to be this foolish, but people need to put a face to their fears. Your father didn't allow him to give them one after the bombing in

New London, so now Sodervall's giving them you. It doesn't matter if you're innocent."

"You have to tell them the truth!" I exclaimed. "They think I killed all of those people."

"Well, you did upload the device that helped us locate the *Piccolo* without broadcasting our own signal and being spotted. What will you tell them, that you were just downloading music to it?"

I lunged at her, but my chair's restraints snapped me back down against the chair. I went to remove them, only to find they were locked. So much for no locked doors.

"Easy, now," Hayes said. "You said no more breaking anything."

I lost the ability to breathe. Everything Rin had told me paled in comparison to this newest revelation. As rapidly as I inhaled, no air seemed able to reach my lungs. My chest was tight, and as I grabbed at it, the *Sunfire* dipped hard. I vomited all over the floor.

"For Trass's sake, kid!" Hayes shrieked.

"That's all right," Rin said. She freed herself from her chair and stood behind me, patting my back. "Let it out."

"I told you he wasn't ready, Rin."

"It wasn't our secret to keep. He's dealt with enough of those in his life already."

I continued struggling to catch my breath as I spit up chunks of regurgitated ration bar stuck behind my teeth. It tasted a lot worse coming up.

"I can't ever go back..." I realized.

"Not like this." Rin positioned herself in front of me and raised my helmet up with two hands. "You wanted to know what we wanted, Kale Trass? The real reason you're here? We've been spread thin for too long. Be the leader Sodervall thinks you are. It's what you were meant to be."

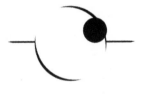

SEVENTEEN

Leader. A leader of the Children of Titan. Was that what my long-lost father never wanted me to be? What my mom hid me from?

All I wanted was to sleep the hours away and shut off my brain, but I couldn't. I couldn't force my eyes to close for more than a second without seeing the final moments on the *Piccolo*, because Rin was right. It wasn't all my fault like Director Sodervall proclaimed, but their blood was partially on my hands.

I wasn't innocent. I knew that the moment I read R's message on Titan and agreed to her trade.

That seemed like ages ago. Only a day on the *Sunfire* and my life had changed more drastically than in eighteen years of living. I had gone from the fatherless son of a sick, penniless, Earther house-servant to the descendant of the single greatest human being in our long history of existence. From a worthless gas harvesting worker struggling to make ends meet to the most wanted man in Sol.

It all left me too exhausted to continue the conversation with Rin. I needed to be alone. At least, partially alone. I gathered as much water as I could and brought it to the airlock. Most of it was for me, but it seemed to be helping Captain Saunders. He shook less and groaned more softly.

"There you go," I said as I laid his head back. "Good as new... almost."

The bullet wasn't stuck in him; I'd inspected him closely enough to discover that it'd blasted through his back. I knew a thing or two about infections, and I was lucky enough to have a space-worthy suit on, so I felt comfortable enough to rub him with some Venta-provided cleaning agents I'd found in the galley. He needed a real doctor, though. He needed one badly.

Unfortunately, there were none for hire in the depths of Saturn's atmosphere. None of my new crewmates would help either. They claimed to have used anything that might've actually helped on Rin's burns and trying to help other Ringer crewmen who rebelled. I didn't want to give up, though. I couldn't. Maybe everything Rin had told me about him was true, but he didn't deserve to die for doing what anybody else would've in his position. Did he?

I patted a wet, unused harvesting rag on the front side of his wound.

"Garghhh..." he groaned. "Stop."

I grabbed his jaw and tilted his face. He squinted through his eyelashes at me.

"Captain!" I exclaimed. "I never thought I'd hear a familiar voice again."

"What the...Where are we?" He attempted to sit up, the effort causing him to grimace and clutch his stomach.

"Don't move."

His breathing picked up. He lifted his bandage and struggled to focus on what lay beneath. The skin surrounding the hole was slightly discolored and oozed pus.

"By fucking Earth!" He poked the area and lurched. "Oh god, it hurts!"

"Don't touch it." I brushed away his free hand and returned the bandage to its proper position, then pulled it as taut as possible.

"We're still on the *Piccolo*?" he groaned.

"No. You wouldn't believe where we were even if I told you." I shuffled backward and sat across from him. "You loved to remind us about the place."

He noticed that one of his hands was cuffed to a pipe. "They took us prisoner?" he said. "Where's the rest of the crew?"

I paused for a moment, then said, "Far away or dead. Don't you remember?"

"We were by the airlock." His weary gaze darted around the room. The color drained from his cheeks. "This one."

"It's not—"

"They took all of my people! John, Orsini, and the others." He scrambled as far away from me as his cuff would allow.

"Captain, you should try to stay still." I wrapped my fingers around his ankle. His stare swept from one of my unchained arms to the other. His eyes opened as wide as they had since he'd come to when they settled on the orange emblem on my chest.

"Don't fucking touch me!" he shouted.

"Captain, relax!" I said. "You're safe here, I promise."

"You son of a bitch... You're one of them!" He sprang at me, but his body was snapped backward, and he face-planted. He screeched in pain. "You son of a bitch!"

"I'm just trying to help you." I went to lift him back into a seated position.

"Don't you fucking touch me, traitor!" He punched my chest, his knuckles crunching against my armor. He roared like he was shot all over again, rolled onto his side, and cradled his arm. Blood started leaking out of his gut, but he didn't have a free hand to help stem the flow.

"I stuck my neck out for you," he panted.

"I know, and I'm grateful," I said. After everything that had happened, it felt good to say that and know I meant it. Whether as a slave or not, he did get me out of the shadows, gave me a chance to see Saturn for the first time. The good feeling didn't last long as I witnessed the mounting revulsion on his face.

"I swear," I said. "None of this is what it looks like."

"You put on quite a show, Drayton," he said. He was sweating so profusely I could've showered under his chin. "Leading on Cora. Pretending to save my life while you handed over *my* ship. My crew. What the hell did you do to them?"

"That's not what happened. Just calm down, and I'll explain everything. You'll aggravate the wound." I picked up my wet rag and held it out for him, smart enough to keep my distance this time.

"Scared of getting sick?" He spat at me, a sticky mixture of saliva and fresh blood. I was able to turn my body just in time so that it splattered on the side of my helmet instead of my face. "I should have never let you back on!"

"Wash yourself, then!" I shouted. I threw the rag at him and shot to my feet. I stopped outside of the airlock's inner seal. "I'm trying to help you, sir."

"You touch me again, and I'll wring your skinny skelly neck, Drayton! You took my ship! I'll kill you." He tugged on his cuff again, then collapsed onto his side and squirmed in agony. The veins in his neck bulged. "I'll kill you!" I heard him groan through his teeth after I decided to hurry away.

My eyes welled with tears. My throat was tight. I made it around the nearest corner, and then screamed at the top of my lungs. I punched the wall repeatedly. My armored fists slammed through a cluster of exhaust pipes, causing hot exhaust to spew onto my face. I didn't stop. I kept punching until my arms were sore and the lights started flickering from damage to power lines buried in the wall.

"Why is this happening to me?" I asked myself as I fell to my knees. "Why me?"

A hand landed on my shoulder. I turned and saw Gareth, expression staid as ever. He signed something to me, slowly so that I could better understand it. He had to repeat the symbols a few times to spark my memory.

"Won't accept help?" I read.

"No," I said. "Because he's an Earther, right? Like your old captain."

Gareth shook his head. *"Would you, as him?"*

"No, I guess I wouldn't." I exhaled. "I don't know what to do..." I collapsed against the wall, steam cascading over my shoulders. Gareth joined me. "I'm just so tired."

"Sleep?" Gareth signed.

"Not like that. I meant I'm tired of being so out of control of everything in my life. All of you telling me who I am. For the briefest moment, I thought I had everything. I saved my mom. I had Cora. A job."

Gareth's hands remained still.

"I don't know why I'm telling you all of this," I said.

"What do you want?" he signed.

"Me? I have no idea. I thought I was doing the right thing helping my mom. Now everyone else I know is either locked up somewhere, refusing my help, or dead, and I'm stuck here in the middle of Saturn talking to the mute who helped put me here... Sorry. I'm sure you were only following orders."

His expression didn't shift. *"What do* you *want?"*

I drew a deep breath. "To fix it. I know my life can never be the same—you've all made damn sure of that—but I guess I failed at keeping my distance from people. At not caring. Trass,

I'd kill to have a drink with Desmond right now, and I never thought I'd say that. I don't know what I'd do to be with Cora." A weak chuckle slipped through my lips.

"Then do it."

"That's easy to say, but I can't. You're stuck here with the most wanted man in Sol."

He shook his head and then stared directly into my eyes. *"Listen to her then. You lead. You choose."*

"I lead," I whispered. I leaped to my feet, having a sudden epiphany. "I lead."

I ran to the command deck so fast Gareth could barely keep up with me. Rin sat at a console, keying commands while she munched on one of our precious ration bars. Hayes scrubbed my vomit off the floor and the back of his chair, visor on, presumably so he didn't have to deal with the stench.

"Rin!" I hollered.

She calmly glanced up from her work. "What is it?" she asked. "Are you feeling better?"

Hayes raised his visor. "Is *he* feeling better?" he said. "How about me? He should be the one cleaning this shit up."

"Quiet."

"By Trass," he grumbled and returned to scrubbing, cursing under his breath the entire time.

"Kale?" Rin said.

I took a few seconds to catch my breath. "I'm fine," I panted. "I... You said you wanted me to lead, but if you've all told me the truth, you operate in separate cells. So what does that actually mean?"

Her expression brightened as much as her disfigured face allowed. "You're considering it?"

"Just tell me."

"The Children of Titan are widespread throughout the Ring, yes. We've never had a single leader, but neither did Titan before Pervenio arrived. Some don't believe that we need one now. They'd rather separately chip away at nothing until we're gone. We won't win a war of attrition, not when they control the trade and medicine."

"So you want to bring the cells together?" I asked.

"Yes, and more," Rin said. "Your father didn't last long enough for the time to be right for him to take the mantle. He may not have wanted that burden for you, but it's no longer his decision to make."

"Why can't you take it?"

"Sodervall already made you infamous for us, plus you have the plight our people will relate to. Lost father, sick mother, stealing just to survive. Me..." She gestured to her face, grimaced. "I'm just a—"

"Fighter," I finished for her, knowing that wasn't what she was going to say. I needed her on my good side for what I was about to propose, and calling her a monster wasn't going to help, even if it was true.

She grinned halfheartedly. "Sure. But we don't need you to be one. Titan needs a new voice. All we need from you is to begin broadcasting publicly, provide a face and name to the coming revolution. A Trass to rally to. You can keep your hands as clean as you'd like."

I regarded the faces of my new companions. They were the strangest group I'd ever encountered, but on second glance, they didn't seem that much different from those I'd worked with in the Lowers. Dexter Howser lost his legs; Rin her face. Every Ringer worth a damn had scars they couldn't hide.

"I'll do it," I declared. "I'll say whatever you want me to say, but you're going to have to do something for me first."

Rin's smile faded as she said, "Go on."

"We're going to break the *Piccolo*'s crew out of Pervenio Station."

Hayes scoffed. Rin struggled not to. "What do you expect us to do, pull the *Sunfire* up next to it and grab them?" she asked. "Unidentified vessel. They'll shoot us down as soon as we break atmosphere."

"I don't care how we do it," I said. "You told me to stop worrying about others, but this is what *I* want. You need your figurehead, you'll think of a way. Then we'll be even for what you did to us."

"Can't lead anything if you're dead, kid," Hayes chimed in.

"No, but would you follow a man who would forsake his friends and crew just to get away?"

Rin glared at me, and even Hayes's usual smirk vanished from his face. They both knew I was serious, and if I could have seen Gareth behind me, I'd have bet he was secretly glad he couldn't talk once he realized he'd inspired the idea.

"Kale..." Rin began soberly. "In a cell on Titan, we might have the people and the resources to save them. But there's a reason nobody's ever been broken out of Pervenio Station: Nobody's ever tried. Maybe we could get in, but where would we go afterward? There's no bridge to Titan."

"He's officially lost it, Rini," Hayes said. "I told you this was a bad idea."

Gareth stomped forward and signed something slow enough for me to understand. Hayes's reaction to him helped as well. *"Would you rather stay here forever?"*

"Better than being dead."

"We can use the hand-terminal I smuggled to get in," I proposed. "You told me it will provide a window into their systems."

"A brief one," Rin said. "My sister was going to use it to wipe as much of the Pervenio medical database as possible. Erase names and births. Make as many Titanborn illegitimate as possible to hamper Pervenio credit records. But they have to plug into their systems to analyze it, and once she gets to work, it won't be long before they realize that and destroy it. She can't do both."

"Yeah, and we all spent months planning for that," Hayes added. "It's the whole reason those people on the *Piccolo* died, kid. It'd take 'em years to replace the data."

"And then we'll be right back where we are," I said. "Nothing will change."

"I can look into it, Kale," Rin said. "You have my word. We can try to arrange something. Keep an eye on them to make sure they're okay."

"No. I didn't ask to be here, but I'm done fighting it. You want more of my help, then it's time you help me. Otherwise, you may as well shove me into the airlock with Captain Saunders."

The room went quiet. All I could hear was a gentle chorus of deep breaths and the vibrations from another storm outside.

"Rin, you can't seriously be considering this," Hayes protested.

She said nothing.

"If we free my friends from the most guarded place in the Ring," I said, "Pervenio will know not only that we'll try to hit them anywhere, but that we *can*. And people won't just hope I'm actually a Trass and listen, they'll believe it, even if I don't." By the end of my argument, I was both breathless and impressed with how much I'd improved at negotiation since attempting to haggle with Dexter.

"You're not going to make this easy, are you?" Rin questioned.

"Rin, c'mon," Hayes said. "This is the same kid that just puked all over the command deck. He's probably unstable after what happened."

"You want to strike Pervenio at their heart." Rin stood tall before me. The ship trembled, but her balance was pristine. "Me too. For too long." She extended her hand. "Deal."

"Deal," I exhaled. I shook her hand before anyone changed their minds.

Her dark, grayish eyes glinted with a hunger the likes of which I hadn't seen in them before.

"I hate my life," Hayes groaned as he threw down his rag.

"It won't be like sneaking around the Lowers," Rin said.

"I know," I replied.

Gareth patted me on the back, and I turned to him. His face remained impassive, but he signed, *"I'm with you."*

"This is insane," Hayes said. "You know I always have your back, Rin, but he's supposed to be a figurehead. Now we're taking orders from him?"

"He's a Trass," she replied firmly.

"He's a kid!"

"You're welcome to stay here alone if you'd like, but it's time we finally get off this ship."

Hayes released a fake, exaggerated laugh. Then he scanned the broken-down room, looking from one pleading face to the next. He sighed. "Well, you'll need a pilot, but I'm making it known I don't agree with this. And don't expect me to take a bullet for him either."

"Wouldn't expect anything else," Rin jested.

"So you have an actual plan for this, right, Mr. Trass?" Hayes asked me.

My high of excitement died swiftly. Between my conversation with Gareth and the command deck, I hadn't really had a chance to think about anything other than how I might convince Rin.

"No," I admitted.

Hayes threw up his arms in frustration.

"Leave it to me to get us in," Rin said. "We'll need my

sister's help again. Kale, you're the expert on smuggling here. Start thinking of how to possibly get people off Pervenio Station."

"People..." I bit my lip. "They're a little bigger than hand-terminals. I don't know if I can—"

"We just need ideas for now. There's nothing too crazy to consider at this point."

"That's for damn sure," Hayes added.

"Can you do that?" Rin asked me.

"I'll try," I said.

"Good. Hayes, get a read on the nearest luxury cruiser and bring us under them."

"Sure thing, beautiful." He saluted unenthusiastically before spinning his chair around and getting to work on the navigation console. "Trass-damned maniacs," he whispered loud enough for us to hear.

"Gareth, evaluate our supplies and munitions," Rin ordered. He nodded. Then she gripped my arm crisply. "Let's crack open Pervenio Station," she said, "and you can tell Director Sodervall who you really are right to his wrinkled, mud-stomper face."

"There's one more thing I need to see before we leave." I stepped past her, ignoring her confused expression, and reached into a supply crate under a control panel. I'd noticed the scanner they used to sort out who had been Ringer, who Earther, on the *Piccolo*. I grabbed two vacuum-sealed needles.

"Can this check DNA?" I asked.

"Sure," Rin said. "Blood type, DNA, and bone density if you go deep enough. Everything to help us figure out who's really Titanborn."

"Perfect." I presented the equipment to her. "I'm tired of being lied to."

She got my meaning. She took the scanner from me and pricked her neck inside of her helmet. Then she switched the needle and did the same to me so she could compare blood samples. I wasn't sure what most of the information that popped up on the screen meant, but she allowed me to watch as she worked the controls.

We were a genetic match. Family. That was the least crazy of the revelations about my life she'd provided, but it was nice to be 100-percent sure that my memory of her wasn't somehow fabricated.

"And Trass. Can it test for that?" I asked.

"We don't have the resources available here or anywhere," she said. "You'll just have to have faith."

"I wish that were easier."

"Few things ever are!" Hayes hollered back.

Rin handed the scanner back to me. "Stop worrying about what may or may not be, and let's focus on surviving what's to come."

"Right." I returned the device, and then the word *surviving* sank in. "Oh, and one more thing: Captain Saunders is coming with us."

"Kale." The healthy half of her lips wilted into a grimace.

"He already knows who I am and thinks it was me, so what does it matter? We'll leave him behind on the station."

She glanced over at Hayes. He smirked back at her. "He's a Trass—remember?" he remarked.

Rin closed her eyes for moment and then nodded. I could tell she wasn't happy, but I was tired of trying to please people. "Fine," she said. "But only if he's able."

EIGHTEEN

THE PLAN RIN CAME UP WITH WAS SIMPLE... AT LEAST THE
initial part. We were going to abandon the *Sunfire* and board
one of the luxury cruisers sailing around Saturn's upper
atmosphere that provided Earther clientele a lavish reprieve
from living under low-g conditions. Not like the pirates of old
this time, however. We were going to sneak on and stow away in
the supply hangar. Hayes sliced into some Pervenio com's
chatter as our altitude rose, and we learned that a decision had
been made from the top that all unessential vessels were being
recalled from Saturn in light of what happened to the *Piccolo*.

The nearest cruiser was already on the ascent, so we didn't
have long. Hayes pushed the *Sunfire's* engines so hard that we
all had to strap in and load up on g-stims just to stay conscious
during the thrust. I could feel the worn-down pieces of the ship
priming to snap off all around me.

Once we boarded the cruiser, we'd borrow the suits of the
cruiser's Ringer workers and infiltrate Pervenio Station. Rin was
also going to have to tap into its long-range coms to contact her
sister Rylah and tell her about the change in plans so that she

could hack into the station's security systems using the hand-terminal I'd smuggled and sneak us into the prison bay.

That was the easy part. Skulking around was my specialty. The impossible part would come after we sprang Cora and nineteen other incarcerated Ringers from Pervenio Corporation's main headquarters in Sol. We'd lose Rin's sister's tech support by then, so hiding for as long as we could in the station's tram tunnels was the best option our collective minds could come up with. Finding enough exo-suits and ejecting ourselves through the vacuum toward Titan was another choice, but burning up in the moon's dense atmosphere was more of a concern than how we were going to land. Commandeering a ship would get us blown to bits by the station's defenses.

It was a far cry from jobs I was used to. Even Dexter Howser's looniest assignment couldn't hold a candle to what we were going to attempt, but it was my one chance. I was in too deep to get out, and if Rin had taught me anything in our short time together, it was that I couldn't escape some of the blame. I'd chosen the quick path to saving my mom, and I would've done it a thousand times over again. But Cora, Desmond, and the others were just in the wrong place at the wrong time. Because of me, they sat in cells, spending every minute fearful of being spaced.

I was going to get them out no matter the cost.

Presently, I trudged down the *Sunfire*'s airlock corridor, using the wall to lug myself along. Even my powered suit wasn't enough to combat the ship's force of acceleration.

"I thought I told you to stay away from me," Captain Saunders grumbled weakly upon noticing me. He clutched a pipe to keep from sliding along the floor, his face glistening with sweat. Dark bags hugged his eyes. He looked thin and pale, skeletal, like my mom the last time I saw her in person.

"I'm taking you off this ship, Captain," I said. "I don't care whether or not you believe me, but I'm getting you help." I grabbed his cuff and yanked it so hard that it broke off the pipe it was linked to. I was getting used to being abnormally strong. He scrambled backward, but I wrapped my arm around his shoulder and lifted.

"Ah, dammit!" he shrieked. He squirmed out of my grasp and crumpled to the floor, puffing uncontrollably and clutching at his wound. "Oh Earth, just leave me."

I knelt and checked his injury. The veins surrounding it looked like the webs of an earthborn spider, and the skin was so discolored it was now yellow. Pink-hued pus oozed out of it as the pain caused his stomach muscles to spasm.

"You need a real doctor," I said. I gave lifting him another shot, but the moment I moved him, he screamed like I'd never heard anyone do before.

"Stop... I can't..." Captain Saunders wheezed.

"I'm not going to leave you."

"Then don't." He attempted to point at something but couldn't raise his arm. Instead, his gaze aimed toward the control panel for the airlock.

"Sir, I can get you out of here," I said.

"If you really aren't behind all this, then I'm still your captain by contract." He had to pause for breath between every few words. "End this. That's an order."

"Sir—"

"Don't make me beg. A captain... a captain should go down with his crew."

"There's still time."

"Kill me!" Captain Saunders roared like a madman. He grabbed hold of my thigh and shook. "Just end this. I can't... I can't..." He struggled for air and fell backward against the wall, his entire body quivering.

I crouched next to him, unable to choke back my tears. I'd expected him to fight me taking him, but not to give up.

"Please, Kale," he said. "I don't know why I'm here, but I'll tell you people anything you want to know. Anything. Please..." His jaw clenched. "The pain is too much."

I wiped my cheeks and took a seat beside him. For two years, he'd been my captain. He'd barked orders and kept us in line. Never once did he waver. He was stern, authoritative, and did his best to seem fair. Or, at least, I always thought so.

"Why do you pay us less?" I asked softly, the question suddenly popping into my head as I recalled all the things Rin mentioned, from his exploitation of Ringers, to why he treated Cora special.

"Kale," Captain Saunders said softly.

"Why?"

"It's just the market. Not personal. Pervenio doesn't leave us fully-manned gas harvesters much room for profit."

"Why'd you name Cora navigator, then?"

It was difficult to recognize the shock through his agonized expression, but I had no doubt it was there.

"She's not a full Ringer," Captain Saunders said.

"That's never mattered to your kind before," I replied.

"Yeah, well, John couldn't navigate worth a shit. She was better. The best. I hope to hell she's all right."

"That's not it. I can handle a wrench better than Culver, but you never would've named me head mechanic, would you?"

"Is that what all this is about?"

"No, but I want to know. Tell me the truth, and I'll..." I swallowed the lump forming in my throat. "Help you."

"I want your word."

I nodded. "You have it."

He drew a deep, grating breath and closed his eyes. "Cora, she's... she's my daughter," he said.

"What?" I said, incredulous. "But her mom was—"

"I know."

I felt like I'd been struck from behind by a hover-car. It was difficult to slow my thoughts enough to formulate words. "Why?" I managed to force through my lips.

"I was young, Kale. Impulsive. I saw a pretty Ringer, had a little too much to drink, and I made a mistake."

I pictured Cora lying next to me on the *Piccolo,* her silvery hair brushing across my nose. She was smiling, wider than I'd ever seen before, and now I knew the person behind the reason she rarely did.

"Rin wasn't lying," I whispered, mostly to myself.

"Not a day goes by that I don't regret it, Kale," he said, "but I tried to make the best of things once I found out. I care about that girl, that's the truth. It's why I never told her who I was. She doesn't deserve to have to know."

"That you're the man who murdered her mom?" I said for him. "That made her an alien to everyone?"

"I didn't murder anyone!" he protested. Raising his voice caused him to wince. "It was a young man's mistake, just like the one that got you stuck on my ship. You can understand that, can't you?"

"Yeah. I think I do now."

"There. I told you." He twisted his body, groaning, and regarded me, eyes red as the surface of Mars. "Now, please... I can't take this anymore."

I rose to my feet wordlessly and walked over to the airlock controls.

"Thank you, Kale," Captain Saunders said. "I knew you weren't like the others."

I placed my armored hand over the screen. My lower lip trembled. I bit it to keep it still.

"Would you mind knocking me out first?" he asked. "I'm tired of feeling."

My finger hovered over the command to close the inner seal,

but I didn't press it. "The *Sunfire* will be devoured soon," I said. "I hope you last that long."

His eyes gaped. "You gave your word!" he shouted.

I signaled the inner seal to slam shut and locked him inside. Depressurizing and evacuating the airlock was as simple as pressing another button, but I walked away in silence. I could hear Captain Saunders banging against the hatch all the way down the corridor.

"Where's the mudstomping captain?" Hayes asked me when I reached the command deck, making no effort to disguise his derision.

"He passed," I said bluntly.

He stopped what he was doing at the navigation console and gawked at me. Rin and Gareth stood behind him, holding on to his chair. They stared as well. Pulse-rifles were latched on to the backs of all their armor, and Gareth had a supply container strapped to his hip. It wasn't big, but it held as much water and ration bars as we could stuff in.

"Are we ready?" I asked after they'd remained silent for a few too many seconds.

It took Rin a few more to finally answer me. "Almost," she said. She grabbed a pulse-rifle off a rack on the wall and thrust it into my gut, so I had no choice but to grip it. "Now we are. Just in case."

I'd never held a rifle before in my life. The thing was dated, its polymerized coating scraped and dented all over, but it made me feel like more than a thief.

"Your father would be proud of you, Kale," Rin said.

"Let's not get emotional until we survive," Hayes said. "We're coming up on the cruiser fast. I get any closer, and their scanners will light up, so this is where we get off. Luckily, nobody knows we exist, so they aren't looking for us."

"All right. Time to fly."

"Wait, what?" I asked. I looked up at the command deck's dome-shaped viewport. Ruddy-colored wisps of wind lashed beyond it, and in the distant clouds, I noticed the large, dark silhouette of the cruiser. I recalled the ads about them all over Darien—ships with every luxury humans of ancient Earth could want, from earthlike gravity, to a conservatory filled with rare plants, to a small, man-made beach.

Rin hit a switch built into my armor, which I hadn't noticed earlier because it was woven into the belt. I heard a *rasp*, and then something popped out of my arm plates. Rin lifted my arm and stretching between it and my hip was some sort of orange-colored fabric.

"The finest tensile nano-fabric Venta has on the market," Rin said. "You ever heard of the winged suits our ancestors used to traverse Titan and help construct the Blocks?"

"I thought they were myths," I said. I strummed the end of the wing, which somehow remained taut no matter where my arm went.

"No, merely outlawed by Pervenio so they could control transit. Until now."

"You're not really a Child of Titan until you soar, kid," Hayes looked back and said, smirking. "Welcome to your initiation."

I laughed nervously. "You guys are kidding, right?"

"Serious as a Q-Zone."

"It's simple," Rin said. "On my mark, Hayes is going to blow the harvesting bay. The blast will shoot us forward, and we ride the acceleration all the way to the cruiser. Now, I don't need to tell you what kind of wind speeds are out there. The armor can handle it, but we use subtle motions to keep our course true. Gusts might knock you around a bit but remember not to panic." She grabbed my arms and raised them to about a thirty-degree angle from my sides. "You extend any more than this, and we'll be waving goodbye."

I glanced up at the faraway shadow of the luxury cruiser again and then back down at Rin. She seemed completely serious.

"There's got to be a better way," I said.

"Not one that keeps us from getting caught," Hayes said. "Your plan, remember, kid?"

Rin rolled her eyes. "Ignore him. The cruiser's storage hangar will be on the aft. Our relative velocities should be close enough for us to grab on to the hull, cut through an exhaust vent, and climb on board."

"'Should be?'" I said.

"I'm not a mathematician." Hayes shrugged. He backed away from the controls, stood, and faced us. "No better time than now, though."

"G-stims," Rin said. "These are strong ones. They'll help keep us alert."

She opened her hand and revealed four of them on her palm —Venta-made like the others they'd given me, but different markings on the casings. Gareth and Hayes snatched one each and injected. I grabbed mine and jabbed it into my neck without arguing. Taking too much of the chems could be bad for the heart long-term, but I didn't have the time to worry about that.

"Helmets sealed, com-links activated!" Rin ordered.

Their faces disappeared behind their visors. I scrambled to close mine. I could feel my heart beating in my throat. Rin reached over and hit a button on the side of my helmet to switch on a built-in com-link I didn't realize I had. It made me wonder why they'd been signing to communicate back on the Piccolo, until I remembered Gareth couldn't talk. That, and fear. It seemed to be Rin's greatest tool, and nothing made Earthers' skin crawl like things they didn't understand.

"Can everyone hear me?" Rin asked, her voice filling the inside of my helmet.

Hayes offered one of his sarcastic remarks on Rin's looks. Gareth gave a thumbs-up.

"Yes," was all I was able to eke out.

"Stow your rifle, Kale," Rin said. "Hopefully, we don't need them."

I looked down and remembered it was in my hand. I anxiously patted the backside of my armor until I found the mag-latch, a metallic strip that the gun's stock attached to.

We stood silently. Nobody moved until Gareth put a hand on Rin's shoulder, as if he could sense how she was feeling. With the other, he signed, *"You okay?"*

"I'm fine," Rin said, shaking him off her. "I hate this place. Thumbs locked."

I wasn't sure what she meant at first, but the three of them formed three sides of a square and gripped one another's hands. Rin and Gareth each took one of mine, ensuring our thumbs locked. I could only imagine the grin on Hayes's face as he positioned himself across from me.

"Ready, Kale?" Rin said.

"I guess—" Before I could finish, she nudged Hayes, and he let go of her hand for a split-second to strike a key on the command console. The *Sunfire* jolted so violently that we were flung at an upward angle toward the viewport. Our suits crashed through it, headlong into the whistling, tearing winds of Saturn.

My armor shook from the turbulence, but the wings held true. Pressure behind my eyes augmented, as bad as it was when I'd first stepped onto the *Sunfire*. Maybe worse. I fought through the pain to open them so that I could see what was happening.

We were skydiving upward, riding a squall like dust on an Earthen breeze.

Rin issued the others numerical commands for path redirections over our com-link. I had no idea what she was talking about, so I held her hand and Gareth's as tight as I could and used them to keep my arms from angling any farther than her recommendation. We veered together, slightly right and left, through the rosy arms of Saturn's eternal haze toward the luxury cruiser's rapidly growing silhouette.

Thunder clapped so loudly it pierced the soundproof seal of my helmet. Lightning sparkled in the distance. My bones chattered. Wind pressure pulled at my joints. It was the most terrifying thing I'd ever done, but as the g-stim kicked in and dulled the pain, I found myself stifling a thrilled scream.

"Wind drag is slowing us!" Rin shouted loud enough for us to hear her over the rushing air.

"One thousand meters and closing!" Hayes replied. "Trust me, we'll be fine!"

If we were slowing down, I didn't have the experience to notice. I had to fight the urge to break away from them and glide through the air like one of Earth's birds. I'd been weightless plenty of times, but it'd never felt anywhere close to this... to flying.

"Five hundred meters!" Hayes said. "Brace yourselves!"

The luxury cruiser now constituted the breadth of my vision. We approached it at roughly a forty-five-degree angle from beneath its backside.

"Kale!" Rin said. "When we land, keep your arms tight to your side."

I nodded like an idiot first, and then replied, "Arms at the side, got it."

"One hundred!" Hayes yelled.

We dipped as we entered the vessel's drift stream directly

under the aft, avoiding the white-hot plasma trails of its dual nuclear-thermal impulse engines. My stomach jumped, and my exhilaration gave way to fright. The others didn't panic at all. Hayes tightened his arm positioning to even us out so that we ran parallel to the lower hull. Our velocities synchronized almost flawlessly.

"Bring us up slow!" Rin said.

Their wings shifted with delicate motions, and we gradually climbed toward the ship. Again, I concerned myself only with not messing them up. We rose until we ran alongside it. I could see the subtle, greenish glow of the glassy conservatory bulging out from its top, where Earthers could pretend they were amongst nature before the Meteorite ravaged their planet.

"Hayes, you first!" Rin said.

Hayes had rotated to be on the side of our formation closest to the cruiser. I wasn't sure what was up or down anymore. He released the others' hands without hesitation, twirled around, and smacked against the side of the ship. His powered fingers dug into the sturdy blades of an exhaust vent, and he deactivated his wings.

"I'm on, Rin!" he hollered. "Gareth, let's go!"

Gareth released my hand before I was ready, but Rin was there to instantly grab me. The mute Ringer looped through the air and landed beside Hayes. He wasted no time removing a cutting torch from his supply bag and getting to work on the vent.

"He's on!" Hayes said,

"All right, Kale!" Rin shouted. She was now across from me, our visors so close that they were almost touching. I could see the outline of her marred face through it.

"We'll do this together, okay?" she said. "Arms tight."

I was short on breath and found myself unable to answer at first. My life was in the hands of the same woman who'd gone out of her way to destroy it. If I went drifting in space during a zero-g repair walk, inertia would carry me in one direction, and there wouldn't be much around to hide me if anyone was looking for me. Here, on Saturn, I'd be whipped around like a rag doll and plunged into a miasma so copious, I'd be lost in seconds.

"Okay," I managed, probably too softly for her to hear.

Our bodies twirled once. I clutched her hands so tight, I feared I might break them. We slammed into the cruiser, my back against her chest. Her arm wrapped tight around my gut. I groped behind me for something to grab on to, found the ship, and went to rotate my body so I was facing it. When I extended my arm, my wing got caught in the wind drift, and I was wrenched to the side. Rin lost her grip on me, and for a moment, I was separated from anything but the atmosphere.

Hayes extended his hand as far as he could and clutched my wrist. "I got you, kid!" he shouted.

Rin grabbed him, and together they hauled me back in. My chest crashed into the cruiser, and I hugged it. Fingers, feet—every appendage at my disposal found a groove in the hull before my muscles tensed.

"No wings!" Hayes said as he reached over and deactivated mine.

"Trass's shit!" I screamed the first words that popped into my mind.

Hayes laughed, and I even heard Rin snicker before she said, "Gareth, how's that vent going?"

He answered her by tearing off the cover and tossing it. My heart sputtered as I was provided a clear example of what had nearly happened to me. The finned piece of metal twisted across the sky and was bent in half in two separate directions before vanishing into the haze.

"All right," Rin said. "Everybody in quick! I'm sick of this planet."

I couldn't agree more. One by one, we followed Gareth into the cramped passage, and I made sure I got in second. Only after I had a solid surface all around me was I finally able to draw a full breath. Every part of me shook, but I'd made it.

One thing was for certain, though. Sneaking around the Lowers was a hell of a lot safer than flying.

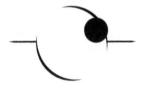

NINETEEN

WE TRAVERSED THE VENT'S INNER PRESSURIZATION SEALS and busted through a grille into the spacious cargo hold of the Pervenio luxury cruiser. It was dark inside, with no need to illuminate a room filled with supplies. All I could make out were the rigid shapes of stacked containers and rolling storage racks. The emptiness did have one benefit, however. There was no reason to heat the room to Earther preference.

I clambered over a tall crate and dropped to the floor between it and another. Never had I been so happy to step foot on a ship. I would've kissed the floor if I wasn't wearing a helmet.

"Still plenty stocked up," Hayes said. "Recall order must have come real early."

Gareth approached a container locked by a keypad. He shoved his powered fingers under the lid and, after a few seconds of prying, yanked it free. It was refrigerated, and cold steam poured out. He waved us over, and inside sat a pile of plastic-wrapped, frozen meat. I had no idea what kind of farmed animal they had been cut from. I'd never seen raw meat in my life.

"Steaks?" Hayes exclaimed. "Remind me again why we decided to hit a shit-ass gas harvester back then, Rini?"

Rin slammed the container shut. "Would you two focus?" she said. "They track stock to keep the crew in line. No touching anything."

"This gets better and better. Kale, tell her we want to see what fine Earther cuisine tastes like. She'll listen to you."

The sight of the meat made my mouth water, but I was lucky: Flying across Saturn had left me feeling nauseous. I fought the urge.

"Listen to her," I said, to a chorus of Hayes's groans.

Rin stepped from behind a row of containers. A blade of light flared from the top of her helmet, revealing the far wall and the only door in or out. Gone were the corroded walls and exposed organs of the gas harvesters I'd grown too used to. Even the cargo hold of one of Pervenio's prized luxury cruisers was a thing of conceived beauty. Pearlescent metal, sleek lines, lofty ceilings with perfect corners; it reminded me of the Darien Uppers.

"Cameras will be monitoring the hall outside that door, watching who comes in and how long they stay," Rin said. "They'd never expect anybody to get in here from the atmosphere, but no way can we sneak out."

"The vents?" I said, eager to propose doing something that I was actually proficient at.

"Not dressed like this," Hayes countered.

"Hayes, you got a read on the coordinates earlier," Rin said. "Approximately how long to Pervenio Station?"

"Six to ten hours, I'd wager, accounting for planet rotation."

"Long enough for the patrons to leave the beach and start clamoring for a meal?"

"Maybe two."

"All right, then we wait. Eventually, they'll send a few

Titanborn workers in here for supplies, and we'll take their uniforms."

We sat in the darkness, visors down and breathing in the scented air. The Earthers had it smelling like flowers, and the air recyclers pumping the room were so noiseless, there was no sound except for the occasional scratching of my armor across a container when I had an itch and couldn't get to it. The floor wasn't even vibrating from Saturn's storms, the cruiser built sturdy enough to handle them as if they were gentle breezes.

Hayes snickered as he and Gareth whispered about something—or at least *Hayes* was whispering. Gareth signed, and I wasn't paying close enough attention to see what they were on about. Rin sat across from me, her thousand-meter gaze aimed over my shoulder toward nothing. She had her pulse-rifle in her lap and continuously took it apart and put it back together again without needing to look.

"You're going to miss it, aren't you?" I said to her.

"Huh?" Rin shook her head as if waking from a reverie, then peered up from her gun.

"The *Sunfire*."

She scoffed. "Like you miss the shadows of the Lowers maybe. You stay in a place for as many years as we were there, and it becomes a part of you. The good and the bad."

"You never got off?"

"Once. Rendezvousing with a Venta transport in a place where the storms never cease wasn't easy, and we couldn't sit around during it. I didn't trust them enough, even with my sister organizing the exchange."

"Did you ever think about stealing it? Leaving everything behind?"

Her attention returned to her pulse-rifle. "You have a lot of questions."

"You have a lot of answers."

A grin tugged at the healthy side of her lips. "I thought about it. Earthers in a different color handed us food and water, guns and armor—everything we'd need to take their ship and disappear. I thought about heading to Neptune and beyond... going until the food ran out. And then I remembered."

"That you were a Trass?" I asked.

"No, that after spending my entire life listening to every word my brother had to say, running, hiding, and taking on names, I could finally have it back. Control something."

"No matter how awful it was?"

"Great a man as your father was, the one thing he never understood was that he didn't have to bear the burden of Titan alone. They were never going to be able to keep you hidden forever. Eventually, the truth finds us all."

"And a part of me is grateful for everything you've told me, but the rest of me—"

"Would rather live in that moment when all that mattered was kissing a girl," Rin said. "I know. You can hate it now all you like, Kale, but once you realize what it's like to stand for something, to truly make a difference, you'll never look back."

"I don't know..."

"I do. I see him in you so clearly. When the time comes, you'll want more than just to speak for us. It's why you proposed this plan, and why I was so eager to accept. You'll want a gun in your hand, leading the charge in the name of Titan, just like he dreamed of doing." She stared longingly down at the barrel of her rifle. "It's who we are. We see a chance at giving our people a real home in the face of hardship, and we build an ark to cross space and get to it."

With my mind now focused, I noticed the glimmer in her

eyes when she spoke of Trass—the austerity of her façade. Our relation to him was more than faith to her. She believed it completely, and for the first time, the notion that it might be true really hit me. I could understand why my father had felt the need to bear the burden alone. To hide. They were planet-sized shoes to fill.

The cargo bay's door whooshed open and promptly ended our conversation. The four of us immediately hopped to our feet, but Rin raised a finger to shush us. We were behind a row of storage containers, and she peeked around the end of them toward the door. I followed.

Two male Ringer workers strolled in, wearing tidy Pervenio staff uniforms. Pointed hats rested on their heads, as if they were attending a formal ball in a Pre-Meteorite era.

"One more meal before we hit zero-g," one of them groused.

"Better than carrying one more drink to a fat mud stomper in a bathing suit," said the other.

"Still, who could be that hungry? Can't they wait until we dock?"

"Apparently not. We better be getting paid a full shift for this, though."

"You know we won't. 'Wasted gas for a weeklong trip is expensive,' they'll say."

They stopped by a pair of food supply crates and started loading them onto a rolling rack. "Trass damn the Children of Titan," one said. "You'd think they realize that they're just hurting the rest of our wallets?"

"I don't think they care," the other replied.

Rin drew her pulse-rifle and stalked out into the aisle. "You're right," she said, aiming at them. Our conversation dropped from my mind, and I remembered who she was. I hurried out beside her, fearful that she might shoot them, Ringers or not.

"Don't move," I warned them. "Don't shout."

Their hands shot into the air. Their jaws dropped beneath their sanitary masks. They couldn't get much paler than they already were, but any hint of color fled their cheeks.

"P... please, don't shoot," one of them stuttered.

That was when I realized I had a pulse-rifle of my own aimed at them. I lowered it.

Rin stomped forward. "Uniforms off," she demanded. "Don't make me ask twice."

"Listen to her, and you'll be fine," I said, hopeful I wasn't lying.

They didn't wait. Hands shaking, they removed their uniforms down to a pair of crummy boiler suits you couldn't get anywhere else but in the Darien Lowers. My eyes darted between them and the barrel of Rin's pulse-rifle the entire time.

"On the floor," Rin said once they were undressed. They crumpled their uniforms and placed them down. "Masks and gloves too." They hesitated for a moment and then decided to do as she asked and risk exposure.

"Good," she said. "Now come this way." She took a step back and beckoned them around the corner. They obeyed, at least until one of them saw my face up close. He stopped in his tracks, eyes wide like he'd seen a ghost.

"By Trass, it's you," he said, incredulous. "Kale D—"

Rin cracked him across the head with the butt of her rifle, knocking him out. Gareth did the same to the other.

"What are you doing!" I whispered sharply.

"Two walked in," she replied. "Only two can walk out. Now get dressed."

She approached their uniforms, but I tugged on her arm. "What are you going to do to them?" I asked.

"Hide them. Or do you have a better idea?" I didn't. She pulled away from me and picked up a uniform. "From now on, you're a servant on the—" She paused and read the tag printed above the chest. *"Ring Skipper."*

"What kind of name is that?" Hayes laughed.

"An Earther one," Rin said. "Help Kale with his armor. There's no time to waste."

Hayes appeared behind me and started removing my suit. Gareth helped Rin. Hayes waited until the top half was folded down over my torso before somehow switching off its power. The tiny needles stabbing my nerves slid out. I instantly fell to my knees, finding that I had to work to draw breath again. The weight of the suit, in combination with my weak natural muscles, was too much to handle. Hayes forced me onto my ass and freed my legs.

"It'll take some time to get used to," he said. "The g-stim we took should help."

He drew me to my feet, and then let go without warning. I stumbled forward, legs feeling like jelly as the gravity of Saturn's upper atmosphere pulled on them. I had to lean against the row of containers to make my way over to the uniforms. Rin held one of them in front of her face, grimacing.

"Not sure you can pass as a man," Hayes remarked.

"Lucky for us, they think we all look the same," she replied. "Get dressed."

Getting it on all by myself was like exercising with heavy weights. I had to take it one exhausted arm at a time for the top half and sit to shove my wobbly legs into the pant-legs. I was puffing heavily by the end of it.

I patted the pocket to find its owner had only an ID chip with him. Then I lifted his sanitary mask. The idea of putting on someone else's was revolting. I washed off both the mask and the man's gloves in a service sink.

I glanced back at Rin as I snapped the mask over my mouth. I'd never seen her out of her bulky armor before. She was excessively skinny, no doubt from having survived on a limited amount of ration bars for so long. Her elbows and knees bulged like beads along a string. The uniform fell loose over her chest so that it was impossible to tell if she had breasts, though not that many Ringer women were well-endowed in that area. A sanitary mask covered the worst region of her facial scars, which surprisingly made her pleasant to look at, though I couldn't help but smirk at the sight of her hair drawn into a bun and hiding beneath a pointed service hat. The trappings of civilian life didn't suit her.

"You look gorgeous," Hayes cackled as he dragged one of the unconscious bodies across the floor.

"Shut up," she snapped, her healthy cheek a light shade of pink.

"Seriously. Forget your sister. I might take a run at you when this is all over."

"I said, shut up!"

He snickered but didn't dare push her further.

"So now what?" I asked as I put on a pair of gloves.

"We need a hand-terminal," Rin said.

"You didn't have any on the *Sunfire*?"

"None that still work. You think you'll be able to steal one?"

"You're joking, right?"

"Unless you'd rather break into the command deck. Rylah's taught me a few tricks, so I should be able to relay a message to her through their com array without them realizing."

I smiled. "Finally, you pick something I'm good at."

"All right, then—let's go. The kitchen is expecting our delivery."

"You two, don't take long," Hayes said. Gareth held open a tall storage container while Hayes stuffed one of the bodies in. "Once we hit zero-g, you'll be expected in restraints."

"We won't," Rin said. "If anyone comes through that door—"

Hayes finished with the body and slapped the container on the side. "Give them a shiny box just like these two. I know."

Rin and I emerged from the cargo bay, pushing the rack that the Ringer staff had prepared for us. We kept our heads down on the way out, wary of surveillance despite our disguises. A crimson carpet with gold frills extended down the center of a gracious hallway. Wonderfully elaborate faux-wood moldings ran along the edges of the tall, white-paneled ceiling, hiding thin air recycler vents pumping in unpleasantly warm air. Golden pendant lights hung from it, high enough for even the tallest Ringer to pass comfortably.

If that wasn't enough, a row of glassy doors to our left opened up to one side of what was labeled the NATURE DECK. Inside, trees with broad, frilly leaves soared toward a latticed dome projecting the image of a clear blue sky inside, like from the stories about ancient Earth. Through them, I could see tan-colored sand with calm waves lapping at it. Lounge seats were arranged along it, beneath massive, hanging light fixtures than shone like the sun.

An Earther with too many rolls to count lay upon one, wearing tinted glasses. He barked at a masked Ringer server carrying a tray of drinks, who'd apparently done something wrong. She remained silent and cowered.

Rin whispered something to me as I slowed to stare in awe. I was too distracted to hear her. "Kale!" she snapped when I didn't answer right away.

"Sorry," I replied. "What?"

"Focus," she said. "We can't look shocked by their deca-dence, as disgusting as it is." She stared straight ahead, concentrated on our task and not fazed in the slightest by the most luxurious space I'd ever seen. "And we have to remember to follow every order we're given," she added.

"I'll be fine. I'm used to having a captain."

"I'm not worried about you."

We turned at the first branch in the hallway away from the NATURE DECK. It looked the same as the last, only without a field of green through the doors.

"Do you have any idea where you're going?" I asked.

"Not at all," she said, "but they do."

Two Earther security officers appeared from around another corner a ways down. They weren't freelance like John and his team. These were legitimate Pervenio officers, in full armor and regalia, armed with pulse-rifles and the newest in shock-baton technology. Seeing one again made me cringe as I remembered what the lit end felt like.

"Aye, you two!" one of them hollered. "Get those back to the kitchen now. We've got hungry customers."

"Staff is stretched thin," Rin said, keeping her voice low and subservient. "They sent us to grab this, but we haven't ever worked the kitchen."

"I hate when they shuffle in new help." The officer rolled his eyes, then waved us along. "Come on."

They rushed by, and Rin and I exchanged a nod before turning the cart to follow behind them. She was smart. With our uniforms on, no Earther security officer would know who or where we were supposed to be.

We rounded another corner and soon approached an ornamental door clad with more fake wood. As we got closer, I actually started to wonder if it was the real thing. Considering most trees didn't grow naturally anywhere in Sol, there was no material more expensive to build with. Even the majority of Earth struggled to foster sizable flora after the Meteorite.

The officers held the door open for us. "Unload quickly," one said. "Servers are already sending out the first course."

We rolled the cart into a sweltering room clad in shiny chrome. Stoves and other kitchen appliances were steaming. Voices of a dozen chefs and prep-men yammered in every direction. The latter were mostly Ringers, too overheated and invested in chopping ingredients to realize we were strangers. The Earthers wouldn't notice we didn't belong unless we wore blinking signs that said as much. Once again, I found sanitary masks to have a greater use than simply keeping germs out of my mouth. They were a scoundrel's best friend.

"Finally!" a stout Earther I assumed was the head chef exclaimed. He lumbered around an oven over to us, wearing a scowl and a ridiculously tall, white hat. "These people paid good money not to wait. Next time, you'll be paying for it."

His thumbprint unlocked each container we'd transported. They opened with a refrain of hisses and steam, revealing more frozen slabs of meat in vacuum-sealed bags. Each one bore the emblem of Pervenio Corp alongside addresses of the industrial animal farms on Earth they'd come from.

"Start unloading, Ringers!" the chef ordered.

Rin held her tongue, and we got to work tossing the blocks of meat onto a counter manned by a Ringer prep-man, who transferred them into zap-defrosters. They were then passed along to cooks to be heated in tremendous industrial ovens. The security officers observing from the corner kept everyone focused. As far as kitchens go, it was extremely efficient.

None of the slabs of meat were very heavy, but by the time we emptied every container, my arms burned with soreness. Sweat poured down my forehead. I was preparing to lean against the wall and take a break, when I heard a *clank*.

One of the prep-men dropped a plate, and before he could apologize, the head chef backhanded him across the face. The

Ringer flew into a counter, the edge of it slamming him in the gut and knocking the wind out of him. The entire kitchen went silent for a moment, but when the head chef turned his attention back to the food, everyone else promptly did the same.

Rin's hands balled into fists. Being trapped on a ship with only her own kind for years clearly had her unused to dealing with Earthers. I prepared myself for the worst, and then someone slapped a finished plate down on our rack. On it lay a steak, cooked to perfection and served beside the greenest spread of steamed vegetables I'd ever seen in my life. Then came another plate, and another, until the cart was full.

"What're you two standing around for? Tables are waiting!" the head chef yelled at us.

I gave Rin a tug on her shirt to get her moving, and we rolled the rack toward a door on the other side of the kitchen. Another pair of Ringer staff appeared with an empty rack right behind us. Focusing on pushing was nearly impossible with the fantastic aromas wafting right in front of my nose. I wasn't sure what smell was what, since I'd never experienced food like this, but it sure beat salt and molten metal. I immediately regretted having gotten a job on a gas harvester and not a luxury cruiser.

"You see any terminals in there?" Rin asked.

"None," I said, though I hadn't exactly been paying attention. The hubbub of an active kitchen was hard to ignore.

We emerged into the ship's galley. Or rather, dining room—it was much too grand and seated far too many people to be a galley. The gentle, harmonious melody of string-instruments emanated from live performers in one corner. One was taller than the musician herself, with a curving bow made from wood and more than a dozen filaments.

Hundreds of Earthers sat at round tables with frilly tablecloths draped over the tops. The tall ceiling was coffered, and I had no doubt that the rich-colored wood it was made of had been cut from real trees. Sparkling chandeliers fell from it in equal intervals, dozens of crystal arms arcing away from their centers.

The hallways of the cruiser paled in comparison. This was now the most ostentatious room I'd ever visited in my life by far, and the sight gave even Rin pause upon entry. Massive paintings on the pearly walls hung above a molded, wooden trim. At first, I thought they were prints, but the brushstrokes had texture. I didn't even know people painted anymore. They were landscapes from ancient Earth, a place nobody would ever see after the Meteorite struck. Blue skies, green pastures—they'd all gone away soon after Trass fled.

Earthers glowered at the food on our rack as if we weren't there. They appeared famished. Judging by the width of their stomachs, they didn't know what real hunger was.

I nodded to Rin, and she returned the gesture. We rolled the food forward and began serving plates to each patron. They cracked their stubby fingers and licked their lips, prepared for a delicious meal. Forks clanked, knives sawed, and all I could focus on were the sounds of teeth chomping on thick slices of meat. Earthers slurped down drinks fashioned with genuine alcohol, poured by additional Ringer staff. They laughed and reveled, celebrating the mere fact that they existed.

At first, I wanted to grab a plate and devour the food, but the more we served, the more I just wanted to shove it down their throats. To watch them choke on portions so excessive they could've fed an entire level of the Lowers for days.

Armed security officers posted all around the room made doing any of that impossible. They weren't watching out for patrons getting too drunk and disorderly—they were keeping an eye on us servers to make sure we didn't attempt to sneak some of the good food.

"Hey, Ringer!" a guest shouted to Rin after we attended his

table. "I thought I told the kitchen I wanted it well-done." It was the same man I'd seen yelling down at the beach. He was so fat, his jowls bounced as he talked, and he hadn't even bothered to change into formal clothes or button his shirt. He raised the piece of meat stuck on his fork for us to see.

Rin froze.

"Are you deaf?" he continued.

"Sorry, I don't know what that means," she replied, with an edge to her tone that made me nervous.

The Earther cackled, bits of food spewing out of his mouth. The others seated at his table covered their mouths to hide their laughter. "Well, how about you get me someone who does. Or better yet, take this bleeding shit back and get me a new one!" His fork clanged against the plate, and then he shoved it toward us.

Rin remained silent. I could see her fingers twitching. Three years on a gas harvester, far from civilization and Earther verbal abuse, and she was probably ready to explode.

"There a problem over here?" a security officer asked, arriving seemingly out of nowhere. His hand rested securely on the handle of his shock-baton.

"Yeah," the fat Earther growled. "This one won't take my plate back. I didn't order it like this."

"It's fine," I said, jumping forward. "I've got it."

I hurried over to take the plate, and as I did, I noticed a rectangular lump in the man's pocket. My heart started racing like it always did when I reached the object of a job. I positioned my back so that the officer's view was obstructed. With my left hand, I picked up the plate, purposefully allowing the loose fork to fall to the floor to distract the Earther. As I bent over to retrieve it, my right hand slipped into the pocket of his fancy tunic. His chubby leg made it a tight fit, even for my fingers, but it also likely mitigated some of his sensation.

"Sorry about the mistake, sir," I said, feigning all the pleasantries of a proper servant.

He snorted and folded his arms on top of his belly. "Fix it." His breath reeked of alcohol, a fact I hoped would keep him from noticing anything was missing until we were long gone.

When I returned to the cart, plate in hand, his handterminal was stuffed securely into the waistband of my pants beneath my shirt. The officer moved along, and I nudged Rin to remind her to focus so we could finish our mission.

We emptied the racks, and then returned to the kitchen. We didn't get far before our cart was topped off with additional plates, each of them bearing a triangular slice of something white and creamy. I'm not sure what it was, but the fragrance was so sweet it was nauseating.

"I don't know if I can handle another round," Rin grumbled.

"You'll be fine." I gained her attention and flicked open my shirt to show her the hand-terminal. "Now let's go feed some Earthers."

We pushed the rack back out, and I felt her pat me on the back in approval as we passed through the door. All my life, I'd worked jobs for fences, mostly on my own. Sometimes I'd be partnered up with another thief, but we were always out only for ourselves. Typically, we didn't converse much more than signing each other from across a room. Even on the *Piccolo*, I didn't scrub canisters to make anyone else satisfied, only my wallet.

I knew I shouldn't—not after the crimes I'd seen Rin and her crew commit—but right that moment, it felt good to be a part of a team. Part of something beyond the pursuit of credits.

TWENTY

The meal didn't last long before the Earthers were shepherded away to be restrained for zero-g. Rin, the rest of the Ringer staff, and I were tasked to help clean the kitchen. Out of the generosity of his heart, the head chef left behind meals for us—the same lumpy goop I was fed on the *Piccolo*. I was glad to eat anything other than a ration bar, but Rin wasn't nearly as enthused and skipped the meal entirely.

"What now?" I asked her, lifting my last spoonful to my lips while I scrubbed down a counter with the other hand.

"We wait." She glared at the security officers by the exit. They would notice if I pulled out an expensive hand-terminal. The rest of the Ringers were too busy and overheated to notice that we were strangers, however. Once again, I found sanitary masks to have a greater use than simply keeping germs out of my mouth. They were a scoundrel's best friend.

"What about Hayes and Gareth?" I asked.

"Worry about us."

I nodded. Her confidence was infectious. I kneeled and scrubbed the grime out of the inside of an oven. Some got on my glove, and I considered licking it off just to get a taste of real steak. Then I recalled my mom's lessons about washing my gloves as often as I could to avoid germs and did that instead.

"All right, Ringers!" one of the officers shouted. "We're breaking atmosphere soon. Finish up and head to holding."

After the kitchen was cleaned, Rin and I stuck to the back of the pack as we traversed the ship. I was nervous that beyond the commotion of the kitchen, someone might realize we were impostors, but Rin seemed calm as ever. A few members of the Ringer staff complained about their sore arms during the walk, but that was it—almost complete silence. I wondered if we would've been noticed on the *Piccolo* under similar circumstances. It seemed impossible we wouldn't have been, but Culver's incessant yelling had a way of making me want to avoid everyone around me. Of having me keep my head down.

The holding cabin was somewhere toward the stern of the cruiser, on a level beneath the cargo hold where the rumble of the ship's engines made it difficult to perceive anything. Unlike the rest of the vessel, the room had a military feel. Rows of bolted-down seats lined the walls. They were fitted with heavy-duty restraints. Officers in the entrance let us sit wherever we liked, so we selected the farthest positions.

I watched the jaded faces of more Ringer staff trickling in once we were seated. Lucky for us, the flow stopped shortly after, and we were left without anybody sitting next to us. It seemed the crew wasn't large enough to fill every seat; perhaps the shortage of willing workers that had plagued the *Piccolo* was widespread.

"Sorry we're late," someone at the entrance said to the officers outside. They allowed two more Ringers in staff uniforms into the room, then sealed the door and left.

It took me a second to recognize the newcomers as Hayes

and Gareth, since their faces were half-covered by sanitary masks and I'd never seen them outside of helmets. They scurried over and took a seat on either side of us.

"I was worried you two wouldn't show up," Rin said.

"Yeah, well, if Gareth didn't take his sweet-ass time," Hayes answered.

Gareth signed something discreetly to Rin. I couldn't see what it was, but she smirked.

Hayes rolled his eyes, then whispered, "We spread everything throughout the cargo hold, so it should take security hours to comb through it all." He stretched out his legs, his knees cracking. "I'll miss the suit... and my gun."

"You get used to it," I said.

All three of them regarded me with blank expressions but said nothing.

Restraints suddenly lowered over our shoulders. My body was forced back against my seat, where an automated g-stim injection jabbed the side of my neck. The cruiser then started shaking violently as its nuclear-thermal engines powered it through Saturn's atmosphere. An incredible pressure built up in the center of my chest and behind my eyes, which would've been unbearable even with the g-stim if I hadn't been getting so accustomed to it. My short stay on the *Sunfire* had bolstered my endurance.

"Ascension has initiated," the calm voice of the captain announced. "Please remain in your seats until our arrival at Pervenio Station. Approximate flight time is five hours and thirty-six minutes."

"So, you two get in contact?" Hayes asked us through gritted teeth.

Rin tapped me on the leg. "Kale, the terminal," she said.

Everyone else in the cabin was too busy dealing with the forces of acceleration to pay us any attention, so I reached into the folds of my uniform and pulled the device out. I couldn't extend my hand much due to the restraints, but my long fingers again helped me out. Rin took it from me and held it between our legs.

"You sure you can do this?" Hayes asked.

"I contacted that brother of yours after we went missing, didn't I?" she said.

His cheeks turned a light shade of pink, and he leaned back without another word. Rin's thumb shifted across the touch screen of the device, rifling through commands. She didn't operate it with the natural grace that Cora did when she sat at a command console, but she knew what she was doing.

In a few minutes, she breached Solnet through the cruiser's long-range navigation systems. In one more, she sliced into the black parts of the vast network, where the fences I'd worked with operated amongst people with far more reprehensible cravings. She entered a contact number—a clutter of numbers and characters that it must've taken her weeks to memorize—then typed a message.

'CHANGE OF PLANS. CAN YOU TALK? —R'

Since we were departing Saturn and Rylah was on Titan, there was a natural delay. It took about two minutes for a reply to come through. Letters arrived, scrambled and nonsensical at first before they each flickered and changed individually to reveal words. The Children of Titan were clearly extremely careful when it came to communications.

'ONLY LIKE THIS. I'M UNDER WATCH. THEY TRACED THE TERMINAL BACK TO ME AND BROUGHT IT HERE,' answered a contact I assumed to be her sister Rylah.

'IT'S NOT ON THE STATION?' Rin asked.

Rylah said, 'IT WASN'T. IT'S BACK ON ITS WAY NOW FOR ANALYSIS. THEY SENT TWO COLLEC-

TORS AFTER ME, ONE A COGENT. I GOT THEM TO
BELIEVE I WAS COERCED... SOMEHOW. THEY'RE
BEING HANDLED.'

Rin said, 'GOOD. AS SOON AS THEY PLUG THE
TERMINAL IN ON THE STATION FOR STUDY I
NEED YOU TO SLICE INTO THE SECURITY
NETWORK AND HELP US REACH THE DETENTION
BLOCK.'

'DETENTION?" Rylah typed. "WHAT HAPPENED
TO WIPING THE MEDICAL RECORDS? I CAN'T DO
BOTH.'

'LIKE I SAID, CHANGE OF PLANS. WE HAVE OUR
TRASS. THE TIME HAS COME. CAN YOU DO IT?'

'NOT SURE. THE OFFICERS WITH ME MAY BE
STUPID, BUT THEY AREN'T BLIND. THEY'LL SEE
MY SCREENS MONITORING THE STATION,' Rylah
said.

'THEN GET RID OF THEM.'

'WAIT.'

The conversation went silent for one minute, then another.
By the third, the *Ring Skipper* had broken through Saturn's
atmosphere, and the ship stopped shaking. Restraints continued
to hold me down, but my body became weightless. It was a
welcome relief.

"What's happening?" I asked.

"I don't know," Rin grumbled. "C'mon, Rylah." She tapped
the device to make sure it was still working.

Much of the Ringer crew had conked out from the stress of
breaking Saturn's gravity well, but a few of them eyed the
device. Though none of them said anything, it made me
nervous. On the *Piccolo,* no Ringer would ever rat out one of
their own for doing something wrong, and I could only hope
that extended to every crew.

"Here," Rin said. A new message came through from Rylah, one letter at a time.

'SOMETHING IS HAPPENING DOWN HERE. EVERY MEMBER OF THE TEAM WATCHING ME JUST LEFT IN A HURRY EXCEPT ONE. SEEMED URGENT. PERVENIO OFFICERS THROUGHOUT DARIEN ARE MOBILIZING.'

'WHAT IS IT?' Rin asked.

'THE COLLECTORS LOCATED OUR BASE BENEATH THE Q-ZONE BEFORE WE GOT RID OF THEM, BUT SECURITY OFFICERS ARE GATHERING OUTSIDE OF THE MAIN Q-ZONE TRAM ON DARIEN LIKE THEY DON'T KNOW EXACTLY WHERE IT IS.'

I noticed a shade of panic cross Rin's face. 'THE DOCTOR?' she asked.

'ESCAPED, SOMEHOW. HER PATIENTS ARE BEING EVACUATED THROUGH THE TUNNEL NETWORK. WHEN AND IF PERVENIO GETS THERE, ALL THEY'LL FIND IS ROCK.'

Rin breathed a sigh of relief. "Katrina will be fine, then," she whispered to me. Though I didn't know enough about what was going on to realize I should've been worried, I found her assurance oddly comforting.

'WHAT'S YOUR STATUS?' Rin asked.

'I'LL HAVE MY WATCHER TAKEN CARE OF IMME-DIATELY,' Rylah answered.

'YOU HAVE FIVE AND A HALF HOURS TO BREACH THE SYSTEM AND PASS US OFF AS STAFF ABOARD A LUXURY CRUISER NAMED THE *RING SKIPPER*. CAN YOU GET IT DONE?'

'I ALWAYS DO. TRANSMITTING NAMES NOW.'

"IDs," Rin said to us.

We handed over the IDs stuffed into the pockets of the

Ringer outfits we'd stolen. They were little more than transparent cards with a data-chip embedded in one corner, and the Pervenio Logo ghosted across the middle, like my real one had looked before it got left behind on the *Piccolo*. You received one for living in a colony run by Pervenio Corp.

Rin sent her sister each of the names. I was Gavin Davier, in case anybody asked me, which I doubted. Messing with IDs was supposed to be impossible, but I'd been finding that claim disproved a lot by the Children of Titan recently.

'DO YOU NEED AN IMAGE OF KALE TO DOCTOR?' Rin asked.

'I'LL MAKE DO WITH WHAT I'VE GOT,' Rylah replied.

I shot her a sidelong glare. Rin shrugged and typed: 'YOU STRAND US WITH THESE AS IS AND WE'RE DEAD.'

'YOU'LL BE FINE. CAN YOU MAINTAIN CONTACT THROUGHOUT?'

'NOT WITH THIS TERMINAL. IT'S STOLEN AND A RISK. I'LL FIND A WAY BACK ONTO SOLNET. PREPARE A ROUTE.'

'GOOD LUCK.'

As soon as the last message went through, Rin switched the device off and used her nails to pry out the power source. The nearest crew member peered at her over the top of her sanitary mask. Rin shot a scowl back at her, so piercing that the woman instantly turned her head and closed her eyes to pretend she was asleep.

"Better rest up," Rin said, letting her head fall back.

"Don't have to ask me twice," Hayes replied. Gareth grunted his agreement.

I tried to take her advice, but I couldn't sleep. Every time I closed my eyes, I saw Captain Saunders's face before I locked him in the airlock. I thought I'd feel guiltier about condemning him to a slow death, even though he'd begged to die. I didn't. I wondered if that was because he deserved what he got, or if I was no different from the people sitting on either side of me who'd murdered half of his crew.

Then I pictured Cora with the blood of a man she didn't even know was her father being washed from her cheeks by tears, and I knew I would've done it the same way all over again.

Ever since I was sent off to work on the *Piccolo,* I'd felt out of control of my life, but that wasn't completely true. I'd chosen to break into an Earther's house, just like I'd chosen to do whatever it took to get my mom right. At every stop, I could've continued along like most people did, gone through the motions, made a simple living. But ever since I was a child, I'd reached into the darkness and grasped for more. I stole what I wanted to, snuck wherever I could, and lied when I had to. The truth was that I hated every second aboard the *Piccolo,* taking orders. I hated feeling like a cog in a wheel.

Was it the blood of Trass in me? Was that the only reason I'd decided to break prisoners out of Pervenio Station—to do the impossible? Or did I actually care?

"We are arriving at Pervenio Station," the captain announced. "Please prepare for disembarking."

Rin's eyes snapped open like she'd been stirred from a nightmare. Hayes yawned awake and had to nudge Gareth a few times to get him to come to. My eyes stung from exhaustion. Five hours, yet I couldn't quiet my mind enough to even nap for a few minutes.

No viewports were available to see into space in the Ringer holding area, but I felt the gentle pull on my body of the cruiser tilting to land on the inner face of the moon-station.

"We can't keep this," Rin said, wasting no time. She slapped the hand-terminal down on my lap.

"What do you want me to do with it?" I asked.

"Ditch it before we hit any scanners."

I nodded and stowed it in my uniform. The ship halted, and then our restraints popped off. The soothing tug of near-Titan-level g drew my feet to the floor. I was sore as hell. The g-stims we'd taken had mostly worn off during transit, but even though it hurt to stand, I was glad to do it. My bones and muscles were built for similar conditions.

A Pervenio security officer appeared in the holding cabin's doorway. "All right, everybody off!" he barked. "No dragging your feet."

The Ringer crew stood with a collective groan. They were all as exhausted as I was, and if we were going to be punished for dragging our feet, the officer would've had to electrocute us all. We shuffled, one by one, out of the cabin and were escorted through the luxurious halls of the cruiser.

First, we stopped at the Ringer dorms so the crew could retrieve their baggage. Despite the majesty of the cruiser, they looked like oversized versions of the ones on the *Piccolo*. We waited to go in last and kept our heads down as we found the only four bunks with any unclaimed bags beneath them.

Then we set off for the main exit ramp, which, of course, was located on the far side of the cargo hold. My eyes darted from side to side as we entered, searching the scores of containers and racks for bodies, weapons, and armor. I was used to handling almost everything on my own during jobs, so it was difficult not to feel anxious. I saw nothing, not even a speck of blood on the stark metallic floor. Hayes and Gareth had taken care of their end impeccably. They'd even reattached the vent cap we'd busted in through.

We passed the container Gareth had stuffed the first Ringer

staff member we'd replaced into. I half-expected to hear the man banging on the inside to be freed, but it was silent. The thought that maybe Hayes and Gareth had taken care of things too excessively popped into my head, but I couldn't afford to let it fester.

"Good as new, eh?" Hayes said, nudging me in the back. "Old Gareth loves moving shit."

Gareth flicked him the middle finger in response. Then he stealthily reached into a nook between two containers and snagged the supply bag we'd brought over from the *Sunfire* so that we wouldn't starve while we hid on the station. In its place, he dropped one he'd taken from the dorms.

"Stop it, you two," Rin whispered. "Focus."

The ramp exited into a massive hangar, larger than any I'd ever been in before. Deep trusses swept overhead, thirty meters into the air at least, their surfaces shining like they had been installed recently. I instinctually turned my head and gazed upon the cruiser in awe. From the atmosphere of Saturn, there was nothing to provide scale, but standing next to it, I realized how tremendous it was. Its top nearly scratched the ceiling, and it extended what had to be half-a-kilometer behind me. A true testament to Earther decadence.

"Focus," Rin repeated directly into my ear.

I looked straight ahead. The Earther patrons were already waiting at the bottom of the ramp, preparing to pass through a security inspection post. The first thing I noticed was how light security was. Only two officers in addition to those who served on the *Ring Skipper* were present. The *Piccolo*'s hangar typically received at least three times that for a crew of only around forty.

The second thing was the plump Earther I'd robbed earlier. He stood with his arm around a woman, likely his wife, barely able to stand. I knew the symptoms. His cheeks were pale, and he appeared hungover enough to vomit at any moment. Drunks always made the easiest Earthers to pickpocket. He probably didn't even remember he'd had his terminal on him and figured it was stowed in his baggage.

I veered toward him. The others followed me, no questions asked. I sped up and purposely bumped into his wife. Compared with him, she was slender, but she was still an Earther—it was like walking into a wall. I reached around her back as I collided with her and dropped the hand-terminal into his pocket.

"Watch where you're going, ghost!" he slurred, then hiccupped. His wife shot me a look of disgust and towed him away.

"Sorry," I said before falling back in line with my companions. Hayes wrapped his arm over my shoulder.

"Nice one, kid," he said.

My grin was swiftly wiped away by what Rin said next.

"Now remember, Kale, you're the most wanted man on the Ring," she whispered. "Don't remove that mask, no matter what. Fake a bad cough, be confident about it. You'll be fine. They won't expect anyone new coming from Saturn."

My throat went dry. I'd forgotten about that little detail. Without the mask, I would be locked up within minutes of being spotted.

We fell into line at the scanners, and I forced out a few grating coughs. There were no decon-chambers on the way back in, only before hopping on a shuttle back to Titan. It maintained efficiency during disembarking, and considering how wiped I usually was after a shift, I never minded. That would help me as long as the officer at the gate was in a decent mood.

The line ticked along. I grew more and more nervous with every step. I didn't even know Rin's sister, and we were essentially trusting her with our lives to falsify the IDs we had. *I was trusting her, and them.*

"ID," the security officer said to Rin when it was finally our turn. I realized then how young he was, probably just out of training.

Rin placed her bag on the scanning belt and then handed her falsified ID over. He ran his scanner over the data-chip, and when her information appeared on the view-screen, his brow furrowed in a way that boosted my anxiousness.

"I'm going to need to see under that mask," he said.

She reached up and slowly pulled it down to reveal the ghastly burns coating half of her face and the sinewy hole in her cheek. The officer looked repulsed. Immediately, I realized that the blemish must not have been featured in the linked identity Rylah provided for her.

"How'd you get that, Ringer?" he questioned.

"Cooking oil spill on board a while back," she replied without a moment's hesitation.

"Well, put that thing back on before you scare somebody. Your baggage is clear—move along. Next!"

Rin passed through the full-body scanner clean, and Hayes stepped up. His passage went much smoother. I was after him, and predictably, my heart thumped uncontrollably. I fake-coughed repeatedly, hacking so it grew phlegmy. I was fortunate I hadn't slept, leaving my eyes red and with a slightly glassy appearance. I repeated my fake name over and over in my head, just in case.

The officer snatched my ID from my clammy hands and gave it a scan. I saw the top of his screen. My face popped up; however, everything from the bridge of my nose down had been altered in a manner that was unexpectedly familiar. My memory of my dad was fuzzy, but I was pretty sure it was him at my age. I feigned a series of even more guttural coughs than earlier and rubbed my eyes.

"Mask," the officer grumbled, clearly tired of repeating the order.

"Is that necessary, sir?" Again, I hacked.

"Just for a second, Ringer. C'mon, you're holding up the line."

"I'm worried I caught something on board... Please. I can't risk it."

He sighed. He glanced back at his partner, who monitored the bags, and they exchanged shrugs. The officer then leaned forward and stared straight into my eyes, so close that I actually did get nervous about germs.

"You do look like shit," he said, lip twisting in revulsion. "Decon-chamber on the way home should sort you out. Let's go."

He placed my ID back into my gloved hand and beckoned me along. I hesitated for a moment, shocked that it had worked, and then shuffled forward. I maintained my cough all the way through the scanner, until I found Hayes and Rin waiting on the other side. Gareth came through with our supplies soon after. Nothing was suspicious about a Ringer hoarding ration bars and water packets.

We were in.

TWENTY-ONE

Pervenio Station's main concourse wasn't anywhere near as busy with foot traffic as usual. Instead, I noticed the overly-packed entertainment venues running alongside it. Security seemed low outside of the hangar as well. I was used to seeing an officer posted on the station at every corner, but all the way down the gently-arcing hall, I spotted only a handful, spread thin.

"Don't need these," Rin said. She tossed her stolen luggage into a trash compactor bin. Everyone but Gareth did the same. Our *Ring Skipper* staff hats also went in, which thankfully made the oppressive heat of the Earther-run station more bearable.

"So how do we contact Rylah?" I asked.

"We'll need the best terminal out there," Rin said. "As minimal transmittal delays as possible."

"Where do you plan on getting one of those?"

"Like everybody else."

Rin headed toward a tech shop nestled between two bars. She strolled right in, past all the screens and automated dispensers displaying Pervenio-made gadgets for sale. Terminals, timepieces, health monitors—all the things people with credits used to make sure they were never late, never disconnected, and lived longer than any human ought to. She strutted right up to the counter and requested the same V3X model I'd stolen from John what seemed like an eternity ago. Five thousand credits. A shift's worth of *Piccolo* work in pay, and that was before Pervenio and USF colonial taxes.

The Earther shop-keep was so short I could see only his big head above the counter. His eyes lit up when Rin slapped her ID down without a care in the world. Like John would have. My real ID chip used to be linked directly to my credit account, so her sister must've done the same to hers... or to the Children of Titan's. For a group that cursed credits, I couldn't help but wonder how much they had.

"You're sure?" the man asked. "I have a few cheaper models over here—"

"No, I want this one," Rin said, oozing confidence. "Been working for years—might as well get the best."

"If you say so." He retrieved the shiny device from his display counter. "V3X, it is. If you'd just have your friends there wait outside, I'll get it registered straightaway."

She glanced back at us, and we took the cue. We stepped into the concourse and waited outside of a bar-restaurant called Pan Fusion. The words NO GLOVES OR MASKS ALLOWED were projected beside the entrance.

"She does a good impression of one of them, doesn't she?" Hayes said.

"Must hurt her," Gareth signed in response.

"Guys, look," I said.

Pan Fusion was separated from the hall only by a hip-height partition, and every single Earther patron on the other side of it crowded around a view-screen. Their drinks were all lowered, and they were so silent it was like they were attending a funeral.

On the screen, a news correspondent stood in the tram

station within the Darien Q-Zone, a place I was all too familiar with. We were too far away to hear her, but the tram was parked in the Q-Zone station, with armed Pervenio security officers swarming about it. Hundreds of sick Ringers were being herded by them, marched along like they'd committed a crime and shoved into the tram cars. I also caught a glimpse through one of the space's narrow viewports of Pervenio dropships hovering outside.

"What the hell is this?" Hayes said, echoing my own sentiments.

Our peoples had one unspoken agreement since the Great Reunion: Leave our sick alone unless all proper precautions are taken. But the decon-chambers at the end of the waiting area were powered off and being used like rotating doors by officers and ailing Ringers. The reporter didn't wear a helmet or a mask, and neither were many of the higher-ranking officers.

Suddenly, a Ring-wide address broadcasted through every speaker and view-screen in our vicinity. The Voice of the Ring, Director Sodervall himself, popped up. He appeared more exhausted than ever. His wrinkles cut deeper, and the whites of his eyes were as pink as mine, like he too hadn't slept properly in days.

"People of the Ring," he announced, his tone autocratic yet solemn. "According to reports from our Collectors, the terrorists behind the *Piccolo* attack are hiding out in caverns somewhere below the Darien Q-Zone. All tram-lines have been suspended until further notice as peaceful efforts are made to displace the residents to a contained area of Darien for a brief period while the investigation commences. I assure you, nobody who is innocent will be harmed. Soon, this war being waged in the shadows will be extinguished, and we will have peace. The fight to ensure our survival rests in all of our hands."

The feed cut out, replaced by the usual talking heads

discussing the director's announcements and defending all of his words. "Peaceful efforts?" This was the greatest show of force I'd ever witnessed in my lifetime. The amassed officers weren't flaunting shock-batons. They wielded pulse-rifles, fingers on triggers, ready to blow a hole in Ringers, even though they were surrounded solely by the frail and dying.

Rage filled my heart. Gareth grabbed the rail of the low divider and squeezed like he was choking the life out of someone. I'd never seen him display such emotion. Hayes's trademark smirk vanished, replaced by pure abhorrence.

"Rylah's in," Rin said to us. We turned to see her staring down at her hand-terminal. Her expression surprised me. It wasn't brimming with the unbridled hatred I'd expected her to radiate after hearing the director's message, but sorrow.

"Rin, are you seeing this?" Hayes asked.

"We have to move," she said.

"Rin!"

"We have to move. As soon as security finds those staff members on the *Ring Skipper,* this place will be shut down tight."

She started walking, leaving us no choice but to follow. She moved at a brisk pace, but I caught her by the shoulder.

"Stop!" I said. "You knew this was coming, didn't you?"

"No," she said.

"You're lying."

She stopped and faced me, breathing heavily. "I have no reason to lie to you! Rylah just informed me the orders to sweep the Q-Zone from top to bottom came from Luxarn Pervenio himself."

"By Trass," I said. "How many people were you hiding under there?"

"Not enough to warrant this. There is a Pervenio army down there. Look around. Security has never been this light on the station, because he dispatched so many to Darien. Rylah said transports arrived by the dozens to maintain order before they went in. The feeds won't show it, but the Lowers are going crazy. Everything is shut down. It's..." She gathered her breath. I could tell that beneath her sanitary mask, her lips trembled slightly. "It's happening."

"What is?" I said. "What's going on?"

"They pushed too far," Hayes said. "Whatever happened with those collectors down there, Luxarn Pervenio's lost his mind."

"Focus!" Rin snapped, startling the three of us. "This is what you wanted, Kale, and now whatever's happening on Titan has cleared our path. All that's left here are men too green to stop this. There is no time to waste. Rylah is inside the surveillance systems watching over us."

"Can she see Cora?" I asked excitedly. "Can she see the others?"

"Everything in the detention block is on a local server. Accessing it right now would be too risky, but logs say no prisoners have been released since the *Piccolo*'s crew was taken in."

I nodded earnestly.

Rin gave my shoulder a reassuring shake. "We'll get to them soon enough," she said. "Now, when I say 'move,' or 'turn,' or anything, follow me exactly. The detention block is only accessible by tram, so we need an officer. Follow me."

"Where—" Hayes began, but Rin stared daggers in his direction to shut him up. "Follow."

She set off in a hurry again, and it took every ounce of my energy to keep up. It was impossible not to notice the newsfeeds reporting on the situation inside of every venue we passed. Earthers who managed to pry their attention off the screens scrutinized us, along with all the other Ringers arriving at the station after the recall from Saturn. The few security officers posted about stood at attention, trying their best to appear calm. I could see clearly that they weren't. With so many on Titan, they were the worst of what Pervenio had to offer. Something contorted their features. Something drew their hands toward the grips of their weapons.

Fear.

Rin spotted the most panicked of them and led us toward him. The young Earther stood alone outside the gate of an empty hangar with no departure scheduled. His hair was matted to his forehead as he perspired uncontrollably. His gaze danced nervously from side to side.

"Stop," Rin said to us, glancing down at her hand-terminal, where Rylah provided directions. We listened. "Wait. Surveillance will be cut in five..." She finished counting down and then approached the officer.

His shoulders rose and fell with each of his nervous breaths. As Rin got closer to him, I realized what she'd meant when she'd said we needed an officer. She was going to take him down— an Earther, wearing armor that likely augmented his strength and a weighted boiler suit underneath. Not to mention that while we were now unarmed, he had a pulse-rifle on his back, a shock-baton dangling from one hip, and a sidearm holstered on the other that wasn't snapped in, enabling him to draw it hastily.

I had no time to stop her.

"Sir, can you help me with something?" she addressed him, utilizing the sort of gentle, unassuming voice I wouldn't have imagined could stem from her mouth. As she spoke, she allowed her sanitary mask to drop.

When the Earther noticed her grisly scars, he froze, giving her the opening to slide to his flank, snatch his sidearm, and aim it at him. Her back faced the corridor, and with the three of us behind, anyone passing by would just assume we were all having a conversation.

His arms rose slowly. She pressed the pulse-pistol firmly against his chest plate with one hand. With the other, she switched off the Pervenio com-link built into the neck area of his armor.

"Arms at your side," she growled. "Eyes on me. Understand?"

He managed a nod.

"What's your name?" she asked.

"Vi... Vick," he stuttered.

"You have a clan-family, Vick?"

"I... uh... Yes. Amissum."

"Well, the four of us are the ones who took down the *Piccolo*. I'm sure you've seen the recording." She typed something into her hand-terminal with one hand and then read information off the screen. "The Amissum clan-family holds their main residence just outside of New London, factory workers. If you don't do exactly what I ask, I'll make you watch as we do the same thing we did on the *Piccolo* to every single member of your family, and then you'll go out last."

His eyes bulged. They wandered toward Hayes, Gareth, and me, but Rin lifted the gun and aimed it right under his chin.

"Eyes on me," she said.

Vick obeyed. Sweat poured down his forehead. He looked like the crew of the *Piccolo* had when we were locked in the harvesting bay, awaiting our inevitable doom.

"Please, don't shoot," he said. "What...What do you want?"

"I need you to get us onto the tram to the station's detention block," Rin said. "Pretend we're detainees en route for questioning for contraband discovered in our belongings."

"What contraband?" Vick asked.

"You'll see. No more questions. Will you help, or do I have to find another officer?" She pushed the barrel of the pistol into the upper part of Vick's neck so hard that he gagged.

"I'll do it!" he yelped. "Just don't hurt anyone."

"That's all up to you. Now remove your rifle. Slowly."

Vick reached onto his back, detached his pulse-rifle, and carefully brought it around in front of him, fingers stretched away from the trigger. Rin grabbed it and handed it to Gareth, who emptied its magazine into our supply bag. She then shoved it back into the officer's gut before taking his shock-baton and smashing the switch used to ignite it against the wall, breaking it.

"There we go," Rin said. "Now walk. Gareth, stay on him."

Gareth took the pistol and fell in directly behind the officer as he started moving. He kept it inside the supply bag, pressed firmly against Vick's back. Rin was behind them, head down and focused on her hand-terminal. I was behind her, as anxious as Vick that we were going to be spotted and mowed down. I could feel Hayes's rapid breaths on the back of my neck.

"Trust her," he whispered into my ear.

TWENTY-TWO

THE SECURITY TRAM STATION WASN'T FAR. VICK LED US toward two officers posted outside the entry, ammo-less pulse-rifle in his hands. Rin typed something into her hand-terminal, and then we all pretended that our wrists were cuffed as she'd instructed earlier.

"Rylah's now got control of the scanners and cameras inside," she relayed to us. Then she leaned over Gareth's shoulder and whispered to Vick, "Take us in. Act poised."

"Bringing them in for questioning," Vick said to the officers as we passed them, his voice shaking only a little. They were too focused on a newsfeed about what was happening down on Titan to notice or even offer him more than a nod of acknowledgment.

Inside, a scanner was planted in front of the tram-line spouting up through the ceiling. A sleek, vertically oriented car waited on the rail. A listless female officer sat in a booth beside the scanner, chin resting in her palm.

"Bringing them in for questioning," Vick said to her. This time, his voice cracked from nerves.

"For what?" she droned.

He took a deep breath. "Found illegal contraband in one of their bags."

Gareth removed the pistol, gave Vick the bag, careful to angle his weapon hand so that it remained aimed at the officer's hip, unseen. Vick placed the bag on her desk. She peeked through the top, and no doubt saw a pile of bullets sitting on top of ration bars. Her jaded expression barely shifted.

"Thought they could get this through security, eh?" she asked. She shook her head and sighed. "Damn, Ringers. You call it in yet?"

Vick stammered and looked from side to side. Gareth nudged him.

"Uh, yeah," he answered.

The woman typed into her computer and read something on the screen. "All right, I see the report right here," she said. "*Ring Skipper* staff caught smuggling ammo." It didn't take me long to realize one had already somehow been forged by Rylah.

"They're unarmed, so they're probably only trying to sell it," Vick said. "No need for alarm, but the director wants them interrogated nonetheless. You know, considering what's going on."

"I hear you. I'll just need to register your officer ID, and then you can take the Ringers along through the scanner."

Vick dug his hand into a pouch along his belt. He stepped toward the desk, leaving Gareth a few feet behind him. One whisper to the woman and we'd all be compromised. I wasn't sure what would happen then, but I could imagine. The mute Ringer's finger threaded the trigger of his pistol, ready to fire.

Vick wisely took Rin's threats seriously. He handed over his ID chip and waited without a word for it to clear. The woman was too disinterested to question the sweat glistening on his forehead. She returned the ID and our supply bag to him before ushering him along.

"All right," Vick turned to us and said, swallowing. "Let's go. In the car, Ringers."

Vick passed through the scanner first and strapped into one of the car's horizontal seats. Gareth went next, pistol and all, and strolled through without setting off even a chirp of an alarm. More of Rylah's handiwork, apparently. The rest of us followed, and before I knew it, we shot up through the core of Pervenio Station, toward the detention block of its security headquarters.

The car was organized so that we all lay in a circle with our feet aimed toward the center. Rock-strewn walls raced by through vertical viewports behind us.

"The detention block itself will be lightly defended, but it's connected to the main security headquarters," Rin said, still staring at her hand-terminal. "Even with what's happening on Titan, there will be a ton of officers only a short run away."

"Can Rylah lock them out?" I asked.

"Good question," Hayes added. "I'd rather not wind up in a cell myself."

"You're all insane," Vick muttered. "You'll be killed in seconds."

"Quiet," Rin snapped. Gareth nudged his pistol against the officer's temple to enforce the order.

"As soon as we arrive, Rylah's going to lock down the block, shut off the emergency alarms, and freeze surveillance feeds," Rin explained. "Fooling scanners and a camera here and there is easy, but once she does that, the researchers analyzing Kale's hand-terminal will become aware of her infiltration and cut her out."

"How long do we have, then?" Hayes asked.

"They'll be blind for about five minutes. Enough time to grab the prisoners and get into these tunnels. According to Rylah, they're listed as being held in row C, but with all surveillance feeds down, we'll have to find the exact cells ourselves."

Our car suddenly flipped 180 degrees to realign us with the station's rotation. I withheld the contents of my stomach.

"What about any guards?" I said, holding my gut.

Rin grabbed the pulse-rifle from Vick and removed the empty clip. Our bag floated from the car's spin, and she snatched it out of the air, then refilled the clip with the loose bullets.

"We do what we have to," she said. "They aren't expecting us, so we'll have the jump."

"What happened to sneaking in?" I said.

"What do you think we're doing?"

"Yeah, but I didn't think—"

"Wake up, Kale," she interrupted, using the same harsh tone she had with Vick. "You wanted into Pervenio Station, and you did your part. Now let us do ours. This isn't like robbing some shop in the Darien Uppers."

My head sank, and I didn't dare respond. Maybe I was going to be their leader one day—whatever that meant—but I wasn't yet. She made sure everybody knew that, and I knew that I'd have to trust her if I had any hope of freeing Cora and the others. Whatever it took.

"It's either them or us," Hayes said. "Get used to it."

"I'm trying," I replied. I looked back up to see Vick staring at me, probably realizing that I was the weak link. All I could do was hope he didn't try anything that would challenge Rin to keep her word.

She sighed in frustration. "You escort us in and then hop back on here and get as far as you can," she said to Vick. "Understand?"

He nodded, eyes still fixed on me as if he could read the

lines of concern riddling my face. I thought about thanking Rin for showing mercy, but the tram began to decelerate.

"Good," Rin said. "Everyone ready? Stick tight. We get out of this together, or not at all."

The tram screeched to a halt at a tubular platform, where Gareth left our supply bag. Vick led us into a long corridor, or at least it felt like one to me. The detention block reminded me of the Q-Zone waiting room. White and chrome everywhere, with bright lights that made me dizzy. I could hear our footsteps echoing as we approached the main lobby and the group of three officers operating the area. They matched the thumping of my heart.

"Walk faster," Rin told Vick. "Eyes forward."

Vick was unarmed except for the broken shock-baton at his hip. Gareth remained directly behind him with the pistol and Rin behind him, concealing the pulse-rifle. Hayes and I took up the rear, unarmed. Four Ringers in staff uniforms marching upon one of the most secure detention centers in the solar system.

Nobody had ever gotten as far as we were, because nobody'd ever bothered trying. There was no reason to. Hundreds of meters of rock surrounded us on one side, and the great vacuum on the other. Only one way in or out without passing through the security headquarters itself, and usually, enough officers at any given time to fill a troop transport. Except for that very moment, when most of them had been dispatched to Titan to handle an unprecedented situation.

Half-a-century since the Great Reunion, and there had never been a day before when the sum of Pervenio's might was required. We were indebted to the Collectors who'd apparently stumbled upon the Children of Titan's secret hideout and caused all of it.

We stepped into the lobby after what seemed like forever.

The three officers inside stood behind a desk, eyes glued to a small view-screen. It faced away from us, but I could hear that whoever was on the newsfeed was discussing the Q-Zone invasion. Word about violent protests in the Lowers were starting to trickle through.

"What do you have here?" one of the officers asked as we approached the desk.

"Four Ringers off the *Ring Skipper,*" Vick replied. "They were caught—"

He was cut off when the lights suddenly dimmed, the result of Rylah initiating a power surge. Gareth jumped forward and shot one of the officers in the throat. Another reached for his pistol, but Rin unloaded into his chest before he could get to it. The third officer ducked down behind the desk and fired blindly. I dived to the floor.

"Intruders in the detention block!" the officer shouted. "I repeat, intruders in the detention block! They're armed!"

I scrambled across the floor, spurred on by pure adrenaline. Gunshots resonated along the unadorned walls. It was deafening. I rolled over and saw Rin creeping around one side of the desk and Gareth the other. The latter fired, earning the officer's attention, and then Rin popped around the corner.

"Nobody can hear you," she said before putting a bullet between the officer's eyes. I stared as the blood leaked out across the glossy floor.

"Kale, watch out!" Hayes groaned.

Sometime during the firefight, Vick made the mistake I'd hoped he wouldn't. The pistol of the first officer Rin shot had skidded across the floor right into his hands. Hayes lay on the floor with a bloody lip after being punched by him. Before I could do anything about it, Vick grasped my slender Ringer body by the collar, heaved me to my feet, and held me at gunpoint.

"Nobody move or I'll blow his head off!" he shrieked. His strong arm wrapped my throat so tight, I gagged. I pawed at it, but the layer of sweat on both it and my hands made it too slippery.

Rin and Gareth took aim at him. I'd seen her angry plenty, but her eyes had never smoldered with the intensity that they did then.

"Drop him!" she snarled.

"You Ringers think you can just do whatever you want," Vick said. "You can't!"

"Gareth?"

He couldn't reply, but the muzzle of his pulse-pistol flashed. The bullet grazed my cheek before blasting through Vick's skull. As he toppled backward, I slipped from his grasp, angling myself away from his weapon.

Rin ran over, caught me, and helped me to my feet. "Are you all right?" she questioned.

I reached for my face, not sure if it was still there until I felt only a shallow scratch along my cheek. "I'm fine..." I panted. "Did Gareth just..."

Gareth's firearm remained aimed, hands steady as a surgeon's, one eye closed.

"Best shot on the Ring," Rin said.

I released a mouthful of air and glanced down at Vick's still-twitching arm. "Thanks," I said.

Gareth nodded and then retrieved two loose rifles. He kept one for himself and brought the other to Hayes, who was struggling to get to his feet.

"Hayes, you okay?" Rin asked.

"Wonderful," he groused, rubbing his cut lip.

Rin checked her hand-terminal. "Area is secure," she said. "Just have to help open the cells." She rushed behind the desk and stopped at the console there. Her fingers flew across the keys while her gaze darted between the screen and her hand-terminal. "There we go. Thank you, Rylah."

Three corridors branched off the lobby in addition to the one we'd arrived from. The doors into two of them slammed shut. Heavy footsteps echoed down the one remaining open hallway.

"Everyone down!" Rin whispered. She vaulted over the desk and ducked behind it. I scampered over Vick's body, struggling not to gasp as I caught a glimpse of the gruesome hole in the center of his face. Hayes and Gareth joined us.

"Wait," Rin said.

The footsteps grew louder. I heard two officers conferring, obviously having heard our disturbance.

"Wait," she repeated.

"By Earth..." one said as they entered the room. "What is this?" He raised his hand to his ear. "Coms are down."

My three partners sprang up and fired. By the time I joined them, the two officers' innards were splattered all over the wall. The few shots they'd gotten off had sped harmlessly into the wrong side of the desk.

"All right, let's go!" Rin ordered. "It's all on us now. Less than five minutes."

She and the others sprinted down the unblocked corridor. I stopped for a moment to choose between a fallen pulse-pistol and a rifle. I didn't have any experience shooting firearms, so I settled on the pistol, figuring I'd be more useful with something small. Then I quickly caught up.

The corridor led to a fanning passage with sealed doors running along one side at a tight interval. Each was labeled, and the numbers of those we passed were all preceded by an "A."

"Row C is two floors up," Rin said.

A curved staircase ran along the back wall in the center of the lengthy passage. She sent Gareth up first, and he crouched at the top, his footsteps light as a feather. Feet scuttled past row B's railing, and he swept them with his arm. As a Ringer, he probably wasn't strong enough to knock an Earther over straight on, but the officer was caught unawares and tripped. Gareth shoved his rifle against the man's neck and fired, letting the man's flesh muffle the shot. Three years on a gas harvester in the heart of Saturn, and now I knew what they'd been practicing the whole time.

Gareth waved us up, and we followed. They may as well have been towing me on a leash, I was so flabbergasted by what was happening. We reached the top of the stairs, and Gareth shot another officer down the row. Footsteps loudly descended the stairs from the next level up. Hayes fired his rifle between the risers, and when two bodies tumbled down, Rin finished the job with two clean shots through their foreheads.

We rushed up the next flight of stairs, when gunfire erupted from behind us. An officer had emerged from one of the row B cells at our backs. I almost tripped face-first in my attempt to duck. A bullet caught Gareth in the meat of his thigh, and he groaned in the only way his tongueless mouth could allow.

Rin leaped over the side of the stairs and rushed the cell, firing to drive him back to cover. She stopped just outside and tossed a stray gun across the opening to draw his fire. She then poked around the corner, and I knew that the screams emanating from within the cell could mean only one thing.

"Can you walk?" Hayes asked, wrapping his arm around Gareth's back to help him stand. He grunted in response. When Rin caught up, we continued to row C, blood dripping from Gareth's leg in our trail.

"Wait," I said. "They'll be able to follow us later." My uniform was well-made, so I pulled it loose and shot through the fabric with my pistol. It was technically the first time I'd ever fired a gun. The rip allowed me to tear off my sleeve completely, and I wound it around Gareth's leg. He grimaced in pain as I pulled it tight, but didn't fight me.

"Ready," I said.

Hayes went to help him walk again, but Gareth shrugged him off and raised his rifle. *"Let's go,"* he signed.

"I opened every cell in row C," Rin said as we reached the top of the stairs. "No time to check who was where, so find the ones you came here for, Kale, and then we leave. We don't have the supplies for any more."

"If they're open, then where is everyone?" I asked.

The cells extended in both directions from where we stood, each of the thick steel doors raised. I'd expected to see my friends strolling through the halls, confused, wondering why they were free. I didn't. No officers were left on the top level either.

Gareth and Hayes stayed by the stairs to keep guard while I stowed my pistol in my belt and hurried ahead with Rin. I checked every cell we passed. They were clean metal boxes, four meters by four meters at the most with ceilings barely tall enough for a Ringer to stand at full height. The floors were entirely transparent, with a view of Saturn's rings that would've been beautiful if I couldn't see the thick, circular frame wrapping the glass, denoting them as airlocks.

The first three cells were empty. In the fourth, I found a Ringer curled up in the far corner, facing out into the void. He shook uncontrollably. I edged into the room slowly, my pistol hand dropping to my hip.

"Hurry, Kale," Rin said, waiting by the entrance.

I got close enough to reach out and touch the man, and then he turned to face me. Even through a thick coating of bloodstains, I recognized his face right away. Desmond's eyes, usually brimming with fervor, regarded me, but it was as if I weren't there. Like he could see right through me. For a moment, he stared blankly, then he cowered backward as far as he could go.

"Don't... Don't touch me!" he moaned. "No more. P...p... please." He extended a trembling hand, his fingers twisted and gnarled as if they'd each been broken in a different direction. Half were missing their fingernails, and as he spoke, I could see that most of his teeth had been knocked out.

"Desmond," I whispered. "Desmond, it's me." I went to grab his arm, but he recoiled and held his shaking hand against his chest. "It's Kale."

Hearing my name seemed to awaken something in him. His gaze focused as much as possible, and when I reached for him again, he poked my arm as if to make sure I wasn't a hallucination or some cruel trick being played on him by his captors.

"Kale?" he muttered weakly.

I'd considered him a pest for a long time, but he'd always been ready to pick a worthy fight or spit out some witty comeback. Now he could barely speak. I choked back tears. I couldn't even imagine what Pervenio had done to break him so thoroughly and in so little time. It hadn't been even three days since the last time I'd seen him.

"Yeah, it's me," I said. "I'm here to get you out."

His eyes widened. "I can't! They'll—"

"You'll be fine, I promise. They can't touch you anymore." I leaned in and extended an arm beneath his shoulders. He didn't fight it, but as I tried to lift him, I realized how little help he could offer me in return. One of his legs was bent awkwardly at the knee. We made it two steps before it gave out and his body folded. He would've collapsed to the floor if Rin hadn't lunged forward to help me.

"By Trass," she whispered. "I hope the others aren't this bad."

"Hold him," I said.

I ran to the next cell and found it empty. I kept going. By the end of that row, my heart pounded against my rib cage. The last compartment was as vacant as the others. I left it and sprinted back toward Rin and Desmond.

"Anyone?" Hayes hollered.

I ignored him. Every cell I passed in that direction was vacant as well. Empty. All empty and sparkling, as if they'd just been washed. My chest felt like it was going to explode. There was only one woman aboard the *Piccolo,* and I didn't see her anywhere. I returned to Desmond without taking even a moment to catch my breath.

"Cora!" I seized him by the shoulders and shouted, "Where is she?"

He winced as if he thought I was going to strike him. Then he raised his hand and pointed with a crooked finger to the cell next to his: C-031. It too was hollow. I raced in and checked the flat, metallic walls for ways out. A vent, something. But the cells shared walls, and there were hardly even seams in the surfaces.

Rin and Desmond stood by the exit watching me. "Where is she?" I yelled.

"The director... made us watch," Desmond said, his voice barely louder than a whisper. His hand lifted again, and he pointed a crooked finger at the transparent outer seal of the airlock behind me. "He said... he said we'd receive the same fate our people granted his if we didn't tell him what he wanted to know."

"What did he want to know?" I forced through quaking lips. "What are you talking about?"

"The *Piccolo,*" Desmond said. "Something about a hidden Q-Zone. They didn't stop. They started sending us out one at a time. I was next, but... but then they all left for some reason."

"You're lying!" I tackled him out of Rin's arms. My fingers squeezed his throat. "You're lying!" I cocked my arm back to punch him, but just before I did, I stopped. His hands covered his face as he shrank away from me, as terrified as a child left alone in the bottommost level of the Lowers.

"I didn't know anything," he whimpered. "I didn't know anything..."

I fell off him and crawled back toward the empty cell C-031. A piece of frozen rock drifted by the airlock window, but there were no bodies lost in the blackness. Nothing. No proof that anyone had been ejected to die. I scanned the cell one last time and noticed a lens built into the small area of wall above the entrance.

"Rin," I said, my throat dry as sandpaper. "Did your sister know?"

Rin shook her head. "Only that they were here. I told you, she had to deactivate all surveillance feeds to get us in and those feeds are all local. From the hall, the cells looked empty. We didn't prep for this, Kale, we're improvising. She—"

"Is she still connected?"

Rin sat upright and withdrew her hand-terminal. "Yes, but not for long."

"Can she pull up the last day of recordings from this cell?"

"Probably, Kale, but we don't have time. They've found her bug and are fighting her. We have to go."

"Ask her."

"Kale..."

"Ask her!" I boomed.

She reluctantly obeyed. She entered communications with Rylah, and I gazed out of the C-031 airlock. Lights from distant ships danced across the blackness. Ice-rock glistened against the swirling rouge atmosphere of Saturn. Rin extended her hand-terminal in front of my face for me to take.

"Here," she said gravely. "We don't have long."

I took it without a word. Frozen on the screen was a silent

feed facing the inside of the cell. Cora sat silently in the corner, staring expressionlessly at the wall, her clothes and face clean. I swiped my hand across the screen to fast-forward through the time. Once, security officers came to take her away. She was gone for hours until she limped back in, her face as bloodied as it was when I'd left her, her right arm broken, snapped at the elbow like a twig. Twice more the security officers came for her, and each time when she returned to her cell, her limp was more pronounced and her body more densely covered in red.

She cried for a few hours after the third time she returned. Until the entrance opened again and in strolled Director Sodervall himself, the time stamp indicating this happened only a little more than an hour ago. I'd never seen him below his shoulders. He wore formal black-and-red fatigues and was unexpectedly short, even for an Earther.

Cora regarded him, and for the first time, I could see the blue of her eyes before she scrambled across the floor. The director leaned in front of her and said something. He didn't grin afterward. Or shout. He merely sighed, as if he was tired of the sight of her, before strolling out of the room.

She watched him go, the dread in her expression matching Desmond's when I found him. I didn't need to see what followed to know the truth, but I watched nonetheless. I had to. The cell's inner seal closed. She gazed up at the lens—right into my eyes—and then the outer seal popped open. Her body was sucked through, gone in less than a second. Like ashes in the winds of Titan.

TWENTY-THREE

THE HAND-TERMINAL SLIPPED THROUGH MY FINGERS AS the recording stopped. I couldn't breathe. I couldn't swallow. I was petrified, like one of Earth's forests frozen over for centuries after the Meteorite struck.

Rin's hand fell upon my shoulder. Not forcefully, but with the concern of family. "We have to go, Kale," she whispered. "She's gone."

"I..." I couldn't find words.

Rin crouched by my side and picked up the hand-terminal. "Now you know what we mean to them."

I turned to my aunt. Gone was her hardened glare. Her eyes were glazed over, a tear running down the ripples and craters of her disfigured half.

"She..." I swallowed. "She didn't even know anything," I managed to say.

Rin propped me to my feet. I didn't have the energy to fight her as she led me out of the cell. I wanted to sit at the airlock and search for Cora amongst the stars, but I knew I wouldn't find her or anybody else.

Back in the hall, Desmond cringed against the railing of the stairs. My assault had caused him to revert to a complete state of terror. Nearby, Hayes supported Gareth, his normally carefree expression rife with anger. Twenty Ringer members of the *Piccolo*'s crew had been detained, and only one of them remained, beaten and broken to within a fraction of his life. He would've been spaced as well if not for what happened on Titan.

"Kale, we have to go," Rin said. "Rylah's been blocked, and reinforcements are incoming."

I couldn't move. I stared at the long row of open cells, imagining the screams that had echoed from within them at the hands of the director before each Ringer was rendered silent despite knowing nothing. But they weren't all gone. I helped Desmond to his feet. His whole body shivered.

"Kale, focus," Rin said.

"They'll pay for this," Hayes bristled. Gareth signed his agreement, though his scowl was more than enough to indicate his feelings.

"They will," Rin agreed, "but we have to get to the tunnel. Our time is up."

I wound my arm around Desmond's back and walked wordlessly with him toward the stairs. He was heavy, and having only one working leg meant he couldn't help me much. Fury drove me. I wasn't sure what was going to happen afterward, but I was going to get Desmond out just to show the director what failure felt like. Even if it killed me.

We followed the others down the stairs. I stopped as my view of cell C-031 was about to be cut off. Through the airlock viewport, as the station rotated, I saw the silhouette of Saturn's largest moon eclipsing the sun—Titan. Orange blades of light encircled it like a crown of fire.

"Kale!" Rin shouted with urgency.

I snapped to and allowed the cell to fall out of sight. Down the stairs we went. Rin took the front since she wasn't carrying anybody. Her rifle was ready. Desmond and I brought up the rear behind Hayes and Gareth. My shoulder burned with soreness and my arm felt like it was going to fall off. A few times, Desmond stumbled, but I didn't let him fall. I wouldn't let him fall.

When we were halfway down the exit corridor, the emergency alarms started wailing. Rylah's interference in the station's systems had finally been purged. By the time we crossed the lobby, every door into the detention block was reopened. A device that had the potential to wipe a million Ringer identities off the grid had been expended to save only Desmond's life. My first decision as the leader Rin hoped I could be.

Officers flooded the lobby behind us, their footsteps clattering like a herd of ancient cattle. We retrieved our supply bag at the platform and jumped to the service ladder rising through the vertical passage just before any of them might have seen us. The tram-car we'd arrived in was gone, leaving only rock, metal lines, and darkness, enough to shroud us.

Desmond could barely wrap his broken fingers around the bars, so I stayed below him, keeping him steady. We climbed, the force of the station's centripetal gravity lessening with every rung. We reached a service landing about forty meters up, where we finally had a chance to rest.

It was a tight fit against a power conduit, but we all shoved in, stifling our heavy breaths by pulling our sanitary masks as tight as possible. Desmond didn't have one on, so I covered his mouth with my sleeve. Getting sick was the last thing he needed to worry about. His gaze dithered as if he was ready to pass out.

"Legs in," Rin whispered. "Tram's coming."

The rocky walls around us rumbled, and I heard a loud humming sound like a shuttle taking off. A beam of light pierced the darkness from above, gathering fast. There was just barely enough room for the tram to zip by. My sweaty face was blasted by a wave of warm air.

"Let's go," Rin said once it passed.

"For Trass's sake, give them some time," Hayes protested.

"There is none now."

The tram stopped. Then a basso voice filled the depths of the shaft, one I'd heard many times before. It belonged to Director Sodervall.

"What in the name of Earth happened here!" he barked. "Spread out. I want the entire block searched. Find these Ringers and put them down!"

Hearing him ignited all the ire festering in my gut. I pictured him leaving Cora's cell without a care in the world before she was taken by the vacuum.

The rest of the group listened to Rin. They prepared themselves to climb deeper up the shaft, where gravity would become imperceptible. Even Desmond stood groggily, expecting me to be behind bracing him. I didn't move. I stared down at the platform where Sodervall had arrived. My hands balled into fists so tight that my nails dug into my palms. I wasn't sure if it was my limbs shaking or Desmond's as he lay beside me, but I felt like I was going to explode.

"Kale, what are you doing?" Rin whispered from above.

"Aren't you tired of hiding?" I answered.

"Kale?"

I released Desmond, pushed off the wall, and dropped through the shaft. I braced myself between the metal of the car and the rock of the walls with my hands and feet. It was no different from a ventilation shaft, and negotiating those was my specialty. My light weight made me noiseless, and once I was low enough, I swung myself around the cylindrical tram-car and threaded through one of its open viewports.

Stacks of horizontal seats rushed by me, my body snaking through the narrow spaces between each level. I grabbed hold of the second-lowest one with my left hand and launched myself through the vehicle entrance, landing directly behind Director Sodervall. Before any of his men could react, my pulse-pistol was out of my belt and aimed at the back of his head.

"Nobody move or he dies!" I screamed.

The host of officers in front of him whipped around, pulse-rifles raised. I ducked so that the director obstructed my tall frame.

"Don't shoot," he said, more calmly than I'd have expected. "Listen to him." He turned his head to catch a glimpse of me.

"Eyes ahead," I snapped, taking a page out of Rin's book.

He chuckled as if I wasn't the least threat, like he probably had after he sentenced Cora and so many Ringers to death. "You think you're the first Ringer to hold a gun on me?" he asked.

"No, but if you try anything, I'll be the last."

"Kale Drayton, isn't it? If only Graves could've been here to see how wrong he was about you."

"Quiet!"

I heard the clank of Rin and the others scrambling down the ladder. The officers trained their sights on them.

"Tell them to put down their weapons and back away," I ordered. "Now!"

"You heard him." Sodervall extended his hands and made a downward motion. His officers slowly placed their rifles on the floor. I honestly was shocked by their willingness.

My impulsive gamble had paid off, at least for the moment. Pervenio wouldn't tolerate the murder of a director at the hands of a Ringer. It showed weakness. The act might earn the indignation of Earthers everywhere, but it'd also reveal what they were trying to hide in every address he issued. From their attempt at covering up the riot in the Uppers to ignoring the widespread protest to their invasion of the Darien Q-Zone—they were losing control.

"What are you doing?" Rin questioned, dropping down behind me.

"Exactly what you asked me to do," I said.

"Do it," the director growled. "Kill me and prove to everyone exactly the kind of animals you people are. You're all the same. We should have wiped you all out when we had the chance."

"Shut up!" I peered around his head and made eye contact with his officers. "Contact the rest of the station and tell them that if anyone fires at us, I'll blow a hole in his head. And the only thing it'll prove is that we can reach you anywhere: Titan, Earth—anywhere."

The officers immediately started chattering into their com-links.

"Kale, what's the plan?" Rin asked. She stepped in front of us, with the others forming a line beside her consisting of exhausted Ringers helping a wounded Ringer stand.

I was improvising, like I was a kid again amid a theft gone wrong. I spun the director around and shoved the barrel of the pistol into his mouth. "The Voice of Titan is going to take us to the *Piccolo* and ride with us down to Titan," I said. "Is it still operational?"

Sodervall's eyelids opened wide, finally displaying the hint of panic I yearned for.

"Is it?" I said.

He nodded.

"Where is it?" I asked.

He coughed a few times, and then glowered at me. "Back to the scene of your first crime, eh?" he said. "It's in a private hangar just through the security headquarters. You Ringers will never—"

I fired a round right past his ear into the ceiling. The sound of the blast caused him to recoil, but I didn't allow him to move far. "Quiet, or the next one won't miss!"

"Fall around Kale," Rin ordered the others, finally grasping what I was up to. "Half of us in front, half behind. Gareth, can you walk?" He snorted in response and armed his pulse-rifle.

"You guys are really trying your best to get me killed," Hayes groaned as he stepped in front of me, together with Gareth.

"Throw us cuffs, or he loses a hand!" I hollered at the officers. A few seconds later, a pair slid across the floor, and Rin slapped it on the director's wrists.

"Walk!" I ordered. I shoved him, and though my weak arms couldn't send him far, it was enough to get him moving.

We reached the lobby quickly, where we were greeted by a group of more security officers. The four of my companions huddled around the director and me like a protective shell. The officers formed a circle around us, matching our every movement but making sure to keep their distance. There were dozens of them, all armed with pulse-rifles. Anytime they got too close, I pressed my pistol against the director's neck and got my finger comfortable on the trigger.

"You'll never escape us, Kale Drayton," the director spat as we crossed the dead bodies by the reception desk. "Collectors will find you and your mother for what you've done, and then I'll show you what real pain is."

"Like you showed him?" I gestured to Desmond, who limped along using Rin as a crutch. "Or Cora?"

"You sent them here."

"They didn't know anything!" I smashed him in the back of the head with the pistol. I wasn't strong enough to knock him out, but his head drooped forward. I grabbed him by the jaw and wrenched it back. "I said quiet."

He cackled, still unwilling to display weakness. "They'll find you as soon as you land."

"No, they won't," Rin responded before I could, probably fearful that more talk from the director would provoke me into pulling the trigger and getting us all killed.

"Kale, stop," Rin said. "Hayes, where are our suits?"

Hayes's face lit up like he understood where she was going. I still wasn't sure. "Latched on to the vent we entered the *Ring Skipper* through," he said.

Rin turned to face the ring of officers surrounding us. "Send a squad to the *Ring Skipper*," she demanded. "Our armor is hidden in the cargo hold in an exhaust vent, third from the back. Have the suits brought to the *Piccolo*."

"They'll find the staff we stole the identity of in there as well, if you haven't already," I said. "Let them go free, no questions asked. They didn't do anything." There was no way I could trust Pervenio wouldn't interrogate them thoroughly after what had happened with Cora, but it was the least I could offer them.

Rin nodded. "That too. If the armor isn't there by the time we arrive, Sodervall flies. If anybody tampers with it, I'll know, and again, he flies."

She established eye contact with me, and when I noticed one side of her sanitary mask lift from a grin, I realized that her use of the word *flies* wasn't accidental. I hadn't thought of anything beyond using Sodervall to steal the *Piccolo* to get Desmond home, but with the wings on our suits, we wouldn't have to land at all.

An officer relayed her orders. I nudged Sodervall to keep moving. He muttered something, but the cold barrel of my pistol against his bare neck rendered him silent.

. . .

The security headquarters wasn't far from the detention center, but we had to move slowly and constantly remain vigilant. Desmond could barely move at all any longer. All his weight was slung onto Rin, who needed two arms to support him and struggled to keep a hold on her rifle. Gareth leaned on Hayes, and to combat the pain had to relinquish his weapon so he could grasp his wounded leg.

We were lucky at least not to be in the Darien Uppers or anywhere where lofty ceilings would provide vantages for sharpshooters. The only officers were directly around us, and any shot would have to go through my protectors before it could hit me. If it came to a firefight, we would lose handily. That was evident. All I could do was keep my attention on Sodervall and make sure that if he did attempt to break free, I took him with us.

The security headquarters was a marvel of technology. View-screens, some of which were entirely holographic, shined amongst a bullpen of desks and surveillance stations. Officers inside gawked as we went by. I caught glimpses of shops on fire playing on the screens at their desks, and hordes of screaming Ringers waving scraps as weapons. Any words were too small to read, but those screens were displaying what was *really* happening in Darien—what Director Sodervall's address and the public newsfeeds didn't want anybody to see.

"The hangar is just up ahead," Sodervall said. "I hope you've thought about this. You murder me, and it'll give Mr. Pervenio a reason to unleash his army on Titan. All of your people will die, and it will be *your* fault."

I ignored him. The tall gate of the hangar was set along the side of a corridor branching off the security headquarters. I could see the fluted hull of the *Piccolo* through a wide viewport.

Officers surrounded it. A perfect circular hole in the side of the harvesting bay had been patched up by a plate and sealant. The broken command deck translucency we'd busted through to reach the *Sunfire* was in the process of being repaired, a shimmering tarp fastened over the breach.

"You might as well just do it now," Sodervall continued. "Kill me and let my death be the reason Luxarn finally gets rid of you ungrateful Ringers like his father should have. Forty-five years I've been stationed here watching over you, listening to you gripe about the lost, 'perfect' world that Trass gave you. He was a coward, helping more cowards run from the Meteorite and never look back. Without Pervenio, you'd be nothing."

"We'd be free!" I growled. It took all my rage-fueled strength, but I thrust him against the gate, where a retinal scan was required. His face crashed into the unyielding metal surface. "Open it!"

He spit out a gob of blood. "Free," he sneered. "Until you get sick and need our medicine again. I wish I'd been there at the Great Reunion. Maybe then we wouldn't have made the mistake of not wiping all of you out. We own you, Ringer."

"Titanborn!" I fired my pistol into the gate, so close to him that the bullet skimmed his biceps.

I heard the clamor of the officers circling us edging closer as he groaned in pain.

"Back!" Rin warned, firing her rifle into the ceiling.

"Open it," I whispered into the director's ear. For all his smug talk, he didn't hesitate. He could try to hide it as much as he wanted, but I could tell he didn't want to die. Why would he? His hair was gray and his face weathered by time, but as a top executive beneath one of the wealthiest men in Sol, he had access to luxuries that could give him twenty or thirty more years easy. There was a time I'd have longed to swap lives with him.

The retinal scanner chirped, and the gate rose. My companions crowded around me, even tighter now as we stepped into the hangar. Everyone who hadn't been dispatched to Titan seemed to be present—at least fifty armed officers, at a complete loss over what to do. All their more experienced counterparts were far away in Darien. From behind Director Sodervall, my gaze swept from vent to vent near the high ceiling to the top of the *Piccolo,* searching for sharpshooters. There were none.

The most decorated officer stood outside of the lowered exit ramp of the *Piccolo*. He carried a large hand-terminal instead of a rifle. Once we were close enough, he began to speak.

"Your suits have been delivered as demanded, and your captives on the *Ring Skipper* let free. They will not be detained." He gestured up the ramp, where a few workers unloaded our suits of powered armor from a large container. "However, before you proceed, Mr. Pervenio requests an opportunity to discuss terms. He promises that none of you will come to harm if you abandon this foolish course of action, and begs that you sit with him to try and resolve the dispute with the Children of Titan. To start with, the one-hundred-credit reward offered for your arrest will be paid in full to you, and to any of your companions who comply."

We stopped a few meters away from him. A chorus of clanking footsteps, shaking rifles, and heavy breaths besieged my ears. The officer raised the screen for me to see, and on it, I noticed a face that was impossible to mistake. I'd seen him live over Solnet during M-day addresses and on a select few ads over the years. Sharp jaw, firm cheekbones, a stern glare: He was as handsome as any Earther model I'd ever seen. A perfect specimen. Luxarn Pervenio.

"Belay that order, sir," Director Sodervall said to the only man in his corporation who outranked him. "I assure you everything is under control."

"Silence!" Luxarn bellowed, and even through the device, his baritone voice commanded respect. I felt as if I could hear the hairs rising on the necks of every officer in the hangar. Mine would've too, but they already stood on end and had been since I'd first grabbed Sodervall.

"I will not tolerate the murder of one of my directors," Luxarn said. "Even one who has so spectacularly failed me. I've already lost too much today." He steepled his fingers on his desk. "Now, Mr. Drayton, name your price to end this madness."

I caught a glimpse of Desmond. He leaned on Hayes's shoulder, eyes almost entirely closed, but I think he was watching me through his eyelashes. I was reminded of something he once told me. That if credits didn't exist, he would be king.

"There is none," I said. "We'll be taking the director down to Titan. Follow us too closely, and he dies. Smuggle anyone onto the ship to kill us, and he dies. Once we're there, you can have him back. Those are *my* terms."

Mr. Pervenio's face contorted in a way I imagine it never had before. Before he could respond, I shot the hand-terminal out of the officer's hand. It exploded into a thousand silvery shards. Rin immediately pushed past the baffled officer onto the *Piccolo*. I nudged the terrified director onward and followed closely behind her.

TWENTY-FOUR

THE GROUP OF MAINTENANCE WORKERS INSIDE THE
Piccolo's cargo hold fled as soon as we entered. Our familiar
suits lay on the floor in a row, orange circles on the chest
arranged front and center. Our rifles were arranged to the side
of them.

"Check all of it," Rin said to Hayes.

He surveyed the suits, tapping the switches and lifting each
side to check underneath them. "Clean," he reported.

"Close the ramp," I said.

Gareth limped over to the controls. The cargo bay ramp
lifted, and I glared at the wall of officers gathered at the base. It
sealed with a prolonged hiss, which was immediately followed
by an exhale from every single one of my companions.

"I told you he'd find us a way out eventually, Rini," Hayes
said, chuckling in relief.

"You have no idea who you just insulted," Director Sodervall grated, gaze fixed on our suits as he probably realized where
he'd seen them before. "You might as well—"

I finally unleashed the wave of fury I'd been holding back.
"She was innocent!" I cracked him across the face with the

handle of my pistol three times in succession. By the time Rin and Hayes grabbed my arms and pulled me back, he was sprawled across the floor coughing up blood and teeth.

"We need him!" Rin shouted.

"Sorry," I grunted. "I'm tired of hearing him speak."

"We all are, but we didn't come this far to die now," Hayes said.

Gareth didn't sign anything, but he approached, tore half of the bloody bandage off his leg, and stuffed it into the director's mouth. He offered me a thumbs-up. I nodded.

"Rin, can your sister broadcast a live feed to the station's security headquarters?" I asked.

"I'm sure that'd be simple for her," she answered. "We've just never had any desire to send them anything."

"Good. Set it up. They'll need to see he's alive if we don't want to be shot down. Hold him." I knelt in front of the reeling director and yanked the gag out of his mouth. He dry-heaved.

"You fucking skellies!" he barked. "I'll space all of you just like the others. Every single one!"

"I hate that word." I raised the pistol to his temple. "Now, use the tiny com-link in your left ear to tell your men to open the hangar." His brow furrowed like he didn't know what I was talking about, but there was a time I'd made a living being good at observing. I'd noticed the com-link at some point while I was next to him. I reached into his ear and removed the minuscule device, no larger than my thumbnail. Pervenio officers had only the best tech.

"Don't make me ask again," I said.

He snatched the device and held it to his mouth. "Open the hangar immediately," he said. "Happy?"

"Are there any officers hidden on board?"

"No."

I hit him with my gun. "Don't lie to me!"

"There aren't! To think that Luxarn actually thought he could talk some sense into you. He still doesn't know how you people really are. I spent too long shielding him from the truth. How you're all animals."

I snatched the com-link from him and crushed it beneath my foot. Then I stuffed the gag back into his mouth. He lunged at me, but a blow from Rin to the back of his head with the butt of her rifle knocked him flat on his face.

"Everyone in their armor in case he's lying," I said. "Keep your weapons on you. Hayes, once you're ready, get to the command deck and power the engines."

"Maybe you forgot, kid, but we kind of blew up the command deck's ceiling," he said. "They have it covered for repairs, but I'm not sure how well that'll hold."

"Do you need to be out there to pilot?"

"Only to lower us out of the airlock, I guess," he replied, scratching his chin. "Then, I think I might be able to plot a course and get us the hell out of there."

"Good. Do it."

He looked to Rin, who nodded, and then he picked up a suit of armor.

"Rin and Gareth, take the others and set the director up in the airlock," I ordered next. "I want Gareth's gun on Sodervall every second. Rin, find something in the medical bay for his leg and to help Desmond. Strap him in outside of the airlock and get him in an exo-suit."

Gareth nodded and wasted no time starting to put on his armor. Rin took me by the arm and pulled me aside. "What about you?" she asked.

"Just get it done," I said.

I brushed her off and stepped before my suit of powered armor. I could feel Rin eyeing me as she put hers on. The first time I wore it, I'd been forced in. Now I longed to hide my face behind the tinted visor.

The others left the cargo bay to prepare for departure, one by one, but I didn't move. Once they were gone, I screamed at the top of my lungs. So loud that I had little doubt the officers in the hangar outside could hear me through the *Piccolo*'s rickety old hull. When I had no more air left in me to release, I bent over my armor and started to cry. I cried until the *Piccolo*'s engine flaring on made the floor vibrate. The ship descended through the airlock, and my tears were caught on the unseen currents of zero-g.

Hours passed. I figured it'd take about six to reach Titan with the way Hayes had the engines humming, and while I had no way of telling time in the cargo bay, I knew we had to be getting close. Accelerative forces towed at my body. I could've put on my powered suit to temper them, but I didn't want the numbness that came with it. Instead, I remained in the cargo bay, holding on to the grated floor so I didn't float away, staring at the orange circle on the center of the armor.

"Everything's been prepared," Rin said. She floated in the room's entrance, body covered by armor. It suited her. Made her look like a fighter worthy of the scars on her face.

"Good," I replied.

"That was an unexpected move, to say the least. You'll be better at this leading thing than I ever was."

"I still couldn't save her."

Rin didn't respond at first. She drifted slowly into the room and pulled her weightless body to the floor beside me. "You know, the last thing Rylah told me is that your mother will be at the safe-house we're going to once we reach Titan. Everyone below the Darien Q-Zone fled there before Pervenio's army arrived."

"I'm glad she's okay," I said.

"Kale," Rin sighed.

"I'm going to kill him, Rin. I know I said I wouldn't, but I lied."

"They've lied plenty of times to us. Whatever you decide, I'm with you to the end. We're family."

"Trass's." I scoffed.

"You invaded Pervenio Station and took Director Sodervall hostage. Impressive for a boy who never thought he'd be more than a thief. If that doesn't make you believe, I don't know what can. Everyone else sure as hell will when word gets out."

"Darien Trass saved people. He didn't..." I exhaled through clenched teeth. "He didn't kill them."

"Tell that to Desmond." She edged a bit closer to me. "All I know is that if your father could see you now, he'd be prouder than any man in Sol."

I turned to her, lower lip quivering. "Like I should care? My father never saw anything."

"That's not true. Alann loved you from the moment you were born. I never saw him cry any other time but the day he let you go. We watched as your mother took you home after his fake ashes soared. You were so small back then. She gave you lettuce, do you remember?"

"I do."

"I'd known him my whole life, and when I saw tears running down his cheeks, I couldn't believe it. He was always so strong, so focused. He and Katrina cried together from afar while I stood next to him stifling a grin. We'd always looked out for each other, so like a fool, I resented how much he loved you both. I told him it was for the best, and when he saw how happy it made me, it broke his heart. We didn't talk much after that.

He sent me to work with Rylah, the illegitimate daughter planted in our mom by some putrid Earther."

"You mean she's like Cora is... was?"

"Yes. I rarely saw Alann again until he came up with the plan for the *Sunfire,* but I'd have given anything to have been able to go back and tell him I was sorry. I never got the chance. Katrina contracted a rare virus, and he traveled to Earth without as much as a goodbye to find the medicine she needed. By the time he located it, our former homeworld had riddled his body with diseases. His only choice was to bomb New London as a distraction so the followers who would've stood with him into the vacuum could steal the medicine. He gave his life to give her one back, Kale. That is who your father was. That is who *you* are."

Hearing her story had me so choked up that I could hardly speak. It made me think of Cora. "I never even got to say good-bye," I said softly. "I loved her."

"I know. And I loved him. And if you embrace who you are and become what he and Katrina were so scared to let you, then nobody will ever have to die for the reasons they did again." She pushed off the floor. "When you're ready, we're all by the airlock. Ship's on autopilot." She drew her body out of the cargo bay without another word.

I understood what she was trying to tell me. It didn't make me feel any better, but I don't think that was the point. I'd never get over what happened. None of us would. But that passion, that love, didn't have to make us weaker. I didn't have to forget Cora; I only had to fight the battle she never could. Destroy the thing that took her mother and almost mine as well. Free the Ring before they made bastards out of us all.

I grabbed hold of my armor and lifted it. My face was reflected in the helmet's visor. I was gaunt, covered forehead to chin in blood and tears, sanitary mask and all. I raised it farther so that the orange circle was directly in front of me, like the ring of flame wreathing my head in the image Director Sodervall had distributed throughout Sol.

I remembered that day in the Uppers when Cora had pulled me out of a riot while I cowered. I was wondering how I'd act in that situation now, after all I'd been through, when suddenly, it hit me.

A ring of flame.

I knew what I had to do. I threw on my armor—no small task while tumbling around in zero-g—and headed for the airlock.

TWENTY-FIVE

"THERE HE IS!" HAYES EXCLAIMED AS I FLEW DOWN THE ceiling of the stern airlock's corridor in my powered suit. "Our fearless leader."

Dried blood was crusted to the floor and walls, most of it belonging to Captain Saunders and the Earthers I'd watched die in the very same airlock. Flashes of that moment assailed my mind as I approached, but they didn't hinder me. Not with the plan I had bouncing around inside my skull.

Hayes was strapped into a seat on one of the side aisles. Desmond sat next to him. A bulky exo-suit used for emergency EVAC repairs on the exterior of the *Piccolo* covered the majority of his wounds, but he appeared less on the brink of death than earlier. Rin was across from them, deconstructing a pulse-rifle just to pass the time, the loose pieces floating before her.

"How far are we?" I asked.

"Two hours or so, last I checked," Hayes answered. "Kind of an issue getting into a command deck that doesn't have a top."

"Do we have any tails?"

"Only about a dozen, all armed with enough ordnance to

blow us to bits if they feel like it. Gareth's keeping them in line, though." Hayes gestured toward our mute companion, who held on to a wall inside the open airlock to stay grounded. He aimed his pistol at Director Sodervall with one hand and held Rin's hand-terminal with the other. The director himself was cuffed to a pipe, the same way Captain Saunders had been on the *Sunfire*. A gag kept the director quiet. He was only half-conscious regardless, and a spattering of fresh bruises on his face didn't make it difficult to imagine why.

"We told them that we'll be landing the ship by a methane lake about fifty kilometers west of Darien and leaving the director behind," Rin said. "There's a storm in the area, so scanners should lose us after we take to the sky."

"What about Darien?" I asked. "Has Rylah provided an update on the situation there?"

"Last I heard, the main tram station in the colony block had been converted into makeshift quarantines while Pervenio forces continue sweeping the Q-Zone. It isn't pretty in the Lowers. Titanborn everywhere are trying to break into the Uppers and riot."

"Good." I drew myself into the seat next to Rin. "How do you guys feel about helping them?"

"Once we're down there, we'll find a way."

"No, now."

Rin's and Hayes's brows simultaneously furrowed. I was too keen on the plan I'd thought of to wait for their response. "Hayes, I need you to go back to the command deck one more time and alter our course."

"What?" he questioned. "Why?"

"I want the *Piccolo* diving directly for the Darien Q-Zone at full burn," I said.

Rin appeared shocked by the idea, and she wasn't alone.

"We'll never get close," Hayes said. "They're monitoring our vector. As soon as I change it, they'll take us down. No way would Mr. Pervenio sacrifice that many men for the director. It's suicide."

"That's why we're going to have to turn at the last possible second once we're in atmosphere."

"Autopilot can't handle a maneuver like that. We could miss by kilometers."

"We won't if you're at the helm."

"The command deck's barely covered. Diving down bow-first through Titan's atmosphere at that velocity...the friction alone will burn the repair canvas up in seconds. I'd never make it."

"That's what our armor is for. We flew through Saturn. It can take it, can't it, Rin?"

"For a short time, yeah," she said.

"We'll wait as long as we can for you. If we hit the Q-Zone now, while our people are in Darien, Pervenio Corp will never be able to recover."

"We don't know if all the sick are gone," Rin said, though her tone didn't indicate she was opposed to my idea. "It looks like they are, but there could be stragglers. We just don't know, since any feeds inside have been deactivated."

"We'll never have this chance again, Rin," I said. "If Hayes pushes the engines as fast as they can go, then nothing will be able to stop the ship."

"Why don't you go out there, then," Hayes countered. "I'll happily walk you through it."

"I'll do it," Rin volunteered.

"No," I said. "He's the only experienced pilot here, and if we miss, we'll never have another shot."

"Nah, screw this!" Hayes blurted. "I've done everything that was asked of me, but not this. I don't care who you are, son of Trass. We've got the director now; that's enough. Right, Rin?"

She stared forward, her eyes bursting with wonder as she likely imagined the same possibilities I had when the idea had popped into my head.

"Rini?" Hayes repeated.

"He's right," she said. "We've been waiting for a revolution, and now we have a chance to gain the upper hand before it even starts."

He shook his head. "No. I won't do it." He snapped off his restraints and drew himself down the corridor away from us. "You're on your own."

I chased after him. He turned the corner, but before I could follow, Rin blocked me with her arm.

"Are you sure about this?" she asked. "A lot of men will die down there. Men with families, kids."

I bit my lip. I knew she was right, but as I prepared to answer, all I could see was Cora's face before she was sucked out to die. If I'd learned a single thing about Earthers since Rin abducted me, it was that it was either them or us.

"I'm sure," I said. "We'll never get another chance like this."

"No, we won't." She gave my shoulder an approving shake. "I'll talk to him, then. He'll listen to me."

She followed him, and I'd started to pull myself back toward the airlock, when suddenly, I heard them arguing. I stopped.

"I know it seems insane, but you know he's right," Rin said fervently.

"It *is* insane," Hayes replied. "With everything that's just happened, he isn't thinking straight."

"But I am. Trust me. You think flying to the *Ring Skipper* was any crazier? You can do this, and our people will never forget. Half of Pervenio Corp's armed forces, gone in a flash. Imagine what we could do."

"Rin. We don't know if it's only them."

"No, but it's what we wasted three years for. A small sacrifice to pay for freedom, if any."

I decided I'd snooped enough and headed back to the airlock. My plan hinged on Hayes's willingness to risk his life. If Rin couldn't do it, I'd have to find a way to convince him.

I returned to my seat and leaned back. After a few minutes, Gareth caught my attention and lowered his pistol for a moment to sign me something. It took me two attempts to understand that he was saying. *"Now you lead."*

"You think so?" I said.

He shrugged his shoulders. *"Trass gave his life to give us the Ring."*

"This is nothing like that. He was a hero."

"You will be too."

I swallowed a dry throat, then nodded. I knew he was right. For killing so many, I'd be a hero. I'd give my people a real chance at changing things for our home. "I wish that weren't true."

"Kale..." a hoarse voice mumbled. "It really is you." I turned to see Desmond awake. Painkillers from the med-bay had calmed his nerves, and for the first time since we'd saved him, it didn't seem like he was staring through me at some unspeakable horror.

"It's me," I said.

"What's going on?" He lifted his arm and realized that he was in an exo-suit.

"We stole the *Piccolo* to get you out."

His helmet rotated so that he could get a glimpse of his surroundings. His gaze froze on the director, jaw dropping. "By Trass, I thought I was dreaming."

"So did I at first."

He looked back at me, and his features darkened. "Cora, I—"

I hushed him and patted his leg. "It's not your fault. Now rest. You'll need it."

He nodded and stopped fighting the urge to close his eyes and catch up on the rest he so desperately needed. I considered joining him, when Rin reappeared around the corner, Hayes trailing close behind.

"He'll do it," she said.

"You're lucky I can't turn down the chance to watch that place burn," he said. "But there's one condition. When they name you king, or whatever, I get to be your jester." His solemn façade broke into a halfhearted smirk.

"I wouldn't have it any other way," I replied. "You're sure?"

"We flew across Saturn, remember? With this suit, and if I'm fast, I should be able to slip out after I make the turn."

"I know you will."

After a long, uncomfortable silence, he said, "I'm going to go check on the numbers." I noticed his lips droop out of the corner of my eye as he turned to pull himself back out of the airlock corridor.

"If you're worried he's going to go hide, don't be," Rin said to me. "He'll do it."

"How did you convince him?" I asked.

"I told him that if he doesn't make it, we'll name a colony block after him," she answered. "And that if he does, I'll person-ally introduce him to Rylah as the brilliant pilot we couldn't have survived on the *Sunfire* without."

"You'd lie to her like that?" I joked.

"No, probably not, but I wasn't going to crush his heart." She snickered, then turned serious. "He didn't need the inspira-tion, though. Hayes has as much reason to hate the Q-Zones as any of us. The one in Ziona left him orphaned before he could talk. Plus, it's a brilliant plan. He knows it's what any of us would do if we could. He just needed to hear it from me.

Beneath all the bluster, Hayes is a good man. Titanborn, through and through."

"You should tell him that, Rin," I said. "Before he goes out there."

She grimaced. "He'll make it. We all will."

The rest of the trip passed in a hurry. I could tell by the silence that the gravity of what we were about to attempt weighed heavily on us all. Especially Hayes. Once he returned from the command deck, he sat alone on the other end of the airlock corridor, staring at the wall. He looked like he wanted to do what I was asking of him about as much as I had wanted to smuggle my corrupted hand-terminal onto the *Piccolo*.

Rin watched him the entire time. She'd sacrificed Joran, one of their own, back on the *Piccolo*, but after all we'd been through, I imagined it must've been even harder for her now. For three years, she'd led them through the bowels of Saturn, and it was clear she cared for them more than she would ever let on. The tears welling in the corners of her eyes were proof enough of that—of the heart she thought she didn't have.

But it wasn't her who'd come up with the idea to murder thousands. It was me.

Gareth banged his pistol on the wall of the airlock, instantly rousing the director and Desmond. He was monitoring our progress on Rin's hand-terminal, and his signal meant that we were five minutes from hitting Titan's atmosphere.

"Here we go!" Rin shouted, mustering her most commanding tone. "Everyone in the airlock."

I'd been shaking in anticipation and immediately pushed off my seat. I took Desmond by the hand and helped him into the airlock. "Hold on to something," I said to him.

Gareth didn't move. He remained filming the director from

the floor so that there was no way for anyone on the other side to see what was happening.

Rin drifted into the airlock and regarded the director. "Should we let him go up in flames with his men?" she asked as she handed me a pistol. "Or make a show of it?"

"Neither," I replied. "Get him in a suit. He's coming with us, for now."

She didn't question me. She grabbed an exo-suit off the corridor walls and carried it into the airlock with us. The director said something and kicked his legs, but through his gag, all I could hear were moans.

Hayes leveled his weightless body outside of the airlock and visibly swallowed the lump in his throat. "All right, I'm going to seal you in and head up," he said. "Pretty soon, it's going to get real bumpy. When we're low enough, I'll release the outer seal. Take it slow out there. I know I'm the best flier here, but I'll be catching up to you from the command deck."

"As slow as we can," Rin promised. She threw him a nod, and he returned one.

"Let's show those Pervenio mud stompers who the Ring really belongs to," Hayes said, pouring as much heart into the words as he could muster.

He raised his hand to close the outer airlock seal, but before he could, Rin shouted, "Hey, Hayes! From ice to ashes!"

He flashed a smug grin. "From ice to ashes, beautiful."

The airlock sealed, and he disappeared around the corner. It was strange watching him through the tiny viewport from that vantage; seeing what John and the other Earthers had before they were evacuated. It seemed impossible that I would ever have wound up where they were, yet there I was.

"Wait until we start shaking, then we cut the feed and suit Sodervall up," I said.

Rin nodded without averting her gaze from the viewport. I

checked Gareth to make sure he heard me. He did the same.

We braced ourselves, and a few minutes of silence later, the ship lurched as we hit Titan's atmosphere. The airlock started rocking, more violently with each second. We were thrown against the inner seal.

"Cut it!" I yelled.

Gareth smashed the hand-terminal on the floor. I grabbed the director and released his cuffs. He squirmed, but he couldn't compete with the strength of my suit. I lifted him, and together Rin and Gareth forced his body into the exo-suit.

"Rin, you take the director," I said. "I don't trust myself."

"With pleasure," she replied.

"Gareth, you'll fly alone and keep a lookout for ships. I'll take Desmond."

"Take me where?" a bewildered Desmond questioned.

I gently lowered a helmet over his head. He wore a similar expression of terror as the director. "You'll be fine," I said. "Just don't let go." I sealed his visor.

"Com-links on," Rin shouted. "Wings ready."

I didn't need any help this time. The nano-fabric wings popped out of my arms and stretched to my sides. I closed my visor and gripped the wall. The airlock rattled so intensely it hurt my joints, even through the suit.

"There you guys are!" Hayes shouted over our shared com-link. His voice was muffled by raging winds, so I had to listen carefully to hear him. Either he was pretending to be having fun, or he really was. It made me feel confident that he might actually be the best flier he boasted to be and escape unscathed.

"How is it out there?" Rin asked.

"Hell of a ride! Repair canvas burned up in a flash and I'm holding on to the console with my legs in the air like I'm riding an Earther pig!"

"Are we on course?" I asked.

"Just one more shift!" As slight as the turn was, at the speeds we were going, the force of it heaved us against the side wall. I grabbed Desmond's helmet just in time to make sure the visor of his far-inferior helmet didn't hit the wall and split open. Everybody else seemed to make it fine.

"There we go," Hayes said.

"Take it easy up there!" Rin yelled.

"Too rough for you?" Hayes laughed nervously. "All right, I can see the Q-Zone—by Trass, I can see it! There are ships everywhere. They're starting to take aim at us."

"It's too late," I said.

"On my mark, I'm releasing the seal. Hold on to your friends, ladies and gentlemen! Five, four..."

My muscles tensed. I clutched Desmond's arms and stretched them around my waist so that he was holding on as tight as possible.

"One!" Hayes hollered.

"For you, Cora," I whispered to myself right before the outer seal opened. The ship fell around us as we were pulled out into the atmosphere, where so many of my people's ashes had been loosed. The wind took me, gripping my wings and twisting Desmond and me about. The force of it racked my brain, but the suit kept me conscious until I could straighten myself out. As I did, Desmond lost his grip on me and fell.

The thick Titanian atmosphere and low g slowed him enough for me to figure out how best to angle my arms to dive toward him. I snatched his body with one hand, causing us to corkscrew through the air. As we tumbled, I managed to draw him against my chest so that he could wrap his arms and legs around me. That allowed me to gain control of my wings, like I'd been flying my whole life. The storms of Titan had nothing on Saturn.

"We're straight!" I yelled over the coms.

"Us too!" shouted Rin.

Gareth snorted loud enough for us to know that his sound wasn't merely distant thunder.

"Hayes?" Rin asked, but he remained silent.

That was when I finally had a chance to look around. I tilted my arms to turn, falling in line with the others at roughly the same altitude.

The *Piccolo* plummeted, a plume of flame from friction enveloping its bow like a red dress. The Pervenio ships hovering around Q-Zone scattered. Others, which had been following us from the station, darted through the upper atmosphere above. Both they and the anti-air turrets tucked along the top of Darien's enclosure kilometers away let loose a barrage of missiles simultaneously.

Strings of dark smoke traced the sky, but they were all too late. The *Piccolo* crashed bow-first at full speed into the lonely plateau that harbored the Darien Q-Zone.

Its nuclear-thermal engines and their reactor detonated instantly from the impact, causing an explosion so bright that I momentarily lost control while attempting to shield my eyes. When I flattened back out, the brightness waned to reveal a mushroom-shaped cloud. The blast painted Titan's horizon in brilliant orange.

I was too high up and too far away to feel the shock wave, but half of the tram-line connecting to Darien itself toppled. Pervenio ships were smacked out of the air like insects. Rocks and debris flew in every direction, so far they peppered the side of Darien's thick enclosure. I scanned the fragments for a flying man in white but found no one.

Rin continued calling for him, and I hadn't the heart to tell her to stop. I knew, though. Hayes hadn't made it, but he took more Earthers with him than anything had since the Meteorite struck their homeworld, three centuries ago.

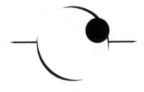

TWENTY-SIX

I STRODE DOWN THE CRAMPED COMMAND CENTER OF WHAT was apparently one of the Children of Titan's many secluded hideouts. Consoles and other equipment were strewn across the floor. Even as far away as we were—within a century-old transport ship buried beneath a string of mountains—the shock wave of the *Piccolo*'s exploding engine was felt. Loose pieces of the ice-rock walls had snapped off, and the provisional lighting systems strung along the low metal ceiling were dim. Wires hanging between them drooped so low that I had to brush them aside while I walked, as if I were trekking through one of Earth's pre-Meteorite jungles.

I was told it took five years to construct the series of tunnel systems leading from beneath the Darien Q-Zone to where we were. Titanborn men and women stood in silence on either side of the room. It was strange to see so many of my people together and not wearing sanitary masks. They watched me go by with a mixture of confusion and reverence.

By then, a few hours after the explosion, the entire Ring knew what had happened. Nobody was sure how many Pervenio officers were killed in the initial blast or how many were suffocating beneath the crumbling plateau, soon to die. Debris had shattered one of Darien's glass farm enclosures, but with my people striking, nobody was inside. Only the plants were left to flash freeze—a small price to pay.

Pervenio rescue efforts to the Q-Zone diverted much of their remaining forces, spreading them thin all across Titan and the Ring. According to Rylah, the central lift to the Darien Lowers had been shut down to retain order as my people protested. Many of them had begun to climb the shafts toward the Uppers in an unstoppable fury. They stormed the intact hydro-farms. Took control of factories, shops, and even docked ships. It didn't matter how weak their muscles were, or how crude their weapons, with numbers on their side.

I passed Gareth. He stood with a cane and a fresh bandage on his leg. He signed *"Now you lead"* to me. Beyond him, Desmond lay on a medical table, an IV connected to his arm. His head was angled toward me, his eyes still drawn wide from the thrill.

On an adjacent table sat Rylah herself. I'd have recognized her in her tight-fitting violet dress anywhere, but the rest of her looked like she'd been through a rough battle. She offered me a nod but nothing more.

The red-haired woman Rin had referred to as the Doctor tended to a wound in Rylah's calf. She was the only person in the entire base who wasn't watching me. She was also the only non-Titanborn. A necklace with a Departure Ark ship figurine hung from her neck, a clear giveaway since no sane Titanborn would wear anything referencing M-day right now. As I got close, I saw the shimmer of dried tears on her freckled cheeks. It made me wonder if she'd chosen to be where she was, an alien to all those around her... just like Cora.

I shook the thought out of my head and forced myself to focus. Rin waited in front of me. She was out of her armor, wearing a simple tunic like everybody else. She didn't even have her mask on to conceal her half-burned face. The grisly sight didn't earn a second glance from me. In her hands, she held a hand-terminal that was set to record.

"Rylah prepared a connection from Darien to broadcast to the entire Ring," she said. "We're ready." Her voice was cold and distant. It had been that way since we'd watched the *Piccolo* explode and Hayes not emerge from the clouds.

"Good," I replied. I went to step past her, but she grasped my arm. "Are you?"

I removed her hand as gently as I could and continued on my way. I still wore every part of my powered armor except for the helmet, so I had to be careful not to hurt her.

My mom suddenly parted the crowd and positioned herself in front of me. As one of the recuperating Q-Zone escapees, she still wore her sanitary mask. The rest of those in her situation were in a nearby cavern continuing their treatment under the watch of the Doctor.

When we'd first arrived at the hideout and she saw me, she wept. I squeezed her so hard I almost broke her back, but as grateful as I was to be with her, no tears escaped me. Once I knew she was okay, all I could manage to ask her was whether or not she knew who I really was, who my father really was. Her expression told me everything I needed to know.

"Kale," she said presently, forcing a smile. "You don't have to do this."

"I need to finish what I started," I said.

"No, you don't. All that matters now is that we support each other."

A week earlier, that would have been enough for me, but more had happened in the short time since I'd left the Q-Zone to save her than in the entirety of my life before then.

"You'll never be stuck in a place like that again, Mom," I

said. "I promise. None of us will." I placed my hands over her cheeks and gazed straight into her eyes. She seemed healthy. The dark rings around her eyelids were gone, and her cheeks were a lighter shade of pink.

She choked back tears. "Kale... don't."

I embraced her, pulled her tight, and pressed my lips against her forehead. Then I placed her frail body to the side and stepped forward. Director Sodervall was on his knees within the airlock that provided entry to the base, hands cuffed behind his back and a bag covering his head. Behind him, a tiny viewport offered a view of Titan's whipping wind. Two armored Children of Titan operatives stood on either side of the open hatch, pulse-rifles at the ready. I stepped in front of them and turned to Rin.

"Recording," she said.

I regarded all the people gathered in the room, then stared into the lens of the device in Rin's hand. Then I cleared my throat. "People of the Ring," I began. "My people. For too long, we have lived in fear. Controlled. Watched. Infected. No longer." I spread my arms, taking care to gesture to the armored men behind me. "You all know my face and what we've done, but what the Voice of the Ring failed to mention is who I really am. The secret he's been keeping since the day they arrived. My name is not Kale Drayton. It is Kale Trass."

The crowd arrayed before me released a collective gasp. I could only imagine the reaction of all the people throughout Titan's numerous colony blocks or around the Ring watching their local newsfeeds, which Rylah had managed to subvert. That was a far simpler task than broadcasting to the entirety of Sol, and my message was, at first, meant only for my people and our direct enemies. It would spread soon enough.

"Trass's blood runs through my veins, as it did my father's," I continued. "Luxarn Pervenio and his dog Sodervall kept us in the darkness, but no longer. Those who think themselves our masters will fall! Here I stand while one of the places we've dreaded for decades burns, begging you as a fellow child of Titan: Rise from your hollows to reclaim our homeworld! Fight toward the light, not just on Titan, but all throughout the Ring and the stations watching over us! Don't be afraid. The spirits of our fallen watch over us from the winds. Our freedom starts today."

I stepped to the side, revealing Director Sodervall. The operatives tore off his hood so all could see his bloody face. He screamed futilely into a gag.

"To all the corporations like his who think they can own the Ring. To the USF and every citizen of Earth, I say this: Retribution is coming. There is a new Voice of the Ring, and we are the descendants of those chosen by Trass. We are Titanborn."

I nodded at one of the operatives, and he moved so I could reach the airlock controls. My hand hovered there as I beheld Director Sodervall's horrified visage. I then turned to the crowd. To my friends and my family. Their jaws hung. Their eyes were glued open.

Rin gritted her teeth and nodded at me.

My mother wept and turned her head away.

I pictured Cora's smile, as radiant as *Piccolo* when its engines blew. Then, wordlessly, I keyed the inner seal of the airlock to close and the outer to open. Director Sodervall didn't scream as Titan's cold embrace greeted him. He couldn't even squirm.

The seconds he was out there felt like a lifetime for me. The room stayed so silent that I could hear the thud of his body collapsing into the hatch. A swipe across the controls signaled the airlock to pressurize again, and the inner seal slid back up into the ceiling. Director Sodervall's frozen body fell through.

As he hit the floor, his head and torso cracked into so many pieces they looked like one of Saturn's ice rings wrapping what was left whole of him.

No one dared say a word. I turned, glowered directly into Rin's camera, and said, "From ice to ashes, Titan."

EPILOGUE

I JOLTED AWAKE. MY HEART RACED SO RAPIDLY, MY RIBS were on the verge of breaking open. All I could see were blotches of white and blurred figures. As I turned my head to survey my surroundings, a respirator covering my mouth yanked it back into place.

That was when I realized I was gagging. I grabbed the respirator, needles popping out of my arms as I moved and pulled. The long tube attached to the respirator slid out of my throat, releasing all manner of phlegm and who knows what else as I gasped for a real breath. And kept on gasping. It felt like I'd been chained to the bottom of an ocean until I was on the brink of drowning, then launched to the surface.

I threw myself off whatever I was lying on. More needles affixed to tubes popped out from every region of my body. My legs were weaker than after a month in a sleep-pod on a passenger liner. Or at least, one of them was. I couldn't feel the other at all, which caused me to stumble forward into a counter upon an attempt to stand. My groping hands knocked over pieces of shiny equipment. Some fell and shattered. My hearing was so distorted that they could well have been explosions.

Fingerlike appendages wrapped my arm and heaved. Muffled voices murmured in my ears. I tore free and attempted to run, but again my numb leg caused me to fall. I grasped at the area in front of me, expecting to find air, but instead, my hand smacked into something rigid and cold.

Once more, someone pulled at me, hoisting me to my feet. I threw them off and hopped along on the leg I could feel while my hands skated across a smooth wall for balance. I continued until one sank through an opening. A door. I grasped the edge, swung myself into the adjoining space, and found the wall again. This time, it was coarse and lumpy, like the face of a cavern.

I clung to it for a few hops, then discovered I wouldn't topple as long as I pressed all my weight on the leg I could feel, as if there were a crutch in place of the other. I'm not sure where I was planning on going, but I hobbled as quickly as I could. Faster and faster, like a kid learning how to ride a bike. Until I slammed into a railing.

I searched for the hand-bar, and once I found it, I slouched all my weight onto my arms. My working leg burned with soreness. Each heavy breath I drew stung deep in my chest, like a blade plunged through my sternum. My vision remained cloudy, but as I rested there, the ability to sense shadows and depth returned.

It wasn't cold enough to be Titan, but I was in some manner of grand hollow wreathed in solid rock. Aged air recyclers rattled through the darkness. An asteroid perhaps? My augmenting senses informed me that the gravity was too weak for it to be Earth or even Mars.

I squeezed my eyelids as hard as I could and reopened them, trying to drive away the blurriness. They were wet with tears even though I wasn't crying, as confused by disuse as I was about what the fuck was going on. I repeated that procedure a few more times, and then I saw.

On the level below me, a group of twenty or so people trained in hand-to-hand combat. Only they weren't ordinary security officers. They wore all-black boiler suits. Their hair was neat and trimmed, almost military-like. Their skin was pale and youthful. Over the left side of each one's face, a yellow eye-lens was attached. The same as the one Zhaff wore.

I fell to a knee. Images of the last memories I could draw on streamed through my consciousness. A gunshot piercing his helmet and leaving only Zhaff's green eye visible through the stormy haze of Titan. Aria soaring away above him.

My breathing hastened until I was clutching my chest as if to hold my heart inside. I stared through glass at the numerous Zhaff-like people below. They'd stopped training, each of their shiny eye-lenses aimed up at me.

I keeled onto my side, my whole body going numb. The corners of my vision darkened as I grew woozy. Glinting yellow dots danced across the room, like stars against the blackness of space.

There *was* a hell, and I, Malcolm Graves, was in it.

The Story continues with Titan's Rise. Or pick up the whole series.

THANKS FOR READING!

To all you wonderful readers out there, we at Aethon Books hope you enjoyed this story. Even if you didn't, please consider leaving an honest review wherever you prefer to leave your bookish thoughts online. Reviews are the lifeblood of authors, and they help more than you could possibly imagine.

And if you *did* enjoyed this story about the growing rebellion on Titan, continue reading the rest of the *Children of Titan* with Book 3, *Titan's Rise,* coming May 7, 2019. Malcolm Graves survived the events of *Titanborn,* but how ready is he to face down Kale Trass and end the Titan Conflict for his employers?

If you'd like to be updated about this series and Rhett's upcoming releases, as well as gain exclusive access to limited content, ARCs, and more, please subscribe to his monthly newsletter below.

Subscribe at www.rhettbruno.com/newsletter

You can also follow Rhett on Facebook: www.facebook.com/AuthorRhettBruno, or join his official fan club group: www.facebook.com/groups/RhettBrunoFanClub

Check out the rest of our catalogue at www. aethonbooks.com. To sign up to receive updates regarding all new releases, visit our website.

ABOUT THE AUTHOR

Rhett C Bruno is the USA Today Bestselling and Nebula Award Nominated Author of *The Circuit Saga* (Diversion Books, Podium Publishing), *Children of Titan* (Aethon Books, Audible Studios), and the *Buried Goddess Saga* (Aethon Books, Audible Studios); among other works.

He has been writing since before he can remember, scribbling down what he thought were epic stories when he was young to show to his friends and family. He currently works as a full-time author and publisher in Stamford, Connecticut, with his wife and their dog, Raven.

You can find out more about his work at www.rhettbruno.com

You can find out more about his work at www.rhettbruno.com

SPECIAL THANKS TO:

ADAWIA E. ASAD	EDDIE HALLAHAN	KYLE OATHOUT
BARDE PRESS	JOSH HAYES	LILY OMIDI
CALUM BEAULIEU	PAT HAYES	TROY OSGOOD
BEN	BILL HENDERSON	GEOFF PARKER
BECKY BEWERSDORF	JEFF HOFFMAN	NICHOLAS (BUZ) PENNEY
BHAM	GODFREY HUEN	JASON PENNOCK
TANNER BLOTTER	JOAN QUERALTÓ IBÁÑEZ	THOMAS PETSCHAUER
ALFRED JOSEPH BOHNE IV	JONATHAN JOHNSON	JENNIFER PRIESTER
CHAD BOWDEN	MARCEL DE JONG	RHEL
ERREL BRAUDE	KABRINA	JODY ROBERTS
DAMIEN BROUSSARD	PETRI KANERVA	JOHN BEAR ROSS
CATHERINE BULLINER	ROBERT KARALASH	DONNA SANDERS
JUSTIN BURGESS	VIKTOR KASPERSSON	FABIAN SARAVIA
MATT BURNS	TESLAN KIERINHAWK	TERRY SCHOTT
BERNIE CINKOSKE	ALEXANDER KIMBALL	SCOTT
MARTIN COOK	JIM KOSMICKI	ALLEN SIMMONS
ALISTAIR DILWORTH	FRANKLIN KUZENSKI	KEVIN MICHAEL STEPHENS
JAN DRAKE	MEENAZ LODHI	MICHAEL J. SULLIVAN
BRET DULEY	DAVID MACFARLANE	PAUL SUMMERHAYES
RAY DUNN	JAMIE MCFARLANE	JOHN TREADWELL
ROB EDWARDS	HENRY MARIN	CHRISTOPHER J. VALIN
RICHARD EYRES	CRAIG MARTELLE	PHILIP VAN ITALLIE
MARK FERNANDEZ	THOMAS MARTIN	JAAP VAN POELGEEST
CHARLES T FINCHER	ALAN D. MCDONALD	FRANCK VAQUIER
SYLVIA FOIL	JAMES MCGLINCHEY	VORTEX
GAZELLE OF CAERBANNOG	MICHAEL MCMURRAY	DAVID WALTERS JR
DAVID GEARY	CHRISTIAN MEYER	MIKE A. WEBER
MICHEAL GREEN	SEBASTIAN MÜLLER	PAMELA WICKERT
BRIAN GRIFFIN	MARK NEWMAN	JON WOODALL
	JULIAN NORTH	BRUCE YOUNG

Ingram Content Group UK Ltd.
Milton Keynes UK
UKHW012220080323
418239UK00004B/523